Six Pounds Eight Ounces

Cardiff Libraries
www.cardiff.gov.uk/libraries

Llyfrgelloedd Caerdy
www.caerdydd.gov.uk/llyfrgelloedd

D0306218

A   55198113

Six Pounds
Eight Ounces

Rhian Elizabeth

Seren is the book imprint of
Poetry Wales Press Ltd
57 Nolton Street, Bridgend, Wales, CF31 3AE
www.serenbooks.com
Facebook: facebook.com/SerenBooks
Twitter: @SerenBooks

© Rhian Elizabeth

Print ISBN 978-1-78172-140-7
Ebook ISBN 978-1-78172-141-4
Kindle ISBN 978-1-78172-142-1

The right of Rhian Elizabeth to be identified as the author of this work
has been asserted in accordance with the Copyright, Designs and
Patents Act, 1988.

A CIP record for this title is available from the British Library.
All rights reserved. No part of this publication may be reproduced,
stored in a retrieval system, or transmitted at any time or by any means
electronic, mechanical, photocopying, recording or otherwise without
the prior permission of the copyright holder.

This book is a work of fiction. The characters and incidents portrayed
are the work of the author's imagination. Any other resemblance to
actual persons, living or dead, is entirely coincidental.

Typesetting by Elaine Sharples
Printed by CPI Group (UK) Ltd, Croydon

The publisher works with the financial assistance of
The Welsh Books Council

Love Poem

I want to write you
a love poem as headlong
as our creek
after thaw
when we stand
on its dangerous
banks and watch it carry
with it every twig
every dry leaf and branch
in its path
every scruple
when we see it
so swollen
with runoff
that even as we watch
we must grab
each other
and step back
we must grab each
other or
get our shoes
soaked we must
grab each other

Linda Pastan

Blue Balloons

My first word was clock only it came out as cock. That was when my mother knew I was trouble. A sign of things to come that was, Hannah King, she always says, but I've got absolutely no idea what she's on about.

I like words though – I know that. They're my favourite things. I like putting them together into something that makes sense, makes colours. I can even tell you the exact day, the exact moment, I fell in love with them. It was when Nanny came back from Ponty market. A Wednesday. It's where she goes every Wednesday but this time I wasn't with her. Now and again she will take me along too, see, like if I'm sick and can't go to school, but when she goes on her own she brings me a present back in her massive navy shopping bag. I like Nanny, and I like her best when she goes to Ponty.

Ponty's got a big park as well as a market, but she never takes me there. Always says that she *hasn't got time* and I know that's a lie because Nanny doesn't have a husband and she doesn't have a job. Nanny is an old person and all old people do is sleep and eat and buy things. That must mean she's got plenty of time for pushing swings and sitting on the other end of a seesaw, but no amount of nagging I do ever changes her mind.

Ponty isn't very far away and to get there Nanny always catches the 120 Stagecoach bus on Pandy Square. That's what we call the place where we live. *Pandy,* not Tonypandy, because we aren't posh. And that's also why we call Ponty Ponty instead of Pontypridd.

My mother says that Nanny is off her head catching the 120, that it goes everywhere before it gets to Ponty bus station. She tries to explain that Nan would be better off getting the 130 because it's much quicker, but Nanny doesn't care what my mother says. She likes the slow bus because it passes the mountain on the way. And this is what Nanny does. She sits down the front, never up the back and especially not on the wheel, cradling her shopping bag on her lap like it's a fat navy cat. Nanny looks out of the window for a while and then when the bus gets near it – the mountain – she shuffles forward on her seat and stares up at the rows of dead people. Nanny knows them. She rubs the palm of her hand over the green stone on her finger and smiles, one of her really burny mints floating like a tiny white rubber ring on her tongue.

My grandfather is up on that mountain and the last time I went to Ponty with Nanny on the 120 bus, when I had a stinking cough and couldn't go to school because my nose was running like mental, she talked about him the whole way. I was absolutely busting for a pee and Nanny promised me only one more stop now love, every single time we stopped. Well, it was my grandfather who gave her that green stone ring she rubs, and it's really special to her although I don't know why she smiles at it because he's dead. I can't count change out like Nanny does when she pays the driver, and I can't tie my laces without them coming undone again straight away, but I do know that being dead isn't something to be happy about. I think she must smile because the mountain makes her remember nice things. She crunches her mint and says she'll be up there with him one day under the dirt and the earth and the flowers and I say *Nan*, shut up, you're still quite young, aren't you? How old are you? Apparently my nanny is sixty-seven years old and I'm not sure if that's *really* old or just old but I know she can climb the steps up to Ponty market as fast as I can and sometimes she even beats me when we have a race, even though she's carrying that heavy shopping bag. So she definitely can't be old enough for dying yet.

But I started telling you about this particular Wednesday when she went on her own, didn't I? And it really was the most important day of my life. That day I wasn't sick, I was absolutely fine. And after school I waited by the window for her to come with my present. I waited hours for that slow bus to bring Nanny back to Pandy from Ponty. I bounced on my toes as I watched her empty her shopping bag, watched her carefully take out the things she bought for herself and put them down on our dining table. Boring old lady things. Potatoes. Some brown tights and a gold can of hairspray and a slimy fish in a see-through wrapper. This fish had an actual real proper eye that stared at me. Yuck! She must've stunk the bus out all the way back. Buses smell quite bad anyway what with all the old people on them and that. I didn't say it though. Kept it in my head where I keep most bad things because I didn't want to hurt her feelings and mainly because I didn't want her to say I was being too cheeky for my present.

So she carried on pulling these things out, like a magician, and I thought it would never end. She'd actually bought the whole of Ponty town centre. Unzipped her bag and tipped all the shops and shelves into it. But then there it was for me, red and sparkling with silvery glitter. A notebook. What did I think it was, a bastard broomstick? Something different for a change and half price in W. H. Smith. I really wasn't being ungrateful. I couldn't help my face. Nanny said it looked as if she'd just whacked me across it with her kipper by there. It was just that I'd been expecting sweets from the market stall. Normally when we go to Ponty Nanny gets a plastic scooper and fills a bag to the top with all sorts and when the man puts the bag on his silver weighing scales she always says, Jesus Christ, how much?

I thought it was boring, this notebook. I picked it up and shook it, ran through the white, light-blue-lined pages with my thumb. The worst present in the world! Of course I didn't say it. I told you, I keep it all in my head. It's kind of like when you fall over really badly and your mother holds a tissue down hard on your knee that's bleeding. And it stops the blood for a while but you know as soon as she takes that tissue off that it's going to start gushing again. Well that's what I do … I push it all down, all the things I can't tell people and the things I know I shouldn't feel. It's not very good I know, because one day I will probably explode, and I thought I would that time, thought my disappointment would spill out of me like green slime onto the table with Nanny's shopping.

But then I found them – words – upstairs, alone in my room. I only wish I'd found them sooner. I realised that I didn't have to keep all those things in my head anymore. I could take my pen and write them down on pieces of paper, bleed them out like black biro blood, let them gush and run and land in between the lines. Lines that soaked them up and never told on me or thought I was bad. I wrote loads of words in my notebook, really neat until they made a story about some balloons. I don't know where they came from. They were just there, blue and floating around my head. My head that felt lighter now, *better*.

The next morning I was so excited. Bouncing on my toes again. I tore the page out and took it with me to school to give in for our St David's Day story competition which was in a week's time. St David's Day is a day all about being Welsh and minging cakes with currants and a dragon. We have prizes and wear stupid clothes and I felt pretty good about my story's chances of winning. But the next day, our phone rang on the windowsill and when Mum slammed it down she huffed and puffed and said that we had to go up to the school to see my teacher. What have you bloody done now, Hannah King, she said. I hadn't done *anything*. Or at least if I had I couldn't remember doing it.

Mrs Thomas was behind her desk in class waiting. And in a serious voice she said we were there to talk about my story and something called The Truth, which was apparently a very important thing. I was next to Mum on one of our red plastic chairs, as excited as she was worried, knocking the heels of my black school shoes together. Mrs Thomas was going to tell my mother that I'd won the competition, that I was absolutely fantastic and lovely and clever, I just knew it.

'Mrs King,' she said, 'the school does not take kindly to parents giving in pieces of work they hope to pass off as their child's. We must encourage Hannah to be creative. To make up her own stories.'

When I stared at my shoes, at the streaky scratches Mum had gone nuts about a few weeks before, and thought about it for a minute, what those big words meant, I felt my head exploding again. I didn't think it was possible to feel happy and sad and angry all at the same time, but it was. I knew my story must've been good because Mrs Thomas thought Mum had written it. My *mother*, who never writes stories, just cheques and birthday cards, who looked funny and huge and awkward sitting on a seat meant for someone much smaller than her. I thought it might collapse and to be honest, I kind of wanted it to. Wanted her to squeal as she flattened the red chair like it was a spider, the metal legs like a spider's legs squashed under her massive bum. My mother, who was there in her best shoes especially polished for walking across Mrs Thomas' classroom floor. My mother, who uses a cooker and a kettle and an iron and who can drive our car. My mother, who is a grown-up. Mrs Thomas thought a *grown-up* had written my story.

She laughed then on the tiny chair in her best shoes and told Mrs Thomas that she doesn't have time for writing bloody stories. But Mrs Thomas went and scrunched my piece of paper up into a jagged white ball anyway, and when she chucked it into the bin at the end of her desk with the orange peel and the shredded green cardboard we'd used earlier that day to make leeks, I wasn't all those loads of things anymore, only angry. Mrs Thomas thought I was a liar. She thought I *stole* words. I wanted Mum to go nuts, as nuts as she'd gone about my shoes. I kicked the metal legs on her chair and tugged the strap on her handbag because she needed to believe me. And she needed to make Mrs Thomas believe me and then once everyone knew I was telling The Truth, she needed to rescue my story from the bin and get the creases out of it like she gets the creases out of my clothes with her iron.

But that never happened. On the way home she said she had too many things on her mind. More important stuff to worry about than words and stupid bloody blue balloons. And then she said that thing our mothers say, the thing that is rubbish and we all know it.

'You know The Truth, Hannah, and that's all that matters.'

St David's Day came and we had our Eisteddfod and that was the worst day of my life. That morning my mother had dressed me in a tall black hat that looked like an upside-down bin on my head. It had this ribbon that went around my neck and choked me to death. And if I didn't look stupid enough already she went and stabbed me with a pretend daffodil through my special Welsh lady's dress that itched me like I was covered in the chicken pox again.

So imagine how angry I was sitting there with my arms crossed in the big hall.

There were songs in Welsh that Mrs Thomas played on her piano but I didn't sing them. And there were minging cakes with currants but I didn't eat any. We talked about dragons and rugby and some blind man, and when it was nearly all over the winner's name was called out. I knew it wasn't going to be me. My words were buried in the bin, but I couldn't believe it was *him*. I had to watch Evan Jones, the stupidest kid in school, sit on a throne that was actually just a normal chair framed in red tinsel while someone placed a spiky crown made of paper and fake jewels on top of his greasy hair. I had to listen to him read his crap story out and while I listened I murdered him twice in my head with my daffodil pin. I had to clap. I had to suck my tears back in.

When I grow up, when I'm much bigger than this, when I can count change and tie my laces tidy, I'm going to be a writer. I'm ginger, poor dab, Nanny says, and I've got freckles all over my face. This means I can't be on the telly, or famous or pretty or anything, but I'm okay with it. I like words most of all and I like my notebook, too. I suppose it's better than sweets because it won't make me fat and it won't make my teeth green and yellow and black. And I like it because I can write anything I want in it. All the things stuck in my head. I can write stories about people I know, even if they're not true. In my notebook I can make people do whatever I want them to do.

But I'm not showing it to anyone ever again. I'll write what I want and when I feel like it. It's easier to tell a piece of paper secret stuff than it is to tell a real person. And real people don't believe you anyway, even when you *are* telling The Truth.

Spaceships

I'm bored. Evan likes Lego but I can't stand it. We're in a terrible mess by here on the carpet. Bricks everywhere. He never wants to play the games I want to play and there's loads of other better things we could be doing in class instead. Like playing with the doctor's set. It's really cool. It's got a white costume and everything. And a pretend thermometer and one of those things you use to listen to someone's heart to see if they're dead or not. I could wrap bandages around his arm and pretend he's been attacked by a massive bear. But he doesn't even want to do *that*.

Evan Jones loves me. He tells me all the time. I love you Hannah King, I really, really love you. And when he says it it makes me feel a little bit sick. He's silly loving me because I definitely don't love him and it must be really rubbish loving someone when they don't love you back. I'm the only kid who plays with Evan but don't go feeling sorry for him because it's his own fault. Light brown hair he's got and I don't think he's ever cut it, not in his whole life. It's quite long for a boy's and it shines with grease as if he's been out the yard playing in the rain. But it's not just his hair. Evan Jones, I think to myself, you smell so bad I have to hold my breath and pinch my nose when we're close together on the carpet like this. Think it, yeah, because my mother taught me that if you haven't got anything nice to say then you shouldn't bloody say it at all. Although I don't always keep not nice things in. It's hard. Sometimes they squirt from my mouth cold and mean like water out of a water pistol. Sometimes my nasty words shoot Evan Jones dead.

And he's got plenty of other things wrong with him as well. His clothes, for example. Jumper sleeves that are too stretchy for his arms and he's always tripping over his laces that are long and floppy like black noodles trailing behind him. Sometimes I step on them and then he kind of goes flying and I kind of laugh, especially when he gets carpet burns, or bleeds ... that's the funniest. My

13

mother says his family are poor. Not poor like kids in Africa with flies in their eyes, it's just that they can't afford new things like we can. Of course I don't want to play with him, but there's no one else. The other kids in class don't like me either. They say I'm weird but I don't know why because there's nothing wrong with me like there is with Evan and I always brush my teeth.

'Are you pretending?'

'No. Honest now,' I tell him. 'It *is*.'

Evan will believe anything. Yesterday I told him my dad's an astronaut who lives on a spaceship up in the stars, and he *actually* thought it was true.

'Well if it's your birthday today, how old are you?'

'Six,' I say. 'And I'm having a party, too.'

'No, you're not.'

'Yeah, I am, after school. It's going to be fan-tastic.'

'Why haven't you got a birthday badge then?'

'Because it's in the house, of course. On top of the telly, nice and safe so I can wear it to my party. Do you want to come or what?'

My mother says that to be a good liar you need to have a good memory, which is lucky because I remember lots of things. I always remember my spellings and my homework and to wash my hands after I've been to the toilet. I've got really good at telling lies. Me and my mother are kind of backwards because when I'm lying to her she thinks I'm telling The Truth and when I'm telling The Truth she thinks I'm lying. Grown-ups are quite stupid really. And so are kids. Especially this one by here. Evan's eyes tighten. The blanket of Lego bricks moves and rattles around us as he squirms. His very small brain is trying to work out if I'm telling The Truth or not today.

He goes and picks a red brick up and screws it down on top of his wobbly tower. How dare he. He's not even listening to me anymore. Doesn't he care about my birthday? I know. I know that Evan likes cake. Every day he's got a cake in his packed lunch. I tell him there'll be a massive one at my party.

'A chocolate cake?'

'Is that your favourite?'

'Yeah.'

'Then yes, a massive, double chocolate cake with chocolate sauce and chocolate buttons and chocolate cream. And there'll be sausage rolls. And cheese sandwiches. *And* crisps. Onion rings and Chipsticks and Petrified Prawns. And Tangy Toms and Skips.'

'What about Wotsits?'

'Millions of them.'

I watch his tongue move slow and fat across his top lip. A hungry, slippery slug.

'Will your dad be there?'

'No.'

'Why?'

'Just won't.'

'Why haven't I seen him pick you up from school?'

'Because I *told you*. He's in space. He's much too busy because he's fighting aliens up in the stars, stupid.'

'Oh, yeah. I forgot. Sorry.'

'It's okay, Ev.'

'I love you, Hannah King.'

'More than Lego?'

'Yeah.'

'More than your mother?'

'Yeah.'

'More than Mrs Thomas?'

'Yeah.'

'Even more than chocolate cake?'

He stops building and instead fusses with his long noodle laces. The bricks break the silence, knock around his nervous, twisty feet. I'm feeling very angry. My insides heating up like a radiator. He isn't allowed to love anything or anyone more than me. That's just not right. So I ask him again … Evan Jones, do you love me more than chocolate cake or what?

'I love you, Hannah King. I really, really…'

I stop him. Stop him before he says something that might get me so angry I'll just have to stamp on his Lego bricks with my black shoes and crush them into plastic dust. I tell him that if he does love me, crosses his heart and hopes to die love me, he can come to my birthday party later.

15

'Okay.'

'Promise you'll come?'

'Yes, Han.'

I sigh. Don't know how many times I've got to tell him. It's not Han, it's Hannah King, or Your Majesty. Say it.

'Yes, Hannah King, I promise.'

'*No*. Say Yes, Your Majesty.'

'Yes, Your Majesty.'

'And you'd better bring me a present to my party or I won't let you in.'

I tell him straight and then I get up. I'm bored of talking about parties and my bum's gone dead on the carpet. He carries on doing his tower massive and I go and play doctors on my own. Even though I haven't got a patient it's better than being childish with bricks. I'm not a builder. It's much more fun being a doctor. Doctors are really important people. They fix you when you're sick. They make you better and then when they're finished fixing you, you can go home from hospital. I take my temperature. I wrap my bleeding wrist up with a bandage and give myself a couple of stitches. It's dangerous fighting bears. I put the silver thing for my heart up my shirt and it makes me jump. Freezing!

I play until the bell goes and I see my mother hovering outside the door in her green coat. She wears it every day and when she lifts the furry hood over her head it makes her look like a lion. Mum says it's very important to wrap up warm. That's why my coat is huge and black. She straightens me out in the corridor because I'm all squiff and bloody scruffy. Pulls and yanks me, buttons every single button and zips my zip all the way up. My coat hangs past my knees and the zip goes over my mouth and now I'm completely, absolutely covered. My coat is probably the reason why the kids in class don't like me. They tell me that I look like a big bug in it. A caterpillar with two legs and two arms. And now she's wiping something off my cheek.

'*Mum*, get off me!'

'Watch your bloody lip, Hannah. And why can't you call me Mam like everyone else?'

Most kids around here call their mothers Mam or Mammy, but

I like to call mine Mum. She says it's because I think I'm posh, something special, the Queen of bloody Tonypandy, but it's not that. It's just that calling my mother Mum gets her all angry and sad, which weirdly makes me feel really good. My mother reckons I'm not normal, but then again she's the one spitting on me and rubbing it in with her Kleenex tissue. When she's done with my cheek we walk home past the blue railings and then she goes and holds my hand while we cross the road.

My mother is like a Russian doll. She's small and round and her hair never changes, always brown and short, so neat and tidy I'm sure she's got someone who paints it on for her every morning when I'm not looking. She's got rosy, blusher-dusted cheeks and a serious thin pink mouth that hardly ever moves to smile. If you opened her up you'd find more of her inside. Tiny, serious mothers getting smaller and smaller in their green coats. Mum's got a big hand though and I try to wriggle free but she grabs me really tight and hurts me with her wedding ring. I need to stop messing around by the traffic. I'll get run over now, you watch, and she doesn't have time for scraping me up off the bloody concrete.

I try and explain to her as the cars and buses whoosh past like shooting stars and rockets that I'm not a baby. I say *Mum*, you don't need to hold my hand, *Mum*, because we've already done roads in school. But this only makes her squeeze me tighter. She just doesn't get it. Laugh their heads off, they would, the boys in class if they saw me holding my mother's hand. Like they laughed at me when I told them my dad is the prime minister. One boy called Robbie Jenkins said it was rubbish because the prime minister is a man called John Major so he definitely couldn't be my dad because my last name is King. Hannah King, the big liar caterpillar bug with two legs and two arms. But it's okay. It doesn't matter that they laughed because I put a butter knife through Robbie Jenkins' football and burst it. He didn't know it was me. He was in the toilet. I took it out of our kitchen drawer and snuck it into my packed lunch bag the morning after he called me a liar. Tucked it under my sandwich foil, in between my crisps and my banana-flavour yoghurt with chocolate flakes on the side and *bang*.

17

Mum switches the telly on when we get home. It's the first thing she does, even before taking her coat off. And next she turns the gas fire on, not up full though because my mother is very tight according to Nanny, and while she's in the kitchen running taps and banging pots I have to sit on the settee and watch a show with letters and a large, round clock. This is what's on every day after school. It's like that clock is a part of our living room, and Carol Vorderman a member of our family.

'That Carol is wonderful,' Mum shouts. 'Lovely teeth, she's got, and if you grow up to be half as clever as Carol you'll be alright.'

Our kitchen is down a couple of steps from our living room. That's where my mother is, wiping a silver pot dry with a tea towel, bubbly white sleeves up her arms as she's going on and on about Carol. She bets Carol never cheeked her mother. Carol must've worked hard in school to get where she is today. Carol this, Carol that. I scrunch my nose up at her. It's not my fault that I'm not wonderful like Carol Vorderman or that some of my new, big teeth haven't grown back yet. I don't care anyway. I just want to watch cartoons. They're on the other channel and cartoons are so much better than clocks. But Mum gets to watch what she wants. She's in control of the remote. It's because she bought the telly and the house and because she pays the electric bill and she also owns the air I breathe.

My mother cooks my dinner too and she's pretty good at it, I'll give her that. We eat it on trays on our laps. We do have a dining table in the living room but we only use it when there's something really special going on like Christmas. Actually, only at Christmas. Mum's tray is plain and red and mine is blue with yellow fishes on it, and plants and pebbles, like a camera's taken a picture under the sea. Today we've got homemade corned-beef pie.

'Where does corned beef come from, *Mum*?'

'From cows.'

'Real cows? Like the ones on the mountain?'

Mum's sitting the other end of the settee. Our settee is dark blue and the cushions are also dark blue. I daren't drop any food. Not one single crumb. If I did then the world would definitely end. And of course corned beef comes from real cows.

'Are you saying there's a cow on my plate? That's just cruel. I can't *eat* a cow.'

'You bloody will,' she says, her voice all crazy, 'or I'll shove it down your gob.'

The people who don't eat animals are called vegetarians and we aren't like them. They're mostly hippies and celebrities off the telly, people who like to make a fuss about bloody everything. I just eat my dinner because when my mother says she'll shove it down my gob if I don't, I believe her, knife and fork and all. I can tell she doesn't like vegetarians much, and I know for absolute certain that she doesn't like it when the door goes and we're in the middle of eating. I listen to her sometimes when she's out the front. She'll tell the person who knocked that she's got to go because there's something on the hob when there's absolutely nothing there at all. Apparently it's okay for my mother to lie though because her lies are white. It must mean the ones I tell are black. Hers fly gracefully from her mouth like doves but out of mine crows come screaming. She puts her tray down on the carpet and huffs and puffs the way my mother loves to do.

'Better not be someone selling windows again.'

They do it on purpose, she swears. They were just waiting for her to sit down and relax before they decided to come bloody pouncing. Me and the double-glazing people, and the Jehovah's Witnesses as well, we're all in it together. My mother goes to answer the door and I'm glad. I lean over and grab the remote while I've got the chance, one hand gripped on my dinner tray, careful not to spill anything. I turn Carol off and switch my channel on and I suppose I'm happy that we're not vegetarians. Cruel or not, real cows taste good. I watch cartoons until I hear the front door shut, and when my mother comes back in the living room she doesn't pick her tray up or sit down. She's just standing there in front of me, hands on her hips, staring.

'What?' I say, mouth full of food.

I'm looking up at her from the settee. She seems much taller, bigger, from all the way down here. What you doing *Mum?* Your food's getting cold. But that's when I notice she's put them in. Her angry eyes. Because up in her bedroom she's got this drawer and it's jammed full of eyeballs. Honest now. They look like fish eggs because they're kept in small, clear plastic cases so that they stay clean and shiny forever. My mother's got lots of different kinds of eyes to match her mood and she changes them like most other mothers change their earrings. When she needs a pair she'll slide the drawer open and they'll roll around loose and noisy and fast like marbles. She'll take them out carefully and they'll squeak as she twists and screws them into her head. They're all different, see. Some are wet and some are serious. Plenty of angry eyes, she's got, and only one pair of happy ones that I hardly ever see her wearing. She uses her wet eyes for sad films and her serious eyes for counting with Carol and her angry eyes are especially for me. They stare at you really hard and nasty, just like they're staring at me right now. They're like ice cubes, frozen and cold, with eyelashes that don't blink, stiff as bristles on a dried-up paint brush. I switch the telly back to Carol and the big clock.

'There.'

'Never mind the telly. I'm *fuming*,' she says. 'Do you know who that was at the door?'

'I'm not magic,' I shrug.

'Don't you cheek me, Hannah King.'

'I'm not cheeking. I can't *see* through walls, can I?'

'I'll tell you who it was, shall I? Poor little Evan Jones standing there with a box of Maltesers wrapped in newspaper under his arm. Going on about some birthday party.'

Oops. I forgot about that. I *do* have a good memory, it's just that I tell Evan so many things that now and again some of them get lost in the sea of stories in my head.

'Did you tell him it's your birthday today, Hannah?'

I open my mouth and set it free. It comes out flapping, black beak and two mean, green eyes.

'*No.*'

'Are you sure?'

'Yeah. Course I'm sure.'

'And is that The Truth, Hannah?'

God. Grown-ups really are obsessed with this The Truth thing, aren't they? To them it's as serious as brushing your hair and your teeth and drying inside your ears and between your toes with a towel when you come out of the bath. It's funny because The Truth isn't important to me at all. In fact, I hate it.

'I don't know,' I tell her. 'I can't be expected to remember everything. I'm only five years old after all. I *might* have told him it's my birthday. *Maybe.*'

Mum's angry eyes get angrier and angrier, icier and icier and crazier and crazier. Any second now they will pop out of her head. She says she could still hear him crying when he turned the corner out of our street and I say don't worry, mun, he's *always* crying.

'Where's those Maltesers then?'

'Excuse me, Hannah?'

'You said he had Maltesers with him. They must've been my birthday present.'

'It's not your bloody birthday, Hannah!'

'Well I know *that.* My birthday is in August and I want a real party then.'

And I tell her exactly what I want, just so she can get planning early. I want sparkly hats that make you look like an elf and stay on your head by the elastic under your chin. I want paper plates and tall curly straws that topple the paper cups over and make blackcurrant squash rivers on the tablecloth. A purple tablecloth, that's what I want. And balloons that don't fly away when you let them go. I want sandwiches, no crusts, and cakes and every kind of crisps and party rings and pink wafers and pasties and sausage rolls and scotch eggs. And squares of cheese on sticks, no pickles or pineapples though because they're both just gross. I want a massive double-chocolate cake with chocolate sauce and chocolate buttons and chocolate cream…

'*Party*? You won't be having a party for the next hundred birthdays!' she shouts, her angry eyes already rolling away down the kitchen steps. 'You're a liar. A nasty piece of work, Hannah King.'

She snatches my tray off my lap. Despite being short, my mother is strong. Her hands drive our car, and they lift irons and kettles and hoovers and heavy bin bags, and soon they're lifting me off the settee by my wrists. She's like a JCB the way she scoops me up. She's quick, too. Before I can run away or duck through her legs she's smacking my bum out of the living room and all the way up the stairs and across the landing until I'm pushed, actually pushed, into my bedroom. The door is pulled shut with a loud thud.

I'm supposed to be thinking about my behaviour. I'm supposed to stay in here until I'm ready to come out and say sorry. So I guess I'll just stay in here forever then, because I'll never be ready because I'll never be sorry. It's not my fault Evan's stupid. If he'd just play games with me then I wouldn't be bored and I wouldn't have to make things up. If The Truth was better than stories then I'd tell it instead of them. And if Dad was here I wouldn't be a liar. He wouldn't have to live in space, wouldn't need to be an astronaut.

Questions

The man's come to fix our fire and Mum wants me out of the way. It's because of my terrible habit of asking questions. But I'm not going anywhere. I want to stay down here in the living room. I need to see how you fix a fire and this man who's doing it, he's got hair down to his shoulders.

He's hunched over on his knees on our carpet and it's disgusting. I can actually see his bum and even more disgusting there's this thin line of black fur growing on it, like a river running down the middle of two peachy mountains. He's picking heavy-looking things out of a red metal box and his jeans are absolutely stinking. They're denim and blue, like my dungarees. My dungarees have gold buttons, go just past my knees, and *my* dungarees are clean. I wear them every day and Mum says she's sick of washing them, bored of sewing the same bloody hole up all the time. I know I wear them a lot but it's only because they're comfy and because if you fall over in them, if you scrape your knees across the pavement, it doesn't hurt as bad as if you were wearing shorts or normal trousers or even worse, a dress … yuck! My mother won't get me in one of them again, no chance. The thick blue material of my dungarees is an extra layer of skin and it soaks blood up really good. My dungarees keep me safe.

'What's that?' I ask him, this man with his bum out.

'It's a spanner, beaut.'

'Spanner rhymes with Hannah. That's my name. So what's all that on your clothes then?'

'Oil. And soot.'

'*Soot?* What's soot?'

'Black stuff up chimneys.'

'So what are you going to do with your spanner?'

He bangs and clanks and our fire rattles. He says he's going to fix it and even though it's turned off, I think he must be really brave. Anything could happen. The flames could suddenly come back on and he could fall into them and *die*. If he did it would be a really good story to tell Evan on Monday morning. It would be The Truth and even better than something I made up. If it doesn't happen then I'll probably still tell him it did. I'll just write it in my notebook anyway, make the flames boiling hot, make his long hair a mane of mental orange, make him *scream*.

'Are you scared?' I ask him. 'Have you ever made a mistake? Have you ever touched a fire? What about burns? Have you had any burns before? How do you...'

'*Jesus Christ*, beaut. Am I on *Mastermind* or what?'

'What's *Mastermind*?'

'Stop asking questions, mun,' he snaps, dabbing the sweat off his forehead in the sleeve of his red check shirt. 'I'm trying to concentrate. Go and play.'

'I don't want to play. Besides, I haven't got anything to play with.'

'Bugger off now, beaut.'

'Why have you got such long hair? I thought only girls were meant to have long hair. What...'

He cuts me off. He throws his spanner down and it bounces on our carpet. And then he says something very silly indeed. If I haven't got any toys to play with then...

'Why don't you go and shit in the corner or something?'

I don't like the man with long hair anymore. You're not supposed to swear at kids and you're not supposed to be nasty to them when they're only asking questions. He's got me all crazy inside, hot as the fire that I wish was on because he's got his arm right in it now. I'll show him. I go over to the corner of our living room and next to our tall gold lamp I undo my buttons. My dungarees drop to my ankles and I'm standing there in just my t-shirt and knickers.

Mum can't see me because I check. She's in the kitchen making the man a cup of tea. The grey carpet beneath me tickles my bare thighs as I crouch, knickers rolled down, and pretend to do it. It's really bad to show your foof to boys, I know, because your foof is secret and special, but I don't care if he sees it. I *want* him to see it except he's not looking at me at all so I make faces and these loud squeezing noises to get his attention. I push hard and hold my breath and blow my cheeks out until my face turns as red as his toolbox. And then something bad happens. Really bad. Badder than showing your foof off to a boy. I try to suck it back up but it shoots out, too slippery and too fast. A squidgy brown letter C shape has landed on the carpet between my legs.

Hide it somewhere, Han, that's what I'm thinking as my heart is pumping like mental, as loud and fast as the man is banging his spanner into the fire, against the pieces of fake black coal. Hide it in the drawer or in the plant pot on the windowsill or behind a cushion. *Anywhere*. But I don't have time to pick it up and destroy it, the stinky evidence, because Mum's coming up the kitchen steps with the cup of steaming hot tea in her hand. It takes her a couple of seconds to work out what's going on. It's like someone's got a remote and is pointing it at our living room and pressing pause. Everything stops, my heart and the banging spanner and the whole entire picture. They press play again and fast forward and then they hold their finger down on the volume button. My mother sees it on the carpet and screams ... Hannah bloody King!

She pulls a tissue out of the box on the dining table and closes her eyes and picks it up exactly how she picks spiders up. My brown C-shaped poo has thick, hairy black legs and two beady eyes and some teeth. I'm dragged into the bathroom then, my dungarees clinging onto my ankles, and after she flushes it away down the toilet she makes me sit on the seat. Her angry eyes are in again. Apparently there's something bloody wrong with me.

'No there's not. The man with the spanner told me to do it.'

My mother draws her breath in sharply, as if my foot that I'm swinging like this over the toilet seat has just knocked her in the knee.

'Don't lie, Hannah.'

'I'm not *lying*.'

'You can't help yourself, Hannah. You tell so many you could fill a book with them.'

'Fill a book with what?'

'Your bloody stories!'

'Maybe I will,' I tell her. 'Maybe I'll write all my stories down and then I'll be rich and famous and I'll be able to buy myself a new mother. A nice one.'

I'm still swinging my legs over the white chrome seat in our bathroom. It stinks of soap and bleach in here and my mother is laughing. A pretend laugh. She says she'd soon bring me back anyway, my brand new nice mother would, once she realised how much bloody trouble I am. She's off to scrub the carpet and I've got to wipe my bum and start to seriously think about my behaviour. And now do you get what I mean about us being all backwards? I'm telling The Truth by here on the toilet seat, it's just that my mother doesn't know it. I think my mother needs some Truth Glasses to help her see it better.

I slam the bathroom door when she leaves, leaves armed with a spray bottle of cleaning stuff and a wet cloth for the carpet. The doors in our house don't come off their hinges like I plan. They're supposed to snap and crash and break into pieces when I bang them, but they never do. I slide the lock across and sit back on the toilet seat, and do what I've got to do until I'm all clean and dry. There are some things a girl needs to keep private. I button my dungarees up and run the tap into a plastic beaker I find on tip-toes in the cabinet above the sink. It makes the water taste like minty toothpaste. I don't normally hang around in our bathroom like this. It's cold and boring, and it smells like soap and bleach, and peach shampoo and Mum's deodorant, but I'd rather be in here than out there. With my mother who's angry at me and the long-haired man who I really don't like at all.

Mum is standing by the sink when I come out. It was very cold in there and I almost froze to death. She's washing the long-haired man's dirty cup in the bubbles and I can see she's changed out of her angry eyes and into her disappointed ones. These ones roll at me like pears on a fruit machine. She is waiting. But the word she wants to hear is clogged in my throat like a lump of fake black coal.

'*Well*, have you got something to say, Hannah?'

I stare at my socks and my eyebrows rise without me telling them to. And then I start to whistle when I didn't even know I could.

'Because if you haven't got anything to say, Hannah, then there'll be no Toys R Us.'

I almost forgot that we're going there. We're going there because my mother wants to buy me some plastic people. She thinks I'm bad, keeps saying she's going to take me to the doctors so they can swap my brain for a normal one. An operation with silver tools and blood and stitches. She's worried because I've got so good at telling stories that people are starting to believe them. I think to myself, if only you knew all the stories I've got, Mum, not just the ones I choose to tell you and Evan and Nanny and everyone else, but the ones in my notebook. Course I don't tell her, I only think it. My mother says maybe I can use dolls to *express myself* instead of lying. She read it in a magazine and I've been looking forward to going to Toys R Us all week. So I cough it up. It comes out all slippery and phlegmy and black.

'*Sorry.*'

I'm told to go to the toilet before we leave for Cardiff, even though I don't need to. That's another one of my problems according to my mother. She says I've got to pee everywhere we go, like I'm leaving my mark, like I'm some kind of dog. Same as that day in bloody B&Q when she never felt so embarrassed in all her life. Here it comes. Mum tells this story to everyone we know, like she's telling it to me right now for the hundred millionth time behind the wheel of our car.

'A Sunday morning it was and tipping down.'

And one minute I was there by her knees nagging her, you know how I like to nag her, and the next I was gone. Quick as a flash! Well she looked everywhere, didn't she? Down the aisle with the tubs of matt and gloss and turps and back up where the rolls of wallpaper and brushes were. She was calling me, crawling under shelves and searching behind the stack of shopping baskets in case I was hiding from her because you know how bloody wicked I am, how I like to play games. Her heart was pounding. She even had them make an announcement over the speakers. Hannah King, your mother is looking for you. Please come to the front of the shop. If anyone sees a small ginger child wearing a purple mac and scruffy denim dungarees, please inform the nearest member of staff.

'And then you found me,' I say, fed up.

She bloody found me alright, dungarees and knickers around my ankles, *again*! Sitting there swinging my legs bold as brass on one of the display toilets in the shop. And I was grinning.

27

'Thought it was fantastic, you did, hearing your name ringing around the shop like that. You thought you was bloody famous.'

We're driving down the fast roads. I open my window and let the wind dry and numb my tongue. This story is rubbish. It always ends the same. She was fuming, felt like smacking me all the way back to Pandy. She pulled my dungarees up and we left B&Q without telling anyone that I'd stained the brand new white toilet yellow with my pee and we haven't bloody been back there since.

I'm just glad when I see the gigantic, colourful letters on the building. We're here. Finally. And through the magic doors that open by themselves, Toys R Us is the biggest, brightest place I've ever seen. There's shelves taller than houses everywhere I look, crammed full of colours and toys and teddies and slimy aliens in pods and loads of other really cool stuff. Toys R Us might actually be the coolest place in the world. We find the aisle with the dolls and it's like being in some kind of pink hospital where they're waiting to be born out of clear plastic wombs. And some on the shelves really look like actual babies, too, their faces so cute and real in the boxes that I stare at them for a while, absolutely convinced they'll blink or burp or smile or scrunch a nose at me if I stare long enough. I stand on my tiptoes and get one down. She's got light hair and blue eyes like me.

'Look at the price on that!'

'But *please*. Pretty please. I'll be good forever, I swear.'

Mum says she'd like that in bloody writing, and she tuts and moans but she lets me have it, because I almost always get my own way when I smile at her like this and my dimples come out. I lay the box carefully in her metal basket and then I pick some more. Barbies this time. Boy ones with hard hair and girl ones with long, soft hair. She even lets me choose clothes for them and shoes and jewellery *and* furniture. I flash my dimples at her more than I think I've ever flashed them before. And I suppose my mother's alright sometimes.

The lady at the till scans them and puts them in a carrier bag and I just can't wait to get my dolls home. I'm dying to twist the silver wires off their thin arms and legs and set them free. I'm a doctor. Doctor Hannah King. I'm going to cut them out of their plastic wombs and save them. In the back of the car I stamp my feet on the mats and beg Mum to drive fast back to Pandy, the fastest she can possibly drive, but I'm sure she goes slower on purpose. We get there eventually though and I burst through the front door and straight away put my baby to sleep upstairs in my bed because she's knackered after travelling all the way from Cardiff. And then I sit behind the settee in the living room and tip the Barbies in boxes out of the bag. I bite and rip them free until the carpet is covered with girls and boys and all their accessories. I bend their stiff legs and sit them down on pink plastic chairs. I give them names. I change their clothes. And when you think about it I'm not really a doctor at all. I'm actually God because I give them *life*.

I do like them and don't get me wrong, I am glad Mum bought them for me. But dolls aren't much good. I just don't get it. Their smiles are stuck and they can't make faces, you know, like the way people react when I tell them lies. Dolls aren't as good as stories because with words I can control everything, completely. I can have whatever I want whenever I want it. I can make the people I know feel and do things the way they should and they don't even know it. So I'm going to go back to making stuff up because playing with real people is much more fun.

Pink Custard

Friday is my favourite day. You probably think it's because tomorrow's the weekend, but it's nothing to do with that. I actually like school. I like it much better than being at home.

The thing about Friday that makes it different from all the other days is that Friday is Well Done Badge Day and Well Done Badges are the most important things in the world. A Well Done Badge is a circle shape that Mrs Thomas cuts out of a glossy sheet of card with her scissors and then she goes and squeaks a smiley face on it with her black permanent marker pen. To get the badge on a Friday morning she has to pick you, has to think you've been the best kid in class all week.

We're in the big hall, me and all the others, and we're waiting to find out who's getting it this week. If you were a fly and you buzzed around the ceiling above our heads we'd look like rows of tomatoes down below because we're all wearing red cardigans or red jumpers. It's annoying. I can't stop sliding. It feels like I'm sitting on an ice rink. The wooden floor of the big hall is shiny and to be honest, I blame my new trousers.

I wish Mrs Thomas would hurry up. She's finished her prayer and now she's reading us a poem but I'm not really listening. I can't concentrate because the butterflies in my belly are having some kind of disco in there. It's all because of that badge she's got in her pocket. It's got to be mine. I've done my best this week, got every word right in our spelling test, the only kid in class to get ten out of ten and Mrs Thomas licked one of her tiny gold stars and stuck it on the bottom of my page. I lined our Biff and Chip books up in alphabetical order on the shelf and I made sure all the Geosafari computers were knocked off tidy. I put lids on felts and swept rubber bits and pencil shavings out of the carpet with a pan and brush, and I didn't pull Evan's hair for one whole day. Wednesday.

But right now I've got bigger things to worry about than Evan Jones. The butterflies in my belly morph into birds and then pterodactyls. Mrs Thomas stands on the edge of the stage, right on the edge now, like it's a diving board and she's about to leap off. She's a much taller lady than my mother. Mrs Thomas wears skirts so long you never see her legs, just her sandals and her toes. She pulls the badge out of her blouse pocket. It's ruby red, the smiley face actually winking at me as she holds it up in the air. It's going to look lush on my jumper I think, and I listen hard with a smile on my own face. She says it was an easy decision this week. Because this person tries really hard all the time. This person is kind to everyone. This person never makes a fuss. Mrs Thomas' list goes on and I nod because it's true. She's right. I really am all those good things. I get ready to stand, step through and over the red tomato bodies and up the steps to the stage but then she goes and says…

'This person tidies his Lego blocks away at the end of the afternoon without even being asked.'

Mrs Thomas doesn't say anything about spellings. She doesn't mention bits and shavings and lids. Nothing whatsoever about Geosafaris. She doesn't say my name, she says his. *Evan Jones. Class 3.* He shoots up off the floor like a pressed spring through the tomatoes and to the stage and I really want him to trip over his black noodle laces face first into the steps, but he doesn't. Mrs Thomas sellotapes the badge to his jumper and makes sure it's stuck down properly with her firm fingers. Evan's smile is as massive as the black permanent marker smile he shows off on his chest, proper puffs it out. I don't like Fridays anymore, and when he sits back down next to me I know for sure that I definitely don't like *him* anymore. I slide over two spaces.

'I love you, Hannah King,' he says as he shuffles closer, uninvited. 'Do you like my badge?'

'Minging,' I tell him. 'Absolutely minging. You can't even see it tidy on your jumper. It's camouflaged.'

'What does that mean?'

I say don't worry, thick-o, and I slide further across and I wouldn't mind if I slid away off the Earth for good. I can tell I've hurt his feelings, can see his lip quivering out the corner of my eye. But I ignore him, Evan Jones and his stupid badge. Mrs Thomas plays the piano and the words to 'Colours of Day' roll down on the overhead projector above the stage. I'm not really singing though, just opening my mouth like I'm a goldfish. I'm too sad for singing, too sad for anything. The morning goes *so* slowly. More spellings in class, and times tables which I just can't do. Numbers are stupid anyway. It pretty much takes forever for the dinner bell to ring and when it does I'm back in the big hall again where there's high windows and scratched benches and paintings on the wall from our last concert, Peter Pan. There's a massive collage of him and Wendy suspended over the stage, some green trees made out of card and tissue paper, too.

I walk around on my own, the warm, sickly smell of cooked dinner, maybe mashed potatoes, turning my belly. I watch hungry kids sprint and skid across the hall floor that actually glows, the long light on the ceiling a yellow moon illuminating the brown wooden sea below. It's a mad race to be first to the best tables for eating on, the ones without wonky legs. Girls never want to sit by boys because boys pick their noses and make disgusting sandwiches. Two pieces of white bread squashed down with mashed potato or peas or carrots or tomato sauce or sometimes snobs if they're feeling really disgusting.

I'm watching Evan. He pulls his jumper off, wriggling and squirming like a greasy red eel, gets it stuck on his head. And then he goes and hangs it up on his hook. I expect he doesn't want to get food on it. If it was my badge I wouldn't want to get it dirty, either. He skips back to his table and carries on eating, like he hasn't got a care in the world. Something happens to me. Something bad but I can't stop it. My legs are walking themselves across the hall. Fast. I'm looking over at Evan who's got his head buried deep in his packed lunch box, foraging for crumbs, something he maybe forgot to eat. A stray piece of chocolate cake. And then I'm by all the coats and the red jumpers hanging clumsily on the curled metal hooks, Evan's limp and scruffy, the material thin and worn and the sleeves chewed and frayed at the ends. I rip the badge off it without thinking twice, absolutely sure that the sound of the Sellotape peeling away is loud but no one else in the big hall seems to hear it. They're laughing and chomping, forking pieces of meat and comparing sandwich fillings. Mouths full of mashed potato, jam and cheese and ham and tuna mayonnaise. They've got no idea that I've just committed a crime. That I'm a criminal.

I button the happy, winking cardboard circle up in the back pocket of my new trousers and get a tray off the counter where the dinner lady's waiting with a net on her head. My appetite has come back, just like that. The dinner lady asks me what I want so I tell her. Pink custard, please Miss. Apparently I'm lucky because it's almost all gone. I carry my tray carefully to our table and dip my spoon into the bowl thick with pink goo. I lick it off my teeth and my sticky lips, so warm and silky and soft and the dinner lady was right ... I do feel pretty lucky today. Evan opposite me says he's very, very sorry for whatever he did that made me pull his hair the way I did earlier and I say it's alright, Ev, I forgive you.

And well of course he cries when we get back to class. Screaming! What do you expect? Once he realises it's missing, his tongue leaps out of his mouth like a jack-in-the-box, orange, stained the colour of the Wotsits he had in his packed lunch. He pats his jumper like he's on fire, pulls the floppy material out of his pockets again and again. Our classroom slowly turns into a crime scene. All of us kids are detectives, each wanting to be the one who uncovers the red badge and indeed catches the criminal who stole it. We strip trays bare and lift up mats and crawl under tables and chairs. We shake books out and empty pots of paint brushes and I look in the big tub of Lego. I plunge my hands into the well of deep bricks like I'm searching for a prize in a lucky dip. My fingers rummage around the cold hard pieces of plastic until I think, what on earth are you doing, Han?

I give up looking. I am nervous though. My blood is beating – I can feel it. I could easily give the badge back, put it somewhere Evan will find it. I could wipe my fingerprints off it first with a piece of blue paper from the dispenser in toilet and no one would ever know it was me. I could even pretend I found it, and hand it in to Mrs Thomas and then bask in the glory of being the best detective in the world. But I don't. I just watch the tears fall out of Evan's eyes like fat rain drops, the snot run out of his nose and down his chin like green glue.

'Stop it now,' Mrs Thomas says to him because he's hysterical. 'That's enough. You should've taken more care of it. Calm down.' Mrs Thomas is right. If it was *my* badge, I would've taken good care of it. I wouldn't have let it out of my sight for a second because there are some very bad people in the world. And soon enough everyone gets bored of looking for evidence, for fingerprints and trails and clues, for the dead red badge body itself. No one cares anymore. Our classroom goes back to normal because more important things happen. Milk and biscuits, a fight between Robbie Jenkins and another boy that ends in a bleeding nose and a chunk of skin bit out of Robbie Jenkins' arm. And even more exciting than blood and Mrs Thomas shouting her head off is the telly trolley being rolled out. Evan is still upset but the rest of us just get on with our day, Friday, the best day of the week.

The last bell goes and I'm glad that my mother's green coat isn't at the door waiting for me. She says I'm big enough to walk home on my own now. And at the school gates Evan somehow manages to wish me a lovely weekend through misty eyes and wet sniffles. My house is the other way to his and that's where I head, a bounce in my step as I walk, a kind of skip down the main road past the blue railings, past the church and the chapel and the post office and the fruit and veg shop, across the road checking up and down twice and all the way until I'm in the dog-poo speckled lane behind my house. I look around first, I'm not stupid. Only careless criminals get caught.

When I'm satisfied that The Coast Is Clear, I unbutton my button and slide the badge out. The lovely red face winks at me in the sunshine, the stench of dog poo strong and disgusting, but it doesn't ruin my good mood, my perfect Friday. I slap it onto my chest, the tiny bits of Evan's red fluff on the Sellotape joining up nicely with the red fluff on my jumper, like it's meant to be there. I turn out of the lane and sprint home, down the street past other people's houses and through my front door. Mum's washing dishes in bubbles that are like white mountains rising up from the sink in the kitchen, exactly where she was this morning when I left for school. I think she probably stands there all day long. On the top step, mental out of breath, I tell her my good news.

'You won what now, Hannah?'

Doesn't she ever listen? I told her this morning. It's *Friday*, Well Done Badge Day. And I won. See?

'What did you get that for then?' she asks me, both her arms submerged in the dishwater.

'For being kind and for excellent spellings. Just because I'm the best, really.'

'Fab,' she says, and she almost smiles at me, and for a silly second I think she might even hug me but she doesn't, just peels the badge off my jumper with her soapy hand. Watch you don't get it wet!

'I suppose we'd better go and get that doll tomorrow now, hadn't we?'

I know which one my mother's on about. She's from the catalogue and I've had my eye on her for weeks, since I first saw her on page 347. She's got long brown hair, red heeled shoes and comes with a fluffy black dog on a lead. Mum sticks the badge on the fridge, next to the magnet one of her friends brought her back from Florida. And I just can't stop smiling. Evan's probably still upset, probably *crying* at his mother instead of smiling, but I'm not sorry for what I did. I've worked it out now, see. It's not the taking part that counts, so don't believe them when they tell you that. That's just another one of their big fat white lies. It's the winning that counts because if winning didn't matter then there wouldn't be a prize for the winner, would there? And there's no point in trying anyway because even when you try your best, which they tell you to do, you don't win.

But it's alright. I'm not sad. I'm just not going to try anymore. I won't tidy things up in class and I won't stop pulling Evan's hair. All I have to do is lie. I can get away with anything. I'm a criminal. I'm the Well Done Badge thief.

Candyfloss

Kyle's doing my head in. We're in the bath together, either end as if we're riding on a canoe, noses scrunched and wet arms crossed, giving each other evil eyes over the popping white bubbles. He blinks first. Always does. We are completely, absolutely naked. He daren't look down at my bits or I'll kick him in the willy. I've done it before and I'll do it again. And he knows it. We don't *want* to bath together. Kyle's a boy and I'm a girl. It's just not right but Auntie Eve made us, filled us belly-button deep in warm water because she can't afford to run two separate baths – something to do with her gas meter. But at least he's by the taps. I'm the guest, aren't I? And I'm far too posh for sitting on a plug. This bathroom is painted the colour of buttercups and up above me some damp is spreading like a black puddle across the ceiling. It's all mental. Me and Kyle are cousins, and this is how it happened.

A long time ago Auntie Eve got fat, well fatter than she already is anyway, and then she went to the hospital and pushed and pushed and Kyle slid out of her. And then they took him away to clean him up and when they brought this baby back to Auntie Eve's fat sweaty arms they gave her the wrong one. It happens all the time because babies look the same. Babies are screaming balls of candyfloss and sometimes people take someone else's home by mistake. My cousin, my *real* cousin, he's kind and sweet and lovely like me, but he's growing up somewhere else with a different family.

Auntie Eve is my mother's younger sister. When I asked her before how old she is, she wouldn't say. Told me it was rude to ask a lady her age but I found out anyway off Kyle. She's thirty-six, which is quite old. She lives with Kyle and my Uncle, Griff, in a place called Porthcawl, in a flat instead of a house. Some weekends, like this weekend, she picks me up in her car and I've got to stay here while my mother and my nanny are busy, while our house is no place for a kid to be, especially a kid who asks questions, so my mother says.

Porthcawl is about an hour away and it's where the beach is. We haven't got beaches in Tonypandy, just mountains and some lakes. That's why it's much cooler here. Porthcawl's got a sea that sparkles and at night the fairground is lit up like Christmas, rides that flash with lights and scream with noise. Kyle is the only thing I *don't* like about Porthcawl. He's a bit older than me but you'd never tell unless you already knew. I'm one head-size taller than him and me and Kyle are opposites in every way possible. I've got light hair and his is dark and honestly, he can't even *read*. It's like this. Some people are born clever like me and some people are born all wax and no wick. I learned that from Nanny. And that's what Kyle is, dull, but Auntie Eve calls it ADHD. I don't know what it means, just that she always uses those four letters to stick up for him when he's done something bad, when he's knocked over a vase in Pound Stretcher or when he's posted his willy through next door's letterbox and peed all over their doormat.

He's always waiting for me on the front doorstep when I get here. Throwing a tennis ball up in the air and catching it, or squirting a water pistol at the window pane or a BB gun at Griff's beer cans which he lines up like soldiers on the garden wall. Blue peak hat and tomato-sauce-stained t-shirt, baggy shorts and a shifty grin on his face. When I shut the car door and get my bag off the back seat I know he's got a nasty plan carefully mapped out for my visit. Kyle likes death. He likes killing things on his video games and in real life, too. I can't say for sure whether it was Kyle who murdered that dead cat we found once by the battered red phone box. It wouldn't surprise me, but then again his victims are usually smaller and he stamps on them because he's the Prince of Porthcawl and the insects are no match for him and his powerful Reebok trainer.

Ants are the unluckiest. He must've killed millions of them. With sly eyes and dirty finger-nailed hands on his hips he stands over them, lunges and makes a bridge with his legs stretched wide apart as they march underneath him, his shorts so baggy they touch the pavement. He watches them swarm, fast and tiny and brown, and then he shouts, prepare to die, crawly beasts! Lifts his mean leg up and splat and twist. Mwhahahahahah! as he rubs his trainer into

37

them like they're on fire, like he's Griff and he's putting one of his fags out. Ants and snails and slugs and ladybirds and spiders. Kyle won't be happy until he's killed all the creatures in Porthcawl. Until we're the only things left walking the streets. He says one day he'll kill a seagull, too, and kill me if I'm not careful.

But Kyle's awful stupid. I'm not scared of him, not bothered about his powerful Reebox trainer. If only he knew all the bad things I've made happen to him in my notebook, and how, he'd soon shut his gob. I just smile to myself when he says it, when he threatens to kill me, and I think, be afraid of *me* you want to, Kyle Thomas Rhys Griffiths. Because one day I'll get fed up of you being mean, fed up of sharing my nanny and my bath water with you. You wait and see. Our staring contest is over. I quickly cover my bits up with a water-heavy flannel but I'm too slow and he sees them. He reaches up into the mouldy basket on the side of the bath and pulls the lids off two shampoo bottles, holds them up to his chest. Apparently they're my boobs.

'Look at me,' he says. 'I'm Hannah King and I've got big nipplers.'

'They're called nipples not *nipplers*, stupid.'

Whatever they're called, he don't care. I've got them and they look funny.

'You've got them too, Kyle.'

He looks down at himself, shocked, like it's the first time he's noticed those two little chocolate button-shaped things on his body. Kyle's skin is very dark, scars and chunks from playing and fighting carved into it like wood.

'And at least *I* haven't got a willy.'

So what? He loves having a willy. He gets up and shows me how good it is, a wave soaking me as he stands there ankle deep in bubbles. And when he wiggles his bum his willy spins and splashes in mid-air like a hand on a clock ticking around fast. See? His willy is *cool*.

'Disgusting,' I tell him. 'Sit down, mun.'

He does as he's told although still holding the lids over his nipples, making kissing shapes and smooching sounds, making fun of me basically. He's really, really doing my head in.

'Stop looking at my boobs, Kyle.'

'But they're funny. Look at that one,' he says, and he pinches it, twists it like it's a volume knob on a radio.

That's it. He's done it now. Tipped me over the edge, pushed my bloody button, as my mother would say. My nipple is killing, red and sore. I grab him by his hair and dunk his head under the water. Kyle is a biscuit in a cup of tea. A chocolate digestive slowly melting. But I'm not a murderer like he is. I'm not going to *kill* my not real cousin in this mouldy buttercup yellow bathroom. I let him up when I can see the bubbles forming in the water around him, when I can tell he's drowning. He gasps and pants and wheezes, holds his pumping chest, lumps of soap like nits caught in his dark eyelashes.

He manages a scream which makes Auntie Eve rush in. I quickly tell her what happened before he can catch his breath. He made fun of my boobs and twisted my nipple. And you're not supposed to touch a girl's privates, are you? And then he got the shampoo, the minty one by there, and squirted it at my eye. Only just missed and to be honest he could've blinded me. He turned the hot water tap on and he swallowed some shower gel. And then he said a swear word that's just too terrible to repeat and I never swear because I'm a good girl.

'Lies!' he screams again.

But Auntie Eve believes me. Course she does. Those are the sorts of things he does every day. She pulls him out of the bath and smacks her handprint onto his soapy bum, bright and red and perfect, full fingers and palm as if it's been pressed on carefully with paint. She calls him a little fucking bastard while he stands on the toilet seat and she dries him with a buttercup-yellow towel that matches the walls, his willy bouncing around again.

I poke my tongue out at him soon as she leaves. He says I'm a fat, stinking liar and I say, yeah, so what? I lie on my belly and stretch out, the whole tub to myself. Lush. This is the sea and I'm a fish. I kick my feet, whoosh my beautiful rainbow-coloured fin around the crystal clear water and make bubbles with my mouth. I glide along the slippery bath floor which is actually made of reef and coral and shells and turtles. I'm having loads of fun but then he goes and disturbs my lovely swimming. He shouts *oi, bitch!* and when I spin around he's standing on the edge of the toilet seat, pointing his willy at me like it's a floppy pink gun.

'Prepare to die, big nipplers!'

And instead of BB pellets or water or rotten pieces of potato, it's his pee he shoots me with. It's as yellow as the walls and the towels, as warm as tea, and it sprays everywhere, all up the tiles, all over me! I leap out so quick it's like a tsunami in the bathroom. I grab him by the skin of his arms and pull him off the seat, and then I grab his hair, harder than I've ever grabbed Evan's. Soon we're fighting, rolling around on the slippery bathroom floor like kittens. He punches me in the belly. Scratching and biting and pinching … his favourite move. Kill me now, he will. I'm dead. But I'm stronger. I hold him down by his shoulders, my legs either side of his skinny brown body, and slap him hard in the face. I'm not a murderer though. I even give him a chance to say sorry.

'Never, big nipplers!'

'It's *nipples!*'

'Nipplers!'

He gets me so angry I reach for the first thing I see. The toilet brush. I pull it out of its holder, speckles of brown poo caught in the wet white bristles and rub it in him like it's a paint brush and his face is a piece of paper. Next I grab his willy and yank it but it doesn't come off. And then he bites my arm so hard I lose my grip. It slides out of my hand like a bar of soap and somehow he wriggles free, runs away naked and slimy and red-marked. But I'm not done with him yet. I chase after his wet footprints in the carpet but they only lead me to the living room and Auntie Eve. Kyle's hiding behind her. Coward.

'What's going on *now*?' she asks us, very angry.

'She tried to pull my willy off.'

'He peed on me!'

Not even a lie this time. But Auntie Eve is having none of it, doesn't want to hear anymore! She shakes her bottle of talc and turns us into ghosts.

'If you two don't make friends then we won't be going to the beach.'

Both still completely, absolutely naked, and under the white, choky cloud, me and Kyle swap evil eyes again. He's made teeth marks in my arm and I almost ripped his willy off, but we lie. We pretend that we don't hate each other's guts because going to the beach is much more important than telling The Truth.

It's Griff's job to lay the yellow towels out on the sand when we get there. One for me and Kyle to share, one for him and Auntie Eve. We're far enough away from the donkeys now, left them further up on the beach with their names hanging on leather plaques around their necks. I do like donkeys, but they poo a lot and we don't want to sit in it. I'm more worried about my bathers though to be honest. When I wear them, green and tight and horrible, I look so fat. I wish I could just stay in my dungarees but Auntie Eve says they look even more stupid on me in this weather and no chance is she putting them through the washing machine mucky from the sand when we get back to the flat – something to do with the electric meter.

I hate that Griff can see all my skin, how disgusting I am. He's smoking a fag and sitting next to Auntie Eve on their towel, face to the sky, and blowing smoke up to the sun. He's my Uncle but I don't call him Uncle Griff. Just call him Griff. I don't know why. He likes to drink cans of beer though, I know that, and Nanny says it's all he does, too. And my mother doesn't like Griff, either. She says that smoking is a filthy habit and if she ever catches me doing it when I'm older, she'll bloody strangle me. Nanny laughs when Mum tells her that Auntie Eve has stuck by him despite the cheating and the booze all these years because she loves him. Nanny knows that love isn't cans of beer and coming home to a messy flat because he's sat on his arse all day watching the telly. Love isn't rows and worrying about the bills. Must be good in you know where, that's all Nanny can say, and it's because I'm sitting there listening to them that she talks in code.

She says you know what and you know where and you know who to Mum when she doesn't want me to know what she's on about. It's all very confusing. I sit there and watch her move her hands apart, like she's stretching an invisible elastic band. He must have a big you know what because she can't for the life of her think

41

what else Auntie Eve sees in him. She's always been the same, Nanny reckons. My mother was always the sensible one. Auntie Eve doesn't sound like my mother even though they both slid out of Nanny. Mum says she lost her Rhondda accent when she started courting *him*. Mum's older but Auntie Eve's much bigger. She's got three chins, I counted, and flabby bits that shake like jellies under her arms. Griff calls them her bingo wings but Auntie Eve goes nuts when he does. And now Auntie Eve's living down the fucking desert with that underhanded bastard and that boy of hers, they say he's got ADHD but if you ask Nanny she'll tell you he's just a chip off the old fucking block. You should probably know that my nanny swears a lot for an old lady. She swears a lot for any one person actually.

But I like Griff, and my mother not liking him for some reason makes me like him even more. He lifts his t-shirt over his head and I see that his chest is covered in fluffy brown curls, like the tops of his fingers and under his arms and all over his legs. He's wearing very short shorts. Him and Kyle have got the same sort of browny-yellowy eyes, eyes which are like the devil's according to Nanny. Because Nanny knows a wrong 'un when she sees one, nose like a bloodhound, she's got. Griff's really huge, the most massive grown up I've ever seen. I can fit both my feet into just one of his trainers.

I'm wearing jelly shoes although I wish I'd never nagged Mum to buy them for me now. They're green and really pretty, go all sparkly when the sun shines on them, but they dig into my ankles and have broken the skin on the bony part and turned them red raw. I'd take them off but the sand's too boiling to walk on with just your feet. I'm fat and sweaty and sore, and to make it worse Kyle's already started bugging me to go up the arcades with him but I don't want to go just yet. I want to make some sandcastles. I've been thinking about them all week back in Pandy. It's okay for him. He's used to the beach. He can make sandcastles every day if he wants.

Griff gets the sun cream out of Auntie Eve's bag, an orange bottle that never seems to run out, and calls me over so that he can put some on me. He doesn't bother about putting any on Kyle but he squirts loads onto my leg, rubs the runny, warm liquid into my thigh, his hand big and hot and clammy. I will burn badly and my mother will be cross if he doesn't do this properly. He also tells me that my freckles are cute.

'Give it here,' Auntie Eve says, snatching it off him. 'I'll do that for her.'

She covers me from head to toe. My nose first, which has already started burning, then my neck, my shoulders and chest and the backs of my legs, until every bit of skin is sticky and white. For some reason she's looking at Griff like he's done something wrong. And then she calls him a fucking bastard and he calls her an ugly, fat pig. I don't know. Grown-ups are always arguing with each other. I leave the three of them there on the towels, Kyle throwing sand at the people sunbathing next to him, Auntie Eve and Griff still shouting and calling each other nasty names, cans of beer and fags like weapons in their hands. I walk down the beach with my purple bucket swinging by my knees that sort of look like two jam cakes covered in cream. The sea is ages away but I don't mind.

When I get to the dark, flatter sand I take my jelly shoes off. *Finally.* My ankles sting as the gentle, salty breeze bites them, but it's a pleasant, soothing kind of sting, if you get me. And under my feet is lovely and cool and wet, like fat slimy slugs are wriggling between my toes. I leave my jelly shoes there on the sand, bury them a little bit. Maybe someone will steal them and then I'll never have to wear them again. Griff will carry me everywhere. But if no one steals them, I'll just get them on the way back. I bend down and catch the muddy water as a tiny wave whooshes really fast into my bucket.

Looking out across the sea it glitters blue for ages and just doesn't stop. It's mental, the way it blends in with the sky and you can't tell if it's the sea ending or the sky beginning. And that, the big black thing out there, Auntie Eve says it's an island for bad people. Bad people and kids who tell lies and make up stories about other people. She tells me it all the time, makes sure I know it off by heart, like how Mrs Thomas teaches us the Lord's Prayer. Sandcastles. You need water and wet sand for making sandcastles otherwise they'll just crumble and fall down. Kyle told me. The three of them look like they're a million miles away up there on the beach. Griff's tiny now. He doesn't look like a giant anymore. Nanny can't understand why Auntie Eve loves him but I know what it is. It's because he's so big and his arms are so strong. When Griff hugs you, you sort of feel safe, like no one will ever get you because he could easily fight them off.

I carry my bucket back towards them slowly, like it's brimming with boiling water, not warm sea. I find my jelly shoes. They're still there sadly, like two sparkling green crabs peeping out of the sand. I accidentally step in shallow, watery holes and seaweed catches between my toes like sloppy green wire, like vines, there just to trip me up. By the time I get to the towels there's hardly anything left inside my bucket, just this pathetic pool swimming around the bottom. Kyle looks inside and laughs.

'That all you got, freckle face? Your freckles look like zits!' Kyle kicks my bucket over and the little water I did have vanishes like magic in the sand. Auntie Eve says nothing to him but Griff, still sitting on the towel, has had enough of his shit now. Auntie Eve is too soft on him and I know Griff must be serious because he wiggles his can of beer into the sand so it doesn't tip over. Griff doesn't put his beer down for just anything. They shout at each other again, Auntie Eve telling Griff he can't help it, it's his ADHD, Kyle's a good boy really. But Griff knows it like I know it. Kyle is a cheeky little fucker. Auntie Eve and her bingo wings has spoiled him, ruined him. Griff will show her exactly what he needs now.

He picks Auntie Eve's yellow flip flop up. Kyle tries to run away but Griff catches him by his scrawny ankles and tackles him to the sand. He's slapped across the back of his legs as punishment, the noise loud but not as loud as his scream. Poor Kyle. How awful. Two beatings in one day! He rolls around like a big baby in the sand, like a fish flung out of the sea. Griff gives me a wink and then when Kyle's calmed down, when he's finished screaming and threatening to call Child Line, he begs me to come up the arcade with him again.

'Why should I, Kyle Thomas Rhys Griffiths?'

'Because you just should, Hannah Freckle Bum Arse Willy Foof Nipplers King. I'm your cousin, aren't I?'

Hmm. I don't bother telling him that he's not really, that he actually slid out of a different lady's belly and his real family are somewhere else but they wouldn't even want him back anyway.

'I'm not coming up with you if you're going to keep calling me names.'

'I won't call you another name for the rest of my life. Swear down.'

I check his fingers and his toes.

'Serious, Han. No crosses included.'

I don't believe him. Not one bit. But I suppose I haven't got anything better to do and Auntie Eve and Griff are kissing now instead of shouting – something that's much worse.

We race up the concrete steps that are steep and crumbling away. Kyle wins. And he just has to do it, doesn't he? Even though he knows they spook me out. He kicks through the flock of massive seagulls at the top, jumps through them like they're a feathery puddle for splashing in. I don't like seagulls. They're scary, creepy eyes and hooked beaks, and they steal your chips when you're only minding your own business eating them on the beach. Today might be the day he kills one, I think to myself and not out loud just in case he does grab one and snap its neck and then the rest of them might come after us for revenge.

I know that everybody's staring at me in my bathers. Kyle's wearing his shorts but not his t-shirt, and his Reebox trainers but not his socks. He steals us both a lolly from a freezer in one of the souvenir shops – a lemonade flavour one for him and a rocket-shaped one for me. Don't worry. We steal lollies all the time and we never get caught. I lick it fast as I can before it drips all over me and Kyle finally decides on the arcade he wants to go in. It's loud and bright inside, *so* bright, a screaming disco of pulsing orange and red lights, flashing buttons and levers, glass chambers that are soft toy prisons. The gambling machines play music, the same happy tune churning over and over, and the crash of coins into collecting trays is as loud as a hundred knives and forks falling out of the sky.

He's an expert at this, Kyle is. He bangs into a machine with his bum until a copper waterfall of two pence coins comes spewing out. He must be in a good mood today because he lets me have a handful. I stand on tiptoes and send them down the little gap at the top but I don't win any more and neither does Kyle. He kicks the machine in temper and calls it a stupid homo.

'What's a homo?'

'A man who bums a man.'

'Oh.'

We walk to the other side of the arcade and watch a lady try to win a teddy on the grabbers, Kyle's nose squashed to the glass as he tells her she'll never win because the machine is fixed. Kyle knows because apparently the woman who gives people change in the kiosk here sucked Griff off. He tells me all about it.

'He went out the back with her. It was late so the arcade was shut and all the lights and the machines were off.'

'How do you know?'

'Because I was here. I was waiting.'

'You were in the dark? On your *own*?'

'I'm not scared of nothing.'

'I'm not scared, either,' I tell him.

'When they came back out the woman put this machine on for me. My father. Sorry ... I mean *Griff* ... he said I could have an hour on it for free if I didn't tell my mother. But I didn't win because it's fixed.'

'What were they doing out the back?'

'I told you. She was doing it to him, what he likes having done. That thing my mother won't do with her mouth.'

'Why won't Auntie Eve do it?'

'Because she's a fat bingo-winged bitch.'

'That's not nice.'

'I don't care.'

And neither does the lady. She's super-sweaty, her forehead dripping like my lolly which I've finished now, as she concentrates hard like there's a skill to it. She pushes the orange flashing button and the wire of the grabber goes down. Go on, she wills it, go *on*. The silver claw wraps around the pink bear's head, its sharp, stiff fingers digging into the black button eyes, but Kyle was right. When the bear is lifted up the claw just drops it back on top of the other bears. The lady doesn't put more money in, and I don't know what Griff did with the woman who gives the change out in plastic pots, I just know that Kyle kicks the machine and says he's bored now, so let's go.

Back in the flat I peel my shoes slowly off the raw cuts on my ankles. Actually peel them, the soft jelly material like orange skin, my ankle the juicy wet fruit underneath. It stings so bad, worse than pulling plasters, makes me shiver, but I don't cry. I change into my nightie, and when I do the sand pours out of me. Sand gets everywhere. That's why my mother doesn't like it, goes mental when I come home and it's stuck in her carpet. But at Auntie Eve's getting sand on the carpet doesn't matter and when Griff spills his beer no one gets a cloth to wipe it up. She's not crazy like my mother. It's the same with crumbs and picking rubbish up and putting toys away. Here there are no rules, and I like it.

Auntie Eve is asleep on the settee now. Kyle's playing a game on his console which is plugged into the telly and every time he kills something blood splats onto the screen. The living room is a museum of empty cans and dirty plates, unironed clothes stacked high in messy towers, Kyle's action figures strewn across the unhoovered carpet. I sit at the end of the settee next to Auntie Eve, hardly any room because I told you, she's fat, and when she's stretched out like this she takes up all the space. Griff is sitting on the armchair that only he's allowed to sit on. It actually has his bum print in the flat, squashed cushion and he won't get up now until he needs the toilet. He's like a portrait in the messy museum, a painting of a king, but instead of a sceptre or a golden orb he's got a fag in his hand, ashtray on one arm of the chair throne and can of beer on the other. He isn't wearing robes and a crown but very short checked shorts and dirty white socks. No t-shirt. Not very regal, but he reigns over the living room all the same.

I feel around inside my bag, my clean knickers and t-shirt to go under my dungarees tomorrow, and eventually I find it. My notebook. My lovely, sparkly notebook.

'Writing stories is for *gays*,' Kyle says in a really annoying voice.

He points his remote control at me and says he wishes he could kill me with just one thumb of a button. Blast my brains out, he would, stab me to death, and I say go on then, I dare you. He goes back to killing and I sweep the grains of sand off the front cover of my notebook with the palm of my hand. It's impossible to concentrate though, with Auntie Eve snoring like that, big and fat in her mustard-coloured dressing gown, with the shots and screams coming out of the telly.

I go and lie on the bed in my room instead, shut the door behind me. It's not really my room at all. It's just where I stay when I come here, like a guest in a hotel. I sleep with the dusty cardboard boxes of junk and Griff's rusty, metal-smelling power tools. I'm not allowed in Kyle's room. He's actually got a note sellotaped to the door saying, *Kip awt Hanah King*. But I know he's got red bed sheets and stripy wallpaper. I know because his badly spelled sign can't keep me out when he's sleeping or down in the garden. My bed sheets are plain and cream and I don't think Auntie Eve changes them because there's a smudge of chocolate by there on my pillow that I made months ago.

I eat my candyfloss. Griff gave me money to buy it before we left the beach. It's as if a cloud's been plucked from the sky like a fluffy, pink fish, caught and trapped in a see-through bag especially for me. It tastes as good as it looks and when it's all gone, I'm really sad. I sit up, lean my back against the wall and fiddle with the buttons on my nightie – hard white hearts. And when I lift the thin material up to my face I'm no longer in the smoky dampness of the flat, I'm back in Pandy. At home where it smells like Persil and clean sheets, like my mother. I don't know what happens to me, how or why ... because trust me, it's never happened before. But for some crazy reason this lump grows in my throat and then my eyes are full of disgusting, wet tears that make everything blurry. Crazy because I do not miss my mother at all. No way. Not one single bit. Never.

I feel horrible, so sick. Like I've scoffed a hundred bags of candyfloss all in one go and the only thing I can do to make myself better is push my fingers down into my throat and throw it all up on the dirty sheets, a sweet pink puddle of poison. But I hear Kyle scream from the living room and it sort of jolts it out of me. He must've killed something he really wanted to kill, got a bonus point or moved onto the next level. I don't know. Whatever he does, I just know that I hate him, more than I can explain. It doesn't make any sense, does it? That he's got a real family, a mother and a father who he sees all the time, and I haven't. I just want to ask someone what I've done because someone must know and I need them to tell me. Why can't I have that? Why can't I be *normal?*

I pick my notebook up. It's there on the bed next to me, the red even brighter against the plain cream sheet. I open it out and find a clean page. This is a story about Griff. Me and him are in it. He's a giant but I'm regular sized and Kyle has gone like my freckles have gone. They just both disappeared, like water in sand, like magic. I'm normal and the world is exactly how I want it to be, right down to the colour of the sky … a Parma Violet purple … electric and stormy, stuffed full of pink candyfloss clouds. There's a beach, too, and an endless glittering sea but in the middle of it there's no island for bad people. It's just perfect. This story is mine, and I write it.

Maybe it's Kyle come to tease me. Show me a spider he's caught, a balled-up one or worse, one that's still alive and squirming, missing a couple of legs because he's pulled them off like a flower … he loves me, he loves me not. But it's not Kyle. It can't be, can it? Besides, the hand that pushes the door open is big, not a kid's, thick fingers covered in fluffy brown curls. I sit up a bit more, back to the wall, nightie and hard white buttons, the smell of Persil, but Pandy is a long way away and I know it. He sits on the bed next to me, makes the mattress springs shake, and tells me that I'm pretty and special, things my mother never says I am. I'm a good girl, his *favourite*, and not trouble, not at all.

He gets up, unties the cord on his checked shorts and stands there with his willy out. Of course it's not like Kyle's. It's bigger, like his hands are bigger, like his trainers, and I know I'm supposed to shout for Auntie Eve but I don't, don't even know if I could if I tried, but I don't try. He rubs his willy against my nightie and tells me that my freckles are cute but I say don't be silly, they've disappeared, can't you see? He leaves me then, when he's done, with the empty bag of candyfloss, and my notebook which I'm done with, too, for now. See, Griff is the only person who hugs me. Not even my mother will. It's like she can't, like I'm candle wax, a light bulb, my skin metal bars under the sun's burning yellow shadow ... too hot to touch. My mother is scared of me but Griff's not.

Today the man selling candyfloss thought I was there all by myself.

'As if,' I said, and pointed over to Griff who was waiting for me on top of the steps by the beach while I went to buy it.

'Go straight back over to your daddy then kiddo,' he told me when he gave me the change. 'It's busy down here today.' I didn't tell him that he got it wrong, that Griff wasn't my dad, just my uncle. But I'm not stupid. I know that while I'm here I'm only playing along. For two nights and two car trips from Tonypandy and then back again. I'm like a burglar, walking around the rooms in this flat with sandy toes leaving trails in the carpet when I don't belong here.

The lump grows back in my throat and then the tears run out, ooze down my cheeks like warm glue. I can't help it. If only you could stop tears like blood, with some cotton wool or a tissue or a damp cloth, press and hold your eyes until they stop. I just wish everything could be like how I make it in my notebook. If I could, I would write it so that everything is okay. I would write a normal family. I would live by the beach. I'd eat candyfloss every single day. It's really not fair, you know.

They don't even sell it in Pandy.

Spit Shake

Jess lives three streets away from me. I see her sometimes on the pavement by the main road going up and down on her scooter. One leg on, one leg off. And she must be crazy because she doesn't even wear a helmet despite zooming as fast as the cars that growl past her. Her mother works behind the till in Somerfield down Pandy. I know because when me and Mum are on the way out Mum always goes to me ... that was that girl in your class' mother, that was, Jessica whatshername ... and I say *I know*, Mum, you told me that the last time.

Her name is actually Jessica Matthews and of course I know who she is. It's just that me and her don't talk about the weather or moan about the price of things like our mothers do. We don't talk at all in school because we like different things. What she does the most in class is use the blackboard but I'm not fussed on chalks. They're messy and the thing is, if I came home with dust on my clothes Mum would go mental, like she does when I accidentally get dinner down me. Nah. I like playing clean games but Jess likes all the dirty stuff. Sand and dough and clay. She presses her hands into trays sliding with runny paint and stamps them onto pieces of card, and when they're dry she'll peg them up on the display line, hands turned to bright green trees, fingers to twigs and leaves.

Mrs Thomas says she's fantastic, very talented and her pictures and paintings are lovely. I don't know how she does it. I just know that I can't. This is why I have to be a writer when I grow up. When I write it's the only time I'm good at anything. My words are like Jess' pictures, I guess. My words make paint and chalk and trees and hands and glitter and shape. My words are colours – the only way I know how to be bright. Except Mrs Thomas never hangs my stories up with a peg. It's because I don't write them for her. I won't have anyone throwing them in the bin again.

Jessica Matthews though. I sit and watch her and I think to myself ... woah, she's *really* cool, far too cool to be friends with someone like me, so I just don't bother talking to her normally. Even her feet are cool. I looked under the table while we were drinking our milk and saw that she's got black shoes with pink flashing lights on the side.

'Excellent shoes,' I say to her, but she doesn't say anything about mine.

Why would she? Mine don't flash. I can't ride a scooter fast, haven't even got a scooter, and I can't make trees with my hands, so I've really got no idea why she's been chatting to me all morning. She even sat next to me at milk-time, I told you, jumped on the seat before Evan got a chance and let me tell you, he was not impressed.

'Did you see his face?' she says. 'Looked like he'd jammed his willy in the Lego box again.'

That happened to him yesterday. I'm not quite sure what his willy was doing out in the first place but anyway, he got it stuck under the lid of the Lego box and Mrs Thomas had to send him to the nurse so she could rub some ointment on it. Jess reckoned it looked like a strawberry mini milk ice lolly, his willy, small and pink but she definitely wouldn't suck it, *that's for sure*. Jess isn't as fat as me, and she's only a tiny bit taller.

'When's your birthday?' I ask her.

'April. What about you?'

I do think about lying, because being the oldest is something that's very important to kids. I've heard them arguing over it. And Jess is older than me but I suppose that just means she'll die first. So I tell her The Truth. August.

'Have you got any brothers or sisters?'

'No. What about you?'

'Nah. I'm an only child, too,' she says. 'My mother can't stand looking at my father anymore, let alone making babies with him.'

Jess says kissing people with your lips and then touching your belly buttons together is how you make babies, see. Jess likes scootering and skipping and painting and she doesn't like it when her Mam and Dad argue but she's used to that now because they do it all the time. My hair is curly, but Jess has got a black bob that's dead straight and it floats above her shoulders when she runs. Green eyes, too, super super green they are. Green is my favourite colour. It's like she has green ones on purpose just to spite me. Oh, and her nose isn't long like her mother's. Her mother's nose is *really* long. Jess doesn't wear school dresses or skirts, she wears trousers and a red uniform jumper instead of a cardigan, just like me.

'Skirts are rubbish, in' they? My mam's always trying to get me in one. Says I've got to be a *lady*, but I don't want no boys looking at my minge when I'm sitting down.'

I know lots of words but I've never heard of that one. What on earth is a minge? I don't ask her to explain. I don't want her thinking I'm stupid.

'Well, I hate washing my hair,' I tell her, maybe that will impress her.

'And me. What's the point in getting your hair wet unless you're going swimming, like? Cause you've just got to dry it again then, haven't you?'

I nod. We're by the blackboard. She's scribbled bubble writing on it with a chalk as green as her eyes.

jess and hannah, best freinds forever

She's put the i and the e in the wrong places, and all I want to do is get that duster by there and rub it out, fix it. It kills me a little bit to leave it like that, but being called her best friend makes me feel better, a warm, slushy feeling inside that I've never felt before, and now I have it I don't ever want it to go away. She slaps her hands together and the chalk clouds rise like green steam. And then she makes this sound as if she's being sick and catches her phlegm in her cupped hand.

'What you doing?'

'Spit shake,' she says, a thin silvery river trickling down her chin. 'Now spit in yours.'

'No way. That's *gross*.'

'If you don't do a spit shake we can't be best friends.'

'Why?'

'Because that's the rules. Are you thick or what?'

Well at least *I* know where my i's and my e's go. I don't say it, that I'm a million times smarter than she is, smarter than any kid in the whole world. I keep it in my head because I've got a feeling Jess will be a really good patient. Much better than Evan anyway who squeals like a little pig when I jab him with a freshly sharpened pencil, a pointy lead needle, very important for playing doctors. How else am I supposed to give him his medicine? She holds her hand out and my belly turns when I look at them, the crumbs from the biscuits we had with our milk earlier floating like brown tadpoles in her spit. I can't go making too much of a fuss, can I? It's mad that someone like Jessica Matthews, that *anyone* actually, would want to be best friends with me because I'm nothing special.

That's why I do it. I want to be special. I squeeze some spit into my mouth from wherever it comes from and swoosh it loudly around my cheeks. I purse my lips and it drops out slowly, like a raindrop that grows into a long string and then I catch it in my hand, hold it, warm and gloopy. I close my eyes and brace myself.

'Hurry up,' I say as I hold it out. 'Do it quick.'

Our palms squelch together, wet and slimy. I think I'm going to be sick.

'You can't go back on a spit shake mind,' she says.

'What do you mean?'

'We've got to be best friends forever now. Can't ever leave each other. Because if you break a spit shake you'll die.'

'As if.'

'You will. Don't you trust me or what?'

'Not really.'

'Well I swear it. A spit shake is a contract. My father told me and my father knows everything. And he plays rugby.'

Apparently he's gigantic. Probably the biggest man I've ever seen in my life, she'd bet a fiver on it. He works up on the quarries and listens to Queen and her mother can't *stand* him. But I'm not really interested in her father. And I'm not going to die because I'm not going to break my spit shake. I told you, I *want* to be best friends. Forever and ever, AMEN.

'That's the bell,' she says, as it rings loud around the classroom.

Does she think I'm deaf? She wipes her hand dry in her trousers while kids race to their coats on the hooks and Mrs Thomas puts her long grey cardigan on, ready to go and get her cup of coffee from the staffroom. Well, what am I doing just standing there? Am I coming then or what? Hands on hips Jess waits for me to follow.

But I never leave our classroom at break time. I like to stay in here and stare at the solar system, papier-mâché planets, cardboard stars suspended from the ceiling on string. 'Come *on*,' she says, sad green eyes that make my heart feel like it's melting. 'Let's go and play!'

I don't know how she does it, but just like that I'm walking with her towards the big hall because it's too wet to go outside in the yard. She tries to hold my hand but I shake her off. I don't like holding hands. So she skips ahead and I follow, our school shoes loud against the black-tiled floor, hers flashing, mine completely normal. It's very loud inside the big hall with all the kids running around and screaming. Me and Jess find a free bench to sit on and she teaches me loads of new things I never knew before, like this song about someone called Elvis Presley. She says I can stay over her house as well since I'm her best friend now. And I can have tea and do I like Turkey Twizzlers?

'I don't know what they are.'

'They're made of turkey. That's a meat.'

'Well I know *that*.'

'Do you like mayo, Han? 'Cause I love it, I do. And chips. Chips are my favourite.'

'My mother doesn't let me eat chips.'

'We'll have them over my house, don't you worry. You don't have to tell her, do you?'

'I suppose not.'

'And I'll get my father to buy us a 99 off the ice-cream van. My father gives me whatever I want, see.'

'Cool.'

'He plays rugby, did I tell you?'

'Yes.'

'What does your father do, Han?'

We're facing each other on the long dark-wood bench, our legs dangling either side of it like we're on a seesaw, and I do the only thing I can do besides tell her a lie. Jess has been my best friend for less than an hour, and I don't want to start doing *that* until we've been friends for at least a week. I throw myself off the bench, land face first on the hard wooden floor, too. Something I didn't plan. She helps me back up.

'*Flipping Hell.* You flew off that then. Must be slippery cause of the rain. You alright.'

'Yeah I'm fine' I say, although I've really hurt my knee. 'Just sing me another song about Elvis Presley.'

Mum is always telling me I should be making friends instead of having my head in that bloody shiny book all the time. She tried to take it off me once but I wrestled it from her. If she didn't let it go I probably would've bitten her, sunk my teeth into her wrist and made her bleed. She just doesn't get it. But maybe she'll be happy now that I've made friends with Jessica Whatshername. Maybe, for once, I'll have done something right, something that pleases her. And I do like having a best friend. I only wish she'd stop asking me questions. She can talk all day about herself if she wants. I don't mind. Just not about me.

Evan has spotted us now. He's like a hawk where I'm concerned. He comes and sits next to me on the bench and Jess leans over and tells him straight, can you leave us alone, please? Can't you see we're having a private conversation about Elvis Presley?

'I only want to play.'

'Well do you know who Elvis Presley is?'

'No.'

'He's the King.'

'The King of Wales?'

'Yes. Now shoo.'

'Hannah's name is King, too.'

'I am fully aware of my best friend's name, Evan.'

'She's not your best friend. She's *my* best friend.'

Jess laughs and tells him straight again. Apparently boys and girls can't be best friends. Another rule. When Evan's older he will find a wife and marry her but right now he's a boy and we don't like him, okay?

'But I want to marry Hannah. I love her.'

'Love? Ha! You don't know the meaning of the word love, Evan Jones. And even if you do love her, Hannah doesn't want to play with you anymore because me and her are best friends now.'

'Can't I be best friends, too? I'll give you my crisps.'

He holds them out to us. Wotsits. I go to put my hand in to take one, but Jess pushes the packet away and they fly everywhere like pieces of orange confetti, trampled under the shoes of kids who are playing tag. Evan's face sinks.

'Hannah can share *my* crisps if she wants to. I've got steak flavour McCoys in my bag in class and they're posher than Wotsits, much tastier. Do you like steak McCoys, Han?'

I don't have time to answer because they start pulling me back and forth on the bench and I just let them. My arms hurt. They'll rip me like a cheap doll any second but I kind of like listening to them fight over me. Jess likes me better and she's got Turkey Twizzlers and steak McCoys and her father is massive and will beat Evan's father up *easy*. Evan loves me though, and love is the best thing in the world and he's got Wotsits, well he did have Wotsits anyway, and we've been playing together for years and years. Jess will knock him out now. Honest to Jesus and God and Allah and Freddie Mercury, if he doesn't go away and leave us alone she'll pull his pants down and kick him in the balls. Evan will ... Evan will tell Miss.

'Is that the best you've got, Jones boy? *Right.*'

Jess is much stronger than him, and with one final, violent tug she wins me. I feel nice, if not a bit sore. I must be special now if she wants to hold my hand and give me her crisps and keep me all to herself. I can't be as bad as my mother says I am if she'd kick Evan Jones in his balls with her flashy shoes just to be my best friend. We slide all the way to the other side of the bench away from him, and he does what he does best. He cries. I don't know why the three of us can't all be friends but I suppose Jess is right. He needs to find boys to play with. He needs to love someone who doesn't pull his hair because it's just not natural to love someone who treats you so badly.

'That's right, stinker,' she says. 'You'll have this in your gob if you come near us again, if you try to pinch my best friend off me.'

She clenches her hand up into a fist and shakes her knuckles at him. Evan just goes away, terrified, slithers off the bench like a snake. He sits on the floor sobbing his heart out, but we ignore him.

'No one can touch us,' she says, 'because we're best friends, alright?'
Alright.

Salt

This is where Auntie Eve works. In a chip shop. She's got to wear a white apron and a thing on her head that looks like a window net. It's not only chips that she sells though. There's all kinds of things in the lit-up tunnel on top of the counter you can buy. But don't touch the glass because it's hot and it will burn you. Trust me. I've burned myself loads of times already today. There's fish and sausages in batter, or wrinkly ones just naked, and pies and burgers and rissoles and potato fritters. Rissoles are disgusting. Most people order fish and chips when they come in and Auntie Eve scoops them out and wraps them up in newspaper like greasy birthday presents.

Mum dropped me off earlier. I've got to stay here while she's busy doing 'stuff'. Talking in code again. Stuff means that she doesn't want me to know what she's actually doing. It means she isn't telling The Truth but because she's a grown-up, it's absolutely fine. I'd be up Jess' house if she wasn't on holiday. Or we'd be in the park or down the lake, scaling the steep hills and terraced streets of Pandy looking for something to do. She's gone on a plane to Portugal which is a place really far away, and I'm kind of annoyed that she left me behind. She'll be back soon enough, I know, fourteen all inclusive days and counting. I just wish she was here or that I was there. I don't miss her though. No chance. Not really. It's just that I'm stuck in this greasy, stinky Hell with Kyle who is almost as annoying as the flies. I've never seen so many. They buzz around the shop like tiny, evil black pixies, and eventually they sizzle and die in the spinning fan on the ceiling.

I watch the blurs of people smudge outside, their blue and pink and yellow shorts going past the window like a colourful train. Kyle sighs. I know how he feels. There hasn't been a customer in the shop for ages. No one's pushed through the door and dinged the bell and I'd much rather be out there than in here. When we left Pandy the sky was cloudy and white above the car but when we got to Porthcawl all the clouds had gone. Auntie Eve won't let us out though. We're staying in here where she can keep an eye on us.

I'm not allowed to sleep over the flat anymore on the weekends. It's because of this bad little secret that everyone wants to bury, like a shell on the beach except the thing about shells is that pretty soon the sea will come and wash them all up again. No one will talk about it. And that's another thing about grown-ups. They can say whatever they want but when you've got something to say, something important to ask, they tell you to be quiet. Mum doesn't want to hear another word about it because as far as she's concerned it's all finished with. Griff's gone and that's that. Auntie Eve won't take him back and let's hope she bloody means it this time. I don't know what's going on. It's all very confusing when people are talking in code, shouting, when you're a kid, when everyone around you is mental.

End of. Be quiet now, Hannah. I don't want to hear it. No more questions. That's enough.

But the worst thing ever happened. She took it when I was in school. My notebook. Slammed it shut in the living-room cabinet, the beautiful red sparkles trapped in the dark, dusty shadow of the drawer. I'm bloody trouble and my words are even more trouble. Those things I wrote, the stuff that came out of my head just wasn't right, wasn't bloody normal. I watched her face get angrier with each word she read. She shook her head and turned pages, and it was as if I was standing there in our living room naked, completely naked, and she was looking me up and down and then she peeled my skin off like I was an onion and studied my bones and decided there was something wrong with them, too. Don't worry. I got it back. Took it out of the drawer when she was down Nanny's and I keep it in my bag now, a black rucksack, and my bag is always on my back. In school, up Jess', when I'm shopping in Pandy with Mum. Right now. The only time it isn't on my back is when I'm at home or asleep and then it lives under my bed like a monster where no one can steal it ever again.

Auntie Eve's depressed according to Mum. When a grown-up is depressed it means they've gone mental. That's why Kyle's coming home with us tonight. Auntie Eve needs a break after Griff left. Last week or the week before, I can't remember which, Mum said she poured a carton of curry sauce over a customer and the way she's going she'll be lucky not to be sectioned, never mind sacked. That's probably why she's snapping polystyrene trays in half and calling the dishwasher nasty names, why Kyle's had more slaps today than usual. I climb up on the counter to get a better look outside. You can see the sea from up here and it looks too lush and too perfect to be real, like the window is a telly and I'm just watching it, one of Mum's programmes where the people go on holiday. I wonder what it's like where Jess is. I wonder what she's doing. Maybe she's met some new kids. Maybe she likes them better than me. A horrible thought that makes me feel as sick as dead flies and rissoles. I shake it out of my head.

I'd give anything to be out there on the beach now, my feet in the water, my toes disappearing in the sinking sand.

'This counter is for glasses not arses, Hannah King. Get down.'

When I turn around I find Auntie Eve glaring at me. She's holding a bag of frozen chips up against her oil-stained, yellow-green drizzled apron, her face trickling with sweat. She hates my guts. That I do know. I'm scared she'll tip hot curry sauce over me, or empty me into the bubbling fat with those chips, so I sit back down quickly next to Kyle on a stool. He's holding a sausage in a piece of newspaper like it's an ice lolly and he's being suspiciously quiet today, hasn't called me fat or ginger or gay once. In fact he's been quiet since Griff left.

'Can't believe she just said *arse*,' I say to him, although I can believe it, it's not like I haven't heard her say it before, I just wanted something to talk about.

'She says arse all the time. And *fuck*.'

My mother never swears and I know that if she ever catches me she'll get the bar of Imperial Leather soap out and scrub it back and forth on my tongue. I'll be coughing bloody suds for months. Bloody apparently isn't a proper naughty word because it's in the Bible. And I tasted it once, Imperial Leather soap. I was in the bath and I was bored because all my bubbles had sunk into the water and my fingers were as wrinkly as Kyle's sausage by there, so I peeled the red square sticker off the top and I licked it. I know it was a stupid thing to do but I just wanted to see if swearing would be worth the risk. It wasn't. I could taste it for days after, even when I burped. *Fuck* tastes like soap.

'Is your sausage nice?'

He shrugs. It's alright. Don't know. Whatever. It's just a sausage. I guess Kyle doesn't want to talk today. He finishes eating his alright sausage and I count dead flies until Mum comes back to pick us up. She didn't take long doing her 'stuff' and I'm glad. Auntie Eve makes Kyle stand still so she can kiss him and of course, he wipes it off straight away. She usually kisses me and I wipe it off too, but today she doesn't even say goodbye to me. And we ask her, but Mum doesn't let us go to the beach, either. That'll mean sand trod through her house and she can't stand the messy bloody stuff. She'll be finding it for weeks in the carpet and God knows where else. No. The sound of the seagulls is shut out with the slam of the car door. I look through the back window as we leave the beach behind. The waves will crash without me, I know. And the tide will come in and out and unearth the shells whether I'm there to see it or not. I love the beach more than anything, but it doesn't really care about me at all.

Me and Kyle are both in the back. I don't ever sit up front with my mother because I'll go straight through the bloody windscreen and die. I'll end up like one of the dead squirrels or foxes we pass on the side of the road, my insides squashed all over the tarmac. Kyle silently counts them all the way back to Pandy. And when we get there Mum shakes my box of dolls out on the floor behind the settee, a tumbling avalanche of plastic pink.

'Play nice,' she says. 'Share your things with Kyle.'

As if. Boys don't like dolls and especially not boys like Kyle. My dolls aren't dressed for war. He'd have them all fighting and you can't fight in a bikini and you can't wrestle in a pair of swimming trunks or shoot somebody with a handbag. I don't know what he thinks he's doing, but he crosses his legs and sits down in the middle of it all, like a grubby Buddha. I tell him not to touch anything without washing his hands first. They're greasy and sausagey, but he grabs a doll and squeezes her. She's a Barbie, blue eyes and thin arms and hard volcano-shaped boobs. She's getting on a bit, this one is, white hair that's turned yellow with playing and her material body has been sewn back together too many times. Mum is like a surgeon when I bring my dolls to her all broken, and her sewing box is an operating table and her scissors are forceps and her pins and needles are clamps and scalpels. Kyle has decided to talk now.

'Look at this one,' he says. 'She's stupid. Look at her eye.'

Well what do you expect? I've played with her a lot. We've had loads of fun over the years and her left eyelid stopped working ages ago. If you open it up then it just falls shut again. She can't help it. Kyle gets bored of squeezing her and throws her back onto the pile. My dolls are ants and snails to him, things with no feelings, things to be punished. He takes their clothes off. He pulls down pants and has a look but of course there's nothing there. They don't have real willies, just smooth plastic peach. He undoes the Velcro on dresses and leaves their pointy shiny boobs and privates flashing for everyone to see. It takes all my strength not to strangle him. But then he does something so terrible. He presses one of my girl dolls up against one of my boy dolls, makes their little red lips kiss. I can't take it anymore. They've already got lives. They've got feelings and more importantly, they've got *clothes*.

'You're messing things up. You're making them cold, Kyle.'

'So? I can do whatever I want.'

'Well you can't play with my dolls.'

'They're only dolls, freckly face. They're not real.'

He laughs and tells me I'm stupid. The cheek of it! He picks my very old doll up again, his greasy sausage fingers and long dirty nails wrapped around her bare boobs.

'Are you real?' he asks her, and he puts her mouth to his ear. 'Does this hurt?'

My mean, horrible, not real cousin Kyle pulls her leg.

'Stop it!'

'See, she said nothing because she's plastic.'

'You can't even *spell* plastic.'

'Yes I can.'

'Go on then.'

'Puh, luh, aaa, sss, tuh, eh, kicking kuh.'

I snatch her off him. She's extremely delicate and I don't know how many more times Mum will stitch her up with her needle and thread before she puts her out with the rubbish. I sit her down on the carpet but when I do her leg falls off. I twist the little circle back into the hole on her body, again and again and again, but it won't stay, it keeps coming out.

'Ha ha. She's *dead*!'

'You're horrible,' I tell him.

'You're fat.'

'You're thick and stupid. You can't even *spell*.'

'You're ginger. Ha! You can't beat that!'

'You're mental like Auntie Eve. And Griff's gone. You haven't got a Dad now.'

He picks another doll up. And with a look on his face I've seen before but never so crazy, with mad eyes and wide pupils and gritted teeth and ants and snails and Reebok trainers and blood and guts and guns, he pulls her head off. And then another head and another head. He twists and yanks and strains like he's unscrewing tight bottle lids. I beg him. Leave them alone. *Please!*

'They're always shouting,' he says. 'They're always shouting about you.'

'Who?'

'My mother and my father.'

'Auntie Eve and Griff?'

'Yeah! She threw his clothes out of the bathroom window and they landed in a big puddle and it's all your fault, freckly face.'

'I didn't *do* anything…'

'He's gone because you wrote lies in your stupid book. She cut his shorts in half.'

He's shouting, the carpet around us an abattoir of peach limbs, of ripped necks and legless torsos. A chamber of horrors. He gets me so angry. They're *my* dolls, not his. And this is *my* house. This is *my* carpet he's sitting on. I grab him by his stupid t-shirt.

'Say sorry, Kyle Thomas Rhys Griffiths.'

'No way, Hannah big fat liar King!'

I pull his hair so hard I'm surprised his head doesn't come off, too. He goes rigid and screams and my mother's footsteps down the stairs follow soon after. What the bloody Hell is going on? Hannah bloody King, what have you done now?

'Nothing. *I* haven't done anything. Kyle's ruining everything. These aren't his dolls. And he hasn't even washed his hands. And Kyle...'

'You selfish little bitch.'

I let Kyle go. It must be the shock of hearing her say it that makes me loosen my grip on his hair. My mother said *bitch*. She said *bitch*. I'm halfway up the stairs before I even know it. I'm running from my mother who actually swore, who said a bad word, who is now smacking my bum on top of the landing. I am spiteful. I am selfish. I am a liar. I am a Nasty Piece of Work. *Trouble*.

And I'm pushed into my bedroom and my door is shut. An all too familiar routine. The shock goes and then I'm just angry again.

I want to scream. FUCK SHIT ARSE BITCH BITCH FUCK FUCK FUCK. But I taste it again, the disgusting, sour Imperial Leather on my tongue. I open my notebook and write it all out instead. I cry like the big baby I am. Salt tastes better than soap.

Danville

I can open the basket by myself. Yeah, *really*. A big job. An important job. So I take it slow, untie the knots carefully. I don't want to cut my fingers on the sharp, silver wire but much worse than that, worse than torn skin and bleeding, worse than anything, I don't want him to think I'm useless.

Got it. And as soon as I lift the wicker lid they fight their way out. It's a mad race to the sky. They flap and flap away, feathers falling in the air behind them like soft grey leaves. No wonder they wanted to get out so bad. I felt sorry for them in the car crowded inside that stuffy basket. I could hear them in the boot talking to each other the way pigeons do. Cooing, I think it's called. I don't mind birds so much anymore. At least I don't mind *our* birds. They've got pink rubber bands with numbers on around their skinny ankles and heads that don't stay still and small eyes that never seem to blink. Our pigeons are the fastest, cleverest pigeons in Pandy.

We get back in the car and I sit next to him. My bag is by my feet. I've also got a carton of strawberry flavour Ribena which he bought me in the garage on the way. He doesn't mind me being up front with him, just as long as I put my seatbelt on and as long as I don't tell my mother. I am his co-pilot and this car is our spaceship. In here we can travel absolutely anywhere we want. Outside the wide glass windscreen there are no limits. The fast grey road is our milky way and we're riding it. Me and him in our spaceship under the hot yellow sun, our celestial God. The trucks and lorries are gigantic Jupiters and Saturns, planets with wing mirror moons. Fumes puff out of exhaust pipes like galactic dust and cars zoom past us down the lane opposite loud and fierce like meteors. The pigeons in the sky are our stars, black dots that are free now, move fast. I clip my seatbelt in even though I know I don't really need to. Nothing could possibly happen to me in our spaceship. I am safe.

It took us hours to get here and I don't know where we are. I only know we're somewhere in England because when we passed the sign he booed and I joined in.

'How do they know the way home, Dad?'

'They just *know*, babe.'

The thing about my dad is, even though I nag and ask a lot of questions, he still likes me. I don't seem to get on his nerves like I do my mother's and I think the reason he puts up with me is because we're the same. People are always telling me how much I look like him. In Pandy they'll stop in their tracks and squeeze my cheeks and say dew, dew, you're the image of your father, you are, love … or beaut or sweetheart, sometimes kid or bach. It's because of the hair and the freckles although he's got loads more of them than I have. I counted them on his face once. Climbed up onto his belly like he was a shiny gold carousel horse. Nineteen.

He pushes the tape in. These are the songs I mess up all the words to. The lady singing is Joan Baez and her voice makes my skin go fizzy.

'You could be a singer like Joan when you're older,' he says to me, both hands back on the wheel now.

'Don't be so stupid, Dad. I can't sing at all. I've got a really terrible voice. Listen now.'

I show him. Lean forward and turn the volume down and clear my throat. I croak a bit of 'Amazing Grace', especially for him, and when I've finished he gives me this look that sort of says, yeah, you're right and all, babe, you really have got a terrible voice.

'Are you going to tell me The Story then or what?'

He smiles and slowly shakes his head. He was waiting for that. Aren't I sick of hearing it by now?

'Absolutely not. Never.'

Am I ready?

'Yes. Yes I'm ready. I'm always ready. Go *on*,' I beg him.

Alright then. Here it goes. Sure I'm ready now?

'Yes!'

Okay.

My dad is at this place, at this very special festival, and there's thousands of people as far as the eye can see. None of them have met before yet they're all there standing together on the hard mud, and the sun is beating like a drum in the sky above. Most of the boys have long hair, beards too, and the girls are screaming for a man called Jim Morrison. It's windy, very windy.

'Yeah. And what else, Dad?'

He sighs. Well, it's like this. Everyone and everything sort of stopped still that day, babe, stopped still to listen. And I don't know why he sighs so hard, out of the windscreen like that, like he's looking at something far away but I can't see it. There's nothing out there, just cars and a big truck carrying tree trunks on the back. Maybe he's bored with this story but I will never get tired of hearing it. I'm told to listen to Joan because apparently Joan can explain it better than he ever could. And then she's turned up, as if to speak to me louder. My dad says when Joan Baez sings the world listens. And that's why he ran away from Tonypandy a very long time ago, before I was born and before he got sick, to listen to her sing songs about freedom.

'What's freedom?'

'Freedom,' he says and sighs again. 'It's complicated.'

'Just tell me. You can. I'm quite clever, you know.'

'Oh, I know *that*, babe.'

'So what is it then?'

'It's something you won't find in Pandy, that's for sure.'

I wish he'd just tell me because I need to know. I don't understand. But I do know the words to this song. 'The Night They Drove Old Dixie Down'. He sways his head back and forth, taps his pale fingers against the black wheel of our spaceship. I look up at the sky but the pigeons have disappeared. I'm worried they're lost but he bets they're back at home already.

'What's Danville, Dad?' I ask him, because Danville, it's in the song we're singing about Old Dixie.

'It's not a what it's a where. It's a place in America.'

'Is it anywhere near Pandy?'

'No, babe.'

'Will you drive us there one day?'

'Of course.'

'Promise?'

He promises. And I'm really glad because I decide that's where she lives, Joan Baez, in Danville, and that's also where she keeps freedom and freedom is her voice, the most lovely thing in the world. It makes me happy. Song after song coming out of the speakers all the way back to Wales … 'Black is the color of my true love's hair.'

'I wish I had black hair, Dad.'

'Why, babe?'

'*Because* … because of the song! Jess has got black hair. You know Jess, don't you? She's my best friend.'

'You've got lovely colour hair. Perfect the way you are.'

Well I know that's a lie for sure. I am lots of things but perfect is definitely not one of them, and I don't like my hair. No one in the whole world likes ginger hair. If ginger hair was so good then Joan Baez would be singing about it instead of black hair, wouldn't she? I suppose I'm stuck with it though. I just don't have black hair and that's that. I never will like Joan's true love in the song and maybe no one will ever love me because of it. But I don't love Jess despite her black hair. Not really. Not like I love Joan Baez who makes my skin fizz and it doesn't stop fizzing until Dad turns the key and the engine stops and we're parked up outside our house.

I'm sad then. I never want these journeys to end. But of course he was right about the pigeons. I rush down the concrete steps out our back garden and see they're there already, safely back in the shed. I love my dad. I never tell him because I just can't, okay? I like his music and The Story, like that he takes me with him to race his pigeons and one day he'll take me all the way to Danville to meet Joan Baez. Most of all I like that he's better now. Mum says cancer is the most terrible thing ever but being better means he isn't in hospital so much, the cold white place with the lifts and hundreds of buttons. I was scared of him there. I was afraid to go near him in the bed in case I hurt him, stepped on one of the thin tubes snaked across the floor and killed him.

It's different now though. He's not there, he's always here and I'm not scared anymore. He doesn't leave and come back and then leave again. He's no longer my secret and when I'm with him, I don't feel like I have to make things up. Because when things are perfect, when you have everything you want, then you don't need to imagine it. He doesn't have to be an astronaut anymore. I've got a normal family, like everyone else. I've got my dad back from space, and I'm never letting him go there again.

Seven O'clock

First Jill came this morning. She was wearing Christmas earrings. Little puddings that blinked with pin-sized green LED lights. I thought they were minging. She drained the bottle of whisky in the cabinet and gave my dad a headache. Jill is Mum's best friend and she's got the loudest laugh in Pandy. A witch's cackle. Dad says when she gets going, when she's holding her belly and her tongue's hissing like a snake's, you can probably hear her all the way up in Treorchy. But the first thing you'll notice when you meet Jill is how she smells. She's got this cloud of strong perfume that follows her around, a toxic cloak. And after she's choked me to death she likes to press my dimples like they're buttons without even asking. People do that a lot.

If it's not Christmas Time she comes over and drinks tea instead of whisky, and while she's here, talking and laughing, she makes me get her things. Pass me a biscuit, beaut, and bring me a cushion for my back and that pouffe for under my feet. Bloody Hell, turn that fire up it's cowing Baltic in here. I'm a good old kid, aye, but awful plain to look at, like my father. Not a very nice thing to say to a kid, or anyone, but Jill reckons it's better to tell it how it is, she ain't got no time for bullshit. That's how she is and no one is going to cowing change her, not now. She tells me how plain I am whilst sponging thick blusher on her creased-up cheeks with some sort of orange pad that looks like a soggy digestive biscuit. I don't like Jill.

Dad doesn't either. He says she's a fruit. It's probably because her nails are always painted the colour of cherries, or maybe because the mole on her cheek when she makes me kiss it is as prickly as a pineapple. Let me get this straight. I don't just go around kissing old ladies for fun. Kissing is absolutely disgusting and I don't even kiss my own mother, not that she asks me to anyway. It's just that I'm slightly scared of Jill. I do what she asks because any kid would be afraid of a woman that loud, that mental. You know she's coming down the street before she even gets here.

Clip clop, clip clop, a crazy laughing horse with red lips and nails and a black leather handbag heading straight for our front door. Jill lets herself in, never knocks.

But she went home eventually, *thankfully*, and without leaving me a present. But when Auntie Eve came a bit later on she had presents. I was shocked because I wasn't expecting anything. It was weird. There was something wrong with her. She couldn't talk tidy. Her words came out wet and fast and Dad kept shaking his head like she'd done something wrong. When she gave me it, a square box wrapped in shiny silver paper, she looked at me nastily and said that I didn't deserve it. Said it … well, actually, she sort of spat it at me. You'll be lucky if Santa brings you anything at all tonight. Santa doesn't bring presents to children who tell lies.

That's right. It's Christmas Eve and Mum's been wearing her big glove and sliding trays of mince pies out of the oven since early this morning, since well before Jill came. Jill ate three. They floated in the china bowl like steaming brown boats on a single cream sea. I don't like them but Kyle absolutely loves them. Last Christmas Day he ate eleven in one go and spewed all over Nanny's brand new slippers. They aren't coming to ours for Christmas dinner this year, for the first time ever, so Mum rolled them up in foil, the mince pies, and told him to take it bloody easy now, no stuffing. He wouldn't get out of the car, not even to collect his presents. He only opened the window enough for Mum to post the mince pies through. Her and Auntie Eve argued on the doorstep. Auntie Eve shouldn't be driving in that state. There was bloody black ice on the bloody roads. Mum ought to mind her own fucking business. Happy fucking Christmas. And then they left.

Christmas has taken ages to come. It feels like me and Jess have been singing songs about frankincense and myrrh and little donkeys in school forever. In our concert Mrs Thomas played the piano and smashed a black tambourine stapled with tinsel into her hand. Mary forgot her words and cried. And Robbie Jenkins was Joseph and an elastic band kept a checked tea towel on top of his head. Me and Jess were angels who flapped around the stage in our nighties to warn everyone Jesus was coming so they'd better hurry up and get to Bethlehem. But Christmas is here now.

Our tree is up and it's sparkling with white lights. It's a rule in our house. No tree and no cards and definitely no opening the door to the carol singers before Christmas Eve. Mum reckons all the palaver means you're fed up of Christmas by bloody Christmas. But I don't understand her. How can you get fed up of *Christmas*? I could easily wake up to presents every morning, and to snow so white it glows outside my window. And even though we haven't got snow this year it's still Christmas, and every other day is rubbish compared to it.

Dad did the lights because he said they were tricky to untangle and he had to lift me up to put the angel on top ... she's got blonde hair and white paper wings ... but the rest of the tree I did all by myself. I stood on a stool and wrapped it in so much tinsel and colour you can barely see the green branches now. There wasn't a bauble left in the box when I was finished. I used them all. Rough glittery balls and soft red velvet bows and tiny fake blue presents, chocolates on strings and plastic robins with sharp feet, stars and that. Mum even let me put the glass baubles up that are really precious to her. They aren't kept in the box with the rest of the decorations but on their own in the living room cabinet, as pretty and delicate as light bulbs. Apparently she's had them since she was younger than me. My dead grandfather gave them to her. Dad says I've made our tree look wonderful. Mum says it'll do.

I lick the envelope and press it down shut. My letter to Santa. I put it on top of the stone arch over our gas fire like I do every year although this year I haven't asked for much. I don't want to push my luck because I know I've been bad. Auntie Eve was wrong about Santa though. He *is* going to come because I said sorry. Sorry is this wonderful word that makes it all okay, like a rubber over all the wrong things you've done. Gone. So I asked for an electric toothbrush. They're really cool, much better than just normal toothbrushes. I know because Jess has got one. She let me have a go of it over her house which Mum said was bloody gross but we didn't mind because we share everything, including our germs. I asked for some new stuff for my Barbies, bits and pieces like, and most importantly a scooter because I want one like Jess.

We can race over the park then, and coming home down the main road from her house will be much more fun on wheels, much quicker too.

Underneath my list is where I wrote sorry. I wasn't specific because it's really hard remembering *everything* you've done all year. It was easy to remember when I cheeked Mum in Somerfield, easy to remember tipping blackcurrant squash on Nanny's cushion and not telling her, just turning it over. Those things happened last week. But the things I might've done in March or April or May, I can't be expected to remember them. I signed my name at the bottom.

So there we are … I'm sorry, Santa, for *everything* I've done. From Hannah King in Tonypandy. xx

Mum's getting ready upstairs in the spare room. It's where she always gets ready, where I'm not allowed to play. Dad's in the kitchen doing the carrots, the most important job of all. We bought loads of them just in case it snowed and we needed noses for white men in the garden. But it didn't. We're off our heads, me and Dad are, and what's she going to do with all these bloody carrots now? Christmas makes my crazy mother just a little bit more crazy. She doesn't care about snowmen, only food and presents. She worries about turkey and Yorkshire puddings, cards getting places on time, and where everyone is going to sit around the table, whether Kyle will behave himself. Last year, before he spewed on them, he balanced one of Nanny's new slippers on her head and she didn't even realise it was there for a whole hour after she woke up. But this year they aren't coming. Mum doesn't need to worry.

Dad's done chopping the carrots. They look like orange fifty pence pieces on the plate. They're for the reindeer.

'How do they fly, Dad?'

'Fairy dust, babe.'

'I thought Santa had elves, not fairies?'

'He's got both.'

'If everyone feeds them carrots, won't they get fed up of carrots?'

'They'll eat anything.'

I've got to go to bed now. My mother's orders. So I put the plate next to the letter up on the arch. I'm wearing my new pyjamas with penguins on. They're Christmas penguins instead of regular penguins because they're wearing red hats. I dive onto my bed ready for my story because every night for the past week, Dad's been telling me all about Santa. Santa uses the stars to find where different kids live and that's how he knows what presents to drop where. Every kid in the world has their own star that belongs to them and no one else. Each star beams like a spotlight to the right bedroom window. He points and shows me mine. In the starry Christmas Eve sky, mine is the brightest because apparently that's what I am – the best. The moon is so massive it's turned my bedroom blue but he hasn't got time to tell me a long story tonight.

Him and Mum are going to the pub at the end of our street. Jill will be there, too, and all the other ladies who drink from glasses and mark bingo numbers on tickets. I've never been to the pub but I hear Mum talk about it all the time. Dad sits downstairs with the men and Mum upstairs with her friends. The toilets in the pub are spotless. Mum knows the cleaner and she's very thorough. Upstairs the rows of tables have ashtrays in the middle of them and Mum and her friends sit by the same one every time. Some of them smoke but not my mother. She has a little drink but she never gets as drunk as Jill. Jill who once fell out of the taxi door and off the kerb and snapped her ankle. Jill who missed calling the tote because she was too bloody drunk to see the numbers.

'Make sure it's not under the covers now,' I tell him.

My stocking which is actually just a brown tight, one of my mother's.

'Will he be able to find it?'

'Yes, babe.'

'But what if I knock it off the bed when I'm sleeping?'

'He's magic. He'll find it.'

I've got one last thing to ask before he goes. And it's quite important so he needs to tell me The Truth now. Is it right? What Auntie Eve said … that liars don't get presents?

'Nah,' he says. 'All children get presents on Christmas.'

Besides, my dad knows that I'm a good girl. Deep down. No matter what I've done. No matter what anyone else says, he knows it. I think he's scared I'll ask him about Griff, so he quickly tucks me under my covers and reminds me that Santa is around so I'd better close my eyes and get to sleep. It's okay. I wasn't going to ask him about Griff anyway. My dad kisses me on my cheek and then shuts my bedroom door. I listen to his footsteps on the stairs, to Nanny coming in and my parents going out.

Mum won't like it, but Nanny will have the gas fire turned up full because she's old and old people get colder than we do. Sometimes when she babysits I sneak down and watch her from the gap in the living room door. She keeps it wedged open with her shoe so she can hear me upstairs. But not only old and cold she's also deaf. The telly's blasting loud and she never knows I'm there. Right now she'll be drinking from a glass clinking with ice cubes, and eating Mum's Christmas twiglets and dates until there's no room left inside her to fit any more, until the pub is closed and my parents are home. Nanny will walk home, it's not far, and then she'll be back tomorrow for Christmas dinner.

I don't want Santa to catch me awake so I stay in my bed tonight, no spying on Nanny. I close my eyes and squeeze, hope for sleep, for time to go faster. I think about reindeers on our roof. Christmas dinner and presents and Quality Street chocolates. The wrappers noisy, and as colourful as fairy lights in the deep tin. My head is a collage of all the things that have been giving me butterflies for weeks. And when I open my eyes again it's no longer blue outside but light. Christmas Morning is here.

I whip my quilt off the bed and throw it onto the floor, excited, frantic, my teddies and my dolls tumbling off with it. My heart is pumping so fast and I'm pulling sheets and lifting pillows, but I soon realise that my stocking isn't here. There's no electric toothbrush. No Malibu Barbie hairdryer or purple ball gown with matching jewelled handbag. There's no scooter. There's *nothing*. He's even taken my stocking because Auntie Eve was right. I've done a lot of bad things this year. So many bad things. I wish I never called Jess spiteful names, even though she deserved them, even though she called me them, too. I wish I hadn't been cheeky to my mother, tipped squash on Nanny's cushion, and most of all I wish I hadn't told lies.

I run across the landing and take it all out on their bedroom door with my fists. I bang the varnished wood so hard I think the hinges will give. Mum soon appears, eyes tired blue planets with black rings around them, the buttons on her nightie done up wrong. She's got my stocking, the limp and saggy tight Dad left on my bed now as full and swollen as a brown balloon. I see wrapping paper and tubes of chocolates. It's seven o'clock, mun, and she's got a stinking hangover. That bloody Jill must've spiked her drink. My mother doesn't come down in the mornings without brushing her hair and spraying it stiff with lacquer, but this morning it's sticking up and out like an exploding firework. Of course I ask her what on earth she's doing with my stocking. Why has Santa put it in her room and not mine?

'Perhaps he made a mistake, Hannah.'

Nah. I tell her straight. Santa doesn't make mistakes. He's the cleverest man in the world. He couldn't have put it in their bedroom by accident. And *no*, Santa can see in the dark so he wasn't confused whose room was whose and anyway, he's been bringing presents to our house for years and I've had the same bedroom all the time so it can't be that, either. Besides, every kid in the world has got a star and my star is the brightest and Santa would just know that so…

My mother sighs. A loud, angry sigh. Her words are like the ceiling and the brass light fitting and the attic above it and the sky and all those stars falling on top of me.

'Bloody stop it, Hannah. Stop nagging. It's seven o'clock. You're a big girl now. You know Santa isn't *real*.'

She filled my stocking up last night when she came home from the pub, didn't she? Put the presents in. And she's absolutely positive Jill put an extra measure in her drink when she went to the toilet. *Spotless*, those toilets are. Well then she forgot to put my stocking back on my bed. Must've fallen asleep. Passed out. That bloody Jill's fault, she'll murder her. She'll get up in an hour. Too early and Dad's sleeping. He's not feeling very well. Shouldn't have gone out really. Not up to it yet.

She closes their bedroom door and I can't find the strength to knock on it again. Can't speak, can't cry. I carry my stocking across the landing and back into my room. I open my curtains and see that the moon is still out except it's faint and no longer bright, almost completely dissolved into the Christmas Morning sky. I pick the quilt up off the floor and make my bed. I sit my dolls and teddies back in their places. A colourful line of plastic and hairy people up against the wall, the oldest teddy down to the newest doll. And then I start to unwrap, crossed legged on the end of my bed in my pyjamas. Shivering because the heating isn't on yet, radiator stone cold.

I tear through the thin brown stocking and then one by one through gold paper, hard boxes and soft packages. I pull bows and untie curly ribbon. And inside all these neatly wrapped presents I find the things I asked for and more. There's the electric toothbrush and the stuff for my dolls, Malibu Barbie hairdryer and purple ball gown with matching jewelled handbag and plastic pets, tiny white dogs and black cats with pink tongues, outfits for my teddies, stickers and glitter pens. And things I didn't ask for and don't really care about or want, like socks and soaps and a new nightie and some t-shirts and a pair of slippers and some knickers. In the very last parcel I find a Barbie with black skin.

I'm not sad because I don't like her, my black doll. I do. I'm just sad because I'm stupid. I think I'm clever but really, I'm not clever at all. All those letters I wrote asking for stuff, all those times I said sorry. I can't believe I thought Santa was real. Of course he's not. Like God. He's not real, either. When we were in the hospital I heard Mum say it. Nanny was leaning over the sink to fill Dad's plastic jug with water and she asked us if we wanted her to say a prayer. Mum shook her head and I was surprised to hear it come out of her mouth. A prayer to who? There's no God, she said, and if there is a God then he's a bloody bastard.

'I know it now,' I tell her, the new black doll with wiry hair and eyelids that flicker as I plonk her down at the end of the line on my bed. 'There's no Santa. And if there is a Santa, well then he's a bloody bastard, too.'

Dad tries to make me come downstairs when he wakes up. He looks tired in his stripy grey dressing gown, rough, like he hasn't slept at all. He says there's more presents under the tree, something with a handle and wheels, it looks scooter shaped to him, but I tell him that I don't want them, any of them, and I'm not coming out of my bedroom ever again. What's the point in Christmas if there isn't a Santa? If there's no snow and no elves and no flying reindeers then it may as well just be a normal rubbish day. Of course he hasn't got an answer for me. I've stumped him. It must be awful being a grown-up and knowing The Truth, knowing there's no such thing as magic. I've only known it for half an hour and already I can't stand it.

He leaves me in peace, says I'll come around soon enough, when I'm ready. I say yeah right, as his footsteps are going down the stairs again. I hate Christmas, I shout, I hate its guts, and lean over my bed and pull my bag from underneath. I write it down, exactly how I feel about Santa, about my mother, about Auntie Eve and Griff and Christmas and Jill, inside a brand new notebook I bought a couple of weeks ago from the craft shop in Pandy. This one isn't as nice or sparkly as my red one, nowhere near. This one has rich, cream sheets of paper and in a way new notebooks are better than full ones. New notebooks mean you can start again, forget about all those things you wrote on all those other pages ... leave them behind.

I empty my head onto a clean piece, and when I read it back I feel a lot better, like I've just been talking to a really good friend who *listens*. Not like talking to Jess because most of the time Jess only wants to talk about herself. This is a friend who understands me, a friend who I can tell secrets to without worrying they'll tell them to someone else or think I'm crazy or weird. Yeah, I know. I know it's also a friend who doesn't exist. How sad can you get?

Just as I'm finishing up writing, I smell it cooking and it smells really good. So good. The smell of Christmas dinner drifting up the stairs like a cruel, spiteful fog. I hear pots and pans rattling, cutlery clanking and the most piercing sound of all ... the sound of my mother nagging my dad. I really was going to stay in here all day, you know. But I'm hungry and my belly is rumbling.

Actually, properly growling at me and telling me to go downstairs. I put my bag back under the bed. I brush my hair and my teeth and get dressed, put my new slippers on.

It's the first thing I see when I open the door. This massive present standing next to the tree like some kind of shiny gold dinosaur, scooter-shaped. I don't open it even though I really want to, want to madly tear the paper off, want to zoom around our living room on it, want to ride up to Jess' house right now and see what she got, if she knows about Santa, too. On December 25 our living room is transformed and so are we. It's the one day of the year we pretend to be posh. My mother would have me changed out of my dungarees and into a dress if I was weak, easily persuaded. We sit by the table to eat with napkins on our laps. Serviettes are shaped into swans and they float elegantly on the especially ironed tablecloth river, cream with a thick gold patterned trim. The posh placemats are wiped clean and we use the cutlery from the posh box in the cabinet. Mum shines each piece of hardly-ever-used silver until you can see your upside down face in the spoons. Crystal glasses like goblets, glasses that I'm too afraid to use because my mother watches me with nervous eyes each time I take a sip. The serving bowls and the plates match, a green floral pattern. And after today I won't see any of this again until next year.

It all feels different today. I'm not excited, only sad. I am a tree with one fairy light blown out. Not quite right. Our posh table is full of food soon enough. And I mean full. You've got barely any room to put your elbows down which apparently I'm not allowed to do. The bowls are mountains of vegetables and roast potatoes and Yorkshire puddings, a snowy one of mash. The white jug holds homemade gravy and others glow with bright sauces, blood red cranberry and thick green mint that looks like something that spills out of a drain. I'm sitting next to Nanny because she likes me to. My dad and my mother are opposite us, my mother sweating because she's been working hard in the hot kitchen. She kisses my dad on his cheek and I don't like it. He's mine, not hers.

We all have our place like the plates and the forks. We are all part of Mum's plan. We have to put our hats on – stupid paper things that don't even stay on tidy. Wouldn't want to ruin her perfect day now, would we? No elbows please, Hannah, and sit up straight for God's sake. Couldn't you have put something decent on instead of those bloody dungarees? You could've brushed your hair.

'I *have* brushed it.'

'You've got your bloody father's hair, I know that. Electric. Like someone has plugged you in and you've gone up like a broken umbrella in the wind.'

I roll my eyes at her, put my elbows on the table on purpose. Can't I manage a smile even on Christmas? I'm an ungrateful little cow, aye. She points her fork at me, stabs the air in front of the table. I haven't even opened my present by there and it cost a bloody bomb. And when you think of those poor kids in Africa who haven't got a thing.

'Just take it to them then,' I say. 'I don't care. They're starving but I'm sure they'd love a new scooter.'

Nanny ruffles my hair. That's enough of my lip now. She usually smells like soap, like most old people do, but today she smells like perfume. I don't know what type. Just perfume. I suppose she must've had it for Christmas and sprayed herself in it. She tells us not to argue now, me and my mother, we're always fucking arguing, like two peas in a pod. Both stubborn and that's our trouble.

'I am *nothing* like my mother,' I snap, angry that she could say something so awful.

'Aye. Wrong baby I picked up from the bloody hospital.'

Well, Nanny's fond of my curls anyway. In fact, she loves me just the way I am, electric hair or no electric hair. But I know she's only saying it because she's drunk. When she pours the liquid from the bottle and into her crystal glass, the fourth helping she's had already, Mum tells her to slow down. Course, Nanny tells her to piss off.

'Pull this cracker,' she says, shaking it at me, floppy and gold.

And as she lifts it clumsily above the things on the cluttered table she almost knocks the glass over and my mother almost has a heart attack. I like Nanny. Because she's old she gets away with a lot of things, which is kind of cool. Like swearing and almost knocking things over, and not doing as she's told. She can pretend she doesn't hear you because of her hearing aid and sometimes, if I ask a question she doesn't want to answer, like where's my pocket money this week, Nan? Or, who do you love the most Nan, me or Kyle? she taps the yellow box on her ear and says it's broken.

Nanny also takes cracker-pulling very seriously. She doesn't let me win just because I'm a kid, which is what Dad does and most grown-ups. Nanny tugs it aggressively with two hands gripped on the bright gold cardboard, false teeth gritted, concentration running through the defined wrinkles on her face, the need for victory glowing in her old, brown eyes. I pull and she pulls, and then it bangs and she screams, laughing madly afterwards. Mum tells her to watch the bloody glasses and Nanny tells her to piss off again. Of course Nanny wins, a pack of mini screwdrivers landing in her lap.

'Load of junk in these,' Nanny shouts. 'Don't know why you bother buying them. Waste of fucking money. What am I going to do with a fucking screwdriver?'

'Maybe you can use it to fix your hearing aid, Nan.'

Cheeky little shit, she says, and she smacks me across my head with the long end of the cracker. It's funny, as deaf as she is she always seems to hear the cheeky things I say. The more Nanny drinks the louder she gets and the more she swears and the more I like her. She tucks the string of her reading glasses behind her ears and rests the frames on her nose, lopsided. She's going to tell us this joke now. Are we listening or what? Nanny loves a good joke, see, especially a filthy one. But Nanny is too drunk to read it properly. She messes it up, gets the punch line wrong. It's not funny.

'Oh fucking hell,' she says with a hiccup, splashing herself with the liquid in her glass. '*Shit.*'

'Mind your language, Mam. Hannah's by the table.'

'You don't mind do you, love?'

'No, Nan.'

'You've got to have a laugh haven't you, love?'

'Yes, Nan.'

'Tell your mother to stop being such a miserable bitch.'

Oh, I'd love to, Nan, I think to myself. But I wouldn't dare.

'What's the matter, love?' Nanny asks me, tiny puddles of brown gravy caught in the wrinkled corners of her mouth. 'You haven't eaten much today.'

'Leave her to it,' my mother says. 'She's bloody sulking as usual.'

'Well, I don't like to see her not eating. It's not like her. Feeling bard are you, love?'

Mum says there's nothing wrong with me. My face is like this, like a slapped backside, because she told me Santa wasn't real. I mean I'm old enough to know now, aren't I? It's about time I grew up. Believing in bloody magic. That's my father's fault as well, like my hair, like how I'm a spoiled brat. And we spend hours out in that bloody car with those stupid birds and down the garden in that filthy bloody shed. Dad doesn't say a word. He's kind of scared of my mother but I'm not. I almost tell her to shut up, that I'm not spoiled and our birds aren't stupid and neither is Joan Baez, but Nanny steps in.

'You believe in Santa if you want, love. I believe in God and Jesus and when you think about it, that's the same thing. What's the difference in a man who brings presents to all the children in the world to a man who turns water into wine? They both sound pretty fucking handy if you ask me.'

And that's her lot. She's full, got a stitch from all that eating. Food was lovely. Turkey wasn't as nice as last year's, mind, bit tough and dry, chewy, but fuck it. She stumbles her way across the living room like she's dancing, a quick step and a hop and a crash. She sort of bounces back up from the settee when she lands on it and then down again. Nanny is definitely ready for her afternoon sleep. I can't quite believe I'm saying this but it's not the same without Kyle here annoying me. Being loud with his new toys, being the naughty one at the table, the one Mum is most worried about around the crystal glasses and the sharp turkey knife. I guess Christmas will never be the same again. This is it now forever. Pretend posh and magic-less.

And I bet you next year something even worse will happen, something worse than finding out The Truth. I'll pull a cracker and it'll explode, smoke, bang! Blow my head off. A little white piece of paper will fall out but there won't be a joke on it for Nanny to mess up. There'll just be words. 'Merry Christmas, Hannah King.' There'll be blood and bits of my brain everywhere, all over Mum's perfect posh dining table, and everyone will be laughing.

Laser Ludlow

Mrs Thomas is all dressed up on the stage. She's usually quite smart anyway, but today she's wearing a crystal brooch, an apple-green flower that sparkles under the light on the ceiling whenever she moves. From the bottom up her normal sandals are polished flat shoes that glitter with silver sequins, dark tights and a brown lady's suit, and I think she's had her hair cut. It's not that funny but Jess hasn't stopped giggling for about ten minutes. Who does she think she is, mun? Princess flipping Diana?

We're cross-legged on the floor in the big hall. Me and Jess are always put in the front row like this. Apparently we talk too much in assembly, and by here Mrs Thomas can keep an eye on us, make sure we're actually singing the hymns instead of honking away like two noisy geese. That's what she calls us. Geese! Can you believe it? She also says we've got a terrible habit of gossiping but I don't see it myself.

'And you know as well?' Jess whispers. 'There's this one teacher who teaches English, right, and they reckon she's crazy.'

She's talking about Comp. Who reckons she's crazy?

'Everyone. She's like, a *legend*. Massive, she is. The most massive woman you'll ever see. And want to know something else?'

'What?'

'She's a murderer. She keeps chunks of kids in her desk drawer.'

'As if.'

'Honest, Han. She saws them up herself with her guillotine 30cm ruler and stirs their blood in her cup of PG Tips with a teaspoon.'

'I don't believe you.'

'I swear it. Don't think I'd lie about something like this, do you?'

'So why hasn't she been caught?'

'Because she's a teacher, in'she? An *English* teacher. That means she's really clever. She's got a voice like thunder, and eyes like two bolts of lightning coming out of them when she's telling you off.'

'Is she old?'

'Ancient.'

'What's her name?'

'Mrs Ludlow. But everyone calls her Laser Ludlow.'

'Why'd they call her that?'

'Because she's evil. Pure flipping evil. When you've made her angry and she looks at you, her eyes burn holes in your soul.'

'So how exactly is it *you* know about her, Jess?'

'God Han, haven't you heard of old Laser Ludlow?'

Everyone knows loopy Laser, mun. She taught her father years ago when he was in school, like she's taught thousands of kids over the years. Taught? No. More like tormented. He talks about her like she's something from a ghost story. Says she's been around for so long the kids have turned her funny in the head. Not funny ha ha, because there's nothing funny ha ha about Laser Ludlow. She's just off your trolley kind of funny. And she's got a posh house because all teachers are rich. Actually, Laser is the richest teacher in the world. Maybe even the richest *person* in the world.

'She's got black iron gates around her house, security cameras and all … barbed wire to keep people out. And a cellar deep underground for the rotting bodies. And a massive dog that she trains especially to growl at kids when they pass her window.'

And Jess knows for absolute certain that Laser Ludlow makes voodoo dolls out of cocktail sausages from her fridge.

'*Sausages?*'

'She sits there all night long by her dining table 'til it's dark with them sausages, Han.'

'Doing what?'

Making her dolls, mun. Sticking the parts onto the soft, pork-brown bodies really gently, the eyes and mouths and noses and hair. Laser's got delicate hands, see, steady as a surgeon, because they've got to be perfect, her sausage dolls. They're her pupils.

'What does she use for glue?' I ask, like I believe her.

I realise that this is what it must be like being Evan Jones. Except I'm not gullible like he is. My mind isn't a sponge that soaks up Jess' overdone fibs. It sees them and squeezes them out, all over the hall floor. Besides, Jess can't tell a story like I can. She's a terrible liar. She can't look you in the eyes and make you believe it, every single carefully prepared word. You can't lie to a liar because liars know.

'Mayo,' she says.

'What about the eyes?'

'Pieces of sweetcorn.'

'What about the hair?'

Jess stops and thinks about her answer. Now this is the thing you shouldn't do. It's easy to forget but if you want to be a successful liar then there are rules you have to follow. And one of them is that you never stop and think when you're trying to convince someone you're telling The Truth. Because if you really were you wouldn't need to make something up at all, would you? It would already be there on the tip of your tongue just waiting for you to spit it out.

'What does old Laser Ludlow use for hair now?' she says, lips pursed and brain thinking hard. 'Hmm. Oh yeah. *Worms*. Slimy, wiggling worms. Ludlow goes out her back garden and digs them up from the soil herself. Not even with a shovel, but with her own two *cuh-razy*, hands.'

'Peppers for mouths?'

'Aye. Red and juicy. And when she's finished she sits back on her dining chair and grins like this,' and Jess flashes her teeth, 'her fingers dripping with warm blood and lumpy worm guts.'

Another classic mistake. Letting the story run away with you. Too much, too many words. But I give it to her. Go on, Jess.

'Does she give them names, Jessica?'

Yeah! Of course she does. She stands the sausages up on the dining table and introduces herself like it's their first day of school. In a soft, calm voice she says … hello, children, I'm Mrs Ludlow and I'm going to be teaching you English today. She's made a whole class of them, see, and they're named after the kids she *really* doesn't like. They're smiling back at her with their red pepper mouths, poor little sods. They don't know what they're in for. Maybe it's better that way.

'And what *are* they in for?'

'Something terrible, Han. Something so dreadful.'

'Go on. Tell me.'

Well she just flips, don't she? Laser Ludlow loses it. She attacks them.

'With what?'

'Umm...'

'A fork, Jessica?'

With a fork. Yeah, a fork! Bang bang bang bang bang bang. She's laughing madly now, like some kind of demented witch. Jess says there's sweetcorn and peppers and sausage and blood and worm guts everywhere, mun, all over Laser Ludlow's face and splashed across her expensive wooden table, all up her living room walls.

'She really hates kids, Han. Can't stand them. They actually turn her physically sick.'

'Then why would she become a teacher if she hated kids?'

'Don't know. Maybe it's like butchers. Maybe butchers don't like animals, so they get a job where they've got to smash them up. If she wasn't a teacher, she'd be a torturer. Maybe old Laser Ludlow's planning to wipe out all the kids in Pandy one by one.'

'But your dad's still alive.'

'Yeah but only just, Han. He's still frightened of her now, all these years later. Still has nightmares, like.'

She's only telling me because she wants to prepare me. This is what we've got in store after the summer holidays. And something else, too, something *really* crazy, possibly worse than a murderous English teacher ... our mothers reckon that when we start Comp we'll also have to start washing our hair more than once a month, maybe even once a week.

'Ha. She'll have to hold me down in the bath first,' Jess says. 'Told her that, didn't I? And then she said she'd get the garden hose out on me.'

'They can't make us be clean.'

'Too right. But we've got bigger problems now, Han. Don't forget, never *ever* make eye contact with Laser Ludlow if you want to keep your soul. That would be an awful thing to lose. You want to keep your soul don't you, Han?'

'Of course.'

'We might not even have her though. Fingers crossed. There's loads of teachers up in Comp. It's a massive place, like.'

'Hmm.'

'I can't wait for art, Han. Apparently they've got a studio and a kiln and everything. You still sleeping over mine tonight now?'

'Yeah. Jess...'

'What?'

'I don't want to go to Comp.'

'Cause of Laser Ludlow?'

Nah. It's nothing to do with Laser Ludlow. And it's not because I'll have to start washing my hair, either, even though I'm really not looking forward to that. It's just because I don't want to go. The reason Mrs Thomas is dressed up all posh for Assembly is because it's the last day of school. The last day ever. She's been crying all morning and now, this afternoon, she's crying even worse than before on the stage in her nice shoes, her brooch flashing a beautiful ray of light, a glint of green each time she turns to the side to wipe her eyes. She coughs, and when she coughs she coughs loud and stares straight at us with massive wide eyes that aren't made of lasers but we know what they mean ... girls, shut it.

'I'm awful sad to see you all going,' she sniffs. 'I'm even sad to see Hannah King and Jessica Matthews go.'

Me and Jess grin, proud. It's like we're famous or something. Mrs Thomas will definitely always remember us, we know that. We won't get forgotten, lost in the blur of thousands of other kids who have run along these corridors in red jumpers and black Clarks' shoes. Through tears and breath Mrs Thomas fans her face with her hand, something ladies do when they're sad and they're trying to stop it. She dabs her eyes with a balled-up wad of white tissue from her suit pocket and now she's *really* crying. Can barely talk. Some of us sitting in this hall will go on to college and university, she says. Some of us will have children of our own one day and some of us might even change the world.

She sighs and whimpers, and truth be told I'm fighting my own tears back now. But they go and rise up all salty and fast inside me, like nasty little bubbles.

'You okay or what?' I ask her.

Don't know why I bother though. Jess would never admit that she's a bit sad, too. She stops and thinks about her answer again and I really need to give her a lesson. One day she might need to lie about something important and I'll feel bad for not telling her how to do it properly.

'Aye,' she says, voice all croaky and broken.

'But your eyes are watering.'

'So? It's just my hay fever playing up. Are *you* okay, Han?'

'Yes,' I say instantly, plucking the invisible hair out with my finger and sprinkling it away. 'Just an eyelash stuck.'

Mrs Thomas is done crying. She composes herself and tells us that Comp will be a brand new, exciting world where we'll learn new things and make new friends. There'll be tens of kids from different schools around the Rhondda to choose from. But she really doesn't get it, doesn't understand a thing, does she? Stupid lady in stupid flat shoes … stupid green brooch! I don't want any new friends. I'm quite happy with Jess, despite her faults and she's got loads. Even though she's a terrible liar and an even worse speller, I happen to like her a lot. And I don't want a new school. I like *our* school, the way it smells and that I know where to go, all the hidden nooks and good places to hide from Evan if we need to whisper important secrets. I like our yard and our big hall and our classroom. I like How Things Are.

Except this morning Mrs Thomas took our name plaques off our work trays and coat hooks. Just like that, like it was nothing to get rid of us, she tore us away and crumpled us up, Hannah King and Jessica Matthews, and dumped us in the bin. I know that next term there'll be a different name on *my* tray in her permanent marker handwriting, that there'll be some other kid sliding their pens and pencils out of it, hanging their wet coat up on *my* hook, but it doesn't mean I like it. I look around our hall at Mrs Thomas' wooden piano and stool, the metal PE apparatus climbing up the wall and the overhead projector, the high windows and the benches, the places me and Jess sat and played, and it suddenly hits me that after today we'll never be coming back.

Comp is going to be big and massive and full of strangers who I definitely won't like, I know. And teachers who won't like me. Teachers like Laser Ludlow. And I'll have no idea where to go. I'll be absolutely and completely lost. And what if Jess decides she wants a new best friend? What if she meets one of those tens of kids, and no doubt they will all, every single girl, be prettier than me, and realises that I'm actually quite boring really compared to them? That I'm not much good at all?

I don't want to share Jess and I tell her straight. I can't share you, Jessica Matthews, and I will not. It's a very serious thing I've just said to her and I mean it and she needs to know, but she just laughs at me like I've said something stupid.

'What? What are you laughing at?'

'Just you saying you can't share me. As if you'd have to share me anyway. Just won't happen.'

'Why won't it?'

'Because it just *won't*. Stop being so dull. Me and you are best friends, aren't we? No one can touch us. Am I right or am I right?'

'But how do you know it won't happen? How do you know someone else won't come along and then you'll just tell me to go away and leave you alone?'

'Because I love you, mun. That's why.'

I punch her in the thigh, dig her hard with my knuckles, because she can't go around saying things like that, that she *loves* me.

'Well no need to punch me, Hannah. We spit shaked, didn't we?'

'You still remember that?'

'Course I do, Han. We're going to be best friends in Comp, don't you worry now. Until we're old and wrinkly and grey.'

Jess will wear floral skirts and a hairnet over her head when it's windy. She'll have a metal hip and I'll have false teeth that need to be soaked in a glass overnight. And we'll have arthritis and liver spots and corned-beef coloured legs. We'll be pretty minging, like, she won't deny it, but it won't matter because we've already shared spit and you can't get much more minging than that. Because we'll be best friends and that means we'll love each other, always, just the way we are.

'Promise that you won't leave me. Promise it and mean it.'

'Promise,' she says, and Mrs Thomas coughs again and tells us with her eyes to shut it, but Jess ignores her, says it one more time because it's important, because I need to understand. 'We're best friends, Hannah King. And I won't leave you. I *promise*.'

Rainbows

The sun makes people mental, that's what my mother says. Only the people in Pandy though. It's because they're not used to it, because they're so adapted to the rain and the clouds, to being bloody miserable. But don't count me in with them. I don't go crazy happy for the sun the way everybody else does.

I'm on my way to call for Jess. I've been calling for her every morning since the start of the summer holidays. She only lives three streets away but I'm sweating really bad after walking up her massive hill. That's the sun's fault, like my freckles, how they've multiplied. They're absolutely everywhere. A hundred million of them all over my skin. It's like I've caught some terrible disease and this is mostly why the sun is no friend of mine. Why it can stay away forever, for all I care.

When I turn into the street I see that Jess' dad's jeep is parked outside their house, its black bonnet gleaming, and next-door's white cat is lazing in a puddle of yellow sunshine on their windowsill. Everything seems normal. Jess is bent down by her front door chalking numbers on the pavement and she looks the same as she always does. Just maybe her skin is a bit darker than usual. But the sun hasn't got to her yet, turned her crazy happy, and I'm glad.

'Alright, Han?' she says, and I lie and say yeah, I'm alright. You?

She's alright too but her shorts are apparently stuck up her arse something chronic. Cycling shorts, that's what she says they're called, light blue and very short and made of thin glossy material that clings to her almost-brown-now skin the way bathers do. And she isn't happy one bit. Be in her jeans, she would, if her mother hadn't made her wear these stupid, sticky, arse-hugging shorts.

'You want to see this dress she bought me,' she says, and then makes a sound like she's being sick. 'Flowers on it and everything. What does she think I am, a flipping *girl?*'

Our mothers say we're tomboys which means we're not proper girls but we're absolutely fine with that. Girls are silly things that aren't very clever, that do stupid stuff like giggle a lot and cry. My mother has given up trying to get me into a pair of shorts and a nice vest like Jessica Whatshername. If I want to walk around like a bloody farmer in my dungarees, then so be it. She's just mental. I'm definitely not getting my legs out. My legs are so white. White as Jess' chalk by there. And I wish I never asked her how she is now because it's not only her sticky shorts she's moaning about. Jess is going on about her mother and her father. On and on and on. She's giving me a headache. Even the cat from next door jumps off the windowsill and disappears under a parked car.

'I hate that cat,' she moans again. 'Snowy, like. What a stupid name for a cat. My father's nearly run it over loads of times on accident. Wish he'd just flatten the fluffy little fuck.'

'*Jess.*'

'What? I can say fuck if I want. Fuck fuck fuck. Don't care if my mother hears me.'

Poor Snowy. Poor me. Jess is in a foul mood today, I know.

'Go on,' she dares me. 'Say it. Say *fuck.* You'll feel loads better.'

I say nah. No thanks. You're alright. And then she wants to write another different bad word on the side of her father's jeep in her white chalk but in the end she doesn't have the guts.

'Why don't we go inside?' I ask her. 'It's boiling out here.'

'No way. It's like World War Three in there. Can't we go to your house?'

'Nah.'

'Why?'

'Just can't.'

Me and Jess may as well be homeless, two tramps who live in cardboard boxes. Except we haven't got any cardboard boxes and we do have homes, we just don't want to live in them.

Jess gets bored of swearing and chalking and decides we should go to the park. I don't mind. I haven't got any better ideas so we skip down the main road, absolutely sweating, but nothing, not even the horrible, burny, freckle-making sun, stops her moaning. Her father this, her father that, she pants, like a thirsty dog.

Something to do with making her mother cry. Something to do with being a bastard. And then the fire engines are screaming past us and it's quite exciting really, these giant red things charging like a deafening stampede towards the mountain. Third time this week now. We stop still on the pavement and squint at the flames in the distance.

'Let's go up and watch!' she says, a crazy look in her eyes.

'What a stupid idea, Jessica.'

She'd probably be up there with her disposable camera taking pictures of the squirrels and the birds being barbecued alive if I wasn't here to tell her how mental she is. Suppose I'm right. And she can't be arsed anyway.

'Do you think if the fire gets really bad it'll spread down? To Pandy, like. To my house and your house?'

'Well I hope not, Jess.'

But Jess says that personally she wouldn't care. She'd actually be glad if the whole world burned down. And so what if she died? No one would miss her.

'Don't say that, Jess.'

Well it's true. Whatever though. She needs a lolly, something to cool her down and she's gasping for a drink.

'Come *on*.'

She's walked off without me realising. I was far away then. Thinking about her dying. I was imagining her skinny, brown body laid out in a coffin like a Barbie in a box. Cold skin and static face. I was thinking that I'd probably have to die too because I've got no other friends and my life would be pointless without her. I walk faster to catch up. Sometimes when we're walking around like this I feel like I should be on a lead so that she can yank and pull me wherever she wants me to go. Jess always decides our plans. Apparently I'm indecisive, a word I've always known the meaning to but she only found out yesterday and now she's using it constantly.

We slide the lid across, both of us together, because it's heavy and hard. We're leaning over and staring into the empty, icy abyss, and Jess is furious. For Godsakemun. What's the world coming to? The freezer is bare. No lollies or Tip Tops, no Cornettos or

Magnums. Absolutely nothing. And to make matters worse the fridges are out of cold cans so she snatches a Fanta angrily off the shelf.

'Warm,' she says, cupping it. 'It's flipping *warm*. Yuck!'

I tell her that it's probably because of the sun. The sun stole everything, because it's spiteful like that. But she doesn't seem to care or even listen.

'Well go on then. Pick the one you want. We haven't got all day, mun. You're awful indecisive.'

There she goes again.

I don't know what I want but I just get a Fanta as well. When we get to the park and find it's packed, that really makes Jess mad. All the swings are taken and the car-shaped climbing frame is full with kids, like a tree covered in birds. It's never this busy. Robbie Jenkins is here as well with some of the boys from school, pushing one of the swings until it's knotted over the top of the bar, but he's far too cool to acknowledge us when Jess waves and shouts, oh, Rob!

We go and make a den in the bushes just up from the park instead. We part our way through branches and leaves and Jess gets her greasy black hair caught on a twig and then calls it a bastard. And as if she cares that Robbie Jenkins blanked her.

'Stupid, stinking boy. Did you see his hat? Wearing it backwards like a mong.'

Deep in the middle of the bushy green we're hidden away from the noise of the park, from everything. It's so lush and cool and shady I'd be happy in here all day but I've got to go to chapel in a bit. We're lying on our backs in the dry mud, the sun spraying through the gaps in the leaves and twigs above us, a greeny yellow kaleidoscope, and for no reason at all she says...

'Snog me, Han.'

'You what?'

'Kiss me. *Do* it. I bet you taste like sherbet lemons.'

My mother was right. The sun has sent my best friend bonkers now. Of course I sit up really quick, my elbows dusty with dirt, and ask her what on earth she's going on about. Is she alright, or what? Course she is. She just wants to play 'Lesbians', a brand new game she's thought of. The best game in the world. Much better than hide and seek or hop scotch or swinging on the swings because 'Lesbians' doesn't have any rules and 'Lesbians' doesn't need any props.

'Just our hands and our tongues and for us to pretend we're in love.'

'But I don't love you, Jess.'

'So? That doesn't matter, silly. My father doesn't love my mother.'

'Well I'm not kissing you, that's for sure.'

'Why? You can imagine I'm someone else if you want when we're doing it. I don't mind. I'll imagine you're Robbie Jenkins. Don't you want to be a Lesbian?'

It's what girls who kiss girls are called. They can also be called lezzas or homosexuals or just plain gays. Jess says most people can't wrap their minds around it because the *normal* thing to do is get a husband and a house and a jeep. But look at her mother and her father. If that's normal then Jess doesn't ever want to be normal. She doesn't even know a single normal person who's happy. Do I?

'Not really.'

'Well then. Let's be lesbians. Like Dusty.'

'Dusty who?'

'Dusty Springfield, you nutter!'

I shrug. Never heard of her but apparently she's a singer. Dead.

'"I wish I'd never loved you". My mother listens to that song when she's hoovering sometimes. And she's vroom! vrooming! it back and forth over our expensive cream carpet and Dusty is screaming the chorus and my mother is crying her eyes out, like a flipping tap. Bonkers!'

'My mother cries as well,' I tell her. 'But not when she's listening to Dusty Springfield. I don't think she knows who Dusty Springfield is, either. She can just be sitting down and then she'll start crying when the telly isn't even on or anything. So I suppose that makes her even more bonkers.'

Yep. Jess says our mothers are crazy, alright. We've got no hope. Doomed. Like Dusty Springfield who was also doomed.

'Doom everywhere, mun,' she says. 'Lesbians and doom.'

Jess' mother thinks lesbians are disgusting, that it's just not natural for two women to be rubbing their bits and pieces up together, and if Jess turns into one when she's older then she'll disown her. It makes her sick to the stomach, but not Jess.

'Love is love,' she reckons, 'and it doesn't really matter who you love as long as you only love them.'

Besides once, on the beach in Portugal, she caught a glimpse of one by accident, a *cock*, and it was the most disgusting thing she's ever seen so she can totally understand why some women play 'Lesbians' every day. Of course I say *no*, Jessica Matthews, I'm not kissing you, so stop asking. I might be indecisive about where I want to go and what I want to drink but I know I definitely do not want to be a Lesbian.

Me and Jess have had many a tickle fight and she's pretty strong, always wins, so when she sits up I'm worried she might try to kiss me. Pin me down and then I won't be able to stop her. I stand up and tell her that's it, I'm off. It's boiling and the back of my dungarees is soaking and the world's crazy and I've got to go to chapel. And she'd better come with me or else I'll tell her mother that she's a Lesbian.

'As if I'm going to chapel. What do you think I am, a flipping *disciple?*'

'Fine then. I'll call in and tell Bev on the way. Break the terrible news to her that her only daughter is a massive, stinking Lesbian.'

Bev is Jess' mother and Bev definitely can't find out that Jess is a massive, stinking Lesbian. So Jess pats the brown dirt off her little glossy blue bum and follows me. We pass Robbie Jenkins in the park on the way out and see he's done that to all the swings now. No one will be able to use them unless they're really tall, like a giant tall, and untangle them. Jess shouts, oh Rob! You're a mong. And when he blanks her again, she still doesn't care.

'Can't believe you've made me come. Blackmail's a terrible thing, Hannah.'

'Oh well, Jessica, so is being a Lesbian.'

'You don't understand. She'd send me to an asylum, honest.'

'At least your mother talks to you. Mine never even told me what a Lesbian is.'

'She makes nice cakes though, Han, you've got to admit it. I love a Mrs King Welsh cake with jam in the middle. And at least you don't live in World War flipping Three.'

It's funny. Jess thinks she knows where I live. Three streets away, five minutes down the main road. But she really has no idea at all. It's just that I don't talk about it like she does, my house, my mother and my father. Right now my mother will be in bed. Up late last night because of Dad. Most of the time I pretend I'm asleep. I don't want to get up in case something bad has happened but last night I did and I wish I hadn't. I found Mum sweating in the kitchen, stuffing bed sheets splashed with brown sick and blood into the mouth of the washing machine. Sometimes he misses the bowl on the floor. She was crying. What was I bloody staring at? Go back to bed.

'It doesn't matter anyway, Han. When we're older we can leave. Pack our bags and go somewhere far away.'

But for now we're stuck here. We're sitting on the steps outside chapel like two witches with a potion, both stirring some purpley yellow oil around a ditch in the pavement by our feet. Got the sticks off a tree in the park. You can still smell the smoke from the fire in the air and I think it's cool the way our bodies are casting black shapes against the ground. We're thin and stretchy and I wish we could stay shadows forever. We might be almost the same height but Jess is skinnier than me and I know she's prettier, no matter what she says. When we're shadows we're exactly the same though. Shadows don't have faces and they certainly don't have freckles.

I think Jess must be wearing all the bracelets she owns. Emptied her jewellery box. They go up as far as her elbow. Some are strings threaded with coloured wooden beads, a mixture of cube and sphere shapes, and some are made of silver.

'You can have one if you want.'

'Serious?'

'Yep. Any one you like, Han.'

'That one,' I pick, purple string and green cubes.

'Not that one, mun. That's my favourite.'

'Well you said any one.'

Hmm. Let's see. With her fingers she flicks through them like they're harp strings, but instead of gentle chiming the wooden beads knock against one another like knuckles clicking. This will look nice on me, she decides, a thin silver band with love heart charms hanging off it. I put it on.

'You can have it for keeps,' she says, squirming on the step because her shorts are doing her head in. 'In case you forget, this bracelet will remind you that we're best friends forever and no one can touch us.'

'I won't forget, Jess.'

'Good. Last chance to kiss me now, Han. You might even like it. It's not like I'm asking to see your tits.'

What? She only said *tits*, for Godsakemun. It's completely normal. In fact, in some countries they have beaches where everyone walks around absolutely naked all the time. Like that one in Portugal she was telling me about.

'My father loves them. He gets to look at all the women's tits and my mother can't say anything or slap him because she's eyeing up the cocks, too.'

'Yuck.'

'I know. I just keep my head down, like. What time does Sunday school kick off then?'

I've been to chapel before but this is Jess' first time. I don't know why Mum makes me go because she doesn't even really believe in God or Jesus. Well, at least, we haven't got a Bible in our house and we don't say prayers. I don't like it much but if I don't go Mum will find out because she knows the Pastor like she knows everyone around here. Chapel will give me something to do besides wandering the bloody streets and getting up to no good with Jessica Whatshername.

'No good? Cheeky cow,' Jess says with a very unimpressed look on her face. 'And Jessica *Matthews* is my name, thank you very much. Mrs King can shove her Welsh cakes with jam up her arse now.'

'I know. Our mothers are lucky to have us.'

Think about it. They moan about our hair and our clothes, and they say we talk too much and nag a lot, but at least we're not like Robbie Jenkins who damages swings, or the kids who start the fires on the mountain. Our mothers should be more grateful. Actually there should be a day where they send us cards to tell us how wonderful we are, not the other way around. Jess hasn't got matches in her shorts pocket and I haven't got a can of petrol in my bag.

'But why *do* you bring that bag with you everywhere we go?'

'Don't know.'

'What's in it then?'

'Nothing. Just stuff.'

'You've got books in there, I know. Writing pads or something. And a lovely sparkly red one. Very posh. I saw it before.'

'No you didn't.'

'I did. You were sleeping so I unzipped it and had a look.'

'You didn't read them, did you?'

Jess tells me to chill my bean. No need to shout, mun. As if she's got time for reading. It was bad enough when Mrs Thomas made us read *Goodnight Mister* flipping *Tom*. She hates sitting still. And why would you bother with all them words when you can draw a picture? Quicker, mun.

'I'm going to be a writer when I grow up.'

'Well that's not very cool, is it? No one's going to want to fuck you if you're a writer. You should be an artist, like me. Now artists, *they're* cool.'

'*Jess.*'

'What? Fuck fuck fuck fuck *fuck*!'

Sometimes it's a good thing that my mother doesn't take much notice. It would be better for her if I did have petrol and matches in my bag. If she knew I was still writing, that I took my notebook back out of the drawer, she'd go mental. Jess shrugs. She doesn't understand and doesn't want to, either. She doesn't ask me what I write about and I'm glad because it's Sunday and far too hot for telling lies.

'What's it like inside?'

'Where?'

'In Chapel, mun.'

Well, Chapel is a small building with tall windows called stained glass, with pretty shapes and colours on them. The Pastor tells you stories about bread and fish and the man who walked through a fire and came out alright after. And they give you biscuits for coming.

'Sounds shit,' she says. 'Apart from the biscuits. So why don't you want to kiss me?'

'Just don't.'

'Don't you think I'm pretty then?'

'Don't know.'

'Do you think Robbie Jenkins thinks I'm pretty?'

I shrug, stir the oil a bit faster.

'*He'd* kiss me,' she decides.

'Would you let him then?'

'Yeah. Course I would. He's lush.'

'You just called him a mong!'

'Yeah, well. Love is like that, Han. My mother calls my father some terrible names. But I wouldn't let Robbie Jenkins see my tits. Do you think God can see our tits? Because he can see everything, can't he?'

'Hope not.'

'That's what my Nan says anyway. She says he's always around. He can see us but we can't see him. Big old perv. That means when you're getting changed he can see your minge. And he's watching when you wipe your arse.'

'Hmm.'

Nah, Jess doesn't believe in God. Her father told her that the Christians are off their heads if they think some man in a dressing gown is going to come down from the sky and save them.

'He said they believe you'll burn in fire if you lie. Like if I say this stick is a giraffe,' and she waves it, drops of thick oil splashing onto her shorts, 'that means I'm going to Hell. Christians and Lesbians, my parents can't stand either of them.'

'That's just stupid,' I tell her. 'If God didn't want you to lie then he would just stop you lying, wouldn't he?'

'Yeah.'

'And he wouldn't make bad people, would he? He'd just make good ones.'

'Aye. And he'd feed the kids in Africa and stop my father kissing Fat Pat Morgan.'

100

'Who's Fat Pat Morgan?'

'Just this woman. And God would make Robbie Jenkins love me if he was a tidy God.'

'Why do you want *him* to love you for?'

''Cause I do. I told you, he's lush.'

Lush? As if. *I'm* lush. And I'm the only person she needs to love her. Am I not enough?

'Of course you are.'

Jess is telling me lies. I don't like them, not one bit, so I ignore them.

'I suppose if God was real he would get rid of my freckles and my curly hair. He wouldn't have given me them in the first place.'

'Yep. God is rubbish, Han.'

I don't say it out loud. I do not believe in God. You're not supposed to just in case he *is* real and then you'll end up in Hell and that isn't a very nice place. I'm just glad Jess is coming to chapel with me. I wouldn't really have told her mother that she's a Lesbian because her mother, old Bev, she's pretty scary. And because I lied earlier, too, in the bushes. I do actually sort of kind of and only a tiny bit love her, and I really don't want her to love Robbie Jenkins. Sometimes I even wish she didn't have a mother and a father that I had to share her with. Sometimes I wish she had no eyes because then she wouldn't be able to look at any other kids, especially Robbie Jenkins. I don't say all this out loud, either. Jess knowing that I care, that would be even worse than going to Hell.

We abandon our sticks and make our way up the steps. And behind the door at the top, away from the noise of the main road, the cars and the buses, the flaming mountains and the screams of the kids in the park, my house where my mother cries and Jess' where her parents are engaging in full blast World War Three, is chapel. A secret pocket of peace and quiet in Tonypandy lit up with rich colours. A warm blaze of greens and reds and vivid yellows from the stained glass, the grand black organ down the front and the polished dark brown pews. Poor Jess, she's sliding all over the place in her shiny shorts.

'You could've told me they don't have tidy seats, mun.'

Jess doesn't like it in here, gives her the creeps. Apparently it smells like old ladies and biscuits and death. I suppose it is kind of eerie though, the way the sun outside is beaming through the stained glass and squirting the light over the tops of the pews and onto the floor like bursts of coloured water. And it's weird how in here everything happens, the whole spectrum of life taking place under one roof. You're a baby brought in a shawl to be baptised and soon a kid listening to stories in Sunday school and then a grown-up getting married and finally you're here in a box.

'And then you definitely won't be coming back ever again.'

'Alright, Han. Bit deep. I was only saying it smells like shit.'

The Pastor is standing down the front by a thing called a lectern, another new word for Jess.

'You're like a flipping encyclopaedia,' she whispers, and I'm impressed with that one. '*My* encyclopaedia.'

He tells us to bend over and pick the hymn books up by our feet. I open the black front cover, the pages inside as thin as rice paper, and it smells very different to the books I write in. This hymn book is full of songs and smells musty, like Jesus and his brown leather sandals, like sins and crosses and red wine and blood and bread and little donkeys. Some people on the pews in front of us stand up and sing. A man in a green t-shirt and baggy white trousers throws his arms in the air like he's on a rollercoaster and shouts yes, Lord!

Jess' cheeks pump and her face turns tomato red. If I pushed my finger into her cheek right now she'd burst. She tries to squash her laugh back down but it goes and blurts out of her mouth and then that sets me off, too. We have to hide our giggles behind our hymn books when the fat lady stops playing the organ and brings the collection basket over to our pew. I feel around the seven sides of the coin in the pocket of my dungarees with my finger while Jess drops a pound in. A whole pound.

'You should've kept it,' I tell her when the fat lady goes. 'I never put my money in.'

'*Han*, mun. Your mother will be fuming if she finds out you're stealing off Jesus.'

'Thought you didn't believe in him?'

'I don't. Not really. But you know. You've got to be careful. I don't want no Jesus ghost killing me when I'm wiping my arse.'

I shrug.

'Well don't blame me if the next time I'm in this chapel is when they're carrying your body out in a coffin, Han'

I see her again then when she says it, in the coffin, lips as blue as her shorts, and dark, decaying cheeks. She isn't laughing the way Jess does. She can't laugh. And she isn't moaning because there isn't a single moody breath left in her cold, cold body. I shake it out of my head, too horrible, and focus on the Pastor who opens his Bible out, a gold tasselled bookmark dangling down its black leather back. Everything is silent then when he starts to tell us a story about a man called Noah and some massive flood. This flood wasn't even like the flood that we learned about in school. The plaque in the big hall was to remember the local flood disaster in 1910 when a wave of water came and killed some kids and a baby and sent someone kayaking down the hill naked in a bath tub. That flood was bad enough but this flood in the Bible that the Pastor's on about, with Noah and his long white hair, killed billions of people all around the world. I put my hand up.

'*Excuse me.*'

'Yes, Miss King?'

I've never been called *Miss* King before. And I like it.

'You just said God loved his people. Did you make a mistake?'

'No I most certainly did not, Miss King. God loves all of us.'

'But if he loved them so much then why did he drown them?'

He must be lying because you don't hurt people you love and you definitely don't drown them.

'Well,' the Pastor says, slamming his Bible shut. 'Everyone was being bad. They were lying and cheating and drinking and disobeying God's commandments. God got tired of it and decided to teach them a lesson.'

'So he *drowned* everyone, just to teach them a lesson? Couldn't he have just told them off instead?'

The Pastor smiles. It's not funny though.

'When you're bad, Hannah, doesn't your mother teach *you* a lesson?'

Oh, yeah. Once she stopped me going out for two whole days in a row just because I stuffed an empty chocolate wrapper down the side of the settee. And she took my notebook away from me because I'm a liar. I couldn't write for days and I almost blew up. That was the worst lesson of all. My mother teaches me lessons all the time, but she isn't God. And she smacks me sometimes but she's never tried to *drown* me.

'But then God gave us Free Will.'

'What's Free Will?' I ask him, because I'm proper confused now.

'It means you're responsible for your own actions. But of course everyone started believing in him again because they had seen how powerful he was. And do you know why he sent a rainbow?'

'Why?'

'To remind us to always be good. And to always tell The Truth. Every time you see a rainbow, just know that God is watching you.'

Jess rolls her eyes at me, twists her finger around by the side of her head. What a nutter. But when we're back on the chapel steps I push the purples and yellows around the oil again with my stick, and it's bothering me. All those animals going two by two on the Ark. Those poor people and tiny babies who couldn't swim died in the water all because of God. Why would anybody believe in someone so mean?

'Do you think it's true?' I ask her.

'What now?'

'That you'll go to Hell if you lie.'

How on earth would she know? But this is what her father told her. Dying is just like going to sleep. There's no Heaven and no Hell, no man up in the clouds and no devil snarling in a pool of lava underneath. The only God he knows is Freddie Mercury. When you're gone you're gone and that's that and there's nothing no one can do about it. Only one thing's for certain in life and that's death.

'Although my mother reckons he only tells himself that because if there is a Hell then he's going straight there and Fat Pat Morgan will be waiting for him by the gates.'

And to be honest Jess thinks her mother's right. That doesn't happen often, either, like with my mother. The thing is, Jess used to believe her father knew everything. Really believed it. He was kind of like God, a superhero, her favourite person. But now she's getting older and less stupid, now that he can't pick her up and put her on his shoulders because she's too big, now that he makes her mother cry, she's not really sure he knows anything at all. Jess used to be *his* favourite person as well but now he prefers Fat Pat Morgan. She sighs, a really sad sigh, and I almost reach over and hug her, but I don't. Can't. I just mix the swirls around the oil.

'That's cool, Han. It's like a rainbow.'

'What?'

'*Look,*' and she nods. 'You've made a rainbow, like in the Bible innit.'

'Jess...'

'What?'

'Do you think God sent that flood that killed the baby?'

'What baby now?'

The plaque in the big hall. A baby died, three weeks old. It happened here, in the very same place where we live. It could happen to *us.*

'Oh aye. I remember him. Poor little sod.'

'But why would God punish a baby, Jess? How can a baby be bad?'

'I don't know, Han. Maybe he shit too much.'

'*Jess.* I'm serious. If he can send a flood once then he can send it again.'

'Come on now, mun. Don't take it all to heart. Besides, we can swim. Got our hundred metres badges, haven't we?'

'Wouldn't be able to survive a really bad flood though.'

'I think it'd be cool myself. All that water and the people screaming. Don't look at me like that. We live on a mountain anyway, and it's boiling. Look. I'm sweating cobs.'

She fans her vest out and wipes the greasy layer off her forehead, rubs her hand dry in her shorts. I know we can swim, and I know that we live on a mountain and it's the hottest day in the history of the world, but he sent a rainbow then and look, he's sent one to my puddle.

'It's just oil mun, Han, don't be so dramatic.'

Nah. It's not *just oil*. The Pastor is right. It all makes sense now. God must be teaching me a lesson, like he taught all those bad people in the Bible a lesson with the flood. God is making Dad sick on the sheets because I've been bad. Next thing you know Pandy will burn down, a really massive mountain fire the engines can't put out, and Jess will die and in this very chapel her body will be laid out in a wooden box made especially for kids, for smaller bodies. And Bev will cry, an uncontrollable sob, much worse than how she would cry if she found out that Jess is a Lesbian because being dead is a lot worse than being a Lesbian. Even her father who never cries will cry, and it'll all be because of me.

I sprint up the steps back inside the sun-soaked, musty chapel. I'm sweating loads but I don't care. Jesus is etched in colours on the stained-glass window, serious, sad eyes that stare at me. I take the fifty pence coin out of my dungarees, silver and boiling hot, and drop it into the collection basket on top of the organ. I don't deserve a normal family. I don't deserve a best friend. God is watching me. He knows everything I've done.

Lettuce Sandwiches

Hands snatch at the back of my nightie, with rough fingers that pinch my skin as they shake me awake. They are my mother's hands. I've barely prised my sleep-caked eyes open but I've got to get out of bed and put my dressing gown and my slippers on and without asking questions, for once in my bloody life.

I'm walking too slow down the stairs, making too much of a fuss. And then we're outside on the doorstep and Mum's bunch of keys is jangling like bells and soon I'm in the car, the air conditioning blowing, like a cold punch that smacks me in the face. That's when I'm wide awake. That's when I realise that I'm in the *front*. With my *mother*. But we can't listen to any music. She needs to concentrate, needs to think. The tapes are staying in the glove compartment and who the bloody hell is Joan Baez anyway?

Those hands are trembling as she starts the engine, and when she doesn't tell me to put my seatbelt on, I really know it. My mother has gone mad. Finally. I've been waiting for it because it's already happened to two of the ladies in our family, Auntie Eve and Nanny. Auntie Eve only recently but Nanny lost it years ago. The plot. Her marbles. Maybe she was even born like it. Crazy Blood, that's what they've got, and it's running through my veins too like a poisoned red river. It'll happen to me one day but right now it's my mother's turn.

She's taking us up to the Rhigos Mountain. She's had all she can take of me and my questions. I've driven her over the edge like she's about to drive our car over the edge of the steep, grassy drop. We'll tumble off it like a big metal ball on wheels, knock the sheep over like they're fluffy white skittles. It's only what Auntie Eve said she'd do. She screamed and cried it down our house phone, so loud I could hear every word even at the other end of the living room. Griff had someone else. *Already*. She was going to drive her car, drunk, all the way up the Rhigos and sail it off the edge. May as well be dead anyway because she wasn't as perfect as my perfect fucking mother. Griff didn't love her anymore. Kyle was better off without her. My mother told her to calm bloody down and of course she didn't do it. Mum said it was A Cry For Help. Auntie Eve would never *really* do it because she hasn't got the bottle. The doctor gave her some pills and Kyle went to stay with Griff so I guess everything's all fixed now.

I turn to my mother and ask her if I'm dreaming. If I am then I'll wake up just before our windscreen smashes into the mud and grass and before every bone in my body breaks.

'Of course you're not bloody dreaming. I'm taking you to Nanny's. Now stop asking questions.'

And soon we're parked outside her house and I'm walking up her steps in the black dark and then I'm sitting in her living room. My mother rushes off, doesn't even say goodbye, and I look down and see that I'm not wearing my slippers. I pick the jagged little stones out of the soles of my feet and wonder whether they dropped off in the car or on the way up the steps, or maybe I never even put them on in the first place. I also never noticed how loud the black arrow going around the wooden birdhouse-shaped cuckoo clock up on Nanny's wall is before. Each tick is a thumping jolt I feel moving through my entire body. I suppose it's because else everything is so quiet, because the rest of the world, or Pandy at least, is still asleep.

Nanny's just been outside for a fag. She smokes them every day in secret, especially in secret from my mother. That's something no one else knows apart from me. She's in her dressing gown like I am, except hers is brown and mine is green. And when she comes in from the kitchen her hands part the bamboo chimes that hang like a curtain on the doorway, the long wooden strands left shivering behind her. I watch until they're all stopped completely still. They came home in Auntie Eve's suitcase the last time she went on holiday and left Kyle behind in the flat on his own. She leaves him a lot. Spain mostly, Costa del wherever the bloody Hell she feels like Mum says, and Kyle's going to end up in care and then prison. Because Mum can't have him. She couldn't cope. Not with his behaviour the way it is, and not with everything else she's got on her plate. Nanny likes her chimes though. She's very proud

108

of them in her living room. Tells everyone who visits how exotic they are, how they've come from a land faraway where the seas are clear as crystal and where the sun always shines.

Nanny's the same as me. She's never gone abroad. Of course I've been on holiday before, but because of Dad we don't go too far, only in the car and across the bridge into England. Nanny though, despite being old and having had plenty of time to get there, she's never even been out of Wales. Nanny's afraid of flying and she can't swim so you'd never get her on a plane or a boat, not for love or money. But I'm not afraid. If a plane stopped outside the front door right now I'd climb up the steps with my bare feet and get on it. Strap myself in and fly away. I'd be more than glad to go.

'Did you find them?'

'No, love,' she says, coughing over me, breath wet and smoky. 'They're not out on the steps. Sure you was wearing them?'

'I don't remember.'

'Fuck it. They're only slippers after all.'

'But I *loved* them. They were green. And they had a zip.'

'Hows about we go to Ponty tomorrow?'

She'll buy me a brand new pair of slippers in the market. Zip and all. And if I'm extra good, no cheek and no questions all the way on the fucking bus, she'll get me something else as well, a present as long as it's not too expensive.

'That sound alright or what?'

I nod my head and smile at her. It's the best I can do. All I've got. I can't quite manage a thank you, Nan, because I'm just no good when people are being nice to me. When people are nice to me my cheeks heat up and I don't know how to speak anymore and I just can't stand it. My mother says I'm an iceberg, hard as nails inside, but she doesn't understand that my lips are sewn together, that my tongue is super-glued down. It's not that I don't have any feelings. It's not that I don't want to say and do the things normal people say and do. It's just that I *can't*.

'We'll get the very first 120 bus down on Pandy Square,' she decides.

This is because like all old people, Nanny wakes up really early. Before the postman and the birds and even before the sun. I don't know why. The cuckoo clock says it's just gone two and Nanny looks tired, yawning like mad. I think Mum woke her up, too. Cup of tea lodged between her wrinkly, blue-veined hands as she sits down on her armchair opposite me.

Four round white Sweetex dropped in and a splash of green top milk. Always. Nanny's a creature of habit and the things in her house are weird. Out in the kitchen she's got this kettle that you don't plug in. Instead it whistles on top of the cooker, screeches like a train and makes your ears ring like doorbells. Her wallpaper is dark brown like her carpet and she doesn't have a telly, just a radio. My mother says she wants to get with the bloody times but of course Nanny doesn't listen. It's her house and she'll have it the way she likes it and Mum can shove her gadgets where the sun don't shine.

Oh yeah, and Nanny has a fire instead of radiators. A real fire now, not like ours. She leans over and prods the coal with her metal fire stick and the leather of her armchair squeaks because she hasn't got her tights on. Her legs looks like bread and butter pudding, skin as yellow as egg, spots dark and round like raisins. The coal comes from the shed out her garden and she shovels it herself. Nanny is very old but she's also very strong.

'You going to eat that sandwich or what?'

I didn't ask for it and I certainly don't want it. It's in two rectangular halves on a saucer on the side table, the lettuce flopping out of the white bread mouth like a green tongue. Nanny doesn't bake cakes like most people's Nannyies do. She can't cook so she makes me lettuce sandwiches, every time I come over. I hate them. Maybe if I ask her questions she'll forget about it and then I won't have to eat it.

'Why haven't you got the radio on?'

Because it's *always* on. On a Saturday she twists the knob until a man called Owen Money's voice comes out of the fuzzy speakers. Then she rings him and asks him to put a song on for her and then she rings us to tell Mum to turn our radio on, *quick.* We wait and listen for Owen Money to say Nanny's name and where she's from and then he plays it, always the same … 'Crazy', by Patsy Cline. Mum says that's what Nanny is, bloody crazy, daft old bat, but Nanny really likes that song.

'Nothing on this time of the morning, love. And that's what happened to Patsy, see. She got on a plane and *boom*. She was a gonner.'

So Nanny will stay in Wales on the ground where it's safe, thank you very much.

'Did he like Patsy, Nan?'

'Who? Your grandfather? Nah. He couldn't fucking stand her. Reckoned she was a depressing cow. Always moaning about something or other. Always someone leaving her and no wonder.'

My grandfather had a good heart but he didn't have no soul. So he couldn't understand poor Patsy. Didn't get her like we get her, isn't that right, love?

'Yeah,' I say, although I don't get it, not at all.

I'm sitting on his armchair. It's massive. I feel tiny, and my naked feet don't touch the carpet. This is how they would sit when he was alive and I can imagine them arguing over Patsy Cline. My grandfather trying to turn the radio off but Nanny wrestling it off him. Nanny a conveyor belt of gossip and cups of too sweet green-top tea, my grandfather pretending to listen while puffing away on his pipe.

There's a photo of him by there, on the mantelpiece above the fire in black and white, eyes that follow you around the room, square gold frame. He wasn't like Nanny. He left Wales loads of times and on her conveyor belt there's plenty of stories about him that go round and round. I've heard them twice over and each time their details change. He fought in the war and sometimes he's brave as a lion and sometimes he's strong as an ox. He's always very handsome but sometimes he's seventeen years old and other times he's sixteen or nineteen and the names of the countries he travelled to also change.

I was only a baby when they put him up on that mountain. And as I've got older I've learned that the mountain is actually called Trealaw Cemetery. It's where all the dead people who live around here are put. We'll pass it tomorrow on the 120 bus and Nanny will suck her burny mint and I'll hear the sketchy stories all over again, and I won't mind one bit.

'How did he die again now, Nan?'

111

'In his sleep.'

'Can *anyone* die in their sleep then?'

'No. He was poorly, love. Eat your sandwich.'

I've got no choice. I can't stall it any longer. I close my eyes and take a bite. The lettuce jams between my teeth and the salt and butter mixes together in my mouth like crunchy sand. Nanny's old so I finish it all off. Fast chews and hard swallows. You've got to be nice to old people otherwise they'll just die and you'll feel guilty forever for not eating their lettuce sandwiches.

'Why do you have so many rings, Nan? You've got one on every finger.'

'They're my treasures. When I cop off you can have one.'

'Cop off?'

'Yeah. When I die.'

'You won't die soon, will you?'

'Why, want me to bugger off so you can have one now, do you?'

As if. Absolutely not. It's just that she can't go leaving me with my mother. Nanny doesn't understand what she's like. Nanny doesn't understand that Mum thinks I'm weird and a liar. That she doesn't ever listen to me. Most of all that she doesn't even *love* me.

'Don't talk daft, Hannah. Your mother loves the bones of you.'

'No she doesn't. I know she doesn't.'

Nanny says I'm talking nonsense, a load of shit, and in any case, *she* loves me. Then she goes and smiles at me like Mum never does, her teeth glowing in the light of the real fire. I can't remember the last time I made my mother smile or if I ever have. And it must be my fault because she smiles at other people. She smiles at the strangers we pass in town and at Jess' mother in Somerfield when she pays for her shopping. I've seen her smile at the nurses in the hospital and she even laughs at Jill when she comes round.

'Just don't die, Nan. You've got to promise me.'

Well she can't do that, can she? We've all got to die. Can't go on forever otherwise how will there be any room for the new babies being born? Nanny doesn't want to live forever anyway. The world's gone crackers. Auntie Eve with her happy pills and my mother with her bagless hoover. And all the rest of the shit that goes on on this crazy, scary planet that Nanny has seen nothing

112

of. *Aye*. She'll be quite happy when it's her time to go and she wants Patsy to sing her off. They can drop her on top of my grandfather up on the mountain and chisel her name in gold letters onto that black stone and she'll be good and ready for it.

'Don't talk like that,' I tell her. 'Dying is scary.'

She shakes her head at me and tuts like I've said something silly, something wrong.

'You don't want to be afraid of dead people, love. It's the fuckers who are alive you want to worry about.'

'What was Mum like when she was younger, Nan?'

'Oh, I can't remember. I can't even remember what I had for my fucking tea last night.'

I tell her exactly what she had. Corned beef pie and boiled potatoes. Mum brought it over for her. She laughs. Of course she did. My mother is a pain in the arse but she does love her. And she loves Auntie Eve, too, despite her faults and even though she only comes to visit when she wants to borrow fucking money.

'*All* mothers love the babies that come out of them, see. Even if they can't show it. But your mother hasn't got a sense of humour like us has she, love?'

'*Definitely* not, Nan.'

'She's more like your grandfather in nature. But you're like me, love. You got a cold heart but a warm soul. Warm as that fire by there.'

'Just don't die. Okay?'

'I'm not going anywhere. I'll be chasing you and Kyle around for a long time yet.'

'*Nan.*'

'Yes, love?'

'Who do you *really* love most, me or Kyle? I won't tell him. Honest.'

Nanny suddenly goes deaf again. She taps her hearing aid with her finger. It's okay. She doesn't need to say it. I know she loves me the best.

'So what ring do you fancy then?'

'Can I have whichever one I want?'

'Yes, my love. You can have your pick.'

She holds her hands out for me to see. They must be heavy,

those two wrinkly chunks of skin and bone and blue veins wrapped in gold and stones. Some of her fingers even have three rings on them. I like the big one she's got. Not just because it's big but because it's beautiful, too. A thick gold band that glows and a polished round stone on top that's the same colour green as Jess' eyes. It's the one she's always touching on the 120 bus when we pass the cemetery.

'That's my special one,' she says. 'Your grandfather gave it to me. But you can have it when I go. As long as you promise to look after it and never lose it.'

'Do you think he's in heaven?'

'Of course he's in fucking heaven.'

'Then why do you go to Hell, Nan?'

'If you're bad. If you've got bad blood, love.'

Hmm. I'm not sure if my blood is bad, but it's definitely crazy, alright. Spending time with Nanny like this makes me realise just how crazy. And if we're the same, like she just said, then my blood must be extra thick with Crazy. Patsy Cline kind of Crazy.

'What about if you lie, Nan? Will you go to Hell?'

It's then that I remember my notebooks and I feel my crazy blood turn cold as ice inside me. I left them under my bed because I was half asleep, careless. If Mum gets home before me she could find them and then my life will be over. Parents can take your stuff, they can take your freedom by stopping you going out with your friends. Your parents can break their promises and they can leave you, but they can't take your truth away. They can try but in the end it's yours and they can't touch it, can't stop you writing it that's for sure.

'Hope not,' she says, 'because I've told a fair few fibs in my time. The things I got up to that your grandfather didn't know about, when he was out on that boat in the Perssifc ocean, some sea, I don't fucking know. Well what he didn't know couldn't hurt him, innit?'

'Is Dad going to die, Nan?'

She goes deaf again. Taps her hearing aid. It's late and she's tired. Got to be up early for that bus.

I still like her, but my Nanny is just as bad, is a liar, same as everybody else.

Room 58

The silver-haired Science teacher who herded all thirty-three of us like cattle into our registration room was abnormally tall and lanky. The top of his head stroked the ceiling and Jess said he was like that because of a chemical experiment that went badly wrong one day in his lab. Of course I didn't believe her. I said alright, Jess, and we found a table that apparently we'll have to sit by every morning now to answer our names on the register. But we've got more important things to worry about than weird-looking Science teachers.

It's the first thing we do when we sit down. We've just been given timetables, and our nervous eyes scroll fast through the days of the week and the subjects typed in the square grid like they aren't really there at all. They sort of blur into one massive splodge of ink. Maths, Biology, Chemistry, Physics, Art, History, Geography, RE, PE, Welsh, French ... and then thirty-three hearts stop beating. There it is in bold black letters.

English
Mrs Ludlow

Jess hides her face with the piece of A4 paper which is shaking, and even Robbie Jenkins is worried. He's swinging on his stool and his face has all of a sudden changed colour. White, as if his cheeks have been coloured in with Tippex.

'Why us?' Jess asks the ceiling.

'Bad luck, that's all,' Robbie Jenkins decides, a ball of chewing gum rolling around his mouth like a white sock in a washing machine.

'Nah,' she says. 'There's only one explanation for it.'

Told me on the way this morning, didn't she? That we were doomed. That she could feel it in her bones. And now we're sitting here in our brand new uniforms, shirts that are stiff and itchy and jumper sleeves that are too long, hair that's freshly, especially *washed*, and this proves it.

'We're cursed, you mark my words. I've got a gift, see, can sense things like this happening before they actually happen, like when I knew my Auntie Paula was going to die because I saw it in a dream.'

Jess knew we'd have Laser flipping Ludlow for English. But what she didn't know, what she couldn't bring herself to even imagine, was that we'd have her first lesson, our *first lesson in Comp*.

Laser Ludlow is a legend, the mythical creature of the Rhondda. What the Loch Ness monster is to Scotland, Medusa to ancient Greece. And seeing her name on our timetable like that has sent a panic across the whole of the classroom, not just between the four of us. Oh yeah. Evan Jones is sitting by us as well but he hasn't said a single word. He's shell-shocked, stiff and staring straight ahead, like he's seen a ghost or been through a traumatic experience, something he'll never get over.

The other twenty-nine kids in here, some from our Juniors, some complete strangers who've come up to Comp from different schools, must know it the same as we do. Must've heard the stories about her, Laser Ludlow who's mental and massive, who hacks bodies with her guillotine 30cm ruler, who stirs blood in her PG Tips and burns holes in your soul with her eyes. Laser Ludlow never smiles and only ever wears black clothes come rain or shine. Always ready for a funeral, always well prepared for death. Apart from the handbag she carries, Jess says, which is weirdly pink.

'Used to be white when my father was here but over the years it got stained from the blood on her hands.'

Just imagine a monster, the most terrifying, angriest monster you've ever seen. Bubbling drool and a murderous snarl. And now picture it in a black blouse and skirt, heels on its feet and red lipstick plastered across its mouth. Are we picturing it or what? Good.

'Because that monster is Laser Ludlow,' Jess says. 'A glamorous monster, but a monster all the same.'

You can't miss her because, you know, she's massive, like. But if you haven't already seen her then you'll definitely hear her coming.

If word gets out that she's on her way down a corridor, to the staffroom or to her own classroom, then kids scarper ... take cover ... hide behind lockers or in the toilets ... *anywhere*. It's her voice that scares them the most. Her shouts rampage through the school like a hurricane, travelling effortlessly from one end of a long corridor to the other, up staircases and through doors, enough to make you jump out of your skin.

'She almost got sacked once,' Robbie Jenkins says, blowing a massive, head-sized bubble and then pop, it splats all over his lips. 'But Ludlow weren't having any of that, was she? She said oh, try and sack me and I'll stab you, school governor. So they had to keep her on. Even the other teachers are afraid of her. Silly cunts.'

Cunt. A four-letter word I just learned, like all the other brand new four-letter words Robbie Jenkins takes us through.

I've got butterflies, the worst ones I've ever had, and Jess' heart is going like mental. She grabs my hand and puts it up against her chest and she's right, I can actually feel it thumping out of her shirt. We stare at the clock willing time to stop or for the fire alarm, for the world to end, any kind of natural disaster will do. But the bell rings. We put our timetables away in our bags. Mine and Jess' are identical, black with zips and pockets for all our things, but Robbie Jenkins only has a boot bag for his crisps and chewing gums. He doesn't need a proper one because he doesn't have any pens or pencils or books, won't be bringing his homework in.

We leave registration, knowing that no one and nothing is going to save our souls. Robbie Jenkins is leading us, me and Jess, and Evan who cried in the induction assembly because he misses his mother even though she's not dead or anything, just in the house and he'll see her in a few hours anyway. Two sixth-form boys we pass down the corridor stop at the sight of us. We know they're sixth formers because they've got different coloured jumpers to ours. They laugh hysterically, point and say *awh*, look at them, look how *small* they are. Which is weird because we're not small, we're quite big. Don't they know that we were the tallest kids in our Junior school? But I suppose it's only now I notice it, how Robbie Jenkins, the tallest boy in the world, is tiny compared to them. Here we're like micro-organisms, ants among beetles and bees and dragonflies. We're not on our way to Laser Ludlow's classroom are we? They make ghost noises, shake their hands in the air ... *ooooooo*.

'Watch out!' one of them warns us, a scruffy, golden moustache across his top lip. 'Don't be a second after the bell or she'll have you!'

'Yeah,' another goes, his body as wide and square as a fridge. 'You aren't going to make it out alive!'

'Nice to know you. Rest in peace!'

We hurry along, Robbie Jenkins strutting ahead with his jumper tied around his waist, walking like some kind of penguin, trying to act all cool. His black hair is messy and his shirt torn at the back from a fight earlier, new shoes scuffed already and only one day in.

Jess' father was telling her this last night, and she doesn't know if it's true now, mind, she's only going off what he said when they were having their dinner, but it's written on the wall down by her classroom. Some kid done it years ago as a warning to others, to new kids like us.

'What does it say?' I ask her.

'*Danger*. In big red letters, in blood. Like what they put on boxes that contain wild animals. Like on Jurassic Park, you know?'

Well Robbie Jenkins don't care. He's got a bulldog in the house called Vince and Laser Ludlow can't be no worse than Vince because once Vince bit him on the leg and he was bleeding like fuck so he bit him back twice as hard and Vince haven't tried to bite him since, have he? *No*.

'You can't bite Ludlow, Rob. She's absolutely bonkers. Have you seen her? She'll crush you.'

'So what? Do you think I'm afraid of old Laser Ludlow? Pfft.'

Robbie Jenkins will fold her homework into a paper plane and fly it straight into her cup of blood tea. And when it splashes in her face and burns her, he'll laugh his head off, make her cry like he made Mrs Thomas cry every single day in Juniors.

'But no one's *ever* made her cry, Rob. She hasn't got any feelings ... heart of stone. She's even colder than Hannah.'

'Oi.'

'Sorry, Han, but you are pretty frosty.'

Whatever. Her eyes won't burn holes in Robbie Jenkins' soul because she won't get a chance to look at him.

'I'll knock her out if I want,' he says, bending his arms and clenching his fists. 'Smash my chair through her window. She'll be crying her eyes out!'

And as we turn the corner into the English corridor we see it, the chunky red letters sprawled on the wall. DANGER. LASER LUDLOW UP AHEAD. PROSEED WITH CAUTION.

'Well whoever wrote it can't spell properly. There's a C in proceed. No S.'

'How can you even *think* about spellings at a time like this, Han?'

'I'm only saying.'

Robbie Jenkins tells us not to worry, mun. Calm down, issit? He'll have her in the eye with one of his peppermint chewing gums.

'I'll show her *menthol* now.'

A really bad joke but it makes Jess laugh anyway, makes her giggle and swoon and say *Rob*, you're so funny, aye, the funniest person I know.

But it only makes me sick.

We're slowly approaching Laser Ludlow's classroom. Room 58 according to the timetable which Jess is holding like a map, and it's right at the end of the corridor. This corridor that reeks of tea and coffee and BO and blood and death.

'There's obviously a reason they put her all the way down here,' Jess says. 'Out of the way. Away from all the other English teachers for their protection. Fencing her off, they are.'

Yep. Laser Ludlow is Comp's dark, dirty secret, and now we're bunched by her classroom door, pushing and egging each other on, none of us wanting to be first in and for a second I think Evan's going to make a run for it. Out of the building and down the hill and all the way back to Mrs Thomas' lovely bright classroom where it's safe, where the walls aren't grey like the corridor walls here, where it smells like biscuits and milk and paint and PVA glue, not like tea and coffee and BO and blood and death. And he still can't manage any words. He just gnaws at his lips, slimy and shivering

119

like wet, pink jellies. Jess tells him to get a grip, big massive gay, and Robbie Jenkins is all like yeah, fuck it, go on then, Han.

'What? Why me?'

'You're the cleverest so you should go in first. You was always good at English in Juniors. Go on, mun, Jess,' he tries next. 'If you love me you'll go in.'

Jess does love him, to bits, but there's absolutely no chance. She's going to throw up now in a minute and look … she holds her hands out for us to see them trembling.

'Like a flipping leaf.'

We stand there arguing for a good minute or so. It's just that we don't want to accept it, believe that we're actually about to meet Laser Ludlow. That all those ghost stories we've been telling each other are coming true. It's like when you have a bad nightmare, a *really* bad nightmare and it seems so real, but then you wake up and you're happy because you realise it was Just A Dream. Well, there's no waking up from this. And when the bell goes again, a deafening shake that vibrates through the corridor, through each grey brick, each bone in our bodies, it makes us all jump.

Robbie Jenkins grabs the back of Evan's jumper and with two hands he lifts him off the ground. It's only then that he finally finds his voice.

'Help me, Han. Help me!'

I shrug my shoulders. I suppose Robbie Jenkins is right. We can't be late. *Someone's* got to go in first. And that someone should be Evan even though I'm the cleverest and Robbie Jenkins is the hardest. Jess is almost about to throw up and Evan is the most uh, what's the word now?

'Dispensable.'

Nice one, Han. Something like that he meant. Well whatever. It's better if Evan dies, right?

'So sorry Ev, butt. Goodbye.'

He's human bait. Robbie Jenkins sends him flying into Laser Ludlow's classroom, arms flapping and grabbing at air, at anything. He tries to stop himself on the doorframe but he goes right through. And since the fire alarm hasn't saved us, and since old Ludlow hasn't had a heart attack like Robbie Jenkins just wished

120

on her, we shuffle cautiously in after him. Evan, who has landed in a heap right in front of her desk. *Laser Ludlow.* There she is, Han, ohmyflippinggodalive, there she is! Jess elbows me repeatedly in the side but get off, mun. I know. I can see her. I'm not blind.

We've got no choice but to walk further into the lion's den, this classroom with its books immaculately organised on shelves, its rows of two person tables lined up in a perfectly symmetrical fashion. There's something very clinical about it, and the way the walls aren't plastered but bare bricks painted a light blue makes it feels as cold as a morgue in here. This is Laser Land and from her desk she reigns over it like an evil ice Queen, deadly rays shooting out of her eyes like spotlights. They blister down on the kids who enter, who know not to cross her or their souls will perish like all the thousands of helpless souls before them.

She doesn't get up from her chair, just lifts her head and glares over her desk at Evan. There's no need to speak because her eyes say it for her. *Get. Up. Now.* He scrambles to his feet like the carpet underneath him is a sheet of ice. Robbie Jenkins laughs out loud but he doesn't laugh for long. She eyes us up and down, revolted, disgusting little children, and we're ordered to find a seat and quietly, unless we want to spend break time today with her in detention?

We don't. We definitely don't.

But all the tables at the back are taken. Of course there's plenty free down the front. No one wants to sit within grabbing distance of Laser Ludlow. The other twenty-nine kids must've sprinted to get here first, a short cut we didn't know about. They're sitting like statues, too afraid to sneeze or cough or make a noise. Me and Jess find a table by the window. It looks out onto the car park and from here you can see the teachers' cars and the grassy banking. Also, notice that the window's got metal shutters on the outside of it ... creepy. Laser had them especially installed and she operates them from inside the classroom with a key that only she is allowed to use, touch even. The reason we can see out today is because it's raining, a light drizzle. Glorious summer days don't come around very often in Pandy but when they do that's when Laser will take the key out of her desk drawer and roll the shutters down. Because it's not enough for her having the kids and the teachers of Comp dangling on strings. Laser has to control the weather, too.

We all listen as she delivers an assured speech. She tells us what work we'll be doing this year, the texts we'll be studying. She doesn't tolerate rudeness or lateness or any kind of *ness*, scruffy handwriting or swinging on chairs. She can sniff out a minty chewing gum a mile off, before it's even been popped out of the packet, and she won't put up with excuses for not bringing homework in. There'll be consequences, you bet, and her voice doesn't stutter, her eyes don't blink. Not once. And to think I used to like English. Back in Juniors, when I wasn't worried about being murdered. I'm too scared to move in case my chair squeaks or something.

And then all of a sudden, and you've got to bear in mind how pin-droppingly quiet it is, Robbie Jenkins burps. A deep, drawn-out roar that seems to go on forever. Our heads turn around in harmony to look at him and then back at Laser Ludlow. What's she going to do? The whole class is frozen and about to witness something awful but exciting happen in the same brilliant, adrenalin-soaked moment. Jess loves him but not that much, not nearly enough to throw herself in front of the pounding lasers that are firing out of Ludlow's evil eyes, that are burning holes in Robbie Jenkins' soul.

He's burped. Actually opened his mouth and burped *in Laser Ludlow's classroom*. Laser can't believe it, either. She's as taken aback as we are but her voice is calm and soft which just makes it all the more scary to be honest. Excuse me. Did you say something, young man?

'Nah, Miss. Just burping, like.'

A collective shriek. Thirty-three cocktail sausages come to life. That's it. Robbie Jenkins is done for. Maybe she won't kill him here and now because there are witnesses, but tonight at her dining table Laser Ludlow will make a Robbie Jenkins sausage and she'll give him sweetcorn eyes and black worm hair and her hands will be covered in guts and mud as she stabs the fork into him, something awful wished with each evil prod. Tomorrow Robbie Jenkins will impale himself on the school gates. He'll choke on one of his chewing gums, get run over by a double-decker bus in the car park. What he dared to say has made her very angry. It's like she's holding an invisible megaphone up to her mouth. Her voice is no longer calm and soft. It makes the tables shake, like the shutters outside the window, and our pencil cases rattle, like there's an earthquake in Tonypandy. Robbie Jenkins is disgusting. The most repulsive little *boy* she's ever come across. Does he want to bring his chair down the front and sit with her by her desk, where she can keep her eye on him? Does he? *Well?* And then something amazing happens. A miracle of sorts. Robbie Jenkins doesn't answer back, doesn't poke his tongue out or call her a silly bitch like he'd call Mrs Thomas if it was her telling him off. Robbie Jenkins says *sorry*.

No tears fall from Ludlow's eyes like planned and he doesn't burp again. He gets up sheepishly and spits his chewing gum in the bin at the first time of asking, and when we're given exercise books he doesn't fold his up into a plane. I write my name as neatly as I can on the front cover of my own exercise book and look across at Jess whose hands are shaking even worse now, who for some reason gasps and drops her pen like it's on fire.

'Oh my God, Han. I've only gone and written it, haven't I?'

She tries to rub it out with her finger, to scrape it off with her nail. She even licks the end of her jumper sleeve and scrubs the cover with spit, but it's no good. It's there forever, plain and clear in black Berol ink. Jessica Matthews. English. Year 7. Laser Ludlow.

'Oh my God. Oh. My. Flipping. God. Alive. Help me, Han. *Do* something.'

'Just ask her for a new one.'

'I can't do that, can I? Because then she'll want to know why I need it and then she'll see that I've called her Laser Ludlow, mun.'

Told me, didn't she? Jess knew it before we got here, when we were walking to school. But cursed, be fucked! Her life is over. She's literally dead!

She holds her head in her hands, fingers over her open mouth like she's done something terrible, accidentally killed her Nan. Jess is desperate but then she has an idea. With her pen she colours over it, layers and layers of ink until the words are hidden under a thick black rectangle. But she holds it up to the light, and if you look really hard, squint like this, you can still make it out. Laser Ludlow. She's bound to see it when she's marking her work.

'Kill me, Han. Kill me now.'

'Just explain it to her, that you made a mistake.'

'*Explain*? Are you serious or what? You can't *explain* to Laser Ludlow.'

The woman might be an English teacher, but she doesn't know the meaning of the word mercy. Jess eyes the door up and then the window. She's really going to throw up now. But there's nowhere to run and nowhere to hide. No way out of Room 58. So she whispers a prayer to whoever's listening, actually closes her eyes, bows her head and puts her hands together.

'Dear Jesus and God and Allah and Freddie Mercury. Just don't let Laser Ludlow see it.'

The prayer is sent hopefully out of the window and up into the grumbling, navy sky. The rain is pelting down now, loud and brutal against the shutters. We just get on with our work. Work being a written piece about ourselves because Laser Ludlow wants to know who and what we are. We've got to write about the sort of things we like to do at home, what we want to be in the future. Jess hates stuff like this, I know. She stares at the blank page in front of her, her face as white as the paper itself, with no idea what to put down. Nosy old cow. What's it got to do with her anyway what she likes doing at home? Jess' words are a traffic jam in her head, all still and stuck and going nowhere, but mine come out so fast I can hardly write them down quick enough.

'See the colour on it?'

'What now?'

'Laser's scarf. Blood red, Han. Colour of *death*.'

It's whispered, like a story meant to scare. We're sitting around a campfire and Jess is shining a torch on her face. Laser Ludlow's got a collection of silk scarves, colours, not black like the rest of her clothes. They're one of her murder tools. She's got her guillotine ruler, of course, and also a shovel which she keeps in her pink handbag, but if she hasn't got them handy she'll use her scarves for strangling. She keeps them hung like dead rabbits on rusty nails in her bedroom back home in her big house. And in the mornings, and you know how vicious she is when she first wakes up, she climbs out of her four poster bed with its black satin sheets and six black pillows and selects the colour according to her mood.

'This is before she brushes her teeth now, Han, before she decides which kids she's going to torment today over a bowl of Weetabix. She's a millionaire, see, and her scarves are made of Mulberry Silk and diamonds and the skin of kids she's flayed herself.'

Jess nods over to Laser who's got her head down marking something on her desk.

'Probably a hit list. Probably a...'

Bang! Laser's like an angry judge with a gavel. She slams her ruler onto the desk so aggressively it bounces back up again. She's caught us talking. Our first and last warning. Do we understand? *Well*? Yes. We nod our heads in unison. Yes, Miss. Sorry, Miss. And trust me, we don't say another word to each other all lesson, even though it's hard to believe but I swear it. We're silent for the next fifty excruciating minutes. It's unbearable, like someone holding their hand over your mouth and suffocating you. It might be the longest either of us have ever gone without talking but we don't chance it again. We just swap this look and with it we both know. We *are* cursed after all. This isn't like Juniors where all we had to worry about was Mrs Thomas putting us at different ends of the classroom or down the front in assembly.

There's no talking at all in Room 58. No laughing. No burping. No chewing gum. No mobile phones. No breathing or thinking too loud. Because you know how the stories go. She'll strangle you with her scarf and stir your blood in her tea. She'll chop you up with her guillotine 30cm ruler and wipe your guts off it in her funeral skirt. Except they aren't just stories anymore. Wonderful things you make up, add to, take away ... things you can control. They're no longer far-fetched myths passed on by generations of disingenuous kids. Oh, no. Laser Ludlow is our English teacher, and Laser Ludlow is very much real.

Stitches

It's only quarter past eight. Why is Jess clapping the letterbox like that, like a lunatic? When I open the door she bursts in. And then she's standing in our passage out of breath and I'm putting my school shoes on at the bottom of the stairs.

'You're early.'

She knows, but she had to get out of that house, couldn't stand it any longer. I look up, bending down tying my laces, and see she's written on her arm with black pen. *It really doesn't matter at all.*

'What's that supposed to mean? What doesn't matter?'

'It's from a song.'

Apparently life's a gas or something, I don't know. But her new, neat hair bounces by her shoulders as she sings it to me. She got it cut on Monday after school. Bev said she needed something smarter because the way she had it, long and messy like a fucking tramp, our headmaster would be thinking Jess came from a poor family. My mother's in the passage now hanging a wet towel on the radiator to dry, and then she goes and strokes Jess like she's a cat.

'You look like Jacqueline Kennedy with it, love,' she says to her. 'Much tidier.'

Jess hates my mother touching her like that, I know, but she's far too polite or scared to tell her. I've got no idea who Jacqueline Kennedy is and neither has Jess. She looks at me like what on earth is your flipping mother on about? But I'm just waiting for it. Here it comes…

'Shame Hannah hasn't got hair like yours, Jessica. Look at it. Electric, like someone has plugged her in and she's gone up like a broken umbrella in the wind. How's your mother?'

Bev is absolutely fine. And I wish *my* mother, my mother who never strokes my electric hair like I'm a cat, wouldn't embarrass me in front of Jess. Go on then, I tell her, get out. And anyway, I like my hair the way it is. She'll never get me down the hairdresser's and to be honest, I liked Jess' hair better before. This morning it looks like she's even brushed it as well. The world has gone mad and my shoes are on and our toast is done. We're out the door and on our way down my street with them, the warm buttery triangles that are dripping in our hands. Mum makes us toast every morning, even though most of the time we aren't even hungry.

'Come on, umbrella head,' Jess says.

'Shut it, Jacqueline.'

'At least old Mrs King was happy this morning,' she chomps, mouthful of crusts but I've peeled mine off and thrown them down a drain.

I tell Jess that it's all a front especially for her. Mum is good at that. She pretends she's a normal mother who goes shopping, who makes toast and strokes my best friend's hair, but Jess doesn't know the half of it. When I came home from school yesterday she was crying again. She didn't even have *Countdown* on, just sitting there staring at the blank telly screen. She didn't ask me if I'd had a good day. If she did then I would've told her that I hadn't, actually, my day was really crap. I'll tell you about that later though. But all my mother does is cry. Cry and clean and make toast like some kind of mental, crying, cleaning, toast-making machine.

'Awh. Poor old sod.'

No. She isn't a poor old sod at all. I'm not crying, am I? So I don't understand why she's got to. Of course I'm not allowed to be anything. I'm not allowed to be sick. I'm not allowed to be sad. Because however sick and however sad I am, it's not important. Not as important as other things. I'm not allowed to ask questions and I'm not allowed to care. I don't have feelings, my mother says, which is lucky really when you think about it because if I did, I would be in big trouble. It's like I'm a ghost haunting our house. I'm here but not really. In the mornings I go to school and then I float home again at half three or later, depending on how fast we walk. I eat my food and do my homework and then I'm out again, up Jess' house or we go down the park. I'm just a cold draft that comes and goes. See through or something. Get rid of me, my mother would, if she could. Exorcise me away if I wasn't her problem, *her* ghost.

127

'Do you want a hug, Han? Cause I'll give you a hug if you want a hug.'

'As if. I don't want a hug.'

'Then what you on about?'

Nothing. It doesn't matter.

We're halfway to school already. Just got to go down the grass path on the side of the bypass now, and then cross the busy road and walk up the steps and over the bridge and then up the stupidly steep hill and we'll be there. We've been in Comp well over a month which means we know absolutely everything there is to know about it. And the things that go on there, within those walls and down those corridors and behind those doors, you wouldn't believe, couldn't even make up if you tried. Just imagine it like this, how I tell it to you, and then times the crazy by a million, and maybe then you might get it. Maybe.

The easiest thing to do is take you on a tour. But the first thing you need to know about Comp is that it's run by dictatorship and operates a strict uniform policy. There's no room for democracy. In the morning you put on your black trousers or skirt and your white shirt. You do your buttons all the way up and knot your striped tie so tight it chokes you. Navy jumper or cardi goes on top and then your black shoes, no high heels or trainers allowed, no jewellery. Now you're good to go, by foot or by school bus. And when you get to the top of the stupidly steep hill and walk through the main gates towards the big brown school building you'll see the carpark where the buses let kids out and where the teachers park their cars.

Around the back of school is The Quarter, which you could say is our yard. Although instead of numbers and snakes and ladders painted on the ground like in Juniors it's just an area of trees and benches and a shelter where you can hang around at break times if you want. It's a place starved of sunlight. And I'm not just saying this to make Comp sound gloomier and sadder than it is – I'm saying it because it's true. The Quarter is a shady pit enclosed by the school building itself, with trees that have had their leaves stolen by the weather or by bored kids, and benches that flake red paint like dandruff. Kids in dark coats fill the corners like packs of scheming wolves and the bins regurgitate empty packets of crisps and fags. You aren't allowed to smoke on school premises but kids do. Rules are there to be broken, after all. Teachers walk through the raucous crowd to and from the staffroom with hot mugs of steaming coffee and tea knowing that if they were to *accidentally* trip over a black-shoed foot or a loose bag strap, they'll be laughed at, humiliated.

That's outside. That's where the Real World ends and where Comp begins. The sign outside reception reads 'Welcome/ Croeso', but really ... you won't find anything welcoming through those swinging doors. Instead you'll face a winding labyrinth of run-down, grey corridors that smell like BO and fags. Apart from down the cookery corridor where it reeks of cheesecake and stale pizza. The notices on the boards are ripped and the panels on the doors are kicked in, the walls a universal sketchbook where graffiti is proudly displayed instead of work. No poems or collages or prize-winning stories here, just insults, and drawings of cocks and tits. There's lots of things you can use to write on the walls of Comp. Tippex, permanent marker, paint, pencils, pens ... faeces. You can even be more creative if you want. At the end of the Humanities corridor a used sanitary pad decorates the ceiling like a bloody piece of art. Jess thinks it's hilarious. I think it's gross.

The teachers say we're animals, but when you're treated like animals, you may as well behave like them. We were captured in nets from our Junior schools where we were happy and free and then they put us here in this zoo and locked us up. Most of the kids in school are like Robbie Jenkins. He was always bad in Juniors, but here he's something else. I don't know. Maybe there's asbestos in the air, or some kind of gas that turns the kids mental. He was suspended for two days after throwing some girl's tampons at our music teacher. A drum cymbal shield couldn't save her from the firing squad of string and white pellets. He says the only reason they didn't expel him is because he holds information that none of the teachers want leaking out. Like how he caught BO Pits Pugh from History and Saggy Tits Tyler from Welsh on the desk going at it over the thoracic cavity model in one of the Science labs, the plastic heart and aorta and the two lungs knocked messily across the floor.

It's kind of like war, us versus them, and we outnumber them ten to one, maybe more. Because the problem with a dictatorship is that there's the little people, us, and sometimes, all the time here, they fight back. Us kids in Comp are like a guerrilla army who kick things over in temper. Lockers, chairs, tables, cupboards … other kids. You know our names because they're chiselled into tables with compasses. Their sharp, pointy tips make good pens and even better missiles. If the teachers liked teaching once, they definitely don't any more. And, bless them, they do try sometimes but in Comp there's more important things to do than learn. We stand up and say it to their faces … seriously? Are you actually going to *try* to teach us? Ha!

They trip up, we laugh. They cry and it's even funnier. And when we spit at them from the tops of staircases we watch the drool fall like seagull shit onto their heads. We make fun of their twitches and the way they speak, that's if we let them speak at all. Pages in books are folded into planes and when we're quiet they think we're up to something. We usually are. They drive their cars down the hill home at the end of the day, relieved, foolishly thinking it's all over, but we aren't done with them yet. Because this is war. We throw whatever we find on the ground at their windscreens, plastic lids and rocks and boiled sweets and pens. The only teacher safe is Laser Ludlow. Because as soon as her Death Black car, with its engine that runs on blood, its windscreen that's washed clean with the tears of Year 7 kids, is seen coming over the brow of the hill, we step away from the road and hide the weapons behind our backs. She wouldn't hesitate to run us over. But the rest of them, we don't give up until they're out of sight. We're letting them know they've got to come back again tomorrow, and we'll be ready for them.

So that's our school. Do you get it now? If you haven't walked those corridors yourself, if you haven't been a name on the register, one of those teachers behind a desk, then maybe you can never fully understand what it's like. Just realise that it's not like other places, other schools. Realise that it's the most completely mental place in the whole world. Not quite the brand new exciting adventure Mrs Thomas promised us a million years ago. Although when I say *we* I don't actually mean me and Jess. *We* always wear the right uniform and do our ties up properly. We bring our homework in on time and only ever talk in a class with a teacher we're not afraid of, which is most of our classes to be honest. We're collecting merits in the back of our homework diaries because at the end of term we'll be able to exchange them for prizes. We're going places, me and Jess are. We're not going to be stuck in Pandy forever. We've got a plan.

And I don't know why but sometimes on the way Jess thinks it's okay to touch me. Like right now. She tries to slide her long white-sleeved arm under mine but I shake her off. Hooking, she calls it, and apparently all the girls in Comp are doing it so why can't we?

'We're not in Juniors anymore, Han.'

Remember how we were then? In the morning she'd hate me. I'd be stealing her pencils and we'd be calling each other all the spiteful names under the sun, but then by the afternoon she'd love me again. Now she just loves me all the time. Constantly. Like a planet.

'What?'

'"Life's a Gas".'

'You're making no sense, Jessica'

'Are you worried that I'm a lesbian, Hannah? That I'm going to kiss you and try to touch your minge?'

'Do you have to say minge all the time? It's disgusting.'

'Oh *sorry*. Vagina then. You're so posh! From now on I'll say vagina, just for you.'

'Just don't say it at all.'

'Say it, I'll *show* you it now.'

'Go on then. Dare you.'

'Not by here, mun. Not on the side of the flipping bypass. I'll catch a chill.'

We try to tell each other over the noise of the traffic everything that's happened since we were last together properly. Only yesterday down the park after school, but a lot of things can happen in one whole night.

'My mother's losing the plot big time. Four stitches he had to have, Han.'

'Where?'

'Down Royal Glam.'

'No I mean like, where on his body?'

'Oh I get you now. On his arm by here,' she says, rubbing the bumpy bit above her wrist.

'Ouch.'

'My mother's got sharp teeth, I know. Like a possessed Chihuahua she was, my father said. She just bit him. You could see his bone. He'd been texting *her*, see, that's what flipped her.'

'Pat Morgan?'

'Yep. Fat Pat Morgan. Minge … I mean *vagina* the size of The Gower according to my mother.'

'Will his arm be okay?'

'Once he's had the stitches out, yeah. But he'll be off rugby for months. What am I going to do if they get a divorce? Who will I live with? Because my mother nags me and my father's tidy. But my father can't cook, Han. What am I going to eat? I can't live off Chinese, can I?'

The normally busy road is quiet now, no black tyres ratting over the cattle grid, so we cross it.

'They're always arguing,' I tell her. 'I'm sure they'll be alright.'

Nah. This was different. This time there was blood and bones and words so nasty they could never be taken back. And you know what? Jess has got a good mind to kill herself. Because wouldn't it be funny if she just stood in the middle of the road … like this … waving her arms, woo hoo…! wait for a bus to come and flatten her. Maybe they'd notice her then.

'Bloody Hell, Jess!'

I pull her out of the road and onto the path by the bag on her back. We almost fall on top of each other. A couple of seconds later we'd have been hit by that blue car that just screamed past us and beeped.

'Bloody Hell?' she says, mocking me. 'Who are you, Mrs King?'

No. I am not my mother. And I will never say that again if it makes me sound like her but *God*, Jess, are you mad or what? What does she think she's playing at? She has no answer. She just shrugs.

'Want to die do you, Jess? Going to leave me here on my own, are you? Thanks. Thanks a lot!'

Alright, mun. Chill out. It was only a joke.

'And besides, no one would care if I died anyway.'

We're walking again now, and I know what I *should* say … my life would be shit without you, you stupid, stupid girl. So shit. And you're lucky you've got two parents, even if they do almost kill each other every day. But I can't say it, can I? I just can't. There are words in my head all the time, constantly, but the only way they ever come out is on paper. Maybe I'll write it on my arm later like she's written on hers. Maybe we can communicate through ink and skin forever.

I care.

Jess may be crazy this morning and her hair is horrible and neat, but I do like walking to school with her and listening to her until she stops for a drink out of her bottle of Fanta. Mornings belong to us. They are ours – the only time we're alone during the day. I'm not on about the other kids. They don't bother me, not even Robbie Jenkins who does take up a lot of Jess' time. But there's this one and when we get to school she'll be waiting for us in The Quarter. Her name is Lucy Williams. She's a blonde girl in our class who is very short but looks taller because of the shoes she wears. Even though you're not supposed to wear high heels to school, she gets away with it somehow. She's why yesterday was so rubbish…

She came and sat by us in the hall dinnertime. Uninvited, unwanted. And I don't know who she thought she was asking Jess over her house after school. I gave Jess this look over our pizza and chips that said she absolutely was *not* allowed to go, but she already knew it anyway. Told her she couldn't because me and her were off to the park. But then Lucy Williams went and gave Jess her mobile number so I had to look through her messages in the park just to check what they'd been saying. Don't worry. I'm thinking of ways to get rid of her.

'DCI King, that's who you are,' she says.

'I just don't like her, Jess.'

'You should be tidy to her though, Han. She's popular.'

'So? And what happened to best friends? To no one can touch us?'

'She can't *touch* us, mun. But you know what I mean. You seen what she did to Danielle Lewis the other day. Do you want that to be you next?'

Lucy Williams made Danielle Lewis cry in front of the whole class. She sellotaped a note saying 'I'm a fat minging Pig' to the back of her cardigan.

'Suppose not.'

But it's not just Lucy Williams. Lots of girls in Comp are like that. They're vicious little things, like bees, and the school bags on their backs are wings. Bags worn on one shoulder, not two by the way, because that's just not cool and if you do put your bag on two shoulders, you'll get picked on for it. Girls are petty like that. They fly around the school corridors feeding on gossip like it's juicy pollen, their lip-glossed mouths glowing with nectar and nasty names. Girls are things that will sting you hard if you don't fit in, don't look a certain way, but me and Jess don't care. We wear our bags on two shoulders because it's easier to carry them like that, and because there's more important things in the world, *our* worlds, to worry about. We aren't *girls* anyway. Girls are mean and stupid. They only care about make-up and hair, not about important stuff, like our plan that I was just on about.

'Bev reckons there's no money in art. Says it's just a stupid dream. What does she know, innit? She works in Somerfield. She wants me to be miserable because she's miserable. Scared I'll leave her like my father keeps leaving her.'

Yeah. Bev doesn't know it, but I do. That one day Jess will have her paintings hung in posh galleries. I'm not just saying it because she's my best friend. I'm saying it because she's that good and always has been. People will come from all around the world to stand in silence on the shiny floors and look at them.

'My mother's the same but we'll do it, Jess. I'm going to have my books on the shelves in Waterstones.'

'Defo, Han.'

It's not just our mothers though. If you listen to the news and the people around here they'll tell you that there's no room for dreams in the Rhondda, no jobs and no future. They think we're just two stupid kids who will grow up here and stay here and that's it, like everyone else. That we won't make any mark on the world at all. And you know how it is sometimes, if someone tells you something enough, that your dreams are silly, you can't be this and you can't be that, that you're a liar, then eventually you start to believe it. But it's a good job me and Jess don't listen to them. I'm going to be a writer and she's going to be an artist. We're going to get out of here. This place where my mother is miserable and Bev is crazy. This place that doesn't believe in us at all. So what if they're dreams? If you aren't dreaming then you're just sleeping, and that's the saddest thing of all. My mother and Jess' mother, they've been fast asleep, in a coma, for years.

We hurry across the bridge and power walk up the stupidly steep hill because we can see black smoke rising above the school building. We pick up the pace, our shoes tapping along the concrete, bags bouncing on our backs. Jess shouts come on mun, Han, something's going on! It's *burning down*! Do I reckon we'll get moved to a new school? Do I think anyone is dead? And while we're deciding what's happened, chasing our imaginations that are much faster than we are, that are there already, a couple of older kids overtake us in the carpark. Apparently a skip is on fire in The Quarter. Some year 7 kid called Robbie Jenkins. They twist through the teachers' cars, elbows bumping into wing mirrors, coat zips scraping paint work, and we're snaking through the cars too and sprinting towards the screams and smoke and Jess is leaping over puddles in front of me like she's Sally Gunnell.

Yeah. Comp is crazy, I know. But we'd rather be here. This place is sad and mental, but even though it's sad and mental, it's *so* much better than home.

Dissecting Snails

Lucy Williams wasn't there this morning in The Quarter. Tonsillitis, Jess says, and she might not be back until next week. How awful.

'Poor sod. She's texting me now.'

When isn't she texting her? Jess' mobile makes this happy jingling sound, as if a fairy is trying to escape from the front pocket of her bag, and believe me there isn't a sound I hate more than Jess' mobile telling her she's got a new text message off Lucy Williams. She's only got it turned on because Laser Ludlow's down the photocopying room. My mobile is still in my bag because Jess is the only person who texts me and she's sitting right by there.

'Her tonsils are the size of golf balls. White and everything. Worst case her doctor has ever seen. She'll probably have to have them out. Can't even swallow water, that's how bad it is.'

Lucy Williams this, Lucy Williams that. As if I care.

'What's the matter with you now?'

I turn my back to her, stare out of the window, even though there's nothing much to look at. Just rows of cars with windscreens that sparkle under the beach-ball-sized sun in the sky like they're sheeted in diamonds. It's a lush day. A day for ice-cold bottles of Fanta, for jumpers wrapped around waists and for some reason, Laser Ludlow's shutters haven't been rolled down. Room 58 is flooded with sunshine instead of darkness and it smells like summer as opposed to death, the breeze floating in through the open window scented with grass from the freshly mowed banking. Jess asks me again and I tell her *nothing*, Jess. Nothing is wrong.

'Where do you fancy going for food then?'

I shrug. Don't care. She keeps on.

'You can pick, Han. I don't mind. Your choice.'

'Okay. Then let's go to The Ritz,' I tell her. 'Where there are so many forks you can't even count them. Let's have *lobster* for dinner.'

136

'Do you even *like* lobster? Actually, you've never eaten a lobster in your life, have you Hannah?'

'Are you saying you won't take me to The Ritz, Jessica? Some best friend you are.'

She can't take me to The Ritz, can she? At least not yet, not until she's rich and famous and then she'll give me whatever I want, anything I desire in the whole wide world but for now she can only take me to Phony Tony's chip van which is just as good really, right? I can have as many forks as I want, too, except they'll be plastic and blue instead of sterling silver.

'So what do you say, Han? Phony Tony then or what?'

He's the man who owns the rusty, white chip van that every dinnertime is parked at the bottom of our school hill. The stench of fat and frying onions can be smelled from all the way up here and behind that sliding window he's got everything, a display of all the things that are banned on school premises. Crisps and sweets and the most coveted of all the items … fags. It's why as soon as the bell rings hungry kids squeeze through the tight corridor doors like a mental stampede and charge down the hill as fast they can to get to the front of the queue.

'Don't you want to go to the salad bar? You know how much you *love* the salad bar.'

'As if, Han. You know I can't stand it, mun.'

Funny that, because it's where we always go lately. To the dinner hall, and we eat *healthy* stuff that we don't even like.

'I haven't eaten chips for weeks, Han. I'm wasting away, mun. Haven't you noticed how fast I walk home? It's because I can't get to my fridge quick enough.'

'But what about Robbie Jenkins?'

Jess says that she loves him. She even wrote it on the front of her homework diary inside a red gel pen heart. Reckons he loves her as well, it's just that he's too cool to admit it in front of his friends. He's why we started going to the salad bar in the first place. Couple of weeks ago in PE Lucy Williams told Jess that he wouldn't fancy her for much longer if she turned into a big heffer like Danielle Lewis, so now we have to eat pasta and lettuce and tomatoes, down it with a bottle of Fanta like it's disgusting medicine. Yes. Lucy Williams comes too.

'Once won't harm, will it? I want a chip butty with mayo. I can jog it off on the way home.'

I say alright. Would've rather had lobster and shiny forks, but whatever.

Laser Ludlow comes back with the photocopying and Jess quickly zips her mobile up in her bag. Every conversation stops, just like that. Like someone has come and abruptly pressed mute on the room. We all go back to working on *Macbeth*, heads pulled down to our books like magnets. Robbie Jenkins is itching to play up. After all, he hasn't got a clue what he's reading. Shakespeare is jumbled-up hieroglyphics to him. He's trapped in here. This classroom is his cage. Just like the rest of them who are counting down the seconds until the dinner bell rings. They think English is boring, torture. Way too hard. But not me. It's just another lesson, I suppose, just another classroom in school, but in Room 58, *I'm* different. I'll try and explain it although this is going to make me sound like a massive loser. I don't care though. This is how it is.

In English I sort of disappear, get lost in the thing that I love most. See? Loser! Taking words and putting them together into something that makes sense. Getting it all perfect, described just right … and when it is, when it all comes together and flows, it's the best feeling in the world. Like a release. And only for a while, for sixty stupid minutes that go too fast, I forget about everything. I don't know how or why but in here I feel like I can do something right for a change, like I'm in complete control of everything. I forget about all the things that bother me and the bad stuff inside my head. They just fade away, out of the window, across the sparkly cars or somewhere else. Everyone else hates it here in Room 58, but I love it. It's my favourite place in the world.

We pack our pens and books away when the bell goes, bags zipped up quietly and chairs pushed neatly under tables. Jess is starving, can't wait to get her hands on this chip butty and mayo, and it's unthinkable that we'd wait like this to be excused, but instead of bolting to the door like we would at the sound of the bell in any other lesson, we wait for Laser Ludlow to tell us we can leave, which she does eventually, orderly and without a fuss, no barging or pushing. But not me. She calls over from her desk.

'I'd like you to stay behind, please, Hannah. Not you, Jessica Matthews. You can go. No need to hang around nosing.'

Well you'd swear Laser Ludlow just slapped her across the face. Jess doesn't say them out loud, of course, hasn't got the guts, but I can see the words rolling furiously around her head like angry little balls of fire. Never been so offended in all her life. How dare old loopy Laser accuse *her* of being nosey. Who is *she* to call people names? Jess? Nosey? Ha! The mental old cow. She's not nosey at all. I'm her best friend, thank you very much. She's got every right to be here.

'What the hell?' she whispers, bent down with her foot on the chair, trying to buy herself some time by untying her laces and then doing them back up again. 'Whatever you do, Han, don't look her straight in the eyes.'

Jess isn't really worried about me. She just wants to know what I've done, why on earth Laser Ludlow has asked me to stay behind. Jess wants a front row seat to witness her burn holes in my soul. Would've brought some Doritos if she'd known.

'Well go on then, Jessica, off you go.'

Alright, alright. Jess is going, mun. Give her a chance. Miss wants her to trip up, does she? Break her neck, like? Just got to sort her tie out, do her zip up tidy on her bag now otherwise all her things will be falling out. She lifts it reluctantly onto her back.

'Well, I'll see you in a minute then, Han,' she says, her words as sharp as the look she shoots Laser Ludlow on the way out.

She struts towards the door, nose lifted high in the air, her shirt accidentally or on purpose rubbing some of the words off the whiteboard on the wall as she squeezes past Laser who is sitting behind her desk. Jess has got a death wish, I swear. She goes and pokes her tongue out at the back of Laser Ludlow's head, and she just can't help but have a sly look in the pink handbag on the floor, hoping for a glimpse of the shovel, no doubt. She takes up position standing in the open doorway, an excellent view inside the room from there, but then Laser gets up. Goodbye, Jessica.

The door is shut and Jess is gone. I can just imagine her staring at the blank door, absolutely gobsmacked. Steam actually puffing out of her ears, her blood boiling. Anyone else but Laser Ludlow and Jess would be barging in demanding an explanation, an apology! Thinking about her out there almost makes me forget what's happening for a second. Dinnertime. It's deadly quiet now. The corridor was very loud but now there's no sound at all, no kids running, no doors slamming. The hungry stampede has gone and maybe Jess has left, too, stormed off in a huff down the hill towards Phony Tony's chip van. I'm in Room 58 all alone with Laser Ludlow who is slowly walking towards me.

I'm still standing behind my tucked-in chair, kind of frozen, but it's okay, she's only coming over to close the shutters. She stabs the tiny silver key in the box and when she turns it they fall down with loud bangs, the car park and sunshine outside disappearing with each jolt of rolling metal. Why is she closing them? It's not the end of the day. I hear Jess' voice in my head. She's very smug and very angry, says it like I deserve it.

'Because she's going to fucking eat you, Hannah, that's why!'

Laser Ludlow speaks to me, or at least I think she's speaking to me. She could be talking to herself because crazy people do that, don't they? Laser Ludlow says that when winter comes around it'll be a nightmare in here. The windows were badly fitted. It means the wind will be howling through the classroom. Obviously I don't say anything back. That's nice, Laser, sorry to hear about your windows … because it's Laser Ludlow, like. I'm too scared to put my hand up in class to answer a question, never mind talk to her when I'm alone in her room.

She goes back to her desk and tells me to bring my chair over. So I bring it. She tells me to sit down. So I sit down. Opposite her, every story I've ever heard blinking through my mind like a slideshow. The shovel in her handbag, that ruler on her desk … her scarf and her laser eyes, those cocktail sausage voodoo dolls. How Jess' father, not afraid of anyone, is afraid of *her*. This teacher all in black who gets her kicks out of scaring kids, the fleshy pieces of the especially unlucky ones floating like fruit in jelly, right by there in her blood-brimming desk drawer.

I feel my bag pulsing by my feet. A growl that vibrates against the carpet. Jess, no doubt, ringing me, or a sarcastic text message. RIP Hannah. Has she eaten you yet? Maybe she hopes I've got the volume turned on so I'll get in trouble. But eventually it stops and thankfully, Laser doesn't seem to hear it. I watch her pour water into a white plastic cup. The water is loud. There's always a bottle of it on her desk. I guess it's thirsty work being so mean. I'm asked if I want some but the answer is easy. And now that I'm thinking about it, I haven't actually seen her with a cup of tea. You know, this tea she's supposed to stir our blood into, like how she was supposed to leave the window shut today so we'd suffocate to death in the heat.

I've never seen her this close up. Laser Ludlow's got shoulder-length blonde hair that's cut in a style with flicks sharp as razors on the ends. It must be highlighted to hide the greys because you can't be that ancient and that blonde, it's just not possible. But despite being ancient she doesn't have any wrinkles on her face and her scarf is green today. A venomous bow because that's what green is according to Jess. The colour of poison and funnily enough also what Laser pours over her Weetabix instead of milk in the mornings.

It was stupid of me really to think Jess would've gone by now. Of course she hasn't. She's still lurking outside. Out of the corner of my eye I can see her behind the glass panel at the top of the classroom door. She's on tiptoes, must be, because the panel's quite high up. All I can see is her head and her neck. She's got her hands wrapped around it pretending to strangle herself, tongue sticking out the side of her mouth and now she's jumping up and down like she's on a pogo stick, her head disappearing then reappearing again. Jess is laughing hysterically but it's not funny. Not at all.

Laser Ludlow is done drinking her water. The plastic cup is scrunched up in her hand and thrown into the bin. She sort of stares at me but I don't look her in the eyes, just in case. And then something weird happens. Something crazy. Something that is more shocking than anything you might've ever heard in any of the stories. Laser Ludlow smiles at me.

'Don't look so worried,' she says. 'I only want to talk to you about your writing.'

Right then she pushes me inside a time machine and locks the door. I'm dislodged from this room and flying through space and eventually I land at Mrs Thomas' desk. I'm sitting on a tiny red chair and staring at my shoes. I'm feeling excited. Expecting … no … *wanting* praise, this thing I'm not used to but this thing I crave. But it all goes away when the piece of paper that means the most to me in the world is balled up in front of my eyes and thrown into a bin. My heart sinks. Actually sinks. I feel it drop. And maybe in that moment it falls out of my body completely, forever. My mother can't be bothered to save me. I'm happy and sad and angry all at exactly the same time.

The only difference is I'm ready for it now. This time it won't hurt and it won't make me crazy mad because I've heard it all before. Yes. I'm a criminal. I steal words. I'm a fraud and a cheat. Just hurry up and say it already. You know I'm trouble. You know that I'm a liar.

'I think you've got a talent, Hannah.'

She's only just finished marking the pieces we wrote about ourselves first lesson, and apparently I'm not a liar … I'm The Best.

I pick at the bobbles of cotton on my trousers. Then I focus on Laser's scarf and then the ceiling tiles. The Oxford dictionaries on the shelf and my shoes. The things on the desk … the half-empty bottle of water and the shutter keys, pens lined up like soldiers, as neat as the photocopying that stands in a perfectly stacked tower, not one slice of paper jutting out of place. I couldn't thank her even if I wanted to, even if I was grateful which I'm not. My cheeks get so hot. I hate her for saying those things and actually, I feel sorry for her. She *believes* in me? I have so much *potential* that one day she knows I will be all of those things that I wrote I want to be? Wow. Everyone was right about her. If she thinks that, then she really must be mental.

I wait for her to take it back. To laugh at me in her chair as she says it. Sorry, Hannah King, I was only joking. I know you. We all do. You're a liar. I even *want* her to say it but she doesn't. She leaves me holding them, these horrible nice words that are like little ticking bombs that will soon explode and blow my head off. I'm just glad when she says that I can go now. So glad that I almost knock Jess over with the door. Not my fault she was right behind it.

We're walking fast up the English corridor and she's tugging at my bag. Slow down, Han. What did she want? Am I going to tell her or what? *Well?* There we are then. Like that, is it? Did she shout at me? Jess couldn't hear a flipping thing behind that door even though she had her ear right up to it. Must be sound proofed. Did she say anything about her exercise book? Does she know that Jess wrote Laser Ludlow on the cover?

'Han, don't leave me in suspense like this!'

'Come *on*. Let's just get out of here.'

This corridor. Comp. I need air but Jess is relentless and nags me all the way down the hill. She calls me a bitch, an absolutely terrible friend, the worst, a spiteful cow, but I'm none of those things and I'll tell her in a minute, once we've got our food. We walk straight up to the chip-van window because the queue is long gone.

'Can't believe it. All the bread rolls are sold out,' she says with a look on her face like someone has died. 'Fucking Laser Ludlow. Shutting me out of the classroom like that, did you see her? Slammed the door in my *face*. I've got a good mind to sue her. And now I can't have a chip butty because of her. That woman is ruining my life.'

Jess decides we're having sweets as well as chips. Because if we're going to get fat then we may as well do it right, go all out and get *obese* like those ladies on the telly in America who have to be lifted out of their houses by cranes. She asks him for two pounds' worth of chewy snails and we watch him scoop them out of a plastic tub and into a paper bag. He's the ugliest man I've ever seen. The front of his apron is slimy and yellow, like it's drizzled in piss, and his cheeks are spotted with black holes that were probably made by chip fat spitting in his face. Jess shouts cheers, Ton, you minger, have a nice day! and then we walk off across the road, sweets in her trouser pocket, our cardboard cones of chips steaming in our hands.

Jess is still fuming that she's missing out on a chip butty, mind. If Laser Ludlow hadn't kept me behind for eighteen minutes, and yes, she timed it on her mobile so she's quite sure that's how long I was held hostage, then she'd be eating one right now. She slings her bag down on the pavement opposite the van, kicks stones and

143

rolled-up granny greys out of the way and makes a space for us to sit. A good place to watch the world go by. A good place to try to come to terms with it.

'Come to terms with what?'

'The fact that I couldn't have a chip butty, Hannah. I'm grieving.'

'Get a grip, Jessica.'

'Nuh.'

We sit on our jumpers, the sun turning my arms pink but Jess' a caramel colour. She forgets about the chip butty eventually and how much she hates Laser Ludlow and turns her attention to Phony Tony. Do I reckon he's a paedo? Or maybe just a plain murderer?

'Because all dodgy men go around in white vans. Good for hiding bodies, see, plenty of dark empty space in the back.'

It's all part of the psychoanalysis. She knows because she's got a book on murderers. Loads of cool, gory pictures inside. Her father bought it for her like he buys her absolutely everything else she asks for. Guilty conscience, see.

'Sorry, Han. I forgot … I didn't…'

I tell her that it doesn't matter. Because it doesn't.

'Well my mother doesn't like me reading it. She says it might give me ideas and I'm weird enough as it is. Cheeky cow. Can you believe it?'

Yes. Bev's kind of got a point.

'It's the same as with Rose.'

'Rose?'

'Rose West. Poor sod, she was. See, to get to the end you've got to go back to the start.'

'What do you mean?'

'It's quite simple really. People are the way they are now because of everything that's happened before.'

We all start off as babies, she goes on, ripping the corners of the mayo sachets off with her teeth. She squirts them in zigzags over her salty, vinegar-soaked chips and then she eats them at a speed that's just animalistic. Apparently it's like this. We all come out of our mothers the same and some of them love us and some of them don't. And we shit and spew and cry and yawn and everything's okay for a while, but then they slowly start to mess us up.

'Most parents don't even realise they're doing it.'

But even if they did, they wouldn't be able to stop. It's just the way it is. Especially with mothers and daughters. You'd think that after they grew you themselves, spending nine months inside them, actually *inside* them, you'd have this connection, this understanding.

'*Nah.* It's actually the opposite. The very second you left your mother's vagina, Han, that was the exact moment she stopped knowing what you need.'

In the glorious sunshine with the big green mountains around us, and as Phony Tony closes the window on his van, Jess solemnly finishes the last chip in her cone and with a slap of her salt-dusty hands, solves the meaning of life.

'So what I'm basically saying is we're both absolutely fucked.'

Our empty cones are thrown onto the road. We should put them in the bin really. It's only by there, next to Phony Tony's van, but we're too hot and lazy to move. Jess announces that she's going to do a show, especially for me by here on the pavement with her chewy snails, small sweets that are made of jelly and shaped like, well ... snails. Her greasy hands are rubbed in her trousers and one by one the snails become people we know. She does an impression of Evan Jones first, a blue snail with tangerine-coloured eyes. He cries because he's forgotten to bring his homework in. She eats him slowly, the last sloppy chunk of his bubblegum-flavoured body left caked to her front tooth like a wad of Blu Tack. She chisels him off with her tongue and then he's completely gone. Lush.

'Who shall I do next, Han?'

'Your mother?'

Okay then. Old Bonkers Bev it is. And here she is, cherry red, an extremely angry mollusc who bites her father. He's sour pear flavoured and plucked from the paper bag, too. Jess rips him apart with her teeth and his blood drips down her chin, green though, not like it was that morning when her mother bit him for real. She makes them fight before eating them both. They're better off dead.

'And look, good old Mrs King in her dressing gown.'

My mother is fat and pink and dancing mid-air, a sticky puppet in Jess' hand. And in her best Mrs King voice she makes it say, brush your bloody hair, Hannah, and why can't you be a better daughter, like Jessica Whatshername who is just absolutely gorgeous and very, *very* funny. She's raspberry flavoured and Jess' favourite, so she doesn't live for very long. I won't deny it though. Jess is funny. We're laughing so hard and so much we actually forget what we started laughing about in the first place. My ribs hurt and Jess has got a flipping stitch, mun, and I wish more than anything that it could stay like this. Right now it's exactly how it was before we came to Comp. Just me and her. I don't want Lucy Williams to ever come back to school, to get better from her tonsillitis. I don't want to share Jess anymore.

'You don't share me, stupid. Baby I'm yours.'

'What on earth are you singing, Jessica?'

It's just a song. I'm hers. Simple as that. But that can soon change if I don't tell her.

'Tell you what?'

'What old loopy Laser wanted you for.'

Jess takes the last snail out of the bag and sits it on the palm of her sticky hand. Green. This one is Laser Ludlow herself, the meanest, sourest snail out of the lot, and it's alright, she knows exactly what she said to me. Jess opens and closes its wobbly mouth with her thumb and in a loud and dramatic voice, says...

'I want to eat you all up, *Hannah King*. I loooove you!'

'As if.'

'Well don't be shifty then, Han. I'm your best friend. Tell me what Ludlow said.'

'Fine. But you'll only laugh.'

'No I won't. Promise.'

'She said I'm The Best.'

'The *best*? The best what?'

'I'm talented or something. I don't know.'

Talented? Am I serious or what? Shut up! And she does in fact laugh when I say yes, that's what she said and she even offered me some of her flavoured water. Jess laughs her head off actually, tears coming out of her eyes and everything. Oh my God, like, she can't cope. What a freak! Jess will show her talented now, watch this. She throws the snail into the middle of the road just as a car is coming, carefully and with precision like it's a dart. Splat. Bull's-eye. The tyres squash her good and proper. Laser Ludlow is dead.

Jess is surprised the crazy cow didn't whack me on the back of the head with her stapler on the way out. Just imagine if she was like Jeff.

'Who on earth is Jeff?'

'You know Jeff … Jeffrey Dahmer.'

One of her favourite serial killers from the book.

'If Laser Ludlow drugged you and then drilled holes in your skull and injected you with some kind of mind altering poison that turned your brain to goo, it would be *so* cool.'

Most of the time she's just Jess. Jess who talks until my ears ring, but sometimes, like now, it's as if we're having a race and the starter's gun has gone off and I've missed it. Jess is bolting ahead of me and I can't catch up. There's always something she's got to tell me, some song lyrics, serial killer, something new I don't know about.

'It sucks, Han.'

'What does?'

'Well nothing good like that happens here, does it? The closest we've got to someone *dangerous* is Laser Ludlow.'

'Maybe she's not dangerous at all. She had her chance today. I was all alone.'

'I hate her, Han.'

'It was only a chip butty, Jess.'

'Not just because of that, stupid. She's had it in for me since the start and now I know why. She wants me out of the way so she can kill you. She knows I'm onto her.'

'As if.'

'Serious. She put me outside class the other day on that chair and I was only crunching a Strepsil. I had a cough, like.'

Bitch. Jess is telling me straight. Bad news for Laser because she's all clued up after reading her murder book. She'll make me stay behind again soon and that'll be the last anyone ever sees of me. She might've had the chance to kill me today, but she's just biding her time, lulling me into a false sense of security. Laser will lie to the police and swear on the Bible that she doesn't know a thing, despite Jess trying her best to convince them that it was her who did it, who murdered me. They'll believe Laser of course because she's very convincing, a well-respected teacher, all the evidence long destroyed.

My chair will be empty and Laser will be behind her desk in Room 58, all in black, her lipstick immaculate, her scarf a bright colour to reflect how she feels. Happy. The happiest she's ever felt in her life. She'll smile to herself as she stares out of the window, across the carpark and up onto the banking. Because that's where I am, buried under the grass and the dirt, and she's the only one who knows.

'I really don't think she's got a shovel in her handbag, Jess.'

Then she sings to me again.

'And now she loves *you* so you're totally fucked, Hannah.'

She says it with a wicked smile. Jessica Matthews. My totally mental best friend.

'Ted'

It better not jump now. It's got a stinking habit of doing that. Probably because she's watched it so many times. Oh well. Here it goes. Jess pushes the tape into the slot on her telly video combo and it eats it like a mouth, the white sticky label on the front swallowed with a noisy gulp. The black Berol handwriting said 'Ted'.

It's really late, early hours of the morning, and Jess' mother and father are finally asleep. We've been waiting ages for them to drop off like we're their parents and they're our screaming, newborn babies. Bev is in the bedroom and Jess' father is downstairs on the settee. Jess' house is pretty much identical to mine in that there's three bedrooms upstairs and downstairs a small living room and a kitchen and a tiny bathroom that always seems to be cold, even when the heating's on. It's where World War Three takes place every day. The rest of the street is oblivious, has no idea that behind the front door each night me and Jess have to dodge nasty words that ricochet around the magnolia rooms like bullets. It's why we mostly stay in her bedroom where we sleep top and tail, where Jess likes to dig me in my ribs and just about everywhere else with her jabbing toes. She sleeps like some kind of massive star that's fallen out of the sky and landed on her bed, in all kinds of awkward shapes.

I like staying over though. We never stay at mine because at my house you aren't allowed to make a mess and you aren't allowed to stay up late. Because I just don't want to be there anymore. And we're safe in here, away from the shouting and the bullets. Jess' bedroom is our own little cocoon. This tiny box room that somehow manages to fit a single bed in it, and a telly on top of a chest of drawers that matches the light wood wardrobe. She's also got a lava lamp. I really like her lava lamp. The fat bubbles float slow and dark and lazy like Black Moor goldfish. It's lush, and when the lights are off like this it glows purple and turns the entire room purple, too.

The walls are painted a peach colour which Jess hates. So she's covered them in her artwork. Not quite the pretty trees she used to make in Junior School because some of the things on the pieces of card and canvas are quite freaky. Spirals and strange flowers with faces and teeth, and this multi-coloured skull thing and a dead cow's head. I don't know. Don't ask me what any of it means. I don't understand it, water colours and pastel paints, different kinds of brushes and pencils. I haven't got a clue what she's on about half the time when she tells me. Every time she comes in Bev, her mother, looks at them with horror, like she's just uncovered an actual real dead body in her only daughter's bedroom.

'I'll start it in a minute,' Jess says, pressing pause on the remote. "It would *really* piss Bev off if she knew I was watching it.'

A film about Ted Bundy. We aren't old enough to watch it but we're watching it anyway, and Jess is giggling like a kid, a kid who *really* isn't old enough to watch it. See, Bev just doesn't understand that crazy people are much better than normal, boring people like her. And no one is better than Ted. Jess has his picture stuck to the wall above her bed. He looks down on her as she sleeps, like a guardian angel. He's in a court room and looking very handsome in his suit. Ted got cut out of a magazine, one of the glossy crimes ones her father buys her on the sly every month. She cut me one out as well but I couldn't have Ted because apparently Ted belongs to her. I got Jeffrey Dahmer instead, blond hair and thick-rim glasses, and when my mother asked me who he was on my wall the other day, that weird-looking fella by there, I told her he was in a pop band and she believed me either because I'm a good liar, or because she didn't really want to have a conversation with me in the first place.

Jess jumps back under the quilt next to me on her bed, legs squirming, trying to get warm again. We're sitting with our backs against the cold peach wall. Her pyjamas are silky and green, a shirt with diamond-shaped buttons and shiny trousers that are too long for her legs, and mine are red with teddies on. I had them for Christmas and Jess thinks they're hilarious. She presses play then, her room pulsing purple, and she's been looking forward to showing me this film for days. But this is Jess. Jess who can't keep quiet for five minutes. The girl even talks in her sleep.

'Yeah I reckon Ludlow hasn't got long now.'

'What do you mean?'

'Before they get her.'

'Who?'

'The police, mun.'

I roll my eyes at her. I'm bored of this.

'Oh *sorry*. I forget that you and Mrs Mental are friends now. Always slips my mind. You'll be round her house next watching videos.'

'Don't be stupid,' I tell her. 'Me and you are…'

'I know. Best friends and no one can touch us.'

She says it in a sarcastic voice and with stony eyes, with a massive yawn. That's how it used to be, yeah, before *she* turned up. I just don't see it, do I?

'What?'

'What she's doing. Do you seriously think she asks you to stay behind after lessons because she *likes* you? Because she thinks you've got *potential?*'

'Oh, thanks a lot.'

'I'm not being mean, Han. But just think about it. She's like a hundred years old and you're very, very young. What can you possibly have to talk about?'

It's not Jess' fault that she doesn't get it. She just can't. I have been staying behind after English lessons quite a lot, but it's not weird like she makes it out to be.

'I'm sick of waiting for you in the corridor. It's boring out there.'

A lovely little club we've got going on. A private club Jess is not allowed to join. She's been excluded. Banned. *Shunned!* God only knows what goes on behind the door of Room 58.

But there's no big secret. I just get my chair and sit opposite Laser Ludlow at her desk. When it's windy the windows howl and when it's raining the shutters are loud and I'm not scared of her at all. In fact I feel safe in Room 58, protected. We just talk.

'As if, Han.'

Yeah. Really … we just talk. She's nothing like the person everyone says she is. I don't know. For some crazy reason Laser Ludlow seems to understand me. And for some even crazier reason she doesn't hate me for it, she's actually nice to me. I can tell her things I'd never dream of telling Jess who I've known for most of my life because Laser's the only person who gets it. Gets *me*. That I need to write … *have* to. She told me that when she was younger she was exactly the same and you've got no idea how good it feels hearing someone say it. That you aren't weird and there's nothing wrong with you. That you're good at the only thing that means anything to you. That you aren't a liar.

'Telling you now, Han,' Jess goes on, determined to make me see that it's ridiculous to think that someone else apart from her could like me, 'there's something dodgy about that woman. You sure you're not fucking her?'

'Get a grip, Jess.'

'If she's trying to groom you I think you should tell me.'

'You're sick in the head.'

She knows. But whatever. Anyway, *shh*. She's trying to watch this film.

'You started it.'

'Yeah well. I've had enough of talking about stupid flipping mental Laser fucking Ludlow.'

'Are you *jealous*, Jessica?'

'Of big massive loopy Laser? *Ha*. As if. Move into her classroom if you want. Watch *her* videos. Marry her if you like. What. Ever. What you smiling at me like that for, you freak?'

I'm smiling at her because in the purple dark I'm happy, warm as morning toast inside. Because Jess is clearly, obviously, beautifully jealous. And when you're jealous it means you care. You care so much it bursts out of you like an unwanted, ugly green foetus, and there's nothing you can do to stop it.

'Jessica Matthews is jealous of Laser Ludlow. I can't believe it.'

'Oh shut up, Han. Shut your gob now.'

My smugness is whacked off my face, literally, by her pillow. Let's watch this now because Ted Bundy is so sexy. Look at him, mun. It's not really Ted, of course, it's just an actor. He bundles a girl's body into the back of his car but then Jess pauses it.

'Do you know why he did it, Han, why he killed all those girls and then fucked them?'

'Because he was crazy.'

'*No*,' she says, angry at me for being so stupid. 'It's not that simple.'

She turns to face me on the bed. Very serious face. It's like this.

Under our skin and bones we've got wires and they're the wires that keep us sane, make us normal. These cables pumping with blood, they send feelings to the right places. They join our hearts to our heads and make us feel all the things we're supposed to feel. Guilt and kindness, forgiveness and empathy, gratitude and all that shit. It's how we know right from wrong.

'Let's call them the normal person wires,' she says. 'And those few hours after we're born is the only time they're ever circuited up properly.'

'Did you read this in your magazine?'

'Nah. Got this out of my head, like.'

Animals don't have these wires, see, only humans do. And as we get older the world starts to knot them up bit by bit with every tragedy, every little thing we go through that hurts us. It twists and ties us, isn't happy until we're spun into giant messes. It's our parents that do it to us mostly. Fuck us up. Course we're all a bit messy, like, but some people's wires are played with so badly they can never be undone.

'Imagine a Slinky,' she tells me.

'A Slinky?'

'Yeah you know, mun. Those things you have when you're a kid, like a massive spring and you put it on top of the stairs and watch it flop down.'

Well one of them when it gets all tangled up and you just can't unravel it no matter how hard you try. That's what your insides are like when you're fucked up. And that's what happened to lovely Ted. He thought his parents were his parents but they weren't. They were actually his grandparents and his *sister* was his mother. He never even knew his father. The world messed him up so he hated the world. Do I get it?

'You can't mess people up and then expect them to be normal, Han.'

'Why you telling me for?'

'Just thought you should know.'

'Do you think we're messed up then?'

'Nah. We're alright. But would you come to visit me if I was in prison?'

'Who have you killed?'

'Bev first. Did her with the iron and then my father with the kitchen knife. I pushed Laser Ludlow down the stairs in school.'

Jess giggles again when she says it. You should've seen her. Right from the top she went, tumbling down like a massive, mental bouncy ball … boom, boom, thud, thud on each step! There was *so* much blood on those stairs, like a trail of dripping red paint.

'Very messy business.'

She's like a magician then when she pulls a bag of blue Doritos from under the quilt. Sneaked them out of the kitchen earlier. Not allowed to eat in her bedroom but so what? She bangs the packet, loud, the way she always opens her crisps.

'Shit,' she says. 'Forgot. Hope she don't wake up now.'

Because when Bev is asleep it's the only time she isn't moaning. Moaning and crying, it's all she ever does. When she hasn't got her miserable, nagging gob wrapped around a fag. But I know. If Jess' father does leave, if they do get the D word, then maybe Bev can move in with my mother and then me and Jess can live here.

'Good idea, Han. They'd get on great, wouldn't they? They could cry together all day long.'

Play is pressed again and we carry on watching the film. Ted is tying the limp, dead girl to a bed with some rope. Her eyes are still open.

'Watch him fuck her now,' she says as she dips a crisp into the pot of salsa she also nicked from the kitchen. 'Go on Ted, boy, smash her!'

It gets me thinking about what she said just now. If every bad thing that happens to you makes a knot in your normal person wires, then me and Jess must be pretty messy ourselves. Maybe I've got something worse than Crazy Blood. Maybe I'm all mangled inside, just like Ted Bundy.

'You're not bad, Han,' she says, her words distorted by the slodge of crisps in her mouth. 'You don't *have* to turn out like Ted.'

'What do you mean?'

Well, we're not all serial killers, are we? There's nearly seven billion people in the world and most of them are fine, despite everything. It's like her mother, innit? She could've killed her father if she wanted to, after what she found out he did with Fat Pat Morgan in the back of his jeep, but she didn't, she only bit him.

'And look at us. We're okay. Even with my parents the way they are and you ... well you know. Our wires might be a bit messy but they aren't completely fucked like Ted and Jeff's.'

But what if she's wrong? It's four in the morning and we're sitting in her purple room eating stolen Doritos and watching a really bad and weird film we shouldn't be watching with Jess' crazy flowers and rotting cow's head above us ... Ted on the wall by there, and my bag on the floor with my notebooks inside with all those things that you wouldn't even want to know ... and earlier, when Jess was in the toilet, Lucy Williams sent her another text message and I deleted it so that she wouldn't see it because I'm horrible and jealous so ... yeah, *look at us*.

'Come on,' she says, telly paused again, quilt thrown off the bed. 'I'll show you.'

We're creeping across the landing like burglars. I can't see where I'm going and the floorboards shriek under my bare feet. I follow Jess down the stairs which also talk, louder than usual it seems now that we need them to be quiet. And in the blackness of the living room we tiptoe past her father who we can't see but can hear snoring on the settee, into the cold of the kitchen where she turns the light on, a clear square glass block on the ceiling that's had those three dead flies trapped inside it for as long as I can remember. Like tiny black fossils preserved in ice.

The new brightness hurts my eyes but won't wake her father, don't worry. Bev reckons he could sleep through a nuclear bomb. Jess leaps across the kitchen lino towards the fridge like a triple jumper. She's Jonathan Edwards in silky green pyjamas. Then she swigs it, the half empty, or half full, carton of milk, wipes the white moustache off her lip in her sleeve.

'Want some?'

I think about everyone else who might've drunk it that way. Bev and her father, all their crumbs and germs and spit, Bev's fag breath.

'Nah, you're alright.'

Suit my flipping self. What else we got in here then? She holds the fridge door open and examines inside. It's all come from Somerfield. Bev gets discount, see. Bacon. Do I fancy a sandwich? Some crumbed ham. What about a yoghurt or a gherkin? Jess loves a gherkin. Her father's expensive, crumbly blue cheese from the Deli counter? She unwraps it and sniffs it. *Minging*! Like an old man's ball sack, mun.

'Come on, Han. Let's eat it all!'

'I'm not hungry.'

'But imagine Bev's face if she woke up and found the fridge empty. Classic.'

'So you brought me downstairs to eat all the food?'

Oh yeah. She almost forgot about that. No. But first things first … she goes and spits into her father's expensive cheese. Actually gobs into the clingfilm and mixes it up with her fingers, the texture's like runny egg and lumpy flour when it's really phlegm and cubes of stilton. That's for making her mother cry, dirty old cheating bastard, she says as she wraps it back up and puts it exactly where she found it on the top shelf of the full fridge. That's for ruining absolutely everything, *prick*.

'Hope he enjoys it on his Jacobs crackers tomorrow.'

She lets out a big sigh. Right then. Obviously we're not down here to spit in her father's cheese. That was just spontaneous but it felt flipping brilliant, fair play. Nah. The reason we're shivering in the kitchen at four in the morning in our pyjamas is because Jess is going to show me that we're not crazy. She slides a knife out of the wooden block on the counter, the biggest of the lot.

'Bev uses this for sawing meat,' she says, the thick silver blade gleaming under the dead fly light. 'Cutting legs off stuff. And for threatening my father as well. Said she'd chop his cock off and feed it to Fat Pat Morgan.'

Come on. Follow me Han, nice and quiet now, the black handle of the knife gripped in her hand, out in front of her like it's a sword, like we're on our way to slay a dangerous beast, some kind of dragon. It turns out we are. The beast is her father who we can see now, the living room illuminated by the kitchen light. The beast is asleep. The best time to attack. Catch him off guard. We're standing over his body, his mountain-sized belly moving up and down under his red Wales rugby shirt, pale thighs the size of washing machines beneath his shorts. He's massive, barely fits on the settee. Six foot five Jess says and that's why she's taller than me but only a tiny little bit.

'I hate him,' she says, a revolted look on her face. 'Know what he called my mother yesterday? A useless, ugly pig. Always calling her names. That's why she's crying all the time. But just look at *him*, Han. Who's he to call anyone ugly? Look at his flipping head, mun.'

It's pumpkin-sized, round and chunky and completely bald. He reminds me of a peeled onion, the wrinkles on his forehead deep and wobbly like lines on a heart monitor screen. He does give me a lift home sometimes when it's raining, and he tells me I'm very polite, always been nice to me, but looking at him like this I'm not really sure why Jess' mother cries over him, or why Fat Pat Morgan would want to do *that* in the back of his jeep anyway. The snores growl deeper and louder from his snarling mouth, a river of dribble escaping out the side. This sleeping brute that could wake at any second.

'Jess…'

'Yeah?'

'Why are we standing over your father with a knife?'

'No need to whisper, Han. He won't hear you. Dead to the world. Dead for real in a minute.'

'What?'

We're standing over her father like this, with this pretty, shiny knife, because upstairs I asked her if we were bad, and now she's going to show me.

'Show me what?'

Jess!

'But he deserves it, Han.'

Her green eyes widen, pupils like throbbing black buttons, as she presses the sharp tip of the knife up against his fat neck. She's holding it with two hands now, shaky, and if he jolted out of his sleep he'd impale himself on it, skin sliced open like a squeezed jam doughnut. There'd be police, yellow tape and all the neighbours out on their doorsteps, hot whispers travelling on steaming breath in the cold dark. A murder in Tonypandy, who'd have thought it? Definitely not at the Matthews' house. They seemed like such a normal family. And that Jessica Matthews and Hannah King, they seemed like such lovely girls. The police would take us away in the car and the worst thing about it, worse than the sirens and the neighbours staring, worse than our mothers screaming and Jess' father zipped up in a bag, is that all that would be happening and I'd be wearing my shameful, red teddy pyjamas.

'Do you dare me to, Han?'

'Jess … stop it … *please* …'

'Why not, Han? Why don't I just do it?'

'Just put it down, will you?'

'Nah. I'm going to chop the bastard!'

That's when she laughs. Says look at you, mun, you're white as a sheet. This is what she's trying to show me.

'What? That you're absolutely mental, Jessica?'

'*No*, Hannah. Just that if I was bad then I'd do it, wouldn't I? I'd push this knife right in and twist him, cork him like a fucking apple, give him everything he deserves like Ted gave all those women everything they deserved.'

That's why I'm not bad, too. 'Cause I look like I've seen a ghost. 'Cause I haven't got the guts, either.

She pulls the knife away and I feel like I can breathe again, a ton of bricks lifted off my chest. She goes to the kitchen to put it back but I don't follow her this time. I'm stuck to the spot, staring at her father who is still snoring and dribbling away like nothing has happened, like his daughter didn't just nearly almost kill him.

'Come on,' she says, munching on a massive, juicy gherkin she just took from the fridge, cool as anything in her silky green pyjamas. 'Time for bed.'

Pear Drops

'Hannah King, will you stop staring at me like I've got two heads? You're going to give me a complex.'

'No I won't, Jessica Matthews. Because you look ridiculous. Your hair … what the *hell*?'

'It's just this stuff Bev's got in the bathroom. Makes it smell like heaven. Go on, give it a sniff.'

Give it a sniff? Is she serious or what? I'm not sniffing her hair. And for some absurd reason her eye lids are pink. *Pink*!

'Don't make a big deal out of it now, Han. It's only a bit of eye shadow. Why don't you try some?'

She shoves it in my face. A square tub filled with stuff that looks like fairy dust and smells absolutely disgusting. Lucy Williams leant it to her. So no. No thanks. I push it away. Why would I want to look like *her*?

You'd swear we're off to a party, not a school trip. Lucy Williams looks like a mannequin, her vile make-up caked on so thick she can barely move her mouth to smile. She's all matching, the accessories around her uniform carefully planned. Her earrings are dainty like pink bugs, just like her lipstick and her eye shadow is pink, like her fake nails and her bracelet and the gem in the ring on her finger. If I stroked her preened blonde hair right now I bet it's what angel's hair would feel like. Not that I would stroke it because if I did, I wouldn't be able to help myself. I'd just have to pull it right off her pretty little head, pluck her like a chicken.

She went and sat herself right in the middle of us, made Jess budge up. It means you're pretty privileged if you get the back seats, the *best* seats on the bus, but I would much prefer it if me and Jess were sitting by ourselves on a two seater. Lucy Williams is the reason why we have the back row all to ourselves. Lucy Williams said we were sitting here, with all the seats to ourselves, so we're sitting here, with all the seats to ourselves. Although I don't know why everyone is so afraid of her. I'm not. She's the shortest in our class, maybe the shortest in our year, but no one would dare pick on her for it, not like she picks on them. We're on our way now. To some theatre in Cardiff to see *A View from The Bridge*, this play we've been doing in English.

Danielle Lewis is sitting by herself on the seats in front of us and Lucy Williams hasn't left her alone since we turned out of the school gates. She's her chosen victim today. She's her chosen victim quite a lot but not always. Lucy Williams will torment anyone she feels like, any day of the week and whatever lesson we're in.

'Watch this now.'

She kneels forward, her blonde head reaching over the top of Danielle's seat. She readies it, a mouthful of spit that splashes noisily around her orange cheeks. Her pink lips are pursed and then she lets it out, a yellow phlegm waterfall that lands in Danielle Lewis' hair. Danielle Lewis turns around, as if to say something, but she doesn't manage a single word.

'Least it's got a good wash now, you fat bitch.'

Lucy Williams sits back down, laughing as she wipes her mouth dry in her cardigan sleeve. She smells like Charlie Red perfume, a choking cloud that follows me and Jess around the Comp corridors, and now on the bus she pulls the thin red can out of her handbag and sprays it over herself. That's better, apparently, because Danielle Lewis has made the bus reek of shit. It sticks to the back of my throat, makes me cough, and now there's something going on down the front of the bus. We don't have to think on it. The three of us say it together. *Robbie Jenkins.*

'Poor old Ivor.'

'Is his name really Ivor? For real, like?'

'Yeah, Luc. My father knows him.'

'Ivor the driver?'

Yeah. Mad, innit? You'd think if you had a name like Ivor the last thing you'd want to be is a driver. Kids are cruel enough as it is. And Ivor told Jess' father straight down the pub before. He's been driving buses for twenty odd years, carting different kids from different schools all over the place, even the ones with special needs, but out of all the thousands he's come across in his time, no kids are as mental as the kids from our Comp.

'He drives Robbie's school bus as well.'

The one that takes Robbie Jenkins to school is a rusty old double-decker that chugs up the hill slower than a stair lift and Robbie Jenkins has told her some tales, aye. First day of Year 7 when Ivor picked them up, Robbie and his friends uprooted the seatbelts and used them as bandanas, and then ... but Lucy Williams goes and butts in.

'You don't want to go believing everything *he* says.'

Lucy Williams thinks he's minging, Robbie Jenkins. He's got bad breath and he's very, *very* immature. Sixth form boys ... now that's what it's all about. She's been with *loads* of them. They're *real* men, not little boys like Robbie Jenkins. And don't get her started on his hair. Does he think he's cool or what with that J shaved into the back of it? Uch a fi. She just doesn't know what Jess sees in him but still Jess carries on with the story about his bus journey to school. When she talks about him, she sort of glows.

'In the mornings they're proper up for a laugh, Robbie and his friends are.'

They get on board and it's *so* funny ... they smudge their bare arses up against the windows. Get some class looks, they do, especially off old ladies going past on the pavements. Then they send their sharp cornered, laminated bus passes spiralling over the seats towards Ivor when he's driving. Like lethal tumbleweed, it is, and once Robbie's pass caught him on the back of his head and cut him open.

'Ivor had to have two stitches, girls, can you believe it?'

Course we can believe it. It's Robbie Jenkins. He's playing up on this bus as well. All the commotion is down to him. He's standing in the aisle steadying himself on the seats either side with his elbows, a conductor directing the mental orchestra of boys. BO Pits Pugh tries to calm things down but his voice is lost in a song about Ivor's wife. Apparently her name is Annie and she's got a wizard-sleeve fanny.

'His wife's not called Annie though,' Jess says. 'And look at BO Pits Pugh. He's worn out already, love him.'

He must've drawn the short straw in the staffroom. The unlucky one chosen to supervise us on this trip. It's his own fault he gets treated so badly though. Can't control a class to save his life so he's an easy target for abuse. Sometimes me and Jess feel sorry for him. It can't be nice waking up every morning knowing that your soul is going to be destroyed for the next six hours, but he doesn't do himself any favours. He wears the same shirt every day, a grimy-looking long-sleeved number with horizontal red stripes going through it, and under pressure, having to deal with all the insults, the books and paper planes thrown at him, he spends his lessons soaked in sweat. And today his armpits are looking particularly soppy, the round damp patches growing bigger by the second. He's got a lisp, too – the nail in his coffin. And this on the bus makes me think about the time he tried, in vain, to teach us about the Battle of Hastings. I suppose this is a real-life war and the bus is the battlefield. Massive, hairy men with steel-padded muscles charging with spears and stones and fire and death and blood, nah … that's nothing compared to this – a day out with the kids from Comp.

The song about Ivor's wife is over, a round of applause to finish off, and now comes the fusillade of scrunched-up foil rocks from lunch bags. Cans of shook-up pop are exploding grenades and HB pencils are as sharp as daggers, sandwich crusts like arrows into eyeballs. We watch the madness unfold from the safety of the back row.

'See what I mean? Robbie's an arsehole. What *do* you see in him, Jess?'

He's thick as shit, yeah, and that J in the back of his hair is a bit silly, but she loves him, doesn't she? They're all serious now. Official, like. He even bought her a necklace from Argos, a 9-carat gold heart on a chain which she hasn't stopped going on about, hasn't stopping pulling in and out of her shirt to show us.

'Cheap tat. Probably only cost him a tenner, if that. So what was it like then … his *cock*?'

Jess goes all shy, squirmy in her seat. Massive girl. Lucy Williams can't go asking her that, mun. It's private. Personal. Between her and Robbie. A lady never tells. But oh, alright then. If she must. A secret she's been dying to scream out. A secret I already know because she rung me the second after he left her house. Because I know *everything* about her, things Lucy Williams won't ever know.

Jess sits up, a grin slowly spreading across her face, her heeled shoes, yeah, brand new *heeled* shoes pressed against the seat in front. Jess has made me look two feet tall.

'Well Bev, that's my mother, Luc, she was on the late shift in work so he came over smelling lush. It's this new Lynx he's got.'

And she made him a glass of pineapple squash because he was thirsty after walking up her massive hill and they sat on her bed for a bit and it was her first time kissing anyone so she didn't even really know what to do. She stuck her tongue in and he stuck his in and it was sort of wet and slimy. Like a slug slithering around her cheeks. He tasted like pineapples though, which was cool. But then he touched her thigh and went and told her everything would be okay because he loved her and he had a condom with him.

'I was shocked. I was like Rob, mun, we can't have *sex*! I'm only just fifteen, like. My mother would kill me and my father would kill *you*.'

Even though she hasn't seen the cheating bastard in three weeks now but that's another story. The shiny square packet crunched as Robbie Jenkins slid it out of his black Manchester United wallet. He'd bought it from a pink shop called Johnnie's down an arcade in Cardiff. He said it was a special one that meant his cock would taste like strawberries and cream if she sucked it.

'Of course I didn't.'

She was back on that beach in Portugal again and the thought of it, thick and dangly, curling with green and red veins like a Twister lolly, something *piss* came out of, turned her sick.

'So you didn't even see his cock?'

'Nah.'

'Didn't you do *anything* with him? Not even a hand job?'

Nah. Jess isn't that kind of girl. She wants it to be special, you know? Not like that, on her bed scared her mother's going to come home early and catch them. He slammed her front door and stormed off back down her hill and told her they were over but they're alright now.

'Not for long. Because if you won't shag him then he'll find someone else who will. Someone skinnier probably. With bigger tits.'

Lucy Williams knows about these things, see. Because of all her experience with the sixth-form boys. Jess looks down at her flat front and I know what she's thinking … she's thinking, you're right, Luc, I do have quite small tits. I know Jess hates them because one night at her house she was going on about them constantly, and how life isn't fair and how it's all Bev's fault actually, Bev's terrible tits genes, but apparently mine were okay. She grabbed them, one squeezed in each hand, without even asking and said they were nice and juicy. Jess will always be skinnier than me and only a tiny bit taller, when she's not wearing heels, but I will always have bigger tits. Something that is kind of cool. A small victory, the only victory I've ever had over her, so I'm taking it.

'Yeah, I suppose so, Luc.'

Maybe next time he comes over she will. Because love is complicated, innit? It makes you do things even though you know you probably shouldn't. Like when Bev attacks her father with the meat knife and the bronze rugby trophies on the mantelpiece and the scissors from the kitchen drawer. And she's crying and checking mobiles and going through pockets and drinking vodka like it's pineapple squash and you know why she does it, why she flipping bothers with all the stress?

'Because of *love*. Love is also the reason why she still washes his skid-marked pants and cooks his dinner and the reason why she takes him back every time he's had enough of fucking Fat Pat Morgan. Love is a pain in the tits, mun.'

I would tell her that love is just a four-letter word but we're there now and nothing I say matters. Jess is a giant with pink eyes and they've been talking all the way and I haven't got a word in edgeways. Lucy Williams gives herself a final check in her little silver mirror, a squirt of Charlie Red all over, and then she's good to go. We follow her down the bus aisle, Jess walking clumsily in her heels. She almost fell over about a hundred times on the way to school this morning, but then if she wants to look stupid, I guess she kind of deserves to break her neck anyway.

Quick head count and BO Pits Pugh leads us across the car park into the theatre, a line that's supposed to be orderly and arranged alphabetically. The small stage inside is lit up by round, neon blue spotlights that hang from the ceiling, the backdrop a painted New York City fronted by a cardboard Brooklyn Bridge. It smells like popcorn in here, sweet and sickly, but like old, sweaty socks, too. We already know where we're sitting. By Robbie Jenkins and his little group of friends. Like the back seats, this was decided long before we left, over a week ago. So we shuffle through the narrow row of seats behind him as he flips them up one by one, slam and bang and kick, stupid fucking place, why couldn't we have gone on a trip to Oakwood or somewhere? Jess sits next to him and he holds her hand in his lap. He tries to get her to feel his cock through his shabby black school trousers but she says no, mun, Rob, not yet, not here. Lucy Williams is sitting in the middle of us both, again.

It's a small place so our class takes up most of the seats. We're the only audience members and we're waiting for the play to start, but not patiently. No one wants to be here. They all agree with Robbie Jenkins. Would much rather be zooming around on Megaphobia right now or plummeting down Speed at a million miles an hour. Our headmaster wants to make our lives miserable. You want to hear the speech we had this morning in assembly. How today we're representing our community. How we need to show pride in our school which is just so funny. Because who'd be proud of *our* school? And who wants to watch a stupid play? I've read it but I doubt anyone else has. I know for absolute certain Jess hasn't because I did her English homework on it for her.

The lights are dimmed and the play starts. And in the near darkness we crunch the sweets and crisps we brought in even though we weren't supposed to. There was a sign in the foyer but we concealed them up our jumpers, in our bags and down our socks. It doesn't take long for boredom to kick in. It spreads like a disease, infecting the boys first. They rock back and forth on their seats and whisper. And the longer the play goes on the more restless they get. The whispers turn to shouts, to dares. Go on, Rob! Go *on!* Alright then, he will, because you can't turn down a dare. Jess holds his seat steady for him to climb up. All the sweets he smuggled in are gone, eaten, so the other boys feed him theirs, confectionary propellants for the cannon. First a Mint Imperial is launched, small and round and hard … a white bullet that lands and cracks into pieces on the stage. And needless to say our laughter is wild when a Fruit Pastille smacks the actor playing Eddie Carbone right in the middle of his forehead.

Poor Eddie messes his lines up. Stumbling and stunned. It's hardly surprising, faced with a hysterical sea of bouncing navy bodies who point and cheer at his misfortune. Robbie Jenkins shouts … hurry up and fucking die, will you Ed, butt? We want to go home! But the worst is yet to come for him. It's like a tsunami. Eddie Carbone is swept backwards by the relentless wave of sweets. More Mint Imperials and Fruit Pastilles, Rolos and Munchies, Skittles that fall like coloured hailstones all around the props. And when a pear drop Robbie Jenkins throws hits the New York skyline and gets hilariously stuck to the Brooklyn Bridge, that's it … absolute pandemonium. Even I stand up and throw one of my sherbet lemons. I don't know what comes over me, but I like it.

Before we know it the main lights are switched on and the play is cut short. It's only then in the naked brightness can you see how much destruction we've caused. Who would've thought thirty-three teenagers could make such a mess? BO Pits Pugh lines us up in the foyer all flustered, looking like he could do with a bucket under each arm.

'Looking a bit hot there, Sir,' Robbie Jenkins says. 'Something wrong or what?'

Forehead dripping, old BO Pits tells us exactly what's wrong. We've been banned from the premises. For life. We're lucky the police haven't been called. And after today the theatre will not be allowing any more school performances ever again. We've spoiled it for everyone. We're a disgrace to our parents and our school and our community. We've brought shame not only on Tonypandy but to the *human race*. Of course we laugh our way across the car park, our hands and uniforms sticky with chocolate and sweets, with pride. They really don't know how lucky they are at the theatre. They should come back with us and see our school, what we do to that … the place we're supposed to be so proud of. Jess says it as we climb up the steps to the bus, and she's right.

'They should be flipping thankful they've still got bulbs left in their neon blue lights.'

Danielle Lewis gets a break on the way back. She's left alone, spared the phlegm and nasty names.

166

'What you looking for?' I ask Jess, who is by the window, Lucy Williams next to her and me on the end.

She's pulling things out of her bag. Pencil case and magazine, mobile, clingfilm with half a sandwich still in it.

'My Snickers. I'm Hank Marvin, mun.'

State on this sandwich, look. Wouldn't give that to a tramp. Jess throws it by her feet on the bus floor in disgust. Earlier she had to pick the chunks of mould out of the bread, round and green like crumbly peas. And the ham smelled like a dead body but worst thing was she had to make it herself this morning. How tragic! Bev was too hung over to get up, let alone make her a packed lunch. Jess had to ring Somerfield to tell them she was having women's troubles but Bev's got no women's troubles at all – Bev's got vodka troubles.

'Like one of them kids in Africa, I am. *Starving*. I've been living off crisps and chocolate these past three weeks. Fridge has been bare. Got it.'

Her Snickers bar, crushed and flattened by the weight of the stuff in her bag. She shrugs her shoulders. Crushed or not crushed, it'll still taste alright.

'I wouldn't if I was you,' Lucy Williams says to her. 'Not being funny but you've put on loads of weight.'

'Have I?'

'Yeah. Must be all the junk you've been eating.'

Hmm. Jess leans back and looks at herself again, pulls at the waistband on her trousers.

'Suppose I have a bit, haven't I?'

She sits up straight, covers her belly with her bag. She sniffs and swallows, clears her throat, anything to stop her eyes from filling up. I know what she's doing. I've seen her do it a million times before, quite a lot lately actually, more than usual. And I know that I have to save her.

'You look just the same to me.'

'What do *you* know, Ginge?'

It's not the first time Lucy Williams has called me that.

'Just saying. Jess is *my* best friend. So I think if she'd put on weight then I would've noticed.'

Jess' eyes are glittering like pretty green baubles when she tells us both to just leave it, mun, that it's stupid arguing over a bar of flipping chocolate. She zips it back up in her bag and says *there*, she's not even hungry anymore anyway.

'Why don't you just eat it, Jess? Don't listen to her.'

Her? Who do I think I'm talking to? Swear to fuck. One more word out of my stupid, freckly mouth and Lucy Williams will sling me off the back row. Lucy Williams, who is one foot tall, whose hair I am so close to pulling out.

'Come on, Jess. Let's go sit somewhere else.'

'*Han*. Just leave it, will you? I've had enough of people arguing!'

Jess can't take it no more. Why? Why does everyone have to argue? Why can't people just get up for work and make tidy ham sandwiches? Why can't the fridge be like it used to be? There aren't even any gherkins anymore. And there aren't any Jacobs crackers. Why can't people just make promises and keep them? Why do people lie? Why do they have to upset each other all the time?

Lucy Williams tells her to calm the fuck down. What's she on about? *Gherkins*?

Jess doesn't eat her Snickers bar, and we don't move off the back row. Her shiny eyes just turn to the window, to the carpark outside, and I'm not shocked. I'm not even angry because I already knew it would happen. I told you. I told her on the last day of Juniors in the big hall. She said nothing would change and I was stupid enough to believe her. It's a metaphorical kick in the guts with her brand new heels. She digs them in and stamps on me. And I can't stop what I do next. Some people cry. Some people just tell The Truth, say how they actually feel, but I guess I'm not like them. I yank the silver bracelet off my wrist and I don't mean for it to break but it properly snaps, the love heart charms falling onto the bus floor with the mouldy sandwich.

'What did you do that for?'

Just did.

'What the fuck, Han?'

She'd better find someone else to get old and grey with because we're finished, I tell her.

'Oh don't be so dramatic. Over a chocolate bar, like!'

It's not because of a *chocolate bar*. Is she thick? Does she think I don't know what's going on?

'What? What's going on? What you on about?'

I know. I can see it. I'm not blind. Heels? And pink eyes? And smelly hair? Well that's just lovely. But she can stop calling for me in the mornings because from now on I'm going to be walking to school on my own. Best friends forever and no one can touch us? *Ha*. Yeah, right.

'And what about our spit shake, Han?'

Oh, that means nothing now. It was just a stupid thing two stupid girls did a long time ago, something that she's broken right now on this bus. And you know what happens when you break a spit shake, don't you? Well I wouldn't care anyway, wouldn't care at all.

'You what? You wouldn't care if I *died*?'

I didn't mean it. I didn't mean for those words to come out. But I can't say No, either ... no of course I didn't mean it. Of course I would care if you died, Jessica. They stick in my throat.

'Come on, Han. You got something to say? I love a good row, I do. Can't get enough of them lately. Like a storm, innit? That's what my mother says. Clears the air. Are. You. Saying. You. Wouldn't. Care. If. I. Died?'

Lucy Williams watches us, nasty little bee, her antennas pricked. In the middle of us as we shout over her. Jess' eyes are so full I think I might actually see her cry for the first time ever. I think right now, with the contrast of the pink and the green, the tears that glisten, I like her eyes more than I've ever liked them before. But she blinks the shiny green glaze away like a pro. Okay. Fine. She won't call me for me anymore. She won't text, won't nothing ... won't ever speak to me again, if that's what I want? *Well?* Is it?

''Cause you can't take it back once you've said it, Han. Do. You. Want. Me. To. Leave. You?'

I throw it, the Last Word like I always do. It knocks her out, leaves her bleeding on the floor of the bus with the mouldy sandwich and the silver love heart charms that she picks up and puts in the front pocket of her bag.

'Yes.'

Fourteen Days

I kick through the leaves in The Quarter, a thin and crispy carpet the colour of fire that crunches under my school shoes like wrapping paper on Christmas morning. I'm angry at all of them. The kids who talk and laugh and squirt water bottles at each other like nothing's wrong, like the world hasn't just ended.

I can see her now amongst them. She's over there on her own, bag on one shoulder instead of two, waiting for Lucy Williams outside the staffroom window, where they've been meeting every morning. She's really funny, Jess is. I mean I always knew it but these days, she's absolutely hilarious. Her one shoulder bag, and especially her walk to school, which is timed to perfection. Miraculously so that when I turn out of my street there she is the other side of the main road and then it's a race to see who can get there first. But I'm in no rush. She'll barge past and overtake me on the bridge, striding ahead in her stupid, wobbly heels, like she's got somewhere important to be, someone important to meet.

Little does she know that in my head I make a silent wish that she falls over, that she breaks her neck. She deserves it. Especially now. And then when we get to class she'll stare at me but if I catch her looking she'll turn away really quick. Of course, she always makes sure that I can see them talking or swapping mobiles and if I happen to walk past them, not on purpose obviously, she laughs loud. You know, an exaggerated laugh that's too flamboyant to be real. Jess is trying to make me jealous. Jess is wasting her time.

Don't feel sorry for me because she didn't leave me. I didn't give her the chance. I left *her*. And if she wants me back then she'll have to come and get me because I won't say sorry first. We haven't spoken in two whole weeks. That's fourteen days and fourteen nights, ten walks to school and home again on my own, two whole weekends being bored stiff. Mum says I'm stubborn and that she's the bloody same, that Jessica Whatshername. We're both walking around noseless, hacked them off ourselves with childish scissors, just to spite our faces. But then again my mother doesn't know what she's talking about. My mother doesn't know anything at all.

I check the time on my mobile and wonder why Lucy Williams hasn't showed up yet. She's always here by 8.45, parading Jess around The Quarter on her arm like she's a brand new handbag. *Hooking*. That thing Jess always wanted me to do … well now she's got someone to do it with. Lucky her. I hope she's enjoying it. Maybe Lucy Williams' bus has crashed on the way to school. The brakes must be really dodgy on those old double-deckers. There's something weird about this morning. The Quarter is much busier than normal, kids everywhere you look. Huddled on the benches and even perched right up on top of the trees, hanging off the branches like bats. I suppose that explains all the leaves on the ground. It's like they're waiting for something. But I don't think on it much longer. Kids are strange.

Jess has seen me, too. An uninterested glance up from her own mobile and then away again, arms crossed, foot tapping. I'm just another nameless kid she passes in the corridor but that's just fine with me. I lean my back against the brown brick wall and look through my homework diary and timetable. We've got crap lessons today. It's the worst, most boring day of the week. When we were picking our GCSE subjects I only chose Drama because of Jess. It was mostly because we wanted to be in all the same lessons together. She couldn't convince me to take Art, no chance, no amount of nagging, so I picked Media instead but it would only mean one hour a week apart. We could cope with that, I told her, could always text each other if we needed anything. Jess wasn't happy though. One hour was forever, apparently, but fourteen days … she seems to have managed that alright.

Then my homework diary is almost knocked out of my hands by one of the strange kids. I keep hold of it, just about, but see how crazy they are? Especially the little ones. *Boys*. They're like demented, scurrying rats around Comp. He charges past me screaming … she's here! She's here! And she's got Jenkins with her! Who's here? *Oi*. I call after him but he's fast, already gone and ducking through legs to get to the front of wherever he's desperate to get to. It's not just him. There's loads of kids now, boys *and* girls, running towards the staffroom window, this rushing crowd of navy jumpers and coats. You'd swear a pop star has just turned up in The Quarter. Some world-famous name and everyone is mobbing them for their autograph.

I put my homework diary in my bag and head towards the back of the gathering. I weave and elbow through and manage to climb up onto the end of a bench where I see them together. My heart starts pumping. Not Jess and Robbie Jenkins, but *Lucy Williams and Robbie Jenkins*. They look odd together. Robbie Jenkins so tall, Lucy Williams so disgustingly short. But nevertheless *together*. Holding hands. In front of Jess! And it all starts to make sense. All these kids are here waiting for a Fight. It's not uncommon. School fights are often pre-planned and advertised like this, as if it's a school council meeting or something. By word of mouth or even a note pinned to the noticeboard next to the times of rugby and clarinet practice. I guess no one told me about it but then why would they? I have no friends here now.

I'm being shoved and told to get off, find my own fucking bench, these kids have been here since quarter to eight to get these seats, but I keep my place and from up here I watch The Quarter turn into the Coliseum. Jess and Lucy Williams are gladiators with leaves instead of sand under their shoes. A ring forms around them, a swarm of kids like flies. And not just kids from our year or the years below, but a group of sixth formers have also come to watch. Go on then! someone shouts. Yeah, what you fucking waiting for? One of them pushes Jess into the middle. Nah. They ain't going to do it. Waste of time. They haven't got the guts!

The Truth doesn't really matter here, only what sounds most exciting. The Comp grapevine is buzzing around me, everyone sure they know what happened and why we are here. Robbie Jenkins got the key to the headmaster's office out of his boot bag and that's where they did it, up against his filing cabinet and then over the photocopying machine. No, mun, they did it on his leather chair as his wife watched from a gold-framed photograph on his desk. It happened on Tuesday morning. Fuck off. You don't know nothing. I'm friends with one of Lucy Williams' cousin's friends so Wednesday afternoon, it was. Definitely. Twice. Three times.

Whatever. Bets are placed. Jessica Matthews odds on favourite to win on account of being the tallest. She looks much harder than Lucy Williams and she's out for revenge after all. Then again it's the little ones you've got to watch.

But soon the anticipation is over. Jess puts her school bag down and takes her jumper off. Lucy Williams' cardigan is unbuttoned and her handbag given to Robbie Jenkins to hold. She steps into the ring with Jess but neither one of them bow. There's nothing gracious about a fight in Comp. There are no rules or customs to be upheld. All we want is blood. The Quarter holds its breath as both sets of white sleeves are rolled up. And then they go. Right at it like angry dogs. Lucy Williams' false nails are bubblegum-pink claws that she sinks into Jess' cheeks. Black hair is pulled then followed by screams, blonde angel hair ponytail grabbed with two hands, even louder screams. Jess is at the Olympics, a pumped-up Russian, and she swings Lucy Williams around like she's a hammer. Actually swings her. My fist clenches itself and I'm shouting yes, go on, Jess! The pleasure bubbling inside me like lava. Lucy Williams readjusts her bobble and then she's back for more. She kicks and slaps and spits! Actually spits in Jess' face. It gets her mad, so mad she doesn't even wipe it off. Teeth gritted ... the punches flying everywhere, like the leaves! It's mental, a brown and red and orange storm blowing through The Quarter. Shirts are ripped like they're made of paper and Lucy Williams' left shoe comes off. She's hopping on one leg but still punching and one of the punches lands on Jess' lip. It's greeted with a roar from the crowd. She's bleeding. Yes! I watch, helpless, or maybe I don't want to help. Maybe I want to scream across The Quarter ... see, Jess, *see* ... I told you so, didn't I? Maybe I'm even a little bit happy as she bleeds and drips all over her screwed-up shirt.

They're both wounded and out of breath. Jess' weeping lip, Lucy Williams' neck that's glowing pink with scram marks, who's just noticed that she's missing a nail. She bends down on her hands and knees and looks for it amongst the leaves but the bloodthirsty crowd want more. There hasn't been a fight in The Quarter for months. They chant the name of the girl they want to win but the sight of BO Pits Pugh running in the distance means it's over. He must've drawn the short straw in the staffroom again. Poor bastard. He's even bullied by the teachers ... go and sort them out, Pugh. Like a lamb to the slaughter.

Disappointed boos as he splits the pair of them up. Lucy Williams looks relieved, saved. She's comforted by Robbie Jenkins as she checks her face for blood in her little silver mirror but she isn't bleeding, just a couple of scratches. Her shirt is ripped though, and she still hasn't located her shoe. Apparently some Year 7 kid has run off with it. Robbie Jenkins puts his arm around her shoulder and that sets Jess off again, like a bull and a red flag. She launches herself at Lucy Williams but BO Pits Pugh manages to hold her back. Just about. Let me go, you smelly prick! I'm going to kill her! You old minging fucking flipping prick.

'What's the matter? Old Saggy Tits not giving you any this week?'

The Quarter laughs. But the wrath of us lot is the last of BO Pits' worries right now. Jess is possessed. He's struggling to keep hold of her as she wriggles and squirms in his locked arms like a slimy fish. Let's go, young lady. Fuck off, prick. He drags her away backwards, still kicking and shouting, actually *drags* her across the ground, and Lucy Williams is left basking in the leaves, in her falsely claimed victory. Queen Bee. Queen of The Quarter with her king, her prize, her new boyfriend ... Robbie Jenkins.

The bell goes and the crowd scatters. The fun is over until next time. Back to normality. Back to boring school. But I don't go to Drama. My heart is still pumping and the adrenalin is running through me so crazy that I don't even care about getting into trouble. I know where BO Pits Pugh has taken her. So that's where I walk, down a dark corridor I've never been down before. Why would I? I've never forgotten to bring my homework in. I've never bunked off or thrown a chair or answered a teacher back. I've never had a fight in The Quarter. But this is the busiest room in our crazy school. Detention.

I peek through the glass panel in the closed door, careful that she doesn't see me. She's sitting on a chair right at the back with her head slumped on the desk like an old drunk. Our headmaster will be here soon, no doubt. Summoned from his office. He'll call

Bev to tell her what's happened and then Bev, Bev will probably, *definitely*, cry. Mum said that Jess' father left their house on the weekend. Packed his bag and buggered off for good this time. It's the talk of the town.

Jess looks so sad in there. Maybe she's sad because of that, because of her father, or because of Robbie Jenkins or even because of me. Because of fourteen days. But probably not. I just know that I don't feel happy or smug or pleased anymore like I did in The Quarter when Lucy Williams punched her. Now I only feel bad, like I want to burst the door open and tell her that I miss her more than I've ever missed anyone and if she wants to talk, talk and talk until my ears ring, then I really don't mind at all. I don't do it though because I have no nose. Because I'm pretending that I don't mind it here without Jess when I do. When I hate it. My right side is cold without her walking next to it. It's like I've gone deaf. And the grey walls down the corridors are greyer, black, and the chips from Phony Tony's van don't even taste nice.

All the other kids here are crazy. They care about stupid things like fights. The girls are nasty and the boys are idiots and they just don't have heads full of *stuff* like I do. I'm not like them. Any of them. I know I was born in the same hospital as they were. And I know I grew up in Tonypandy and that I wear the same navy uniform and walk around in the same black shoes – it's just I'm different somehow. But there's nowhere else to go apart from home and home is even worse than here. I still don't go to Drama and I still don't care about getting into trouble. I know she's got a free lesson so I walk the corridors all the way to Room 58 where the shutters aren't up yet, where she'll make me feel better because for some stupid, crazy reason, Laser Ludlow is the only person who knows how.

175

The Club

She's got something to show me and it's very, very important. The most important thing in the world. And about time, too.

'What is it, like a secret? Or an actual thing?'

'I'm not telling you. You'll have to wait and see.'

'You're so annoying, Jessica.'

'Maybe, Hannah. But you've just got to trust me.'

Trust *her*? Funny. Jess and her secrets, which aren't proper secrets at all. She kept the last ones in a silver box and then smoked them in full view of the school CCTV camera, the whole time grinning and waving at the screen like she expected our headmaster to be sitting in his office watching the show.

We're going the long way round to her house. Up across the mountain on the dry mud path that's flanked either side by a bendy, chicken-wire fence. This way takes ages, and it's cold and windy and the air smells like horse shit, but we can't pass my house or the main road where there are cars and spies.

'Don't know why you're so worried, Han. What's she going to do? Ground you?'

Imagine it. What on earth are you two doing out of school? And Jess has got her Mrs King voice on now, strumming her fingers along the silver chicken wire. Get up that hill, you pair of bloody hooligans!

'Yep. She won't be happy, Han. She'll march us back up there herself in her dressing gown, whip us all the way with her slipper.'

We run down the mountain. You can't *not* run down it. Your feet just take you fast all the way to the bottom. Easy for Jess now that she's a normal-sized human being again, only a tiny bit taller than me. Her face is back to normal, too. No pink eyes and no stupid-smelling hair. And when we're off the mountain we keep our heads down, as if our fringes are disguises from any cars that might come past. Our mothers know everyone around here. It's not just something silly I'm saying, they actually do. And if they don't know you then they know someone who knows you. That Jessica Matthews and Hannah King were bunking off school, can you believe it? Bold as brass they were running off that mountain in their uniforms. And their poor mothers as well. All they've had to cope with already and now those two selfish girls putting them through that. It'll be whispered over the washing lines and through the trees because the trees in Pandy are like the trees in Narnia. Even the horses on the mountain will rat us out.

'State on that,' Jess says.

She's on the pavement now examining the yellow, supposed to be white, net curtain hanging inside Evan Jones' front window. It's all ripped and holey and behind it there's a telly on. Probably his mother. Jess says she doesn't work, lazy bitch, and then she gives me this look, this evil grin. I've seen it before. I've seen it too many times, so I know exactly what's coming. One foot in front of the other I ready myself for it … the fast bang of her knuckles against the glass. Run! she shouts, and we're running alright, as fast as we can through the terraced street, weaving in and out of parked cars and leaping over drains. Laughing like the naughty kids we are, that we'll always be no matter how old we get. And not satisfied with just Evan's house, she knocks every single window we pass.

'Go on,' she dares. 'Go *on*!'

So I do it. One house and then the next, knocking knockers and clapping letterboxes. Jess kicks someone's milk bottle over on their doorstep and it hangs in the air for what seems like days before it lands. Then smash! Shattered glass and a freezing, full-fat white wave engulfing us. Another milk bottle and another, over they go house by house like skittles, Jess' swinging foot brutal and merciless. Too bad no one's up this early to stop her. Smash! A river of milk chasing behind us on the pavement, a runny trail of devastation left on this sleepy, Wednesday morning in Tonypandy when we should be in school.

We don't look back. We don't slow down. Can't be seen. The spies are everywhere. But we get to Jess' house unscathed, uncaught, and her hands are scrambling with a massive bunch of keys. Don't know why she's so nervous. This isn't *her* first time.

177

The door is slammed behind us and locked and we're safe now, in her passage. Safe and out of breath.

'You're mental, Jess.'

Tell her something she don't already know, mun. Apparently I love it, the fact that she's mental. And what's life without a bit of danger now and again? Without a little bit of crazy? I look down at my shoes which are covered in mud and milk, my black laces soaked in white. I go to kick them off by Bev's umbrella stand like usual but Jess tells me to keep them on.

'What about Bev's expensive cream carpet?'

'Fuck Bev's expensive cream carpet. Come on then, Han!'

My chest is still burning from our last run, but I chase her up the stairs, an on-the-way-to-her-room ritual we've followed since the very first night I stayed over nearly ten years ago now. I reach out and snatch her ankles at the top and tackle her to the floor. Face first she lands on Bev's expensive cream carpet with an almighty thud. I haven't hurt her though because she's laughing. And calling me a giant prick to boot as she gets up and dusts herself off. Not the first time I've caught her, but the first time she's called me that. I've been a cow and a minge, but never a giant prick.

'Where's Ted?' I ask her when we get inside her room.

Gave him his marching orders. Kicked him out. Evicted! Ted just had to go.

'What about your drawings?'

Yep. Them too. What a weirdo she used to be.

'But you spent ages on those. And *used* to be? It was only a couple of weeks ago.'

Yeah, well. A lot can happen in a couple of weeks. She burned them all out the back garden, a lovely bonfire of paper and paint, like she burned her magazines. That Jess was a right freak. That Jess got dumped by Robbie fucking Jenkins and no wonder. Don't worry, she burned his stupid gold necklace as well.

'That girl is dead, Han. Cut her up and buried her myself. You won't see her again.'

Okay then. Fair enough. Whatever she says. This shiny new Jess has moved in and completely transformed the place, given it some kind of makeover. So much so that it's like being in a different room altogether. The walls are still peach but they're plastered with stuff I've never seen before, like this creepy thing hanging on a silver hook. It looks like a dead crow, limp black feathers coming off a circular wicker carcass.

'It's a dreamcatcher, stupid.'

'So *that's* your big secret?'

'No, mun. That's just for catching bad dreams. My nightmares.'

But she doesn't think it works because she keeps having the same one all the time, nearly every night. And it's awful weird. She's in the café on Pandy Square and she's just ordered fried egg on toast and she's sitting there in the booth waiting for the big fat Italian lady to bring her the tomato sauce and all of a sudden her teeth start falling out on the table. It's minging. They're just crumbling out of her mouth and splashing in her egg yolk. So she comes over with the sauce and Jess doesn't know why but she's not the big fat Italian lady anymore, she's her Auntie Paula.

'But your Auntie Paula is dead.'

Well she knows that. She had a tumour, something to do with her lung. Smoked too much. Jess says it with a fag hanging out the side of her mouth. She reminds me of one of those lollipop men munchkins from *The Wizard of Oz*.

'And I told you before that I dreamt she would die before she actually died for real. I've got a gift, haven't I?'

But anyway, in her café dream everything's purpley pink, right, the cups and the serviettes and the menus. Even her dead Auntie *Paula* is purpley pink. What do I reckon it means?

'No idea.'

Because to be honest, I'm still in shock about her room. I just wasn't expecting it, that's all. I thought she'd open the door and everything would be exactly how I tried to forget it. Her lava lamp is still here, and the bed and the furniture hasn't moved, but everything else is different. She's stuck loads of pictures up. Not ones she made herself but actual photographs and posters. Where Ted was pride of place above her bed, that space belongs to someone called Freddie Mercury now.

'Those cheek bones and hips. And those teeth!'

Out of all her men … yeah, *her* men … he's the one she'd like to fuck the most.

'Which one do you like best, Han? Go on, don't be shy. Have a good look.'

It's like Jess' room is a portrait gallery and these skinny men are glamorous princes. A montage of fur coats and big hair, smoky eyes and massive lips, leopard print and guitars and feathers and glitter. Lots and *lots* of glitter. I'm thinking to myself that she must've used a whole pack of Blu Tack, maybe even two packs, putting them all up but then I find him, the one I like best. It's his eyes, I think. They're pretty and sad and I don't know why I like them so much but I do. His hair is a mane of messy brown curls and in this particular picture he's wearing a blue velvet jacket that sparkles with a collar of coloured studs.

'That's Marc Bolan, Han. He was a poet, not just a singer. Better than Freddie in some ways. His words were like … I don't know … like liquid diamonds running down your ears. But Freddie was the showman, you know?'

'Not really.'

'Well Marc was really young when he died.'

'He's *dead*?'

'Yeah.'

'How?'

'Big massive tree. Right…'

First things first. We aren't sitting around in our uniform all day. Our trousers are alright but just looking at these navy jumpers makes her feel physically sick. She gets two t-shirts out of her bottom drawer, one for her and one for me. White. Never seen these before, either.

'Bought them with Bev's credit card.'

Bev is awful careless with her purse. And as Jess is wriggling her face through the hole she says the band on the front are called The Mamas and The Papas. I tell her she looks stupid when she knots her school tie around her head like a bandana but she doesn't listen, only calls me a giant prick again.

'Just do it, Han. Take it off and tie it up.'

I sigh. Sometimes it's just easier to give Jess what she wants. She'll only nag.

'We look ridiculous.'

'No we don't. We look like *rock stars*. I'll order some proper ones on Bev's card later.'

Bev doesn't notice fuck all. In a world of her own, just like she'll never know that Jess hasn't gone to school again today.

'Same as your mother, Han, so I don't know why you're worrying. She won't have any idea unless they ring her which they probably won't.'

They'll just think we're off sick. A bug we've both caught. Because no one would expect *us* to bunk off, would they? Not lovely little Jessica Matthews and clever Hannah King who are good girls, who never do anything wrong. Maybe this brand new Jess is crazy, even crazier than the old one, but she's also kind of right. I'll go home later and Mum won't ask me about school. She'll be busy cooking or cleaning. And even if she did ask me, if hell froze over and she turned around and said how was your day in school, Hannah? I would look her straight in the eyes and lie to her, and she would eat it all up. There's no need to worry. My mother has no idea I'm here. She doesn't even know that me and Jess are speaking again, didn't ask.

'Who've I got on my t-shirt then?'

'Jim Morrison. He's dead, too. Like the rest of them.'

'There's more?'

'Oh aye. All the good ones die young.'

'Like a curse?'

'Not a curse, Han, *a blessing*.'

And I don't want to go getting coincidence and fate mixed up, either. They've got a club up there in the sky, see. Freddie Mercury and Marc Bolan and Jim Morrison. And Cass Elliot and Jimi Hendrix. Lots of others floating around. Young and dead and beautiful.

I shrug.

'Haven't you heard of *any* of them?'

I've never told her, and I don't tell her now as we're sitting on her bed that I know Jim Morrison better than she does, that he's one of the main characters in the best story ever. That dark stage and all those people, and the tents and the fires and the flags. Joan Baez sang 'Let It Be' and everything was right with the smoky, windy world. I suppose Jess wouldn't like Joan because Joan isn't dead.

'They're all over there,' she says.

On the CDs and vinyls and tapes rising up from the floor. Another new addition. They're standing like skyscrapers in the corner of her room.

'Got every album T Rex and Queen ever made. And most of the others.'

She gets up off the bed and, on her knees, looks for the ones she wants to show me. Then they're laid down gently on the quilt like they're made of glass, like they're newborn babies. I'm given my very own dead rock-star slideshow. The skinny men with long hair on her walls made them – the best music ever and nothing like it since. Electric Warrior. The Slider. Unicorn. Sheer Heart Attack. A Night at the Opera. Electric Ladyland and Strange Days. L.A. Woman, innit. And fuck, yes ... If You Can Believe Your Eyes and Ears. Not forgetting Bubblegum, Lemonade and ... Something for Mama.

'This is Mama Cass. But call her Cass Elliot cause that's who she was in the end. Don't call her Mama, okay?'

'O ... kay.'

Jess pops the disc out. Am I ready?

'Ready for what?'

'This is it, Han. The Big Secret.'

'Cass Elliot is your big secret?'

'Yeah. Well, not just her. All of them.'

But I *need* to hear Cass Elliot first. I need to listen, and listen good! Because if I die without ever hearing her sing, my life won't have been worth living at all.

Crossed-armed I wait for it ... this big secret, this thing that's so important. I don't believe her. I don't believe that my life has been worthless up until this point. This new Jess is just as dramatic as the old one. She pushes the forward button and then twists the volume right up. It comes out of the speakers, 'Make Your Own

Kind of Music', and I'm not ready for it. It happens to me again when I tried so hard to forget how it felt. Cass Elliot does something to me I wish she wouldn't. She goes and makes my skin fizz, exactly how Joan Baez once did.

'I've got videos, too. Look.'

The white sticky label on the front says 'The Mama Cass Television Program', the same black Berol handwriting that once sprawled things like 'Ted' and 'Myra' and 'Poor old Jeff D'.

'But Cass isn't my favourite.'

Jess loves her, don't get her wrong, and Jim Morrison and Hendrix, and Marc Bolan loads and loads, but Freddie Mercury is her favourite. He's got a massive cock, see. Well, he did, you know, before he died. Apparently you could make out the shape of it in the leotards he wore. That big bulge and the sequins on top glistening. I'm ordered to look at a picture on the wall when to be honest, I don't really want to. And she points at it grinning with wide, excited eyes, Freddie Mercury's crotch.

'Shiny, huge, cosmic cock.'

She licks her lips when she says it.

'How did he die then?'

'Too much bumming. But Freddie had fun, that's all that matters.'

She goes through them all, her dead men and Cass. Like we're in school and she's my teacher and I need to sit up and listen. Freddie Mercury. He liked women *and* men but it was the cock that killed him in the end. And Marc Bolan, he was a passenger in a car and his perfect face got smashed into a tree. Now Jim Morrison died in a bath in France but some say he's still alive.

'And Hendrix, don't confuse him with Morrison because Jimi Hendrix is black and Jim Morrison's not. Hendrix died quite boring really. Too much wine.'

I know him as well. He's part of my story. Course I don't tell her.

'*Cass Elliot*. Lovely, beautiful Cass! You won't find a better voice than hers.'

Fuck your Courtney Loves and your Joni Mitchells and your Michelle Phillipses. Do I know why they're still alive? She'll tell me exactly why they're still alive.

'Because they're shit. Nothing special. Not like Cass who was *far* too special and too beautiful for this world.'

The myth is that she choked on a ham sandwich but that's rubbish. It's simple. Cass Elliot's heart was just too big.

I really haven't got a clue what she's on about, can't take it all in. Has it been two weeks since I was last here or two hundred million light years?

'I'll show you, I promise. I know it's weird but it's like … it's like I've seen the light, Han, and it's glittery and cosmic and feathery as fuck.'

She'll play me songs and we'll watch videos until my ears bleed and my insides ache. But for now Cass is turned off and her silver disc put back the right way round because it really gets on Jess' nerves when people don't put CDs back in their cases properly. She sits next to me on the bed again and lights another fag. Steals them from the stash in the kitchen. Bev never notices because most of the time Bev is off her tits.

'Smoking's bad for you, Jess.'

'*You're* bad for me, Han.'

'How?'

'Because you are, mun. Look at you, making me bunk off school like this. And did you think about poor old Laser Ludlow's feelings? What did she say you were now when you gave your Macbeth essay in? Academically gifted or something, wasn't it?'

'Yeah.'

'Well she's sitting there right now crying her eyes out on her desk because you're not in.'

'As if, Jess. This was your idea.'

'I know. I'm only messing.'

'What if you die of a tumour like your Auntie Paula?'

'Then, oh well.'

'I'm serious, Jess.'

'I am not going to die of a tumour, Hannah.'

'How do you know?'

'Because I'm going to die in a car crash, stupid. Before I'm thirty and if I don't I'll be proper pissed off.'

'So you're planning on leaving me, are you?'

'No. You'll die as well. God's going to save us.'

'What do you mean?'

God, like. All the good people die young and it's not a coincidence, like she was saying before. God puts his God-size gardener's gloves on and plucks them from the planet like flowers, these perfect little things that he won't have wilting. He takes them and saves them, puts them in some kind of frame in the sky for us all to look at and enjoy forever. This way they won't ever get old and miserable and shit. You know, like all the has-beens you see, all the saggy, wrinkly rock stars still plodding on. They're just tragic, no better than the people who walk around Pandy like the living dead. Born here, die here.

'That's almost poetic, Jess.'

'Well you know me, Han. Eloquent as *fuck*, I am.'

'Hmm.'

'And if time's getting on and we haven't died then ... then I will learn to drive just so I can kill us. We'll have Cass blasting out of the stereo, 'Baby I'm Yours', and I'll put my foot down and drive us straight into a tree. That's how much I love you, Hannah King.'

'Wow. Thank you. You're so kind. But I don't get it. If they were so special then why didn't God just let them carry on?'

'Because they were *too* special, I just said. Who wants to live forever? Do you, Han? Do you want to live forever?'

'It just makes no sense. If they stayed alive then they could've made so many *more* beautiful songs. Like Joan...'

Jess cuts me off. I just don't flipping get it, do I? That's not the point. The point is they already made those songs, already changed the world. God didn't want them ruining it by getting old so he took them. Saved them. And they do live forever now, but in lyrics and on record. Preserved like lovely pieces of art. That's what The Club up in the sky is. Exclusive to the young and dead and beautiful.

'It's all good if you're getting better, see, Han, but none of them do. Not really. Once you get old you just sort of fade away.'

'"Forever Young", like Joan sings.'

'Fuck you on about, Han? Who the hell is Joan?'

'Never mind.'

185

Weirdo, I am. Jess says if you aren't getting better then you should just go away, disappear or die, one or the other. This is why God is definitely going to take us when we're young. Because we're special, too.

'It's only a shame we weren't born in the 50s because then we could've seen all the greats live.'

She'd have fucked Freddie's brains out. Smoking and fucking … never needing to leave their cum-stained, satin-sheeted, leopard-print-pillowed, four-poster bed. And me and her, we'd have gone to see Marc Bolan live on stage. He'd have sat crossed-legged and sung to us, whispering liquid diamonds. Partied with Cass Elliot and laughed until we died. Literally.

'We'll die in the same car crash, Han.'

There'll be blood and glass and shrapnel, but we'll be young and dead and beautiful forever, in The Club with Cass and Marc and Freddie.

'So smoke. Have a fag and chill out, mun. We're not going to get tumours.'

We were meant to get old and grey, but I guess it doesn't matter, as long as we die together. And I suppose it's true. I just never really thought about it, the reason why people are as grey as the sky. It's because they got old and miserable, because the blood in their veins is normal blood, flat like pop without any fizz. But the blood running through our veins is electric, not crazy. It glitters like strobe lights. I give her one final chance. My mother. I take my mobile out of my bag but the screen only laughs at me. Sorry, Han, no one cares. No one's even noticed you're gone.

'When will your mother be home then?'

Oh I don't need to worry about *her*. Bev's scanning packets of chicken and cartons of juice and weighing grapes. Thrilling.

'Doesn't she care that you smoke?'

'Nah. Bev don't care about much anymore.'

She passes me a fag. The men on the walls make it look so good, like the glowing sticks hanging out of their mouths are as much a part of their faces as their big eyes and big lips. But for all I know about smoking I may as well be about to drive a car. I'm sitting in the leather seat with my hands on the wheel and I haven't got a clue what I'm doing. My legs aren't even long enough to reach the pedals. But I roll the lighter with my thumb. I turn the key. I only wish my mother could see me. *Smoking*, how terrible … a crime on a par with murder. I cough my guts up. Jess laughs.

'Prick.'

'Oi,' she says, still pissing herself. 'Don't you call me a prick, *prick*. Know who you are, Han? Little Miss Strange.'

Oh come on. Black Jim, mun. Ah, don't worry. She'll play the song for me later and when I listen to it I'll realise that Jimi Hendrix wrote it about me. Even though I wasn't born. But still. We lie back against the cold peach wall, the weird dead bird dreamcatcher and Freddie Mercury in his check leotard above our heads. Our ash is flicked into a makeshift ashtray, one of Bev's floral cereal bowls which Jess misses now and again. It lands on the expensive cream carpet, and I think she's doing it on purpose.

'Won't be long now,' she says.

'What won't be long?'

'When we can say goodbye to Comp for good.'

'Hmm.'

'I'm not going back after GCSEs, Han. You don't want to stay *there* do you?'

'Not without you.'

'Exactly. And we've got better things to do.'

'But what about our plan?'

Maybe the new Jess doesn't want that. Maybe she doesn't want to be an artist. Like it was a silly, stupid dream, another one in purpley pink. One her dreamcatcher caught and shredded to pieces like a fan. Like she was asleep and it was lovely for a while, but now she's wide awake.

'Course I still want it, Han. Fucking Hell … you've got no *idea* how much I want to get out of here. Want to get out of here right now?'

'We can't. We don't have any money. And my mother…'

Jess laughs at me again. I wish she'd stop it. She doesn't mean run away, mun. We don't even have to leave her bedroom. She bends over almost upside down and gets it from under her bed. A full bottle of vodka.

'My mother will go mental.'

'Oh, *fuck* your mother Han. And you know what? Fuck my mother, too. And my father. Especially fuck him. And fuck Lucy Williams and fuck Robbie Jenkins. Fuck Laser Ludlow. Fuck Comp. Fuck it all.'

Fuck everyone apart from me and her, she says, because me and her is the only thing that matters, the only thing that is right and always has been.

We're ignoring the massive elephant in the room. It barely fits in here, bright pink with a gigantic, long trunk. It's wearing a tight-fitting, glittery leotard like Freddie Mercury and its tusks are made of solid gold. It's over there in the corner just staring, reminding us that I left her or she left me, something we promised we'd never do to each other, something that neither of us understand. I wish it would leave us be, but it won't. I don't know what happened. But I do know that we can't talk about it and that we're bunking off school and smoking. And we've got our ties wrapped around our heads and we're laughing about our deaths and Freddie Mercury's cock, and no one even cares. And it's weird. The more vodka I drink, the less disgusting it tastes. The more I drink, the less disgusting I feel.

Frankensteins

Jess has got to say, records of achievements make excellent cushions. We're sitting up on the banking and they're keeping our bums nice and dry, these hard, ruby-red A4-sized books are. She's plucking blades of grass out of the damp mud and throwing them to the mercy of the wind. Give her an hour and she'll have picked the entire banking bald. We could've left already but instead we're just sitting here, staring out at the carpark, like the massive weirdos we are. And I'm bored.

'Why don't we just go?'

'Not yet,' she says, and then she shakes her head at me, disgusted.

'What?'

'Look at your trainers. Look how *clean* they are.'

Converse high-tops. Mine are purple and hers are red. And even though we bought them at the same time, Jess' are absolutely filthy and mine are still immaculate.

'So? Just because you're minging and I'm not.'

Nah. She's not minging. This is how she likes them. Apparently there's nothing worse than a new-looking pair of trainers. We haven't worn our school shoes for weeks and weeks. Something that has got us in loads of trouble. A bit like everything else we've been doing and saying. For years I wondered what it was like inside the headmaster's office, this room where only *really* bad kids got taken when detention hadn't worked. Well, there's cream blinds on the windows. And he's got a rubbish bin next to his desk, this massive dark wood desk, and it's stuffed with blackened banana skins and balled-up paper. I found out one Wednesday afternoon, and then lots of other afternoons after.

Me and Jess have been in there so many times it's hard to remember exactly why we were there and on what days. But mostly for bunking off and for smoking in The Quarter, because of our criminal, rule-breaking trainers and our attitudes which are *bad*.

Laser Ludlow marched Jess there a couple of weeks ago when she didn't hand her GCSE coursework in. Jess really went to town on her in front of the whole class. It was only a matter of time though. They'd been building up for years waiting in that corridor, all the angry words she never had the guts to say before. Laser Ludlow was a crazy bitch who hadn't murdered anyone at all, who wasn't a legend like in the stories but just a sad, lonely old lady trying to make friends with a teenager when she really ought to get a life. And the very last time we got called to his office together our head master stared at us all serious on his leather chair, fingers and thumbs pressed against each other in a triangle shape. Thought he was Don flipping Corleone. We were sitting opposite him on far less posh chairs and we just couldn't keep our laughs in when he told us that we'd changed. Off the rails. Yep. Free falling, we were. Weeeeeeeeeeeee! Bright girls, we used to be. Bright girls with bright futures.

Did he think he was telling us something new or what? That we hadn't already heard it all before from our mothers? Jess felt like pulling one of the sloppy banana skins out of the bin and slapping him with it but instead we just told him to fuck off. Actually said it together as if we'd rehearsed it. And when those two lovely words came out of our mouths they were like a beautiful poem.

'Right then, Han. It's time.'

She slides her record of achievement from under her bum. We were given them earlier, during the *special leaving assembly* we had in the hall. It was absolute madness. Some people from our year were crying. Actually crying because for some absurd reason they're going to miss this place, going to miss each other. And the funniest thing of all was when the teachers stood on that stage and wished those of us who were leaving well for the future. The very same teachers we'd traumatised for the past five years. Even BO Pits Pugh was going around the hall with his pen smiling and signing school shirts with good luck messages. Me and Jess only let them sign ours for a laugh, to see what the losers would write. Course there were some people we wouldn't let anywhere near us with their pens. There were some people who Jess would've stabbed to death with her Berol if they'd even come close.

We stopped to look around that hall with its plaques and its stage and long brown curtains. We took it in for the very last time and then spat it back out, threw it up all over the shiny floor. There were no tears from us. We weren't going to miss this place. It was small and stupid, as dull as the dull curtains and the dull kids. Not like me and Jess. We've got plans. We're glitter and disco balls. And then Laser Ludlow went and scribbled her own personal lie on my shirt in black marker pen, in the neatest handwriting you'll ever see...

Do it to them before they do it to you. I'll miss you. L.L. xx

Jess starts tearing the sheets of paper out with dramatic rips and when she clicks her luminous green lighter against the corners her eyes glow as bright as the flame. Slowly, page by page, certificate by certificate, her record of achievement disappears in a blaze of burning orange. Don't need this. Don't need that one. Ha. What's Jess going to do with a first aid certificate, mun? *I'm* the only person in this world she'd save if they were choking.

'Thanks.'

'Quite alright, Han.'

'Be careful.'

Silly of me, really. Jess is many things but careful is not one of them. Every single certificate she's ever been given is destroyed. Merit awards and attendance awards, a first place prize she got for a nationwide art competition back in year 9. This piece of paper was like the holy grail to her then. *Saddo*. Her photo was in the *Rhondda Leader* and everything, do I remember?

'Course I remember. My mother cut it out and put it on the fridge.'

Gone. Ta-ra! Remember how long she spent on that ceramic plate down the art studio? And remember Laser Ludlow thinking I was *talented*?

'Hmm.'

'Want me to burn yours for you?'

'Nah.'

'What you going to do with it then?'

Keep it. Don't know why. I stuff it in my bag with everything else, a hard ruby-red corner poking out when I zip it up. I've packed enough clean clothes to last me ages. And my notebooks obviously. Most of them are full, very old words, but some are brand new and ready to be filled. I'll write at Jess' house. It won't be all vodka and Queen.

'But mostly,' she says, and next she sets her tie on fire, the stripes and the Comp logo very quickly sizzled down to nothing. 'You going to tell me what you wrote then or what?'

She's on about the envelope I've just taken out the front pocket of my bag. The thing is, I wouldn't care about Comp going up in flames, Jess can burn that too if she likes … but I would care if Laser Ludlow died. She's the only thing I'll miss here. And when I think about all the new kids who'll be walking up the hill next term, it makes me smile. They'll be like we were that first Monday morning. Scared … in perverse awe. Those kids will hear the stories and they'll believe them but the stories about Laser Ludlow are wrong. She's the best thing about Comp. No … Laser Ludlow *is* Comp and the *only* good thing. Jess won't ever find out what I've written on the letter. She'll never understand how Laser Ludlow changed everything for me. She was the only person who ever told me I was good at something, who believed in me and made me think for a stupid minute that all the things I ever wanted to be, I *could* be. The world isn't full of strangers. Even though there are so many people who *don't* understand, who try to change you and tell you that being yourself isn't a good thing to be, in amongst all of them are people who are just like you and they feel the same things. You aren't absolutely alone. If you find them you're lucky. And if you didn't even have to look, if you just ended up in the same place by chance, in some blue-bricked classroom on top of a hill in a mental school, then you're *really* lucky.

I don't tell Jess either that I still find it weird that we're leaving school. That I'm badly, stupidly jealous of all those kids Laser Ludlow will be teaching next year and the thought of her maybe liking one of them, talking to them after class, makes me feel sick. She'd probably slap me and I'd definitely deserve it.

'You can burn it,' I tell her.

The letter. I give it to her. Don't open it!

'Alright, mun. But what's the point in writing someone a letter if you aren't going to give it to them?'

I *was* going to. I didn't just write it for the sake of it, did I? I was
going to explain why I can't stay here, why I won't be coming back
to her A Level class next year, but I was just being stupid. Being a
massive loser. Laser Ludlow doesn't care about me. Why did I ever
think she did? If she really thought she'd miss me, if I was as special
as she said, then she would've tried to make me stay but she didn't.
Didn't even bother.

'Don't worry, Han. You don't need her. We don't need any of
them.'

It's just me and her now, and Cass Elliot who she knows I love
most of all, and Marc Bolan and Freddie Mercury and the two
Jims. They might be dead but they're all a lot better than the people
who are alive. I watch the last piece of envelope disappear.
Whatever I wrote doesn't matter now. The ink is melted, only a
golden flake left glinting in the Comp grass.

'Come on then,' she says, finally deciding that she's ready to go.
'Let's get it on. Bang a gong.'

Needles of grass are stuck to the back of her trousers when she
gets up. Probably on mine too but I can't be bothered to pat them
off. We walk out of the main gates of the building and I take one
last look at it … Comp. I don't know. It's like we weren't meant to
be born here, this place where you aren't allowed to think
differently or even think at all. Because dreams in Pandy are like
balloons except they aren't free to float, to soar over the green
mountains and up into the sky somewhere different, somewhere
better. Instead they're popped with pins by people who don't
understand.

'Fuck you!' Jess shouts into the CCTV camera. 'Fuck you all!'

She stabs two fingers up at the tiny black screen whether it works
or not and then down the hill we go in our signature-covered shirts,
a rainbow-coloured collage of kisses and bullshit, until Comp is
out of sight, still there and not burned down but nonetheless gone
forever. The walk to Jess' house is kind of quiet. No news. No
gossip or bitching. Not even any singing. The best she can manage
is…

'You alright, Han?'

And all I've got is yeah, I'm cool.

Bev's got the day off today. She's in the kitchen when we get there, smoking and eyeing me up and down like I'm an insect Jess has brought in from outside, like one of the flies stuck up in the light fitting. I was crawling around the pavement, legs and wings and beady eyes, and now I'm standing there with my bag on my back, caught and trapped under the lid of a glass jar and Jess is asking if she can keep me. In her bedroom. We won't make any mess, she swears. Won't nag for nothing. Won't even know we're there. Course Bev goes and rings my mother. They love a good talk on the house phone. It's like some kind of sex chat line but instead of talking dirty to each other they just moan about us.

Me and Jess sit on the bottom step of her stairs in the passage listening. Mum's voice is just a faraway buzz, can't make out what she's saying, but Bev is clear as crystal. I know it's awful but what can we do, love? Jess is sixteen and won't be long til Hannah is as well, love. I know, but they're not kids anymore, are they? Tell me about it, love. Mouth on Jessica is disgusting. Full of lip, she is. Some of the names she calls me don't bear thinking about and all I do is try my best. They've got to make their own mistakes. But what can we do, love? Lock them up? I know, I know. But they're better off in my house than wandering the streets all summer holidays. Perhaps they'll see sense give it a couple of weeks. I don't know, love. I don't know why she won't come home. Oh I know, love, worried sick.

'She's going to say no,' I turn and tell her, Jess who is picking at the loose wallpaper on the wall. 'You watch. She'll be up in the car now.'

No problem, love. Joined at the hip, these pair are. Just glad they're talking again because Jessica was moping around like a little lost sheep. No I don't mind. Okay, love. Yes, love. Will do. Ring you tomorrow. Ta-ra now.

Bev puts the phone down and now she's standing in front of us on the stairs, hands on her hips and inhaling the air around us that's thick with shame and disappointment. We brace ourselves for The Speech and here it comes alright, hand gestures and everything, pointing fingers and rolling eyes, sighs and shaking heads … the absolute Works.

194

My mother isn't happy about me staying here but she's agreed to it. One day we'll regret this, me and Jess will, leaving school and throwing our lives away. And to think we used to be clever. I've been coming here since I was this high in my bastard scruffy dungarees and she never thought she'd see the day when we turned into … into *monsters*. Now we think we're the bee's knees, all grown up. Heads full of big ideas. Stupid, we are. We think we can take on the world and win but soon enough we'll realise that it isn't all it's cracked up to be and don't she fucking know it, old Bev. We could've been something but now look at us, sitting there on her stairs smirking.

'Just shut up, Mam. You're such a fucking *embarrassment*. Go and make yourself a nice little drink, issit?'

Insolent little shit. Showing off in front of me. Jess isn't too old for a bastard clout, you know.

But Jess isn't worried. She only laughs at Bev whose speech is over, who's all out of patronising words for us to slam back in her sad, tired-looking face. She watches us race up the stairs, shell-shocked and helpless. The door is thumped behind us and Jess' small, three-bedroom terraced house shakes, the way she's shook it so many times before in anger. Yeah. They're right. We used to be their daughters but now we're monsters. *Rawr*. And if we are monsters then they're the ones who made us … Jess' mother and my mother … they're our very own Frankensteins.

They've got no idea, have they?

I can't tell you exactly when they did it. I don't think me and Jess even really noticed it happening, either. But in her room we turn the volume up as loud as it'll go because we need her. We need Cass Elliot to sing to us. We need her to make us better … fix all these horrible things inside us that no one else can.

Bruises

We've renamed Bev Blotto Bev. She was Bonkers Bev for a while and then Brown Bev on account of the weather. She's absolutely loving it. She likes to sit out the back garden on her plastic patio chair, literally naked, with a glass of vodka and pineapple squash in her hand, until her skin is turned the colour of gravy. Jess says she's walking around like a fucking Egyptian. Well, the cheek of it. She came into our room this morning without permission, without even knocking, and started nagging us as usual. It's really rubbish when she's got the day off work. Apparently, since we've got no intention of going back to sixth form, we've got to get ourselves jobs. And that wasn't all. She kept on and on. On and on and on. We can't spend all the summer holidays like *this*, lazing around in our own filth, in our pit, smoking her fags and listening to that fucking racket. Giving her a bastard headache, we are, but Jess told her straight, like she's telling me now.

'It's the vodka that's giving her a headache, not poor old Freddie Mercury.'

Blotto Bev opened the curtains and the window, first time they'd been opened in days, and glared at us like we were two tramps. But there's nothing wrong with our clothes. Jess and her black cord trousers and me and my black denim jeans, a band t-shirt on top and our Converse trainers. Jess has got *so* many band t-shirts you wouldn't believe and she lets me borrow them because I'm running out of clean clothes. Even though plenty more of my clothes are just three streets away, hanging up in my wardrobe, I'm not going home to get them. I'd rather walk around Pandy naked than see my mother again.

Anyway, there's a Cass Elliot t-shirt in green which Jess always lets me wear, which I'm wearing right now actually up on the chapel roof. You don't get much of a view from here. It's not like being up on the mountain. We'd trek there when we were kids, all the way to the top just to look at it, our valley, to stand with the wind blowing through our hair and clothes and feel like we owned it. Tonypandy. With the hundreds, maybe thousands, of terraced houses slanting like rows of sad dominoes, with our old Junior school and Comp, the chapel and the shops on the main road. And when you see it in panoramic view like that, as green as you can get for miles, people say it's beautiful and breath-taking, but me and Jess, we only hate it now. Every house on every street, every single blade of green grass, and we definitely, absolutely, do not want to look at it anymore.

All you can see from up on the chapel roof is the main road down below. The cars that rev past us, engines loud and windows rolled down. And buses, Stagecoach ones that take people to the town centre and back with their Somerfield carrier bags. They're really funny when they stop and stare at us. It's mostly the old ladies that do it. They shield their eyes from the sun and then they realise who we are. That Hannah King, poor bugger, and that Jessica Matthews whose father ran off with that big fat woman and left her mother with the mortgage. Monsters who once skipped happily down these pavements but now cast shadows on them as they strut defiantly in their Converse trainers.

But they needn't worry. They can keep their stupid town because we aren't staying. We're getting out of here and when we go we're not coming back. Oh, they'll know that we left. We'll walk away just as the fireworks are banging, glittering silver and red and green and gold, sizzling down the dull and grey Rhondda sky. We'll get out of Pandy alright, like rock stars leaving the stage after blowing the minds of all the little spellbound people in the crowd. Born here, die here. Not us.

'I hate this weather,' I tell her, because today the sky is bright blue, not grey, and the heat is making me feel sick as a dog.

'Don't be such a misery guts, mun. I'm no way going home yet. Can't be dealing with my mother.'

Jess is basking in the sun – leaning back on her hands and soaking the rays up like some kind of beached seal.

'*Seal*? Fucking charming.'

'We could go to the park? Hide in the bushes like we used to.'

Nah. Never going there again. The park reminds her of him. Her father. The Prick. He used to take her there, see, when she was really little. He'd push her on the swings as high as she could stand before her belly leaped out of her body and she begged him to stop. He'd sing her songs and she swore to God that's where she'd end up if he carried on pushing her any harder.

'Where?'

'The ballrooms of Mars, obviously.'

She liked to mount the car-shaped climbing frame, and when she finally got up and under and lifted her legs over poles and bars and sat down on the hard seat, she imagined that's where she was going.

'Turned the wheel and drove all the way with my lizard-leather boots on, I did.'

'Are you okay?'

'Course I'm fucking okay. Why wouldn't I be?'

The only thing she is is starving and so am I. Blotto Bev reckons that if we want to play at being grown-ups then we've got to cook our own food like grown-ups have to. Not that we could anyway because the fridge is always empty.

'Can't fry fresh air or eat a fuck-all sandwich, can you?'

'No, Jess. No you can't.'

We're like neglected children living off crisps and chocolate, and it doesn't help that summer in Tonypandy reeks of barbecues, the scent of burgers and hot dogs and onions caught on the still air.

'Mmm, yeah. I could murder a burger,' she says as she flicks her finished fag over the edge of the roof. 'With cheese and mayo. And bacon. And maybe an onion ring.'

Her fag lands in the grass on the overgrown patch beneath us. Green weeds wind like snakes with spiky yellow flowerheads up the steps where we once used to sit and prod puddles of oil with sticks. Sometimes I do think about it but then I stop myself. The chapel's been closed down for years and is now an abandoned building with boarded-up windows. Kids smashed them in with bricks and if you look hard enough in the grass you can still find some of the stained glass. Jagged shards of rich reds and beautiful yellows hiding in the blades, poking out of the mud … pieces of a broken Jesus.

'Would you fuck me if you were a boy, Han?'

'Where did that come from?'

'My head.'

Well, would I or not?

'Probably. I don't know.'

'Why don't you ever think about it?'

'Think about what?'

'*Sex*, Han. Cocks and balls and cum and skinny, naked bodies. And wanting someone so bad it makes you ache everywhere, makes you hurt in places you didn't even know could feel anything at all.'

I don't know.

'Do you think he tells her that he loves her?'

'Who?'

'Robbie Jenkins. Because that's what he told me. Why do people lie?'

'Maybe they just can't help themselves.'

'She was right though. I should've just done it when he brought that stupid strawberry condom over.'

'Nah. You're special, Jess,' I tell her, and right now I'm not lying at all.

How can I say that? If she was so special then Robbie Jenkins wouldn't have left her, would he?

'The dirty bitch even gave him a blow job.'

'What exactly is a blow job?'

'You know … when a boy puts his cock in a girl's mouth and … *you know.*'

Spit or swallow. Course Jess would swallow because spitting is a right dirty habit. She can't believe I don't know what a blow job is but then again I haven't even kissed anyone, have I?

'And you know when it all happened … when I was telling Bev … do you know what she did, Han?'

She laughed her head off. Said Jess was *too young* to know what love is but Jess isn't thick, she knows exactly what it is.

'Love is just a four-letter word,' I tell her.

'What?'

'It's a song.'

Jess has never heard of it but whoever sings it is right. Lucy Williams is welcome to him. She doesn't care anymore. Love can suck her cock. And she's glad she didn't fuck him because the first time she does it, it won't be with a prick like him. It'll be with someone like Freddie Mercury.

'I don't think you'll find any rock stars in Pandy, Jess.'

'You never know. He could be out there right now. You watch, next bus he'll be on it.'

'Rock stars don't travel on buses though. It's Cadillacs and Rolls Royces.'

'Check you out, Han. My little rock and roll encyclopaedia. I've taught you well, haven't I?'

'Yep.'

'Well whoever it's with it's going to be romantic anyway. And when it's all over, when he's fucked my brains out, he'll sing me to sleep.'

'Rockets, bells and poetry?'

She grins at me. That's right. That's *exactly* how it'll be. And up here on the chapel roof we break into it. 'It's Getting Better', by Cass Elliot. One of our favourites. We're singing and singing, belting it, but then Jess stops. She starts laughing for no apparent reason at all.

'What's funny?'

'Just the song,' she says, black mascara rivers streaming down her cheeks.

But I still don't get it? *What* about the song? I stare at her blankly as she tries to compose herself. Deep breaths in out and out. Fans her face with her hand the way massive girls do.

'Well nothing's getting better, is it? It's all absolutely, completely shit.'

Look at me, mun, Han. Look at *you*!

That starts her off again, hysterical she is, and seeing her in such a state makes me laugh as well. Because she's right, isn't she? Look at her. Jess who steals fags and vodka from the kitchen and then makes Bev think she's losing her mind when she wonders where they've gone. Jess who is an arsonist, who has to burn absolutely everything she can get her destructive, lighter-clicking hands on.

And look at *me*. I don't even like smoking and I'm smoking. And I haven't been home in two whole weeks, too ashamed, too scared, to even talk to my own mother on the phone and I don't really know why.

'Exactly!' she says. 'What a fucking beautiful mess!'

It *is* all absolutely, completely shit. So shit it couldn't get much shitter really. We're laughing and laughing and trying to sing, messing the words up badly because we're laughing too much. The next bus stops and Freddie Mercury doesn't get off it like we already knew he wouldn't. Just a couple of old ladies, one with a shopping basket on wheels and the other with a fist full of heavy-looking carrier bags. We shoot them four fingers when they gawp at us. Have they got a problem or what?

We don't care if we look mental. They already think it anyway, that we're bad because of All The Things That Have Happened To Us. Piss off. Leave us alone.

We calm ourselves down. Just about. Cheeks and eyes dried in the collars of our t-shirts. Jess is silent and smoking, lost in some glittery, feathery fantasy of throbbing, cosmic cocks and big, biting teeth and sweaty after sex a cappella. We stay up on the chapel roof until it's late, or at least until she's had enough of waiting for Freddie Mercury who doesn't step off any of the buses in a fur coat and sunglasses. And Blotto Bev will be pissed by now, like she was last night and the night before that. It'll just make our mission easier.

No doors are knocked on our way back. We're feeling generous tonight. Let them sleep, let them watch their tellies in peace. We walk side by side under the smoky summer sky. Alive and intense with pinks and purples, these swirling clouds that look like bruises, the colour of Turkish delight. *Pretty.*

'Red sky at night, shepherd's delight,' she says. 'Such a stupid saying because it isn't even red it's fucking pink ... look. Everyone just talks so much shit. What does it even mean?'

'It means tomorrow will be as sunny, as disgustingly hot, as today.'

And well there we are then. If I say so. Think I'm Sian fucking Lloyd, I do. Jess hooks under my arm and I let her. It's no big deal,

I just do. She's gone a bit chilly, goose bumps all up her arms, feel them. Her t-shirt is dark navy, a print of the Unicorn album by T Rex on the front. I like it on her. She looks really nice tonight, as pretty as the sky, and yeah, her arms are quite cold. I don't have a coat otherwise I'd let her wear it. I'm not cold at all. But my coat is at home with the rest of my clothes.

We see the light on through the curtains, a dull orange glow, which means Bev must be still up. Jess growls. Actually growls. Great. Now we won't be able to steal anything. This is why we mostly take what we need during the day when Bev's in work. She's got a drawer full of fags and Jess helps herself to those whenever because Bev doesn't mind too much, or just doesn't notice. They're Spanish. She gets them on the cheap from some woman in work. But the vodka is a different story, much more precious, much harder to get. Bev really ought to get a lock for that cupboard, you know. We've got this trick.

It involves an empty vodka bottle under Jess' bed. And a lot of skill. What we do is we take it downstairs and into the kitchen and get one of the full ones out of the cupboard. Unscrew it, carefully fill our empty bottle up halfway without spilling a drop, and then put the other one back in the cupboard except it's been topped up by the sink so it doesn't look like we've taken anything at all. Clever, aren't we? Blotto Bev is so oblivious that she doesn't even know that the only thing she's off her tits on is tap water.

Luck is on our side tonight. First time for everything. Bev is passed out on the settee when we get in, a full ashtray on the arm of the chair. She's fallen asleep with the telly on, some American chat show where fat black ladies are screaming at each other.

'I think she's dead,' Jess whispers.

She jabs her in the cheek with her finger. Bev stirs and grumbles and swats her away.

'Shame.'

Jess slides the drawer open and takes a pack of fags. Just one pack. We aren't greedy. She stuffs them into the back pocket of her cords. Tidy. And next, the vodka. Twelve tall, slim, red-topped bottles waiting for us when she opens the cupboard door, the crystal clear liquid glistening in the kitchen light. The drinks cupboard at the Matthews' isn't like the fridge. Bev's vodka looks like turps and tastes like turps, but when we down it, it works like medicine. And Jess is feeling particularly sick tonight so we aren't going to bother transferring bottles, we're just taking one. Having it all to ourselves and tomorrow, when Blotto Bev counts them and scratches her head swearing to God there were twelve here the last time she checked, Jess will tell her she's losing her flipping marbles, mun, off her fucking rocker. She holds the bottle in her hand like it's a trophy.

'God, I love stealing,' she says, as if she's just taken the Crown Jewels out of the Tower of London. 'I feel alive. Dangerous.'

But Jess doesn't feel dangerous for very long. Shit, Han. *Fuck. Fuck.* She panics and shoves the bottle up her t-shirt. I don't know why she doesn't just put it back in the cupboard. It's like a game of musical statues and someone has just turned the music off. We stand there still and in silence, teeth gritted, hoping, *praying*, that Bev doesn't see the kitchen light on. She's awake, coughing and spluttering, calling out for Jess. Are you in the kitchen, love?

There's nowhere to run. The back door is locked, Jess checks the handle, and we don't have time to look for the key. The telly is turned off and then Bev is stumbling into the kitchen on jelly legs. Beverly Matthews. I've known her nearly all my life. She may as well be a member of my own family. Her house is my second home. And before she went bonkers, or before I turned into a monster, she used to like me. She'd make me dinner when I stayed over, ask me questions about my mother, and complain about the weather and whatever illness she was suffering with that particular week. I know all her business, all her secrets. I've watched her argue with Jess' father and I've tried on her shoes and her bras although she doesn't know about that. I've smoked her fags and drunk gallons of her Somerfield own-brand pineapple squash. But in all those years and all those things, I've never seen her this drunk.

Yep. Blotto Bev is exceptionally Blotto tonight. It takes a while for her to come to her senses, to realise that we're all standing in the kitchen like this. Jess looks nothing like her mother. Bev who is petite and blonde. Jess looks like her father but don't tell her that, she'll probably knock you out. I don't know how long she's been asleep or how long she sat on that sofa drinking vodka and watching fat black ladies fight, but Bev shields her eyes from the blinding kitchen light as if it's just punched her. They're smudged with make-up, her mascara caked and crispy. I think she's been crying.

'Sort yourself out mun, Mam. You look like a fucking panda.'

Why did she speak? Why didn't Jess just keep quiet? For once in her life. We could've said goodnight, Bev, and made a run for it up the stairs. But no. The bottle is clearly visible under her t-shirt. Jess is a brilliant arsonist but a terrible burglar. Bev swipes it. What you doing with my vodka, you sneaky little shit?

'I'm only borrowing it, Mam. Chill out. Don't be so tight.'

Bev's voice is all slurry and spitty … fast. And right now in the kitchen she reminds me of somebody I used to know. *Tight*? Jess has got some nerve, aye. Living here for free, we are, and she's got the cheek to call her fucking tight. She isn't too old for a bastard clout, you know.

Jess snatches the bottle back and then they're wrestling with it. I stand back and watch. Suppose if I helped Jess we could beat her, yank it off her. Tug of war. Two against one. But I won't lie, Blotto Bev is scarier than normal Bev and Normal Bev gave Jess' father four stitches.

Jess pulls and Bev pulls, like the bottle is a Christmas cracker. I'm amazed it doesn't break in half. World War Three was over for a while. There was peace between the magnolia walls but now it's started back up again. Different enemies this time. Fingers stab shoulder blades, pierce the nasty, toxic air. Jess' t-shirt is pulled and Bev's nightie buttons are popped open, dressing-gown string unravelled. The spit flies like the mean words. Jess is a thief. A weird fucking Goth. Bev is a stupid old bitch. A minging, wrinkly drunk with panda eyes and it's her fault Jess has got tiny tits. Jess is an ungrateful little cow. A fucking mistake. Jess should've never been born.

'Nice one, Mam. No wonder Daddy left you, you spiteful old twat!'

Left her, was it? He left Jess, too, she doesn't want to go forgetting that. Things were alright before she was born. Better!

They had fun then. They had a life and they were *happy*. And Bev's got a good mind to fuck off herself. Pack her fucking suitcase and leave.

'Go on then,' Jess dares her. 'Piss off and leave me. Everyone else does so you might as well.'

It's horrible. Neither one will let go of the argument or the bottle. I back away from them even further, scared that Bev will turn on me with her nasty words or her teeth, afraid she'll throw me out of her house completely. I've never felt so awkward and so aware of my body in all my life. My five foot four frame and my deathly pale, despite the weather, arms. My legs and my stupid, electric hair that's even more stupid and electric in this humidity. The bag on my back. Cass smiling on my t-shirt. I just want to disappear. Slither like a snake out of the kitchen, unnoticed. I focus on the flies in the light. Three little black corpses that were there the day I ate those first Turkey Twizzlers and will be there until the end of time itself. And then the kettle and the toaster, and the knife block on the unit, the wooden wedge and the six black handles coming out.

A horrible series of images runs through my head. I watch Jess snap, her normal person wires obliterated. The heat and the screaming, it's all added to it, turned her mad once and for all. She picks it up like she did before, the thickest handle, the widest, shiniest blade, but this time she does it for real. Jess stabs Bev in the chest like she's a microwavable meal from Somerfield, macaroni and cheese. She's covered in Bev's blood. I mean, *really* covered. Like when she was a newborn baby and she left Bev's vagina, the exact moment when Bev stopped knowing what she needs. And she's yelling at her as she's stabbing. Doesn't she know what she's done? Doesn't she understand that Freddie Mercury is not a fucking racket? It's bad of me to think it but Bev is bleeding on the kitchen floor, and Bev sort of deserves it.

Of course it doesn't really happen. Jess even lets go of the bottle. Gives up. Bev might be petite, but she's got a firm grip. And Bev can shove her vodka up her fucking arse. Bev can leave … Bev can *die* for all Jess cares.

I chase her up the stairs but we're not racing and I don't grab her ankles. She presses the forward button fast, her thumbs shaky, desperate, until she finds 'Cosmic Dancer'. Nothing else will do. Marc Bolan sings it as fragile and as beautiful as only he can while Jess is flying across the room almost poetically, gliding through the air in slow motion, through each heart-breaking note. She lands on her bed, face first on purpose. It's pointless though. I know she's crying. Her whole body is shaking but I just stand over her like the useless, awkward mess I am. I should pick her up and hug her, I know, but I *can't*. Her mother is crazy and mine doesn't care. And now we haven't even got any vodka to make it go away.

Sixteen

'Not still sulking because old Mrs King didn't bring your card up, are you?'

I want to get a grip. You know what Bev said she said on the phone. Card's down here on the table and if you want it then you can come and bloody get it.

'She's my mother, Jess. She should bring it to *me*.'

I'm only three streets away after all. If Mum stood out in the garden and shouted Happy Birthday then I'd probably hear her. But whatever. I don't even want her stupid birthday card anyway.

'There might be money in it though. Tell you what, we'll hide in the street behind a car until she's gone out and then get it. *Steal* it.'

'Nah. Fuck it. Fuck her.'

Jess grins. Proud. That's my girl. She loves it when I swear. She loves it when I'm filthy.

She's standing up on the bed looking down at me. I've been kicked off and onto the floor, the black-orange fag burns patterned like leopard print in Bev's expensive cream carpet all around me. This is my birthday present. She didn't make me a card like usual because, well, she couldn't be arsed to be perfectly honest. And she hasn't got a clue how to make a cake.

'Go on then, Han. I'm all ready to go by here, mun.'

Been warming the old vocal chords up for hours, she has. Apparently I've got to get up and press the button myself. Jess clears her smoke-phlegmy throat. *Play*.

'We are the Champions'. Jess sings it with Freddie, very loudly and very dramatically into her empty bottle of Fanta, each word perfectly enunciated. She's taking it all extremely seriously. She jumps off at the chorus, the mattress springs still vibrating as she lands.

But don't go thinking she's done this especially for my birthday. I often have to sit through The Jessica Matthews Show. Her mattress is her stage and below her on the ruined carpet I count for the hundreds of thousands of people who have come to hear her sing. The music blaring in the background, like this, and Jess dancing around her room clicking her fingers and shaking her arse in my face. Empty bottle of Fanta microphone or teaspoon microphone or deodorant-can microphone. Yesterday she was Marc Bolan and one of Bev's lilac bras was a feather boa and I was her woman of gold and not very old, ah ha ha.

She takes a bow when the song finishes and thanks me very much for coming. And happy birthday! Jess goes and makes me smile and I absolutely hate her for it. How dare she … I'm not fucking happy. Not at all.

'Aren't I going to get a clap, or what?'

No.

Whatever.

We're on top of the quilt then, backs against the cold peach wall, with our legs horizontal across the bed. My very clean purple size 5s and her very dirty red size 6s dangling over the edge of the mattress. Bev's floral bowl in the middle of us for our ash. *Innuendo* on quiet in the background. Curtains closed. The sun and the world shut out. Perfect.

'Why are your feet so small, Han?'

'They aren't small,' I tell her straight. 'Size 5, they are. That's average for a girl.'

And my hands, look. I've got tiny hands as well. We press them together. See? And why are my little fingers bent like that?

'I don't know, Jess. They're not tiny anyway. Just because you've got massive serial-killer shovel hands.'

'Nah. My hands are normal-sized hands, Han. Yours are just *weird*. Bet you'd have a tiny cock too.'

'As if. I'd be massive.'

'Would you shove it in me?'

'Definitely. Where would you like it?'

'In my mouth please, if you don't mind.'

I won't lie, we're kind of drunk. Don't judge us though. If you can't get drunk at four in the afternoon on your sixteenth birthday when your own mother hasn't even sent you a card and your best friend wants to suck your imaginary cock, then when can you?

Right now Freddie is singing 'The Show Must Go On' and this song has sort of become our anthem. We know that Brian May wrote it for us because that's exactly what our lives are ... pantomimes. So crazy and ridiculous, far too crazy and ridiculous to be taken seriously. We pass the bottle back and forth, our very own party game. I'm not worried about sharing spit anymore. That's the good thing about being drunk. You're not really worried about anything. Not the fact that you're swapping germs with your chain-smoking best friend. Not the fact that you haven't written a single word in weeks because you can't, because weirdly, for the first time ever, there's none in your head. Not that fact that your own mother hasn't sent you a birthday card.

'Oh stop keeping on. She'll be on the blower to Bev later, mun.'

'Well I'm not speaking to her.'

'My father ruined my birthday once. He was supposed to pick a cake up on the way home from work but he went down Fat Pat's and forgot. Didn't even have a candle to blow out on my birthday. How tragic is that?'

'Very.'

'Want to know a secret, Han?'

'Always.'

'He hit her.'

'Who?'

'My father. He hit Bev.'

'You never told me.'

Do I think she tells me everything or what?

He must've had a crap day in work or something because he came home and went *nuts* because Bev hadn't cooked him what he fancied for dinner. Not just shouting nuts or nasty words nuts. *Proper* nuts. He was demanding something else to eat, there and then, but she wouldn't cook it for him. She's all like, get Fat Pat to cook it for you, love. So they're arguing in the kitchen like they always do ... did ... Fat Pat's a slag, minge the size of the Gower, and he's a lying cunt. Bev's a miserable, depressing bitch and she brings him down and this house and this life is bringing him down and he's had enough of it. Jess can't remember the other words in between but it was like she froze on the spot, you know?

'I lost my count.'

'What do you mean, "your count"?'

Jess was counting the punches. Not just from him, mind, Bev was giving as good as she got but Bev is tiny and her father is massive, in he? Well the last punch knocked her down and she didn't bother getting back up. She just lay there on the lino crying and he never came back.

'That was the night he left. Fucking steak and kidney pies.'

'What?'

'That's what she'd made him, a steak and kidney pie. Was up the walls and everything. Like dog shit. He's been gone months now, Han. Hasn't even bothered to ring me.'

Never mind her father. She didn't tell me all this. I never knew about steak and kidney pies. Maybe I was wrong to think all this time that *I* was the good liar. I thought she was terrible at it but Jess has been keeping secrets, too, like the bottles of vodka under her bed, the fags under her pillow. I don't like it. What else hasn't she told me?

'Nothing, Han. I tell you everything. Apart from that.'

'Hmm.'

'Swear it.'

'So do you miss him?'

A question I wish I could take back now because I've got a can of my own disgusting little worms that I don't ever want to open.

'Men are all the same, Han. Exactly like my father and Robbie Jenkins.'

They're all pricks. Except for Freddie and Marc, of course. She doesn't want to see her father's stinking, fat, bald, minging head ever again.

'So no, Han, to answer your question. I do not miss him at all.'

And there goes another one. It's not how long she took to answer, or because she can't make eye contact with me. I know Jess is lying because she hasn't burned them like she burns everything else, especially the things she can't stand to look at. The CDs we put on every day are his. He left them behind like he left her and deep down, in that dark place we only go to now and again when we're drunk and listening to a dying Freddie Mercury tell us he

210

still loves us, Jess cares. I don't offer her any nice words though. A good best friend would say that he's the one who's missing out. She's much better off without him anyway, because he can't see it like I can, how special she is. None of them can. She's got me and it wasn't her fault. How could it be? She didn't ask to be born. And he's just a sad mess like all the other messes in the world who can't be happy because they got old and miserable, because they wilted years ago, because their once bright petals fell off and now they can never be stuck back on. Yeah. A normal person would say those things but not me. A person who isn't cold as ice and hard as nails. But I know Jess anyway. If I did, if I leant over Bev's floral bowl right now and hugged her, she'd probably push me off the bed. What are you fucking doing, you gay fucking fuck? After all these years we both know where we stand. It'll be alright. And fuck them. That's about as close as we get to showing our feelings. We talk and communicate over our own self-built walls, through lyrics we stole from dead people, and that's fine with us.

Bev's home from work. We can hear her pottering about downstairs. Been there since seven this morning so we've had a peaceful, nag-free day which is now over. She pops her head around the door and scowls at us in her Somerfield polo shirt. You two still here, are you? Yes, Bev, we're still here, unlucky for you. Have you been home Hannah, love, or rung your mother because it's your birthday and she was in the shop this morning looking awful upset? Piss off, Bev, it's none of your business what Hannah does. Don't suppose you've put the hoover around have you, Jessica? No, Bev, we've been very busy, see.

'And we're still monsters so fuck off out of my room and leave us alone, dickhead.'

The look on Bev's face is priceless. We're pissing ourselves laughing as she closes the door. Silly old cow. Jess gets up to change the CD. What do I fancy? Bit of Electric Ladyland? But just as she's looking through them we hear Bev crying from her bedroom.

'What's the matter with her now?'

'Maybe it's because you told her to fuck off.'

Nah. Jess tells her to fuck off every day so she doesn't know why that would set her off. She bangs her wall with her fist and tells her through the peach paint and plaster to shut the fuck up but Bev doesn't shut the fuck up at all. Her crying just gets louder and Jess just gets angrier.

'She's doing my head in, Han,' she says, breathing heavily through her nose.

Jess just wants to move on. She knows her father's gone, like, she knows he isn't coming back so her mother doesn't need to keep reminding her. Bev is lonely, she gets it, and Bev is terrified of being alone. The Black fucking Dog. But Bev's pathetic. She's got the landing light on every night in the hope that he'll come back through the front door with his full bag and empty sorries. Because Bev would rather be miserable than be alone. And Bev reminds Jess of this every day … how Jess isn't enough to make her happy. She reminds her when she cries, all the time like a big fucking baby.

'And it's like in this house there's no ceiling and it's always raining. It's like everything is grey and horrible and cold. Like Hell on Earth, you know?'

'Yeah, Jess, I *do* know.'

Right. That's it. She can't stand it any longer. We're leaving. *Now*. And it would be exciting, Packing Our Bags and Running Away, if we hadn't done it already. We left for good on Monday and last Friday too, and loads of times before except we always come back when it gets dark and cold, when Bev's Spanish fags and Jess' anger run out. Nevertheless I play along. I pull my mobile charger out of the wall and wind it up. My clothes go in my bag, the ones I can find on the floor anyway. I stuff them down until I can barely do the zip up although there's more room in there since I let Jess burn my record of achievement. She packs her bag as well, doesn't leave a single t-shirt behind in the drawer. A few pairs of knickers and some odd socks and a clean bra, the bandanas she bought in Cardiff with the money off Bev's credit card and half a box of tampons. I'm trying to find my socks but she says sod your socks mun, Han, there's no time.

This Is It and she means it. We aren't staying a second longer in this house. We leave Freddie behind on the walls with Marc looking beautiful in his blue velvet jacket and sparkly collar. I don't even say goodbye to Cass but it's okay because she knows I'll see her later. Each melodramatic stamp on the creaky stairs is a heavy message to Bev. I hate you! We're off! Don't try to stop us because we're never coming back, alright! Goodbye!

Jess slams the front door behind us and obviously, she knocks windows on her street as we pass them although they're more like punches against the glass today. If Snowy the cat was still alive she'd probably punch him off the windowsill, too. I know we're off to the chapel roof because Jess won't go near the park anymore and there's nowhere else to go. Literally, nowhere in the world. She powers down the main road and I tell her to slow down or what? But she ignores me. It's mental warm in these jeans and my bag is heavy, the back of my Jim Morrison t-shirt soaked with sweat. It's not her fault that I carry all those stupid notebooks around with me. I'm a weirdo. I should've let her burn them. Whatever.

She gets there before me but waits for me to catch up. And then we climb the crumbling wall behind chapel together, jump the gap and land on the roof. The black slate is scorching under my hands.

'Shit. I've only got seven fags left. Why didn't you remind me to nick any on the way out mun, Han?'

'You said we were in a rush. Didn't have time for sodding socks.'

Yeah, but socks aren't as important as fags. I'm useless and it's all my fault. I'm supposed to be the one with the brains. She slams the lid down on the silver box like she slammed her front door.

'We'll just get more later when we go back.'

'We ain't going back, Han.'

She's sick of listening to her mother crying and sick of that fucking house, sick of this fucking *place*, sick of fucking everything. But it's okay. If we smoke them slowly they'll last us the night and then we'll go back tomorrow when Bev's in work.

'*Tomorrow*?'

'Yeah. It's no big deal. I've slept up here before.'

'No you haven't.'

'Yes I have.'

'When?'

'Night my father went. Took my quilt off my bed and kipped up here. Left Bev crying on the lino.'

213

'Why didn't you just come to mine? Why didn't you text me?'

She takes her time with her answer, flicks her lighter on and off. Classic mistake, Jessica. You never learn.

'Just didn't think to, that's all.'

As if. Does she think I'm stupid? Of course she would've thought to. Jess tells me everything, irrelevant stuff. Before I moved into her room she'd text me a million times a day. If we weren't together I'd know what she was watching on the telly and what she was eating, thinking, what she was drawing in her sketchbook. And once she even text me while she was on the toilet to tell me the shape and size of her shit. Sleeping rough on the roof of a chapel is kind of important. Your father beating your mother up is kind of important. She obviously didn't tell me those things on purpose. Or maybe they didn't even happen at all. But I know for sure that I've lost my touch and this is the worst birthday I've ever had. Quite possibly the worst birthday anyone in the world has ever had.

I lie back and then Jess lies back, too. Our heads to the roof and eyes to the sinking sun, a yellow smudge on the blue but cloudy sky. They're all kinds of things today. An eagle and a seahorse, an old man with a hooked nose. A cactus. And of course Jess spots a cock-shaped cloud.

'We should be on one of them,' she says, looking at it through her fingers, the plane, a tiny dot that sprays a white paint track behind it on the blue canvas. 'We go every summer but I expect he's going with Fat Pat now. Do you think he is?'

I'm angry with her so I don't answer. I don't know if her father is going on holiday with Fat Pat and I don't really care. I just know that she's a liar and that I've never been on a plane. Up here, on the chapel roof, is the closest I've got to flying away. Jess can see that I'm pissed off so she keeps on talking, the thing she loves best.

'Can't wait until we're rich, Han. When you write this book we can have our own private jet, can't we? Go wherever we want in the world.'

Yeah. If she says so.

'What's the matter?'

Nothing. Nothing at all.

'Will you write about me in your book then?'

Don't know. Maybe.

'You can if you want. Make me famous, Han. I'd love it.'

I don't need her permission to write about her. I've been writing about her for years. She's just never known it.

We lie in the sun smoking until Jess gets bored and sits up. She looks sadly into her pack of fags which now only has two left. Make that one. I sit up as well as she blows a line of rings that ripple and bounce across the sky like white stones across water. The air smells meaty and smoky again although I haven't heard a fire engine today. Then again we've had Queen up pretty loud. Not that Jess would care if the mountain went up in flames anyway. It can all burn. In fact, Pandy could disappear under a mushroom cloud and it wouldn't bother her one bit.

'Just imagine if something like that did happen,' she says. 'Something really terrible.'

But we always imagine it. She's not asking me to do anything new. We've talked before about hurricanes and floods and earthquakes. Asteroids hitting the earth. And killer diseases and nuclear bombs.

'It's amazing though, innit? How the most horrific things are usually the most beautiful things as well.'

'Yes. Wonderful, Jessica.'

'Would you save me, Han? Say I was stuck in my bedroom and the house was on fire. Would you save me?'

'That's a stupid question. I'd be with you, wouldn't I?'

No. For some reason I'm outside but she's still indoors. I can see her trapped up in the smoky window. She's frantically banging it, screaming for help, choking to *death*. Bev's already dead.

'I'd call 999.'

'But your mobile's out of battery.'

'I'd knock next door and use their phone.'

She sighs. Okay. Fair enough. But the firemen haven't come and she's still stuck and if I don't run up the stairs and drag her out then she's definitely, one hundred percent, going to die.

'I'd never be able to lift you over my shoulder, Jess.'

'So you'd let me burn alive? *Thanks*, Han.'

'Oh well. We've all got to die some time.'

Fucking Hell, mun. What's wrong with me?

'I told you already. Nothing.'

She tosses the last fag hand to hand and silently deals with it. How everyone's left her, let her down, and now up on the chapel roof she's discovered that the only person she thought she could count on, her best friend, the person who's supposed to have her back, has gone and let her die in a metaphorical fire without even trying to save her. I was lying anyway. Of course I would save her. But if she's going to lie to me then I'm going to lie to her. That's the way it works.

Buses come and go and Jess huffs and puffs. I watch the craving grow bigger and bigger as she plays with her dirty laces, fingers itchy, absolutely desperate for that last fag. She's placed it on her knee and she stares at it in the hope it'll multiply before her eyes.

'Just smoke it if you want, Jess. I don't mind.'

Am I sure? Yes, I'm sure. She's getting on my nerves fussing like that. And just as she's lighting it, a car stops below us outside the chapel.

'What a beauty!'

But it's hardly a Cadillac, is it? It is different, I guess, not the sort of car you see going up and down the main road. And we've spent so much time up here watching the world go by that I think we pretty much know every car in Pandy and who drives it. Not seen this one before though. It looks like some kind of spaceship. Clean and white. On the back where the boot is, two pieces of polished metal jut like wings. The lights are neon blue and the silver wheel trims are actually gleaming as bright as the sun up in the sky. A boy gets out of the passenger side and Jess looks disappointed. What? Did she really expect it to be Freddie Mercury?

'Who he is though, Han?'

'How do I know?'

He's got long blond hair and he's wearing a jumper and blue denim jeans. A *jumper*, on a day like this.

'Bet you fancy him.'

'As if, Han. Who does he think he is? Kurt Cobain or what?'

'But you like boys with long hair.'

'Yeah, but I can't stand Kurt.'

'Why? He's dead.'

'Not tidy dead. Kurt killed himself, didn't he? There's nothing rock and roll about that.'

'But he still died young.'

So? Doesn't count. If you kill yourself then you aren't allowed in The Club. Let her explain.

'The Club is a party for the young and dead and beautiful, right Han?'

'Yeah…'

And in The Club there's disco balls that hang from the ceiling and they're actually *made* of glitter. Marc Bolan's lying across a cloud sprinkling everyone with his own personal, twinkly stash that he keeps in his velvet pockets. Like confetti. And Freddie Mercury is fucking everything, wining and dining the cherubs on a palatial chaise longue. It's a paradise of halos and cocks and tight, well-groomed angel vagina. Cass Elliot is high up on a seat in the sky swinging and singing and Jim Morrison's off his tits in a corner somewhere. Jimi Hendrix is playing guitar, of course, riffs that are so delicious, as sweet as the chocolate-coated strawberries served in gold-plated bowls, riffs that get you as drunk as the expensive champagne. And then there's a knock on the door and everything stops. It's Kurt Cobain who's standing there, his head dripping with blood from the shotgun wound he inflicted on himself.

'Kurt crashes the party because see, the thing is, Kurt wasn't saved. He just gave up. He simply can't come in.'

'Where does he go then? Hell?'

'Nah. Somewhere much worse than Hell. Kurt Cobain gets sent to Heaven … and you can't do fuck all there without God having a go at you.'

The boy who we've never seen before walks up the chapel steps and then stops in the overgrown grass. He crunches the pieces of glass under his white trainers, no idea he's stepping on Jesus, no idea Jess has decided that he isn't good enough for the most exclusive, most wonderful club in the world.

'Fuck's he doing, Han? Doesn't he know this is *our* chapel?'

Hello? Can we help you? No answer. What the fuck is wrong with him?

'Throw this at him, Han.'

'No way. You do it.'

Alright then, she will. Intruder! Party crasher! One eye closed she aims her luminous green lighter at him. She'll knock him out now, Kurt Co-flipping-bain. He even bends down and steals a piece of our Jesus glass and puts in his pocket. Fucking thief, Jess will show him now. But then another boy gets out of the driver's side of the space car. He's bounding up the steps and shouting at Kurt Cobain. His accent is the same as ours, deep and Welsh Valleys, although we don't recognise him either. And then he shouts at us.

'Do you girls fancy coming to a house party or what?'

Jess asks him if he's got any fags on him. He says yeah, course he's got fucking fags. A shitload. And well, that's it. Jess doesn't need asking twice. She puts her lighter in her back pocket and leaves the empty pack of Spanish fags on the roof. Bags on backs we leap across the gap again like eager cats chasing a bird or a bug. We climb down the crumbling wall without hesitation or really thinking about it, what we're doing, and then on the grassy chapel steps, *our* chapel steps, we're all standing together.

We get a better look of them and no, we still don't recognise them. They're not from our school anyway. The school we *used* to go to, but they seem a lot older than us. Too old even for sixth form. Kurt Cobain in a jumper and jeans doesn't speak at all, just stares at his trainers. He isn't that much taller than I am but the other boy, the driver of the car, he's massive and very skinny. And I'm not sure why Jess is staring at him like that because he's totally not her type. Not rock star at all. No big hair and no big teeth, no tight trousers or sunglasses or fur coat. His dark hair is even shorter than older Freddie Mercury's. He's wearing slack black shorts that stop just below his knees and a grey vest that shows off his almost brown skin.

These boys are strangers, those bad things our mothers would warn us about when we were kids. But we gladly get into their car.

218

Please. Just take us. If our mothers are wrong about everything else, then they're definitely wrong about strangers, too. The Truth is that strangers are actually better than the people you know.

We sit in the back giggling like it really is a spaceship come to rescue us, to take us away to a better planet. And okay. So we don't quite leave fireworks behind us, and the little people aren't spellbound … in fact, they don't even know that we're leaving at all … but we *do* leave and that's what matters.

'This poof by here is Billy,' the tall one driving says about Kurt Cobain. 'And I'm Marley. And I've got a *massive* cock.'

Dead Dogs

Tell her then … why do boys have to walk so fast?

I crash into her, almost *fall* over her, when she stops dead in front of me without warning. But she doesn't apologise, just unties the purple bandana off her head and uses it to dry her tomato-red face, the sweat absolutely pouring off her. I've never seen her in such a state. Two patches have formed under the armpits of her yellow *News of the World* t-shirt.

'BO Pits Matthews,' I say.

'Shut up. Least I haven't got freckles all over my nose.'

True. But it's not my fault. The sun is a heartless, yellow bitch, what can I say? And now it's picking on her.

'It's nothing to do with the weather, Han.'

It's like … it's like yesterday she was a star…

'A *star*?'

Yeah. You know … an actual star. A ball of exploding gas. And she felt bright and twinkly as fuck up there in the sky but then she started dropping. Unstoppable, reckless, shooting star. Jess says she's still coming down, that's all. Not the sun. Not the walking. She puts her bandana back on and blows her breath up her face, holds her side. She feels sick and definitely not in the mood for this, mun, but the boys don't slow up for us. Why would they? We just get going again, faster, Jess eager to catch up with Marley. Those very long, abnormally skinny legs stride ahead of us and not once does he look back to see if we're okay or actually, if we're even still there at all. Marley's lucky. His dark skin is especially made for this weather, for this horrible, disgusting yellow sun in the sky that won't leave me alone. On Tuesday we were parked up in the car with the windows wound all the way down and Marley's thin brown arm was hanging out of the driver's side when some kid walked past and called him a Paki. Well Marley went nuts. He turned the key in the ignition and screeched up onto the pavement, and I swear if the kid hadn't jumped out of the way he would've mowed him down. Marley's no Paki, alright? Marley is Welsh. As Welsh as the sheep on the mountain. As Welsh as Tom fucking Jones.

Marley like Bob Marley, he told us. Not his real name but we didn't want to know that anyway. And that's what did it. It didn't happen when she was staring at him on the chapel steps, this dark stranger who'd just turned up in a space car. It wasn't the fag he gave her, or even because we had nowhere else to go. Marley got Jess' attention when he said he was named after a dead person. Got it and kept it, and hasn't given it back to me since. But at least we've caught up with him now. Fag in one hand, drink in the other. Strutting. He likes to strut.

'Why does everyone call you Marley though?' Jess asks him.

'Because I'm Bob Marley's bastard son.'

See, many moons ago, Bob came to Gilfach. He was in the middle of a UK tour and he found himself up on The Estate looking for some ganj.

'Big black limo. Big black cock.'

Jess giggles. Giggles like a massive girl. She could murder a bottle of Fanta, aye. Twenty bottles of Fanta, come to think of it. One after the other, ice cold and fizzy. And so could I. I'm boiling. The sun is burning my shoulders even through my t-shirt. White. 'Bohemian Rhapsody' video. The four faces ... you know the one. My bag isn't helping but the sun doesn't care how heavy notebooks are to carry around, doesn't care about peeling noses or freckles that multiply or how Jess has just fallen out of the sky. Doesn't care about anything.

'Give me a sip of that then,' she begs him, the cold can of Coke which glows a brilliant post-box red in the sunshine, the silver rim gleaming.

I'd much rather a Fanta, sweet and orangey, but right now anything will do. It looks divine, like the most beautiful thing I've ever seen in my life and I'm so thirsty that I'd probably drink it, despite it being on a boy's lips. But Marley downs it in front of us, every last quenching drop, throwing the empty can into the bushes when he's done. He wipes his wet lips and burps. Grins at Jess with spiteful, sugar-stained teeth. Nah. Sorry.

'And where are we even fucking *going*?' Marley asks him.

Billy, who is so quiet sometimes you forget he's even there at all. He must be twice as hot as we are because he's wearing a jumper, the same woolly grey jumper he had on on the chapel steps. The same woolly grey jumper he has on every day.

'You'll see,' he says, a silly, childish smile spreading across his face.

We're walking along the Taff trail, the three of us trudging behind Billy on the dry mud like a line of fed up kids on a field trip. The trail is this massive long footpath that follows the flow of the River Taff. I only know what it is because we did it in Geography once. It goes on for miles, all the way from Brecon to Cardiff. Or at least I think it does. I can't remember the facts exactly, never did like Geography much, and I've got no idea what we're doing down here. Billy's idea. But everything's turned 3D green. Dense bushes either side of us, blackberries sitting like tiny purple brains on leaves. The thought does cross my mind to pick one and squeeze it into my mouth, let the cool juice land on my tongue which feels like a dried-up sock, but knowing my luck I'll end up in hospital having my stomach pumped because it's some kind of poisonous berry, not a blackberry at all.

And with the birds tweeting and the flawless blue sky, and the intense green and the mud and the trees and the heat, we could be deep in the heart of an Amazonian rainforest instead of just down the road in Ponty. Yeah, we're on the part of the trail that goes through Ponty Park and somehow I'd forgotten that it's the summer holidays. But when we walked through the park I realised that the world has kept on turning without us. Kids were crammed into the over-crowded outdoor pool, at least fifty of them fighting for space in the water, like baked beans in a big blue tin. Ponty Park is a sort of Mecca for families around here. It's just over the bridge from the town centre and it's got a bandstand and some gravel tennis courts, swings and slides and a sandpit. And if you're a kid from Pandy you'll have definitely dipped your toes into the murky, lukewarm water of the outdoor pool. Or seen a squirrel running up a tree and squealed in excitement like it was some kind of exotic, extinct animal you'd just spotted.

Me and Jess smiled at each other. Just a half smile. It was all we could manage feeling so hot, so sick. But seeing the pool we both remembered the day Bev took us to Ponty on the quicker 130 bus. We were about seven, maybe eight, and Bev sat up on the grassy verge smoking her fags but me and Jess were down by the slippery pool side giggling at the kids who were splashing in the water and happily soaking it up, *drinking* it even, with no idea that seconds before we were in it too until a cloud of hot yellow pee purposely puffed out the side of Jess' bathers.

Today we didn't get to Ponty by the quick 130 bus or the slow 120. We got there faster than the speed of light in Marley's space car and we must be far away from the park by now. There are no people around, just us and the bushes and the river. No sound apart from the birds. And Marley's loud voice.

'I know the guy who did that,' he points, pink graffiti sprayed across the arch of the grey bridge. 'He's from Barry Island. Thinks he's fucking Banksy.'

And you want to see what it's like down there, through that dark, grey stone tunnel down by the river. It'd take you the best part of a day to pick all the needles up off the ground. They form a thin, silver nest that crunches like egg shells under your feet. A slushy carpet of orange tips and soggy, discarded bags, the drugs inside them long gone. Sniffed up noses or rubbed into gums or shot into veins. Or swallowed by hungry beaks.

'Yeah. Stupid as fuck, birds are,' he says. 'Ducks can't tell the difference between a chip from The Mighty Cod and a lump of Phet.'

They eat it, the dumb fuckers. Dip their nosy beaks into the bags that are buried in the mud. The birds in Ponty are off their tits, almost as off their tits as the druggies in Ponty. Marley knows them all on a first-name basis.

'When it rains they shelter under the bridge in the shadows and wait for the sun to go down. Then they rise like werewolves under the moon.'

And Marley pretends to be a werewolf himself. Head to the melting sky, *a-ooo*.

He can get you whatever you need and whenever you need it. And Jess grins when he says it. She still looks like she just ran a marathon but listening to Marley talk about it perks her up a bit. Speed … her new favourite thing. Likes it even better than vodka. At least she thinks it's Speed because half the time she doesn't know what it is exactly that Marley gives her. Coke, Blow, Phet, Whizz … he's got lots of different names for it. But all she knows is that she loves it. And that's all that really matters, right?

We're walking fast, breath lost half a mile back, sweating stones off, but Marley's still talking and talking, cool as anything. Our own personal tour guide.

'It's all 'Banksy's', the graffiti. If you caught a train you'd see it under every bridge on the railway line from Treherbert to Barry Island.'

Banksy from Barry Island wears this white apron, right, always in this apron now, paint down it like he's a butcher with a cleaver, just chopped up a cow with rainbow blood. And he goes out in the middle of the night, two, three, four in the morning with his cans of paint, and he's mad as a fucking snake because the speed those trains go past with the coal and shit on the back of them, all he's got to do is stumble onto the track and they'd kill him.

'Heroin. He hasn't got a clue where he is most of the time.'

And it's pitch black and the rats are by his feet wondering who this mental cunt in an apron is, and the tracks are rattling and the trains are tearing past and he hasn't got the foggiest. Yeah. Marley knows Banksy from Barry Island and Marley knows everyone. Like he knows absolutely *everything* there is to know and if he doesn't know it well then it just isn't worth fucking knowing at all. His boasting is only cut short when Billy finds what he's looking for, the reason we've been walking for a hundred million miles … the capital D shaped gap in the scruffy bushes. These ones don't have blackberries on them but if they did, I would definitely be squeezing them into my mouth, poison or no poison. I need a drink so bad.

Billy parts the leathery leaves with his hands and Marley pushes in front. He decides he's going first, so tall he has to kind of crawl through, the branches and nettles catching on his vest as he goes, grabbing at the black material like kittens' claws. Me and Jess get through alright. And behind those bushes we find a steep bank and at the bottom by the river's edge, there's a flat patch of grass and mud and stones. Nothing exciting. Just a place to sit and even more green everywhere you look, messy trees that lean over the still river, their branches thin fingers dipping into the water. This Is It, apparently.

'This? *This* is what we've been walking years for?'

Well what did Jess expect? That Billy was leading us to some kind of tropical private beach with white sands and palm trees? Where naked men with cosmic cocks buried under hula skirts would serve us brightly coloured drinks that bob with ice and curly straws and umbrellas and cherries on sticks?

'Yes, Han. Yes I did!'

'Gutting.'

Marley and Billy race down the bank but me and Jess go slowly, like two old ladies walking on an icy pavement. Last thing she wants to do is fall arse over tit in front of Marley, mun. It's bad enough she's sweating like a pig. Does she look minging, tell The Truth?

'Yes.'

'Piss off, Han. I'm lush and you know it.'

Tell her she's lush.

'You're lush, Jessica.'

Good.

Jess stands behind me and holds onto my bag. I feel like a parachute jumper. She's on my back waiting to pull the cord. If she's going down then I'm going down with her, she says, which is really nice of her. But we get to the bottom with our dignity intact. Marley hasn't seen her fall over, she hasn't embarrassed herself. That would be the worst thing in the world. He's kicked his trainers off and he's cooling his feet in the river now. Jess takes hers off, too, a pair of dirty, sweaty red Converse that she stuffs her socks in, throws at me and tells me to hold. They absolutely stink, gone-off cheese, and are falling apart badly, the black rubber line around the bottom picked off ages ago, the grubby material torn and the off-white laces frayed. She really is minging. Mine are still pretty clean despite the walk through the Amazonian rainforest.

'I'm going in,' she says. 'Cool myself down, like.'

Jess used to talk about a lot of things, but now all she really talks about is Marley. If they were together she'd get him out of those shorts and vest and into a pair of skinny leather trousers and velvet shirt. Maybe paint glitter on his cheekbones, blacken his eyes with liner and paint his nails. First things first though – make him grow his hair. It would be all dark and beautiful like Freddie's. Marley would be this, Marley would be that. And I'm fed up of it, of having to tell her straight all the time. Fed up of prizing her dumb-struck, stupid green eyes open for her because for some reason she's walking around with them closed. Is she crazy? What's wrong with her?

It's Marley she's talking about. Marley who calls her Tiny Tits. Who makes fun of Billy's long hair and calls him a girl. Who I'm pretty sure would never in a million years let someone put make-up on him. He isn't a rock star, he's a drug dealer, and his car isn't a Cadillac, it's a Peugeot 106. Marley's not a poet. All that comes out of his mouth is filth. And has she forgotten that all men are pricks? I tell her all of this again but she's having none of it. She never does.

'Stop nagging me, Han. You going to come in with us or what?'

'*Us?*'

'Yeah. Jess and Marley. Or Marley and Jess? Do you think it sounds good?'

'No.'

Jess sighs. Whatever. Suit myself. Stay by here if I want. I'm a miserable cow sometimes. Thanks.

She tip toes barefoot across the grass, careful not to tread on any stones or something sharp like a piece of glass or a contaminated needle. I drop her trainers to the ground. Stupid, stinking things – I'm not holding them for her. I go and sit next to Billy, denim knees to his chin. He's not going in the river, either. He's halfway up the bank, his messy fringe pasted to his forehead with sweat, like yellow feathers stuck on with glue. His long hair is looking extra especially greasy today.

'You must be boiling in that jumper. Why don't you take it off?'

He shrugs his shoulders, plays with the ends of his furry sleeves. Anything but make eye contact with me. Billy isn't a liar. It's just that he's shy. Jess says he fancies her, she can tell, but she'd never fancy him because Billy is about as far away from a rock star, as far away from *special*, as you can get. I wouldn't believe everything she says though. Jess is up in the sky or falling down and when she's taken Speed she thinks everybody fancies her. Probably even thinks I fancy her which I don't because I'm not a lesbian. But I am hot even if Billy isn't. I fan my t-shirt out and let the breeze dry the sweat on my belly and my back. It feels lush.

'Do you like it here?' he asks me.

'I don't know. It's only Ponty. It's just the Taff.'

'But this is my favourite place in the world.'

I look around us at the overgrown bushes and the Tesco carrier bags caught on branches. There's a shopping trolley, too, a hunk of broken metal protruding from the mud further up the river like an abstract piece of art, and every time the breeze blows it's fragrant with sewage, with rotten eggs and Jess' cheesy trainers. Billy wears a jumper in the boiling hot sunshine and Billy's favourite place in the world is up on the bank of the polluted River Taff. Billy is no rock star and Billy is weird.

'Maybe I am,' he says into the ground. 'But we all need a place where we can go to get away from it.'

'From what?'

'*Everything*. Don't you have that kind of place, Hannah?'

Billy's voice is much softer than Marley's and he never calls me Freckles, which is what Marley calls me. And Jess doesn't like it at all.

'Well, do you?'

'What?'

'Have that kind of place?'

I could tell him about Room 58, I suppose, a place sort of like that, or at least the only place I ever really liked being, but that would be against The Rules. I'll tell you about The Rules but right now a balloon is floating over the river. Quite spooky. Billy notices it first. It bobs above the trees and up until it's almost disappeared, just a blue drop lost on the already blue sky. It probably came from the park, I tell him, probably slid through slippery little fingers.

'I wonder where it'll end up.'

227

I shrug at him. I can shrug, too. I don't know. How would I know where balloons end up? Just burst, I expect. Go nowhere at all.

He looks at me all disappointed, like I've just gone and actually burst his own balloon, stamped on it. But I catch a glimpse of his eyes then, only for a couple of seconds before he turns away again. Blue, *very* blue in the sun, and they make me think about 'Dove', one of my favourite songs. Marc Bolan at his poetic best. I think it would be nice if Marc Bolan was here. If he had his acoustic guitar with him and he sung to us in the sunshine. Crouched down in the grass, strumming. Marc Bolan could make anything, any moment, lovely. Even make the River Taff seem beautiful … leafy blue.

Jess would play it all the time in her room and when I asked her what she thought it looked like, leafy blue, she gave me this lecture about colours. Back when she had other things to talk about. Colours are all to do with feelings, she said. For example, yellow is a bit of a mental colour, so bright it makes your eyes widen when you look at it, so that means yellow is the colour of Crazy. Red is Love, the thing that's a pain in the tits. Pink is Happiness, like piglets and strawberry laces, like candyfloss. Black is the sexiest colour … Death. And green is the worst colour of them all. It's the colour of Jealousy, of evil and poison and snakes.

She didn't say what leafy blue looks like exactly, just that it shivers and trembles and hurts like Marc Bolan's voice. But it is beautiful though. It's the colour that's left behind, the only colour you can see and feel when the death black and the crazy yellow and the love red and the happy pink and the toxic, jealous green has gone. We decided that leafy blue is the saddest, most misunderstood colour in the world, exactly how we both felt inside. And up on the bank of the River Taff, it's also the colour of Billy's eyes.

'I wish I was a duck,' he says, forgetting about the balloon now.

There's three of them across the river on the opposite bank. We watch them waddle awkwardly down the mud then gracefully slip into the water.

'Why do you wish you were a duck?'

'Because it must be nice to spend your day floating. Nothing else … no care in the world … just floating.'

'Why don't you go in with them then?'

'With the ducks?'

'*No*. With Jess and Marley.'

Yuck. Just saying it sends my insides somersaulting, leaves a disgusting taste in my bone dry mouth.

Billy says yeah right. Have I got any idea how dirty the water must be? And dangerous. There are weeds and undercurrents. And he bets the river bed is like a rubbish tip of dead dogs.

'Dead dogs?'

Yeah. Dead dogs. This mass grave of paws and fur and teeth at the bottom. Dogs that ran away from their owners and drowned.

'*Terrifying*,' he says, shaking his shoulders, his neck and his greasy blond hair, his whole top half like a dog himself, a wet dog. 'And even if I wanted to go in I can't swim anyway.'

'Well, you'll be a pretty shit duck if you can't swim.'

'That's a good point. Can you swim then, Hannah?'

'Yeah. Course. I had lessons when I was about five.'

He holds my gaze again, for a bit longer this time. It's as if his leafy blue eyes are giving me an X ray. I know what he wants to ask me next. How old are you now then, Hannah? But we don't ask them questions and they don't ask us. The Rules – and this is how we like it. This is how me and Jess *decided* it was going to be. There's no point in asking questions because there are no answers. Because whatever happened back in Pandy, whoever those girls were, they're not us anymore. We're like criminals on the run. We've got new identities, new lives we can shape whichever way we want. We worked it out for ourselves. It's like this … if you don't let people in, if you never allow yourself to trust them, then they can't hurt you. That's why we didn't want to know Marley's real name. It's best to keep people at a distance. Me and Jess are in control now. And we might've known them for over a week, but Marley and Billy will always be strangers. It works for them, too. They don't want to know that we're just sixteen. Not old enough to drink or to be driving around in cars with boys.

Billy doesn't ask me any more questions and I'm glad. We just sit there in boiling hot silence watching Jess and Marley because no more ducks and no more balloons have floated past. They've waded further into the river now, Marley so tall that the water barely wets his ankles but Jess is knee deep in it, her cords rolled up past her thighs. Marley's brown skin is getting darker by the second and Jess is actually glowing like the sun itself in her yellow t-shirt. I don't like it. I don't like that they're down there and I can't hear what they're saying, what it is that's making Jess laugh so loud. I suppose Billy is leafy blue and Marley is black and for some reason he makes Jess a disgusting mix of red and pink but all I am is green like the 3D world down by the River Taff.

I'm the most toxic shade of green you can get.

Van Gogh'd

We're on another planet.

This planet is known as the The Estate and it orbits in a far-off galaxy called Gilfach. Gilfach is only six miles away from Tonypandy but it might as well be in a different stratosphere. One spin on its axis will see day change to night like any other planet, but Life is different here. Life is turned up full volume, soundtracked by police sirens and domestic disputes, the thunderous roar of space cars that zoom around without insurance. Its magnetic field is what pulls the police cars and riot vans in, and when the galactic winds blow they shake the dirty trainers that dangle from telephone wires. An atmosphere that is hostile, that's poisoned with the smell of burned-out cars and the dog turds which form craters in the pavements. This is where they live together, Marley and Billy, like some kind of very odd couple.

The Estate – one hundred and sixty-five houses on top of a big bendy road. Detached council properties that are grey pebbledash replicas of one another, apart from the ones that are special – the windowless ones, panes of glass blown out by asteroids in the shape of bricks. Marley and Billy don't have jobs but Marley doesn't need one. He makes his own money and plenty of it. Ask him and he'll tell you that the Normal World is crazy, not us up here spinning in the cosmos. Just think about it. We're getting fucked all day long while they're busy working and paying their bills. Marley has a lot to say about the Normal World. Marley has a lot to say about everything.

He's the closest thing to God here. There isn't a house he hasn't been in on The Estate and he can tell you the names of every dodgy, otherworldly fucker who lives in them. And when they come down, when they're no longer stars high in the sky, they're as hostile as the air. They stare at us, me and Jess. We're aliens who were abducted and brought here in a Peugeot 106 spaceship, except we came uninvited. But they don't need to stare at us. We're fully aware that we don't belong here. We're from Tonypandy, a planet we once thought was weird but now realise is actually quite normal compared to here. We had dreams and they were nothing like this. This isn't home but it *is* where we live now. Where we're like caterpillars, chrysalis in a fucked-up cocoon. One day we'll break out, when we find a way to push through. Because we're still butterflies. We *are*.

It's not really much better inside the house. Every room smells of damp and old socks, a warm stew of wet towels, weed and takeaway food. And when Jess can't quite manage to swallow it back down, it smells of sick, too. The Artex on the ceilings is a smoke-stained yellow and the hot water runs out of the taps when it feels like. You won't find any things … the things that normal houses have like photographs and ornaments, clocks and lamps, or a telly or a washing machine. Not even a settee. Just empty rooms and plain white walls, a threadbare brown carpet that's grimy with God knows how many years' worth of spilled beer and ash. Me and Jess sleep on the floor upstairs in the small spare room that is no more than a cold box and we brush our teeth with our fingers because we left our toothbrushes back in Pandy.

But we mostly spend our time out in the kitchen, sitting around a wooden table that wobbles, four equally shaky chairs. The two of us are in the kitchen right now and spread out across the table is a crumpled, silver takeaway tray and a half empty bottle of vodka, an orange lighter and a pack of fags. Not the cheap Spanish ones Jess is used to, but Jess would smoke a shoe if it was all she had. Oh, and Bev is here. She's on the table as well and it's got me thinking. Mothers are funny things really, aren't they? Mothers are like a jigsaw puzzle and you're the piece that was always missing but they never knew they lost until they found you. And no one forces them to but they do it anyway. They have sex with your fathers and then nine months later you come out of them and they sort of like you for a while. You're small and sweet and a tiny part of them that can only ever be theirs but then years and years later, when they've decided you're old enough to look after yourself, they expect you to be thankful for All the Things they've Done For You, reminding you every single day that you should kiss their feet because they're the ones who gave you Life. Hilarious!

I haven't heard my mother's voice in well over a month and it's odd hearing Bev's again. She isn't really on the table but Jess' mobile is, and Bev is on loudspeaker.

Why won't you just tell me where you are, Jess?

'Because it's none of your business, Bev.'

Jessica.

'*Beverly.*'

Where are you, Jess? We're frantic here, love. Both of us are.

'*Both* of you?'

Yes. Hannah's mother's going spare.

Jess shakes her head and smirks, annoyed at how silly she was because for a second, she thought Bev meant that her father was back. What an idiot, she is, to think he might've still cared.

'Do you really want to know where I am, Mam?'

Yes. *Please.*

'I'm on another planet. Didn't you get my postcard? I sent it first class.'

Is Hannah with you?

'Hannah King is dead.'

This isn't a joke, Jess. Are you with your friends or what? That Lucy girl you used to bother with? Is that where you are?

'*Ha.* Oh, Beverly. You are a fucking funny one, aye. Crack me up you do, mun.'

Just tell me if Hannah's with you.

'Yes, Bev. Hannah's here. Happy now? Or do you need me to take a picture of her holding today's newspaper?'

Just come home, Jess. You've made your point now.

'And what point is that, Bev?'

That you're angry at us. We know. We're sorry. We...

'Look at you. You're giving me an headache, mun. We're not coming home, alright? We're sixteen. There's nothing you can do about it. We're *free.*'

Jess leans across the table and presses her lips to the speaker. Jess is a bit drunk. Jess is singing ... 'I Want to Break Free' then drops back in her chair, hysterical. We're sitting opposite each other in absolute stitches but then Bev goes and spoils it. She starts to cry as loud as we were laughing, starts to beg. Stop it, Jess, just stop it … her voice is broken and desperate. Please, love. *Please.* Just come home. She tells Jess that she loves her very much which really does it. Jess picks the mobile up and puts Bev out of her misery. She hangs up on her with an aggressive stamp of the button, the stupid, massive baby. But Bev only rings back, a loud buzz against the wooden surface, the mobile slowly nudging itself towards the edge of the table. And again and again and again. She's relentless. Buzz buzz fucking buzz. We just stare at the screen as it pulses green until eventually Jess turns it off.

'Thinks she can guilt trip me into coming home, does she?'

She kicks out at the wobbly table leg by her foot. It sends ash bouncing out of the tray that's still swimming with last night's barbecue sauce, a stodgy blood-red river floating with chunks of leftover chicken balls. Jess lights a fag with the orange lighter and then angry clouds are puffed into the sweet, damp reeking air. Why on earth would we go home, back *there*, when we've got it made here? It's a bit mental, she knows, and we don't have our toothbrushes and she can't get the taste of sick out of her mouth very good with her finger, but at least here there's no one shouting, no one fucking nagging – crying.

'Right?'

'Yeah. I do miss Cass though.'

'That's because you're a filthy lesbian, Hannah King.'

As if. I just miss it, that's all.

'Miss what?'

Staying up all night long in the purple, lava lamp-light, watching *The Mama Cass Television Program* on repeat. We've played that tape so many times I know the script and all the songs off by heart. It's like we've gone deaf, like we've Van Gogh'd ourselves. I suppose Jess has just forgotten all about her.

'I haven't forgotten her, you tit. How could *anyone* forget Cass Elliot? 'Monday, Monday'. Is it Monday?'

'No, Jess. It's Thursday.'

Well whatever. Do I remember that album, the one where Jimi Hendrix is all orange?

'Yeah. Why?'

'Little Miss Strange, that's what I used to call you, Han. I might

234

not know what day of the week it is but I haven't forgotten *everything*.'

It's not just the music though. I do miss Cass' voice the most of all but I also miss Jess' walls. The glitter and the feathers. And I miss waking up to Marc Bolan and his lovely, sad eyes.

'We'll get new posters, mun.'

'How? Where?'

Jess doesn't know how or where but we will. Is it seven yet or what?

'Don't know,' I say.

'Well have a look at your phone then. I'm not turning mine back on tonight. He said to go up at seven.'

I know what he said. I'm not thick.

'He's going to make you look like a ghost, Han.'

'What do you mean?'

Dark as chocolate, Marley's skin is. Like … like someone's gone and painted a melted bar of Galaxy all over him with a brush. Mmmm. She could murder a bar of Galaxy. Or some Rolos. Or a Crunchie or a Twix. Actually, a Snickers!

'He's black, almost. And you're a ghost. Almost. Look at your arms. Look how *pale* they are.'

Jess is spitting lemons at me across the table. Her breath is sickly and bitter and her tongue is sharp. They jump out of her mouth like yellow stones and smack me right in the face. She's been pointing out my faults for the last hour. How I haven't kissed anyone before. How many freckles I've got. He'll be rough and I'll probably bleed and catch something nasty because he's more than likely riddled so I need to make sure I use something, okay? And he doesn't fancy me at all, did you know? It's just because I'm *there*. Jess ain't bothered though, is she? Why would she care that he doesn't want her?

'What time is it now, Han?'

I get my mobile out of my bag which is under the kitchen table. Half six. Jess taps her fingers against the wooden surface, a soundless piano, clicks the orange lighter on and off. She rips tiny pieces off the fag packet and then lights them, watches them burn to nothing. Jess can't sit still.

235

'You scared, Han?'

'Not really.'

'Bet you are. I would be if I was you. I bet Marley's used to skinny girls. Not that I'm saying you're fat or anything. Have some of This. It'll settle your nerves.'

The kitchen is full of This. It's like a sweet shop in here but instead of pick n mix bags there's money bags and they're kept up in the broken-doored cupboard above the sink. Jess pushes it across the table. This money bag is stuffed with white powder like sherbet. Marley gave it to her this morning.

'I'm not nervous, Jess.'

She sighs at me, disappointed, bends down and digs around inside her trainer.

'What about one of these then?'

'Where'd you get them from?'

'Took them from Billy's room,' she grins as she shakes the tiny, see-through bag of pills at me.

Oh he won't notice, mun. Even if he does, so what? Billy won't mind. Especially now that she's fucked him. This morning, upstairs in his room.

'No idea why I ever thought it would be special though. I should've known better, really. It was just *fucking*.'

And Jess explains it the way only she can. In beautiful, disgusting detail. They were kissing on his bed and his tongue felt like a fucking eel, and then she pulled his jumper off and she wishes she hadn't because it was absolutely minging.

'You want to see his skin, like. All up his arms and on his chest. Like some kind of burns victim.'

Billy likes to cut himself with whatever he can get his hands on. Razors, pieces of glass, knives and scissors. Jess reckons that's why he stole our Jesus glass from outside chapel.

'Why though?'

'I don't know, Han,' she says, tapping one finger against the side of her head. 'Because he's bonkers. Because his mother's dead or something. I wasn't really listening. Told you, he's Kurt Cobain.'

Billy would be dull enough to kill himself as well.

'Rockets, bells and poetry,' she snorts. 'Ha. As if.'

236

It was awkward, clumsy. It didn't even feel good at all and his cock, it was *tiny*.

'Because you're such a cock expert, Jessica.'

'I saw loads on the Algarve beach when I was on holiday. And I saw my father's plenty of times in the bath. So no, I'm not a cock expert, *Hannah*, but I know a tiny cock when I see a tiny cock, alright?'

Alright.

She lights another fag and blows even angrier, more lemony smoke rings at me. And with a melodramatic gag she says it went everywhere, mun.

'What did?'

'His *cum*.'

All over the pillow and all over her knickers. Like hot candle wax up her back. Absolutely fucking vile.

'And then he went and told me that he loves me. Have you ever heard anything so ridiculous in all your life?'

Yeah. How ridiculous. To think that someone could love you. Although she is right. Billy doesn't love her. He can't possibly love her because he doesn't know her, not like I do. No one could ever love Jess the way I love her.

'He's got nice eyes though, I suppose.'

'Oh, like I care about his eyes, Han. Eyes are just things in your head.'

Jess says you can't fuck a nice pair of eyes, can you? She just wishes he was special, that's all. That he glittered like Freddie Mercury or made her skin tingle like Marc Bolan. But Billy will live until he's eighty-seven years old and die of something boring, like a stroke or just close his eyes in his bed one night and never wake up. No car crash for him. No dramatic, beautiful, sudden death. That's why she nicked these. Got to have something to show for fucking him, something to numb the Shame. She opens the bag and places one, tiny and round and white, on her tongue, gently, as if it's a piece of unleavened bread at communion.

'Go on, Han. Have one. You aren't going to die. *Please.*'

I wouldn't be surprised if she wanted me to die. Because if I died then I wouldn't be going upstairs in eleven minutes … she asks me to check again ...wouldn't be about to do something she says doesn't bother her but Jess forgets that I know her inside out. She sends the pill sliding across the table like an ice hockey puck, and it pleases her when I swallow it down with a mouthful of vodka that tastes even deadlier than Bev's.

'So what about Marley? How will he die?'

'Don't know. Don't fucking care.'

'Maybe he'll die of AIDS, like Freddie, if you say he's riddled.'

'No,' she scowls, horrified. 'He absolutely will not die like Freddie fucking Mercury! Marley will be old. Very old. Even older than Billy. One hundred and seven. Pissing and shitting himself. Liver spots and hair growing out of his nose. Fingers folded over with arthritis.'

Jess says Marley will be so senile he won't even recognise his own minging, Paki reflection in the mirror. Look shit in a leotard, he would. Don't know why she ever fancied him! Yuck. And apparently it's quite funny when you think about it.

'What is?'

'Nah. Never mind, Han. Not saying. Forget it.'

'Just *tell* me.'

It doesn't take much dragging out of her. It's been lying on her chest all day like phlegm and now she coughs it up, yellow and lemony and sour ... all over me.

'Well, this is kind of like Robbie Jenkins and Lucy Williams all over again.'

'How is it?'

'Just is. One of my friends getting with someone I like. *Liked.*'

'Jess, this is your idea. I don't even want to ... I'm not ... I won't if you don't want me to.'

Why wouldn't she want me to? She never said that so don't go putting words in her mouth now. Besides, I've got to.

'I've *got* to?'

'Yeah. You don't want to be the only sixteen-year-old girl in the world who hasn't had sex, do you? *Do* you?'

No.

'And we don't want them throwing us out because then we'd have to go back home and we can't do that, can we?'

238

No.

And more importantly, I can't let her down. We promised we'd both do it today and best friends don't break promises. We said we'd be normal, for once in our pathetic fucking lives. She'd fuck Billy and I'd fuck Marley because for some absurd reason, despite all my problems, all those bad things she's been telling me about myself that I already know, he wants me and not her.

'So go on then, Little Miss Strange. Get lost.'

Jess smiles at me. The worst, most sarcastic, painful, fake smile you have ever seen. I tell her to look after my bag and don't you dare go in it. But as if she would. Wouldn't want to touch the bag of doom, would she? The bag of mystery!

'Shut up, Jess.'

'Whatever.'

I get lost, leave her in the kitchen with her lemon-sick breath and fags and vodka and stolen drugs. Billy's gone for a walk. Something to do with the wind turbines up on Gilfach mountain. I'm halfway up the stairs when I stop and wait for it. I don't know what to call it … but for the feeling to kick in, the thing that Jess says makes her an actual star in the sky. I'm waiting to be shot Up, catapulted to a better place where I'll want to stay forever. But it doesn't happen. I'm still here.

Racetracks

We're like a family. We all have our positions in our family car. Marley drives and Billy sits next to him up front. And then in the back Jess is behind Billy and me Marley, his seat rolled as far as it'll go. My legs are crushed. I am never comfy in our family car.

Right now Jess is using the window as a pillow. Her eyes are red and bloodshot, like those plasma globes you get in science-type places, the ones you touch to make zaps of colour inside the orbs. She's massaging her temples, desperately trying to knead the self-inflicted pain away with her fingertips.

'You'd better not spew in here,' Marley warns her.

Because he swears to God, she'll be ejected out onto the fucking motorway. And I believe him.

Marley's car is like his baby. Customised wheel trims that look like UFOs and an engine that growls like a lion. A sound system especially built in, its pumping speakers black and round like massive vinyls behind us on the back seat. We hate Marley's music though. Marley's music is heavy with drums, not guitars, and the last thing Jess needs when she's feeling like this, when she's actually, properly dying. His precious Peugeot 106 is washed and waxed every day without fail and each time we leave the house he has to walk around and inspect it. People are jealous things and people on The Estate are handy with their keys.

In the back of Marley's car it feels like you're on a rollercoaster. My belly does somersaults as we plummet down the big bendy road out of The Estate. Jess cups her hand over her mouth and then swallows hard, makes a face and shivers. Dying looks disgusting. She isn't wearing a bandana and her long black hair is shimmering with grease and just to annoy her a little bit more Billy, with his white trainers up on the dashboard, turns the music down because he's got a story to tell us. He's pointing at the wind turbines we pass on the mountain. Jess is rolling her eyes.

Billy had this friend called Rhodri Davies and he lived in number 21 on The Estate ... the house with the front wall with some of the bricks missing, have we seen it?

'His father accidentally knocked them out with the bonnet of his red Escort, the same night they just disappeared, Rhodri and his mother and father.'

People said they owed money to the housing association but they were probably wrong because they were the same people who reckoned Billy and Rhodri were brothers.

'That's because your mother was a slag,' Marley tells him. 'You haven't got a clue who your father is so for all you know, Rhodri's father could've been your father.'

Billy says no. Absolutely not. So what if they both had blue eyes and blond hair? That was just a coincidence. It was gossip. Nasty, vicious gossip. Because gossip on The Estate is like the rain when it pours down. It doesn't stop. And the people, they're like drains and they suck it up and then spew it back out when it gets too much to keep in. Billy doesn't want to talk about his mother anyway. He wants to talk about Rhodri Davies and the turbines.

'Fucking poof. Homo. Shit-stabber!'

Billy tells Marley to stop. Just *listen*. Him and Rhodri Davies would bunk off school and trek up the mountain. Take them an hour to get there but it was worth it. They'd lie on their backs on the grass under the turbines and when they're going off around your head like that, it's *so* amazing and the noise is just immense. They'd have a picnic with the mushrooms, too, the ones they'd picked on the walk up.

'It's such a buzz when you find one. It's like unearthing gold. Magic mushrooms look like tiny jelly fish. These mushrooms mess you up really bad.'

Before you know it you're in the back of an ambulance and then you're on a ward in the hospital on a bed and these loud, patterned curtains are rolling across the rails like traffic going past you. And then you're throwing your guts up in a monkey-nut-shaped cardboard bowl and your sick is grey, almost silver, and you've got a Chinese nurse rubbing your back and she's got six heads and six stethoscopes and she's trying to listen to your heart but you don't know where that is, you think it dropped out in the ambulance on the way.

'Then…'

But Billy's story is over when Marley turns the music back up. Shut it, poof, no one cares about your gay windmills, alright? And Jess is glad. Rather listen to the monotonous drums than Billy's voice. He's boring. Maybe he wouldn't have been if he'd choked on his own sick and died in the hospital. But Billy is alive. Billy doesn't glitter one single bit. Then an idea pops into her head. It lights her up, makes her sit forward in the seat.

'Can you get us magic mushrooms?'

'Are you fucking serious, Tiny Tits?'

Stupid question. Marley can get his hands on anything, can't he? So of course he can get us magic mushrooms. And he will. If she's good.

Gilfach slips further and further away in his wing mirror. I watch it. Jess smiles to herself, feeling a bit better, more awake, now that she's opened the window. I'm waiting for her to say it, which she does soon enough.

'Fingers crossed. Today could be our lucky day, Han.'

And what a day for it! *Dying.* The sun is shining and the wind is blowing through the car. Lush. It'll be like on winter mornings, when you've got to chisel the ice off your windscreen. Only it'll be our brains that'll need scraping off, lumpy and soft and red on the just-waxed glass like strawberry trifle. Our bodies will be lifeless, two china dolls thrown across the road, our faces smashed into the concrete.

'Old Mrs King will be beside herself,' she says. 'And Bev will be hitting the bottle big time.'

This is why we aren't wearing our seatbelts. We never do because we're waiting, *hoping* for it. Failing brakes or burst tyres, a car into the back of us or even better, a massive heavy goods lorry head on. Something that sends us revolving out of control. Something that makes Marley's UFO wheels spin until the next thing we see is glass and then blood and then concrete and then God and glitter and disco balls. Jess always thought it would happen to us but now she's absolutely positive. Because our lives are at risk every day in Marley's car when we're skidding around corners, around the tight roads of the Valleys that are made even tighter by the cars that park either side. Other vehicles on the road are just obstacles to us. Things we dodge, things that try to slow us down. Sometimes we make dents and scratches, clip wing mirrors and smash bumpers, but whatever. We can't stop. No time. Red lights and pedestrian crossings, old ladies with walking sticks and mothers with prams and speed cameras, fuck them all. The streets of the Rhondda are our racetrack and we ride it, *fast*.

I don't tell Jess The Truth. I don't want to ruin it for her, make her lose hope. Because if she thought she wasn't going to die then she'd have nothing left to live for. Marley does slam his brakes on quite often, and he does drive through red lights and sometimes we only narrowly, by split seconds, miss other cars and lorries, and trucks and motorbikes and walls and lampposts, but we miss them nonetheless. Always. And do you know why? Do you know why we're still alive? It's because Jess is wrong. We are not going to die. Not today or tomorrow and not before we're thirty, either. Once we might've. If Jess had done something with her art and if Laser Ludlow was right about me, if I was actually talented, if I'd written books and changed the world and hadn't turned out to be such a massive disappointment. But not anymore. We popped our own balloons. We let go of our dreams, just watched them float away. Now me and Jess aren't worth saving, aren't special, at all.

We aren't on our way to The Club, we're on our way to Barry Island. We go lots of places. Family outings. Marley takes us with him to drop things off and pick things up, and when he disappears behind front doors with Billy, me and Jess are left waiting in the back of the car.

'Aren't you excited, Han?'

'For dying?'

'*No*. For Barry Island, mun.'

Why would I be? Not like I haven't been there a million times before. Barry Island is the same as Ponty and Porthcawl in that you won't find a kid from the Rhondda who hasn't been. It's a place of pilgrimage when the sun comes out even though it's only an hour away on the train from Pandy and definitely no exotic getaway. The fairground is run down and rusty, and the sands are a dirty yellow and the sea is tinged a browny-blue.

'But don't forget Fred,' Jess says, 'who blows in the wind with the grains of sand and sea salt.'

Marley turns the music down again.

'Who the fuck is Fred?'

'Fred West. Haven't you heard of him? Him and his wife butchered loads of women. Poor old Rose, mun. Buried the bodies in their garden.'

'Yeah course I've fucking heard of him.'

'Bet you didn't know that Fred's ashes were scattered down Barry Island though, did you?' she says, determined to impress him, to say something once, just once, that he might be interested in.

But Marley is not impressed. Marley is very selective about his morals. He thinks it's fucking stupid, fucking *sick*. Not the best advert, is it? Come to Barry Island. We've got a fairground and a sea and a mini golf course and oh yeah, don't forget, a murderer buried on the beach. He tells Jess to shut it, stupid slag … she's giving him a headache talking bollocks. Jess keeps on though.

'It's not like he's still there. He would've blown away years ago. You're not going to be eating your chips and a bit of Fred West lands in your gravy, like.'

'Fred West was a freak. And I said shut it, Tiny Tits. Do you want to walk the rest of the way?'

I know she's dying to climb up onto her soap box and explain that there are no such things as freaks, or good people or bad people, only people who were born and then those people got taken nicely or dragged down different paths. Fred West was dragged. Fred had a bad childhood. Not as bad as Rose's but they both had their normal person wires messed up so it wasn't their faults how they turned out or what they did. Obviously Jess doesn't tell Marley that he's wrong. She wouldn't dare, wouldn't want him to think she's a freak, too. So she changes the subject.

'Do you remember that school trip we went on to Barry Island, Han?'

We weren't bothered about the rides or the arcades, were we? We just wanted to find a crab and then we were going to bring it home and keep it as a secret pet in one of Bev's Tupperware tubs.

And when we got there we searched that entire beach with our spades for hours and hours, until the bottoms of our feet were freezing and raw, but we just couldn't find one. Remember?

'Yeah. I remember Jess.'

'Maybe this time we'll have more luck.'

Because Marley promised her that we'll go to the beach today ... we'll make the most of the last dregs of summer. Jess is bored in the house, bored of driving around in the car. She's used to having a holiday abroad, isn't she? White sands and stunning blue seas, naked men on nudist beaches. But no holiday was planned this year, not even before we left. And now September, and summer, is nearly over. It's all very tragic – all very unfair. But we soon see the sandcastle sign for Barry Island and Jess is a kid again, as overexcited as she was that day on the school bus. So we're not in Portugal, or wherever else she would go with her parents, but we are out of the house and away from the bleakness of The Estate. Jess is going to push me in the sea, apparently. Going to eat her bodyweight in sticky doughnuts. And we *will* find a crab.

'Oh, and rock,' she says, clapping her hands together. 'I want rock ... stripy blue rock!'

We're bombing down the road. The weather is okay. It's not cold and it's not hot. It's just okay. On the right-hand side of us there are small boats stagnant in a muddy dock and up ahead in the distance cracked red letters that spell out *Log Flume.*

'We're *definitely* going on it,' Jess decides.

She needs to get out of the car. *Now.* We have to find a crab and eat some doughnuts and buy a stripy blue rock ... and she needs to stretch her legs really bad, even though I'm the one who's been stuck in some kind of foetal position for nearly an hour. Marley tells her to calm the fuck down. How old is she, fucking seven? First we've got to pay Banksy from Barry Island a little visit anyway. Remember 'Banksy', don't we, the crazy cunt in an apron? One of Marley's best customers.

We drive past the Log Flume, turn the opposite direction to the sea. Marley powers up hills and charges through lights and screeches around roundabouts because the streets of Barry also make excellent racetracks. Me and Jess slide clumsily across the backseat until with a jolt we're parked up outside a tall block of council flats that are as grim looking as the houses on The Estate. We're coming in too, Marley says, taking his key out of the ignition, turning buttons off. Why? Well why not? Would we rather just wait in the back for them again like a pair of fucking dogs?

So we get out of the car. We don't need to be asked twice. I stretch my legs and Jess stretches hers. I tell her that her lace is undone but she can't be bothered to do it up. She lights a fag and so does Billy. Billy smiles at her but she doesn't smile back. This is a right shithole, she moans, when are we going to the beach? But Marley doesn't answer. He's obsessively making sure every door on the car is locked. He checks the handles twice, three times – that every window is shut properly. We are a very strange and dysfunctional family.

'Banksy' sounds mental, spraying graffiti on bridges in the middle of the night on the railway lines. 'Banksy' is a druggie and this place looks really dodgy … if our mothers could see us now walking towards it. Jess even says it, exactly what I was thinking, like she knew, like it's written right through me like a stick of stripy blue rock.

'Imagine Mrs King's face. Or Bev's if she thought I hadn't brushed my teeth tidy in weeks or changed my knickers since fuck knows when.'

Hmm. I don't really want to imagine my mother's face. Or Bev's. Or the fact that Jess hasn't changed her knickers which is pretty disgusting, I didn't know *that*. Yesterday I even borrowed a pair of hers and I won't be doing it again.

We're walking up a never-ending flight of twisting stairs inside the building now and our trainers are loud and echoey against the stone steps. Jess trips over her lace. It makes her embarrassed and nasty although apparently she doesn't care so stop gawping at her like that, alright?

Alright.

It smells as bad as it looks in here – really strongly of pee. I feel dirty just being here although I feel dirty anyway. My teeth have grown a layer of tacky skin. My hair is itchy and heavy.

'Could be on the beach now,' she moans again, out of breath, and she bets all the crabs will have fucked off by the time we get there.

246

Eventually we reach the top of the stairs. I look down at this infinite zigzag of grey steps and feel a bit sick. We're very far up. Lactic acid kicking in and great – Jess has got a stitch now to go with her Headache of Death. And her back. Her poor back is killing because of sleeping on the floor every flipping night like some sort of…

'Some sort of *tramp*.'

Moan moan moan, a skipping record.

Then Marley leads the three of us along a dingy corridor, the air wet with damp and the weird silence broken by our different footsteps that echo once again. The drab white doors of the flats either side of us are identical, letterboxes and metal plaques with numbers on, but not one door. We find his around a corner and it's like a pocket of colour, of life, in this comatose building. His door has been completely graffitied over. There's pink stars and ice-blue diamonds, fat cartoon-style balloons twisted into dogs and swords and flowers with brightly coloured petals. White rabbits with droopy ears, green eyes and pink top hats, and in the middle of it all, the focal point, is a clown with a yellow afro.

We're staring at it, hypnotised, when Marley tells me and Billy that we are not coming in.

'Me and Tiny Tits, we won't be long. You two stay here.'

'Why can't we come in as well?'

'Because you can't, Freckles. That's why.'

Marley grins down at me, sneakily. He smells like petrol and this close to him in the doorway, I catch the beer and smoke on his breath. Jess shrugs. No big deal, Han, just wait by here. And I think she likes it, you know. I think we're back in school outside Room 58 and she's shutting the door in *my* face. In her head, Jess slams it. It knocks me out. How do you like it, Hannah? I'm just left there with Billy who looks as if he's about to cry.

'What's wrong? Why can't we go in?'

'I didn't know,' he says, pitiful.

'Didn't know what?'

Billy won't answer me. In fact he walks away down the corridor so I follow him. He's hanging over the stone bannister now, looking down into the pissy chasm of grey steps. Maybe he'll jump, I think to myself. It's the sort of thing he would do. And what would I say to him if he told me right now that he was going to? If he climbed up and threatened to leap off would I say no, don't do it? Would I bother to talk him out of it because really, Billy has nothing to live for anyway, does he? Billy is even worse off than me and Jess are. At least I've got her and she's got me. All Billy's got is Marley and Marley doesn't care about anyone but himself and maybe his car.

I start to undress him there and then with my eyes. I pull his jumper off over his head and then when he's half naked I see the cuts. The cuts Jess talks about with such disgust. The old white scars and the brand new red ones and all the bad stories behind them that we'll never know, never care to. I almost feel a bit sorry for him but that goes away when he begins to cry … and he's proper sobbing into his sleeves. I wish he would just jump off now, please. Plunge through the air and land face first at the bottom, smack! Legs and arms bent and broken into a letter Z, blood seeping into a puddle around his smashed up blond head … *anything* but cry.

I don't get to ask him why, why are you crying? Because he runs away again, this time so fast I know I couldn't catch him even if I tried. His feet clatter loudly down the steps. I look over and watch him go. He jumps them … two, three, four steps at a time … and then he's gone. Out of the building. I'm on my own. I'm standing outside the door and knocking on it, punching the clown in his round red nose with my knuckles. But no one comes out. I knock again and then I push it, shoulder it. The door's been locked from the inside. I get my mobile out of my bag and ring Jess' but then I remember that she left it in the house because Bev's been doing her head in texting her non-stop all week.

My heart is beating so hard it hurts. I've got butterflies that make me feel sick and those butterflies only settle down when we're back in the car and even then, I can still feel them going. I don't know where Billy is and we don't drive around to look for him, either.

'Fuck him,' Marley says, and I agree, because he left me, he left me on my own.

Thrown himself off a cliff into the sea, he reckons, or jumped in front of the Barry Island train and good fucking riddance. He'll be back soon enough. Or maybe not.

Jess smokes one fag after another, *devours* them actually, not smokes them. I count … eight. Jess smokes eight fags in fifteen minutes. That's a hell of a lot, even for her. Marley stops to put petrol in and for a few minutes we're left alone while he goes to pay. She doesn't speak to me, just stares at the back of Billy's empty seat burning holes in the shiny leather with her plasma-globe green-red eyes, poking clumsily at the bag of thick white powder Marley took out of the glove compartment and threw in her lap before we left. I can see him standing in the queue in the garage, towering above the people in front of him, and I do think about saying it. Come on. Let's just go … let's go *now* before he comes back, Jess. We're somewhere near Cardiff, that's all I know, and there are no houses around, just open road and signposts, but we could thumb a car down … we could *walk* back to Pandy if we really wanted to.

I sit there in the smoky silence though instead waiting for her to tell me what just happened but not a single word is swapped between us. I don't know why I don't ask her anything. I've got a hundred questions that I need to scream out. Maybe I don't want to know the answers. I just watch the people on the busy garage forecourt, the people who belong to the Normal World, going about their Normal Day. And the reason I don't say it, the reason I don't open Jess' door and drag her along the side of the motorway, is because all those people outside the car are aliens now. Because there's no way we can go home.

We're passing the wind turbines that spin sleepily on the mountain, the burned-out cars and the boarded-up windows and the trainers dangling from the telephone wire. We didn't find a crab or a stripy blue rock and we definitely weren't ready to come back yet. It's like waking up too soon from a really good dream.

March 1972

I had to wake up. Come on, Sleepy Head!

But it was five o'clock. AM, now. That meant we'd only actually been asleep for an hour but Jess was nagging, relentless. You know how she gets when she's got an idea in her head. She said we were alive, mun, and sleeping … sleeping was just a waste of *life*. My eyes were heavy, closing themselves, but I got up. If I didn't she was going to tip her bottle of beer all over me. And then when she looked she saw that she had an unopened text on her mobile from Bev. Bev must've sent it earlier in the night but Jess was too drunk then to see her own hands in front of her face, wasn't she? Let alone tiny words on a tiny green screen. It said…

r u ok love? text me back. mam x

And that's exactly what Jess did. Two words, uppercase. The same two words she always texts Bev back with. FUCK and OFF.

Now it's six o'clock. PM. And we've been drinking vodka for all those hours and Jess hasn't really stopped talking since Bev replied with a sad face emoticon. Jess is like a toy you can't switch off.

'You look cute in that t-shirt,' she says to me. 'I'd fuck you.'

Turquoise Marc Bolan, gold Gibson Les Paul guitar. No she wouldn't.

'Yes I would, Han. As long as when I closed my eyes and licked you out I imagined you were Freddie Mercury.'

'But Freddie Mercury didn't have a vagina. I do.'

Am I sure? Because she reckons it's all ice down there in my knickers. Yeah. She bets my vagina is like a giant Tip Top. Cold as fuck, sting your lips kind of cold … and if she licked it her tongue would stick to it and she'd never be able to get it off and then we'd have to walk around like that *forever*, her face on my minge.

'Sorry, I mean *vagina*.'

We're lying on our backs next to each other on the landing. The space is narrow. We don't really fit in it at all. We're looking up at the square in the ceiling that leads to the attic. Jess is wearing her yellow

Queen *News of the World* t-shirt again and to be honest, I'm sick of looking at it. She holds my hand and threads her fingers through mine, strokes her little finger against my little finger. I wait for it.

'It's so funny,' she says. 'How it's bent. Like *you're* bent.'

'You're the one who just said they'd fuck me.'

She was only joking, stupid. And nah, she loves my bent little fingers. And my tiny hands. Wouldn't change them for the world.

'Why are you saying that for?'

'Because it's true? Because they're cute, Han ... like you.'

Hmm.

I play with her fingers, too. Rub the flat of my thumb against her smooth nail. Pick at the crusty scab down the side of her hand. Sliced it open on a smashed bottle a few days ago. We're just lying here touching each other's hands. It's weird.

'Wonder what's up in the attic,' she says.

'Just junk, I expect.'

'Then why did Billy tell us not to go up?'

'Don't know.'

Well Jess knows. It's because he's got bodies up there. This is his cover – pretending he's all shy and sweet but that's what all the girls thought, the ones he lured off chapel roofs long before us. And now they're up there in the attic. If we slid that square across right now the smell would hit us seconds after the flies flocked out like bats.

'Dead bodies smell like bacon, did you know?'

Like old, rotting meat. Billy chopped them up himself and you see? It all fits. That's why he cuts himself. Not to feel better, not because he's sad about his dead mother, but because he's practising with skin and blade. He covered their torsos up with dustsheets and duct-taped their organs and other various bits and pieces up in cardboard boxes. The skulls were wrapped in newspaper like fragile china plates and the brains bubble-wrapped like glass bowls. The bones were finely ground and then smoked with weed in joints and the teeth kept as souvenirs in pretty trinket boxes.

'What about the fingers and toes?' I ask her.

'Oh, they rattle around shoe boxes,' she says, 'like a collection of badges and buttons and guess what?'

251

We're his next victims.

I would say Jess is drunk and that's why she's talking rubbish, but Jess has been talking rubbish since we're seven years old and back then the only thing we were drinking was blue-top milk in cartons with biscuits.

'That's it,' she says. 'I'm going up. Coming with me?'

'No chance.'

'Coward.'

Jess lets go of my hand. Climbs up onto the bannister and walks the thin wooden rafter like she's a gymnast on a balance beam. I tell her to be careful. She tells me to fuck off. She manages to slide the square across and then hoist herself up through the hole. The mobile in her back pocket becomes her torch. DCI Matthews who's disappeared now, off in search of bodies. I hear banging and the sound of Sellotape ripping and then everything she finds is shouted out like she's on the *Generation Game*. A mirror. Toys and cars. Wigs and shit. *Cool*. Some perfume. A lamp. Photos. *Minging*. Who the fuck would wear that? A toaster. A tin of tomatoes, what the..? A human brain. Two livers and one kidney. A severed cock and a bowl full of bitten-off nipples. Some kind of blender. Balloons. Party poppers. A hairdryer. Batteries. A house phone. An eyeball and a dismembered arm. Clothes. Loads of clothes, Han. Black bags … *God alive*, like Aladdin's fucking cave up here!

Her nose is grey with dust when she pops her head through the hole again. She's going to throw some stuff down now and I've got to catch it, alright?

Alright.

We sit crossed-legged on the landing and go through it all, this Jenga tower of cardboard boxes she's built. Look. *Shampoo*. She waves it at me. Minty, liquid gold. We've been washing our hair with soap and cold water. Or at least *I* have. She lifts the lid up and sniffs it. Smells okay to her. There you go – have it. She throws it at me. Maybe now I can stop moaning, yeah? Jess doesn't care about washing. What gets her excited is the black nail varnish she finds, its top stiff and caked down with a crusty black skin but eventually she prizes it open with her teeth. We haven't painted our nails in ages. The black we came here with was picked or bitten off weeks ago. She paints mine first and then hers and you'd swear we'd just had a professional make over at a posh salon. With just a few flicks of a wet brush we feel brand new, or just like ourselves again. Like losing something precious and finding it.

It doesn't take us long to work out that these things must've belonged to Billy's mother. Billy did tell Jess one night after they'd fucked, that she died of something boring and now Marley lives here with him or some shit, but she fell asleep halfway through it, the most boring story she'd ever heard. Even worse than that book MacfuckingBeth.

'*Macbeth* was a play.'

'Well *sorry*. I'm clearly not as academically gifted as you, Han, am I?'

The things that should be downstairs, the things a normal house has, have been stuffed up in the attic, hidden away exactly like dead bodies.

'Maybe we should just put it all back, Jess.'

We're like grave robbers going through Billy's private things like this. Excavating … disturbing bones.

'Chill out, Han. Don't be so dramatic.'

'Just put it back, yeah?'

'Not likely. There's loads of stuff we can use by here. Wonder if there's any tampons.'

Because Jess is sick of stuffing tissue up her minge. It's just not civilised, mun. She's elbow deep in a box like it's a lucky dip now, but no tampons are found. She's squirting perfume bottles and sniffing the misty air. Opening a leather purse but there's no money inside. We come to one box marked photos and she really shouldn't but Jess tears the brown tape off anyway. I rub the skin of dust off the front of the frame she gives me with my finger and see it's a photograph of Billy. He's wearing a green school uniform. He's got the same haircut he's got now, the exact same thick blond fringe and leafy blue eyes. Jess snatches it back off me. Why am I looking at him like that? Boring, miserable prick. She slams it into the box on top of the other glass frames, not bothered if it smashes.

'They'll be in sixth form by now, won't they?' I say to her. 'Evan and all the rest of them.'

We didn't even bother going to collect our GCSE results. Jess will have failed English, but not Art. She gave *that* coursework in.

'So? Didn't mean I cared.'

'Do you think he's taken English for A Level?'

'Who, Evan? Fuck knows.'

She bets Lucy Williams has taken art though, the stupid bitch. She can't draw a nose to save her life.

'I really loved art. I miss the smell of that room. The dough and that ... the paint ... you know?'

Jess stops ripping boxes and for a second, she looks a bit sad. Like she's just remembered something, a memory she threw into a hole in her head and buried underneath a mountain of lyrics and vodka a long time ago. Yes, I know. I miss Room 58. And I sort of even, only a tiny bit, hardly anything at all really, miss Laser Ludlow.

'Well don't bother,' Jess says, brutally stripping Sellotape once again. 'Because she doesn't miss you, that's for sure.'

What do I think Laser Ludlow's doing? Sitting there in Room 58 crying, wiping her tears away with her scarf because I'm not there in my chair anymore, because her favourite little academically gifted pupil has gone and left her alone with all the thick-os of Pandy?

'Get a grip, Han. Anyway, let's not talk about school anymore.'

Jess sorts the stuff she wants to keep into a box and then carries it downstairs to the kitchen where Marley and Billy are. Marley is standing by the sink, Billy sitting down at the table. He stares vacantly at the box in Jess' arms knowing that we've been up in the attic, that out-of-bounds place he warned us not to go. We've gone through his private things, stolen them, but he doesn't say a word, like we knew he wouldn't ... couldn't.

'We found balloons, *look*. Let's have a party!'

No one's up for a party, Jess. There's nothing to celebrate. We're tired. But she is. She'll have a party all by herself then, boring bunch of bastards. Especially me.

She blows them up until the grubby lino is lost under an inflatable blanket of blue and purple and green and pink. Jess is drunk enough already but she drinks some more anyway. Swigs

from a bottle of vodka, from half-drunk, stale ones of beer …
whatever she finds. Billy still looks like he's seen a ghost. Marley is
shaking his head at her, childish fuck. Then a pink balloon is
punched at me, served like a tennis ball into my head. Jess finds it
hilarious. It bounces off my chest and floats in slow motion down
to the floor. Apparently I was supposed to catch it.

'What's the matter with you all, mun?'

Us? What's the fucking matter with *us*? Is she having a laugh or
what? Marley tells Jess that she's the one with the problems. Big
problems. Mental. Absolutely fucking psychotic, she is.

'And you'll be tidying all this shit up later, putting it back where
you found it.'

As if we live in some sort of palace!

He's by the draining board filling money bags with a dessert
spoon, trying to concentrate, and if he spills any then he swears to
God, she'll be sleeping out in the garden tonight, tied up to a pole
like next door's Pit Bull. And like next door's Pit Bull, doesn't
matter how hard she cries she won't be let back in, alright? And I
don't know what possesses her to say it, why she doesn't just sit
down and shut up …

'Oh cheer up, *Paki*.'

Yeah. The party is over. Jess has gone and crushed a nerve. You
fucking what? What did she just fucking call him? He slams the
spoon into the empty sink. Sense of fucking humour? Alright. He'll
show her sense of humour now. Something really fucking funny.
Billy holds his hands over his ears as Marley goes around the
kitchen stamping on the balloons, one massive bang after massive
bang like gunfire, until there's carnage, limp pieces of wrinkly
rubber everywhere.

'See this?' Marley says, so angry he spits, waving a just-filled bag
in her face, a wad of white. 'And this is the funniest part now … I
was going to give it to you but now I'm not going to fucking
bother.'

Thinks he's joking, does she? Mad eyes as dark as the blacked-
out windows of Bob Marley's limousine. Nah. If she wants it then
she's going to have to suck someone else's cock, not just 'Banksy's'
… work for it. She's going to have to suck every single cock on The

fucking Estate until she's choking on cum, until her insides are swimming in cum. She'll be crying cum and pissing cum and shitting cum, and every time she speaks she'll be *spitting* cum.

'Tell him to give it to me,' she says to him, but Billy is still holding his hands over his ears, pushing them into his skull so hard now I think it'll burst, like one of the balloons.

Marley holds the money bag above her head, teases her with it. His arms stretch so high Jess has got no chance of reaching it. She's snatching at the air, can't grab it, no matter how high she jumps. He's laughing and holding her off and she's screaming and shouting. Give it to me, you spiteful cunt! Just fucking *give* it to me, you prick! She pulls his vest and pinches the skin under his arms, tries to wrestle it off him but Marley is much stronger than she is. And his final act of revenge – he shakes the bag out onto the kitchen floor, the white powder falling like sleet. Jess is on her hands and knees trying to catch it, scooping it off the dirty lino with her fingers. I can't watch this any longer. I tell her that I'm going upstairs, is she coming? *Jess.* But she doesn't come.

I close the door behind me, on my back on the floor of our room now. It's very dark in here, only the orange streetlight burning dimly through the shut curtains. I look at the time on my mobile, my mobile which never beeps with messages and calls like Jess' does. 9.38 PM and pitch black already. It's almost the end of October and the nights are getting dark earlier and earlier. I feel around and find the thin blanket Billy gave us a couple of weeks ago when it started to get really cold. It stinks of fags, of Jess actually, like her bedroom back in Pandy which always stunk of fags, the sheets on her bed and her cushion covers. I think about the two of us there, top and tailed in the purple light, stabbing each other with our toes for space on the mattress, and then a lump the size of a melon grows in my throat.

I swallow it down, *breathe.* Just lie there listening to cars coming and going outside, the hopeless howls from next-door's garden, Jess comes up eventually. Maybe half an hour later or something. I hear her trainers land on the floor. One thud followed by another. She stumbles and fucksakeHans over one of mine. I haven't bothered to undress and neither does she. She lies next to me on the floor and steals the blanket which I then steal back and eventually, after lots of kicking and pulling and toe stabbing, we come to some kind of silent agreement that it's sufficiently covering the both of us. Although I feel bad when she shivers so I let her have a little bit more.

'Thanks,' she manages through chattering teeth.

'You smell really awful, Jess.'

'Do I?'

'Yeah.'

She spins over and puts her nose to my chest, inhales me.

'So do you, Han.'

'Do I?'

'Yeah.'

We laugh. For a few seconds and then it's not funny anymore. The dog is still crying next door, wolf-like howls that only make the darkness more spooky, more perfect.

'Why are we always on our backs?' I ask her. 'On the chapel roof and in the bushes and on the landing.'

'What do you mean?'

'We're on our backs in the dry mud and shade, the sun spraying through the gaps in the leaves and twigs above us, a greeny yellow kaleidoscope. *Again.*'

But Jess doesn't know what I'm on about. I ask her if she's alright.

'Of course I'm alright. Why wouldn't I be, you prick?'

I don't dare ask her any more questions. What happened after I left the kitchen, anything at all … so it's not my fault that she cries. She cries so bad it makes me cringe.

'*Jess.*'

'What?' she snaps. 'I'm fucking *sorry*, alright? I'm sorry for crying.'

'I just don't like you crying, that's all. Why are you crying for?'

'Because the world's shit, Han. Why is the world so shit?'

I can't pluck up the courage to turn over and hug her. It's not that I don't want to. It's like … it's like my arms are cemented, bolted down. Like I'm strapped up in a straitjacket. So instead I tell her about all the other much worse places in the world where we could be. Merthyr, for example. And what about Africa? Kids there have to walk miles for water and when they find it there's pigs swimming in it. And Iraq, where there's always a war going on. What about places where they cut off your hands and your feet just for stealing?

'But what's the point of it all?'

Because sometimes she feels like doing it, you know. Getting Billy's razor and slashing her wrists open. Bleeding until there's nothing left inside her. Not one single drop.

'Don't say that.'

'Well I'm fucking saying it, aren't I? What's wrong with me, Han?'

'Nothing. Nothing at all.'

Well, there must be. They all knew it, didn't they? Robbie Jenkins and her father. And Marley. Even Bev would rather get pissed than hug her. But why would she want to hug Jess though, innit? Why the fuck would *anyone* love her? Or want her?

'But imagine we'd had it easy growing up, Jess. We would've turned into normal human beings. How awful.'

I don't get the chance to finish. I was about to say that she's off her head, yeah, completely and absolutely mental, the biggest mess I know, but that's the way I like her. That I wouldn't change a single thing about her and that I'm glad none of them want her because I need her all to myself. I don't get the chance because she climbs on top of me, stamps her hands either side of my shoulders.

'I am sorry, Han. You know that, don't you? And you know what for, don't you?'

Yes.

'And you know I love you, right? That I'm just a big massive mess and I can't help it.'

'Jess … I think we're probably the messiest girls in the world.'

'How can you just say it like that? Why aren't you sad?'

'What do you mean?'

'I mean … why aren't you *ever* sad?'

She's only just realised it. I never cry and I'm never drunk, not drunk drunk. Not like her. And I'm never angry and I'm never sad at all. Never fucking *anything*.

'It's because I'm an iceberg,' I tell her. 'Or maybe there's something wrong with me, too.'

258

Jess doesn't lie and tell me that there's nothing wrong with me like I just did for her. She presses her lips to the middle of my forehead and holds them there. And then she moves them all the way down my nose, Eskimo kisses, and onto my cheeks, dabbing me with even smaller kisses there that are soft and wet, down to my neck where she stops and buries her head.

'*Jess* … please stop crying.'

I lift her mouth up onto mine. She tastes like apples. I don't know why.

'Don't you tell me where to kiss you, Hannah King.'

She regains control of her shaky voice, like a pro. Grabs my t-shirt at the collarbones, two fistfuls of material. She'll kiss me wherever she wants to fucking kiss me, alright?

'Alright.'

But she kisses me right there again, her tongue twirling around mine like a salty, appley snake. She's shivering badly now, her hands especially as she tries to undo the button on my jeans. It's apparently my fault that she can't.

'You and your stupid fucking awkward jeans.'

'You and your massive shovel hands.'

I laugh. I can't help it.

'What the fuck are you laughing at? Are you laughing at me?'

'We're lying on our backs in the dry mud, the sun spraying through the gaps in the leaves and twigs above us, a greeny yellow kaleidoscope. *Again.*'

'Are you off your tits or what?'

'Do I taste like sherbet lemons, Jess?'

What? Shut up. I should just shut the fuck up. She takes her t-shirt off and then her bra. She's so fast and rough with it I think she's snapped the clips right off. And when the button on my jeans is prised open exactly, and I mean *exactly*, the same way the top of the black nail varnish was earlier, she slides her hand into my knickers and I'm not even thinking about how mental this is, how it's Jess, *Jess*, but about how disgusting I am now, too. I haven't changed my knickers in four days and if there was ever a time for having clean knickers on, This Is It.

'I love you,' she lies.

It's a lie because she doesn't love me at all. She loves Freddie Mercury and that's who I am right now, like I would've been Robbie Jenkins that day in the bushes. Freddie Mercury is who she's kissing, not me. I've got big, piano-key teeth and a massive, cosmic cock. I've got a voice that changes the world. I'm someone special, not just Hannah King.

But I can lie, too. In the orange dark she doesn't have to be Jess, either. I pick the prettiest face of them all. I take her bandana off and launch it across the room because she wears top hats, not bandanas. I mess her greasy hair up around her head with my hands until it's all mental and knotted because it's March 1972 in London and she's singing 'Telegram Sam' just for me. How are you, alright? It's good to see you. Mickey Finn is shaking maracas and Jess has got glitter-drop cheekbones, lips like lightning. She's cross-legged on the stage, strumming an acoustic guitar as the screams leap out from the crowd. Velvet jacket and blue flares. Sweat and lights. Beautiful and trembling.

In the orange dark we are silhouettes and we kiss some more. I'm Freddie Mercury, I know, but she's got no idea that she's Marc Bolan.

'Tell me you love me, Han.'

'Why?'

'Just say it. Even if you don't mean it.'

'But *why*?'

'Because I need you to.'

'Well I can't. Sorry.'

She punches me hard in the ribs and hurts me.

'Fuck, Han. I didn't mean it.'

She'd never hurt me on purpose. Never ever do that. It makes her cry again. It's okay, Jess, I tell her. It's *okay*. But I still don't have the guts to tell her that I love her. If I didn't love her then I could just say I did because it would be a lie and that would be easy. So I sing it instead … the chorus to 'Life's a Gas'.

That's when she climbs off me. That's when she throws the blanket over my face, buries me in it. That's when she tells me to shut up, *Lezza*.

Banana Milkshake

I didn't want to go. Couldn't be bothered to get dressed but he was adamant, keeping on about History and how me and him, we were going to make it by watching the moon pass between the Earth and the sun. It sounded really boring to be honest, and the only reason I got up and washed my face and put my trainers on was because he promised that afterwards, he'd take me to the café on Pandy Square.

For making History we had to wear these special protective glasses that made everything red when I put them on. I stopped and checked my reflection in Woolworths' wide black window and I won't lie, I looked really cool. These glasses had thick square frames and plastic arms, so big they pretty much covered my whole face. We got them at the counter in Somerfield when he paid for his newspaper. Bev wasn't working. We saw her and Jess in Pandy as we were walking through. Jess was wearing these glasses as well, said something about Bev making her come, but we didn't stop and talk for long. We had to find somewhere to sit which was difficult because Pandy town centre was so packed. I don't think there were any people left in their houses. Apart from my mother, of course. My mother had too many things to do to be worried about making bloody History.

Lots of those people talked to us. They mostly asked him how he was feeling. We saw Jill even though we prayed she wouldn't see us. But she did. She pressed my dimples with her disgusting, red-nailed fingers and told me I looked like cowing Roy Orbison, mun, even though I had absolutely no idea who he was. She wasn't there to see the eclipse. She was picking her prescription up from the chemist. Her leg had been giving her jip all weekend and the cowing doctors were useless and ta-ra now take care, beaut. We were very glad to see her go.

But everybody else was wearing special glasses like us. He had to take his normal ones off to put them on and the reason I was

261

staring at him funny like that was because he looked weird. He just didn't look like him without them on. And that's when Pandy just sort of stopped still, sort of froze in time. Everything went quiet as if the volume had been turned right down on the red world. People were like statues gazing at the sky but we were sitting down on a bench as the moon passed between the Earth and the sun. It was boring like I knew it would be, but at least we were going to the café next.

I still kept my special glasses on even though it was all over. Everyone else went back to looking at the world in green and blue but I liked it better in red. The pavements and the lampposts were red, and the shops and the cars, and the pigeons pecking at the ground were like mutants. The coolest thing of all though was that the clouds in the cherry sky were pink like candyfloss, like the biggest, fluffiest balls of candyfloss you can imagine. I walked by his side through the rosy world all the way to Pandy Square where the 120 bus drove past us on its way to Ponty. That was also red, the windows and the wheels, and the driver, too.

We picked a table in the corner, the same table we always picked, a booth with red leather seats. I knew they were actually really green but I had my glasses on, didn't I? The café was empty apart from the big fat Italian lady who was putting cakes swollen with cream and jam onto plates and into a glass display cabinet thing. And when she came over I asked for a banana milkshake, please, which she wrote down on her pad of paper with her Biro pen. He ordered a coffee and then she turned around and left us.

That lady was so fat you wouldn't believe it. She was the fattest lady I ever saw. I watched her slowly waddle from the counter back to our table, my milkshake and his coffee balanced on a silver tray. She carried it so carefully. My milkshake came in a tall glass tumbler with two stripy straws sticking out. I blew them until the cold pink bubbles that I knew were actually yellow rose to the top and tickled my nose.

'Why don't you take them off?' he went to me. 'I can't see your lovely face like that.'

I said nah, I'm probably going to keep them on forever to be honest, and he just shook his head and smiled. It was times like that I actually felt happy. I don't know why I didn't the rest of the time because it wasn't like I didn't have any friends or anything. I had Jess who, despite us falling out every day, I knew liked me deep down. I had a mother who bought me things, who didn't ever leave me, not like my cousin Kyle whose mother left all the time, whose father got a new girlfriend every weekend. And I had nice clothes and expensive trainers unlike a lot of the kids in my class. But there was always something there. Something that nagged me, made me feel like I was itching inside.

In the café booth and in the car, it was like I was in a bubble and nothing else mattered. The café wasn't as good as the car, mind, but I liked the screams of the coffee machine and picking the squashy foam from the rips in the leather seats. He drank his coffee and I really wanted to tell him that I loved him but I couldn't. I just sort of hoped he knew. He had his normal glasses back on in the booth. He read the back pages of his newspaper, and he looked like my dad again.

They took his glasses off when they put him in the coffin. I shouted at my mother and I tried to explain that he couldn't even read his newspaper without them so wherever he was, he was going to be in trouble. But I was being bloody stupid. He was dead … and dead people didn't need glasses. She kept them on top of the telly at first with the gold frames opened out on the black ledge. She'd even polish them with her duster. It was like he was still there, you know? Like he hadn't really gone. He was in the living room watching me eat. He was in The Quarter when Jess showed me drawings in her sketchbook. And when I stayed over her house he was there in her room listening to us talk. He was spying on us as we ate chips from Phony Tony's van on the pavement and when I was happy in English he went and ruined it. He was outside the window standing in the car park staring at me. He was in books. He wouldn't even leave me alone when I went to sleep and when I wrote things in my notebook he was behind my shoulder reading them. That was the worst thing he did to me.

But then one afternoon I came home from school and the glasses were gone off the telly. My mother had put them away in the drawer. Got rid of them like she'd already got rid of his clothes and his pigeons. I wasn't upset. He was finally gone, like Nanny was gone, and I was glad because now I didn't have to think about him all the time. I soon forgot what he looked like, how many freckles he had on his face. I stopped thinking about the Bad Things ... the smell of sick and hospital food and bleach, the automatic doors on wards and the buttons on lifts, the doctors and the tubes and the blood.

I refused to go to the cemetery, that place me and Nanny would pass on the 120 bus. That's where he was now and that's all he was ... another stone up on a mountain. And all I had left was my mother who didn't listen, who broke her promises and lied to me. Everything will be okay, Hannah ... the biggest lie of them all. She had no right to tell me it would be okay because she didn't know anything ... not even who Joan Baez was. But Mum was lucky. I wished that I'd never known Joan Baez, either. I wanted to forget her voice like everything else, all the other Good Things because they were even worse than the Bad Things. So I threw the tapes from the car in the bin and I didn't ever open that drawer with his glasses in because now I could write again, the most important thing in the world.

I sorted the bad things into sentences and paragraphs and similes. I emptied it all onto paper, like how it must feel to empty your wrists with a razor. So yeah, this is why I'm never sad.

Rocketshaped

That's the twelfth. I've been counting again. When Jess is worried she smokes even more than usual. She finishes it and posts it like a letter out of the small gap at the top of the window and then it somersaults all the way back up the road.

'It's fucking December,' she says. 'Too cold for the beach now.'

Another fag is lit. Lime-green lighter. Another pissed-off face pulled as she sucks on it, drawing every iota of nicotine, of comfort, out. She hasn't mentioned dying since we left the house which is weird because if ever God had the opportunity to take us, then today would be the day. Black ice lurks in dark, dangerous patches on the frosty ground, waiting patiently for overzealous tyres – for careless, spinning UFO wheels. Billy says yeah, it is cold. But at least it's Christmas soon. Something we already know.

'*Ha.* We haven't even got a Christmas tree. What's the point in Christmas without a tree? And Christmas dinner. There's just no point is, there? No. *Pointless.*'

Christmas can suck Jess' cock. And I just get back to staring out of the window, not wanting to talk or even think about it at all. I see my reflection in the frozen glass and I won't say something ridiculous, like I don't recognise the person staring back at me because I do. That person is me, just a little bit skinnier than before. My jeans are really loose on me now. My t-shirts sag. The white lines on the road below merge into one long, continuous colour as we're speeding past the other cars like we've got a tank full of rocket fuel. Billy is rolling a joint on the dashboard, still talking rubbish. Maybe it'll even snow. Marley turns to him.

'Well if it does then you'll have to tie tennis rackets to the bottoms of your trainers.'

Because just as kids need presents on Christmas, druggies need their fixes. And no way will Marley even *attempt* to skid his car out, are you fucking serious? The big bendy road will turn to a slope of pure ice, like the pavements, and see, when the boilers break down in the houses, and when the dog turds are covered over and the space cars are buried in white and the shop is closed, it's not bread and milk they worry about running out of. But I don't think it'll snow at all. It's just been raining nonstop. It's made The Estate even greyer, more miserable looking, than usual. From the kitchen window we've been watching fountains spit out of cracked drainpipes and mothers in waterproof coats pushing prams down the pavement, their babies under the rain covers like dolls in cellophane boxes. Maybe it will snow, I don't know. Maybe it won't. Either way, we don't really care.

I see the sandcastle sign for Barry Island, the boats in the mud and then the Log Flume in the distance, and so does Jess but she's not excited like before. She only lights herself another fag. It's *winter*, she says again, too cold for the fucking beach … but I like the weather this way. In winter the world just seems cleaner, crisper. It's like I've been asleep all year and now I'm wide awake. Winter means my freckles are gone. Winter has cleverly coaxed Marley out of his vest and shorts and into a black hoodie and grey tracksuit bottoms. And I like him better the less of him I can see. We weren't holding our breath but it turns out he was telling The Truth today. He parks the car in a space on the front and we're told to get the fuck out, before he changes his mind. An hour, that's all we've got, and he'll pick us back up by here and he won't wait around.

Jess gets out quickly. She shoots two fingers at the space car as it flies away at a million miles an hour, the neon-blue lights turned on because that's how dark and grim it is, despite it only being three in the afternoon. It leaves us both shivering on a cold and windy Barry Island front. Jess' hair thrashes around her face like a greasy black whip which doesn't impress her one bit. She spits out strands like they're poison and screams at it … stupid fucking wind! Why have we come here in flipping December? Should've just stayed in the house. And she doesn't know why Fred West wanted to be scattered down here because look at it, mun … it's an absolute *shithole*!

The wind is raw and it sobers us up, or it sobers me up anyway, like a splash of freezing cold water in my face, like I've suddenly got my senses back again. The salt spicy air itches my nose and when the seagulls screech in the overcast sky above us, it actually hurts my ears. The main fairground is closed today. The small rides out on the front, the teacups and a turnaround train, have also been chained up and the patio tables and chairs, packed with people eating fish and chips in the summer, have been put safely back indoors. Barry Island has shut up shop for the winter. Life has gone inside to keep warm. But not us.

The wind tries to push us back but we fight it. Walking along the yellow-stoned front without any coats on, we must look mental. My arms are rough with goose bumps and my numb fingers are glowing a rosy red. Jess finds a suitable spot for sitting on the wall, her back to the beach because the beach, like Christmas, can suck her cock. There's no one else here apart from us. Not a single soul in sight and it's quite eerie, like a perfect postcard that's been coloured in all wrong. With black and grey charcoal pencils instead of blue and yellow watercolour paints. Jess is struggling to light her fag, so frustrated with the wind blowing the flame out it looks like she could cry. I make a shield around her with my body. She doesn't even say thank you.

'*December*,' she just moans again, her cheeks smacked red.

Jess is the most miserable girl in the world. I stand facing her with my foot up on the wall. She's got her favourite t-shirt on. I'm not allowed to wear it. Any of the others but not this one. Marc Bolan on black cotton. Born to be a unicorn on the back in white ironed on letters and on the front he's sitting in some grass in a pair of red dungarees playing an orange guitar. He looks the most beautiful he's ever looked. I'm wearing Jimi Hendrix on red and I can't remember when I last changed out of it.

'And that fucking bag on your back. You're like a snail, mun. Why don't you write anything anymore?'

'I do,' I lie. '*Sometimes*.'

'Well I haven't seen you. You always used to be scribbling something, you scribbling snail.'

'What do you think's going on in Pandy?' I ask her, because I don't want to talk about writing, don't want to admit that I can't *think* straight anymore, let alone write … that there is nothing in my head.

267

'Why you asking me that for now?'

'Just making conversation.'

'You mean in Comp, do you?'

'Yeah.'

Well she doesn't think, she knows. That place never changes, like the paint on the walls never changes. It's stuck forever in some kind of time warp. Headmaster will be pacing, a robotic march up and down the corridors. Lucy Williams will be drawing shit noses down the art studio and Robbie Jenkins, his face will be plastered in juicy, puss-filled zits, his cock itching from the chronic genital warts she's given him. Kids will be smashing the shit out of things for no reason at all. Laser Ludlow will have forgotten my name already. It'll all be exactly as we left it.

'Should've burned it down while we had the chance, Han.'

'Don't you think it's weird though? Like, we're here and they're there just getting on with their lives. It's like … I don't know. It's like we died and no one noticed.'

Jess shrugs. Apparently we may as well be dead anyway. I take my trainers off and stuff my socks inside.

'Fuck you doing now?'

'I told you earlier I'm going on the beach.'

'Why?'

'Just because.'

'You're off your flipping head, Han. It's freezing!'

'Come with me?'

As if. Jess will stay up here, thanks. Her nipples are like fucking marbles, mun.

'Nice.'

I roll my jeans up to my knees. Watch my bag. Won't be long. I walk down the ramp. Jess is facing the beach now, shaking her head as she watches me go. She gets smaller and smaller on the wall as I look back, lovely Marc Bolan a blur but somehow I can still make out her miserable face. It's so extreme and defined that satellites out in space are probably picking it up on their radars. I wave but of course, she doesn't wave back. I think I can see her putting her two fingers up at me but then again she could just be lighting a fag.

The sand is *so* cold. I'm on the hunt for a shell and after looking for a bit, I find a good one. The tide is in today so I don't have to walk very far to get to the sea. I dip the shell in and scoop the dirt out of the grooves with my finger until it's completely smooth and clean. I put it in my back pocket and then walk in, let the freezing water swish the sand from between my toes. The December sea takes my breath away. The dark grey, almost black, waves crash around my feet, grab at my ankles like angry, wet hands, and I realise now that I should've stayed up on the wall with Jess. Because that's the problem with forgetting things. Sometimes, even though you try hard not to, you can't help but remember them. And when you do they come back twice as bad, twice as nasty, as if to punish you for being so stupid as to think they would leave you alone.

I remember it, how I'd stand exactly like this, on the cusp of the sea looking out at the massive black island where bad people were sent. People who lied got taken there and that's exactly where I'd end up if I told anyone lies about Griff. I'd be sent on a boat if I wrote any more bad stories about him in my notebook and no matter how loud I screamed or how hard I kicked and stamped and rocked the boat it wouldn't matter because I'd be too far out, with nothing around me but sea, for anyone to hear. But I was just a kid. It took me longer than it should have to realise that it wasn't an island for bad people at all. I should've been smarter because what I actually saw was land, another place near the sea, just like Porthcawl or Barry Island. A place where in the summer old ladies sit on stripy deck chairs with polystyrene trays overflowing with chips and wrinkled sausages resting on their laps, where in the winter, everything is dead. I can see myself on the beach with my bucket right now. A little girl in her bathers, jelly shoes cutting into her ankles as she tries to catch the drips of juice falling from the rocket-shaped ice lolly on her tongue.

I want to swim across and tell her that she can stop staring at it now wondering when she'll get sent there on the boat because her big fat Auntie Eve is lying to her. I wouldn't tell her that it's all going to be okay though because then I'd be lying to her, too. Because it's not going to be okay. It just gets worse and worse as she grows up, no matter how many things she makes up to make herself feel better. And then one day, when she's sixteen years old and wearing a dirty red Jimi Hendrix t-shirt, she'll be back on a beach again and she won't even be able to write anymore.

I hoped that Jess would make me feel better, say something funny, but I forgot about her face. I slap the sand off my feet and put my socks and trainers back on, try to rub some feeling back into my arms that are pink and stinging. I give her the shell. It was supposed to make her smile.

'Where's my fucking crab, mun?'

'Sorry.'

Never mind. We sit on the wall staring at the sea, our legs swinging over the edge with the dark brown sand below us. The wind blows it in thin, wispy clouds across the beach, and there's a ship out in the distance although you can't see it properly, it's just a black smudge on the murky canvas. Jess' eyes are unblinking as she gazes out at the grey postcard view in front of us, a dreary sky that fizzes with rain now. Tonight my hair will be extra curly, an electric ball of knots that I won't be able to brush because, you know, we haven't got a brush. I ask her what she's thinking about. She must be thinking about something.

'Not really. Just that I hope it's today.'

'That what's today?'

'The day we die. On the way home. I'm ready, Han.'

'Well I'm not.'

'Why?'

Seriously, why don't I want to die? Go on … give her one good reason why I want to stay *here*.

'Don't you want disco balls and glitter, Han? Don't you want to meet Cass Elliot?'

'Yeah. Of course I do. I love Cass. Just not today.'

'What is it, Han?'

'What's what?'

'That. *Love?*'

I'm swinging my legs, knocking my sandy heels against the wall. I'm looking up at the moving clouds that are getting blacker by the second, at the angry sea that thrashes with waves and foam and spit, and the ship that has disappeared ... just like the answer. I don't know what Love is.

"You said once that love is a pain in the tits.'

'I think Love is like socks. Or maybe it's just the people that are socks,' she says.

'*Socks?*'

Yeah. People, innit. People are like socks because socks aren't meant to be together, either. It starts off alright ... you're in the packet fresh and clean and new because you were made for each other. And you're together and it's lovely and you look good and one without the other is useless. But once you've been together for a while, once you've made holes on sweaty feet and spun around the washing machine a million times, you get lost somehow. You lose each other in the drawer or down the back of the radiator or you find yourself balled up in a wad with some other sock you like better now. Some fat, stinking sock called Pat Morgan.

'And Billy is trying to turn me into a sock but what if I don't want to be a sock, Han? What if I want to be a glove?'

'If you want to be a glove, then you be a glove, Jess.'

She will! She flipping well will.

'And if your own father can't *love* you, if he left you ... then you're really fucked, right, Han?'

Yeah. I suppose you are.

She launches the shell I gave her as far as she can across the beach. I don't see where it lands but I do know that inside Jess is as crazy as the crazy December sea. Her blood is crashing around her veins, foaming and spitting in waves, too. But she's forgotten about her mother. That Bev still texts her, that she calls and leaves her messages, that she still cares and always will. Jess has forgotten that I do actually know what it's like to be left and for me it's even worse. The people who left me are never coming back.

It's then that her mobile goes off, a happy jingling sound in her back pocket. She lifts her bum off the wall and takes it out. Bev again?

'Nah, it's him.'

'Who?'

'Marley.'

'*Marley?*'

'Yeah.'

They'll be here in a minute.

'How's Marley got your number?'

'Just has,' she says, and she stops and thinks, one of her fatal mistakes and she just never learns, does she?

It's no big deal, mun. Stop looking at her like that. Come on.

We're fighting the wind again and the wind is coming out on top. Pushing us back, stealing our breath and our words, making us eat our own hair.

'So are we like socks then?'

'What?'

'I said are we like socks then! Me and you!'

'What do you mean now, Han?'

'You said people are like socks. Does that mean we aren't meant to be together, either?'

Nah! We're different, she shouts, her cheeks flapping, hair whipping around her face again. Me and Jess are like chocolate cake and custard, like guitars and glitter, like thunder and lightning. She doesn't know why Billy loves her or why her father doesn't, and she definitely doesn't know why we're down Barry flipping Island in December. All she knows is that Freddie was right.

'What?'

'I said all I know is that Freddie was right! Too much love will kill you. That's if you don't kill yourself first.'

Those seven words rattle behind her, scraping across the yellow-stoned ground like tin cans trailing a wedding car. Wait up, Jess, and you don't mean that … but she's eager to get back and so am I. Back to the car where the icy wind won't bite our ears. And it doesn't take long for the Barry Island drizzle to turn to torrential, pissing-down rain. The weather is just as we left it and how sweet of it to be waiting for us when we get back. It's not just the streetlights that light The Estate up now but the fairy lights, too, and if I squint my eyes like this then the colours outside the window are like a fuzzy kaleidoscope. I think we're the only house that hasn't trimmed up. All the other windows are pulsing with whites and greens and reds.

The car's parked. Button on the key ring pressed and alarm tweeting like a baby bird. Every door handle checked twice, three times. And even in a monsoon like this we're made to stand and wait while Marley completes his extensive security checks. I look up at the telephone wires. They smack about like thin, wild black belts under the sky which is electric, clouds sinister shadows that move like they're running away from something. There are no stars out. Maybe there haven't been any since we got here. They could've fallen out like Cass Elliot said and we wouldn't have even noticed.

We're absolutely drenched by the time we get in the kitchen. Jess moans, as usual, slaps the soggy packet of fags down on the table. Don't know why she's so worried. Marley will give her more. But she empties them out anyway and attempts to dry each one individually by blowing on them. Her t-shirt is soaking, too. Poor Marc Bolan's going to catch pneumonia but it's not Marley's fault we haven't got coats. Actually, that's a good question. Why the fuck haven't we got fucking coats?

Jimi's wet too but it's my socks that are the worst. A stodgy sandy mixture that's like gravel in my trainers. They squelch when I curl my toes. But there's no towels to dry with here and no heat ever comes out of the radiators. Marley announces that he's going to bed because apparently, it's hard work being that fucking cool. This is what he does sometimes. He'll go to sleep now, at 6 pm, and then he'll wake up in the middle of the night. Maybe he'll stay in the kitchen drinking with us, or maybe he'll disappear somewhere in his car. But sleep, like time, like eating and washing your hair and drying your clothes ... none of those things matter here.

He leaves the three of us sitting at the table. I'm opposite Jess whose t-shirt has glued itself to her arms, a new layer of black cotton skin. She's got her legs up on the empty chair beside me and her trainers really do stink. Billy is sitting next to her and his grey jumper looks black and his soaking wet hair more brown than blond. He's hunched over the table making a joint, drips falling slowly from his fringe onto the wooden surface. Jess rolls her eyes at me. They mean ... why the fuck can't he go to bed as well and leave us alone? Because she's decided that she wants to play I Never.

'What's I Never?'

Is he having a laugh or what? He seriously doesn't know how to play I Never?

'Nope.'

Fucking hell. *Everyone* knows how to play I Never. Jess sighs.

'Well you've got to have a drink in your hand, right, and you each take turns in saying things like, I have never stolen something, or something like that … make it as outrageous as you can.'

And if you *have* stolen something then you've got to drink. If you haven't, then you don't drink. It's simple. Even for Billy. We used to play it in Jess' bedroom all the time with a bottle of Bev's vodka but it was kind of stupid because we already knew everything about each other. There were no shocking revelations, or at least, we kept those things to ourselves, things like Bev getting punched in the face, things I kept in my bag. We were almost as good at keeping secrets as we were at getting drunk. Tonight we're using cans of beer. Marley stopped in the shop on the way back. Not as good as vodka, but it's all we've got.

'You do one, Han.'

'I can't think. You go first.'

Jess grins. Alright then.

'What you grinning at?'

I'll soon see. Her eyes are pulsing at me, mischievous, and with pursed lips she says.

I never *fucked* a girl.

She swigs the can with long, loud gulps. And when it's empty she shakes it, slams it back onto the table with a smug look on her face. Billy's eyes nearly jump out of his head. And go on then, I'd better fucking drink.

'Oh, like that is it, Han?'

Ashamed, am I? There we are then. Jess has got the message. Loud and flipping clear. And she also decides it's her turn again.

I never told a lie.

Jess downs another can and then one is slid across the table towards me. Apparently I need to drink a fucking keg of it, never mind a can. I drink. Maybe Billy drinks as well but he's no longer playing, we've decided. It's just me and her armed with embarrassing questions, who can humiliate the other the most. We're like human cans ourselves. We've been shaken violently and now we're opening each other up. I suppose it was bound to happen sooner or later. We've been waiting months, maybe years, to explode.

I never broke a spit shake.

'As if, Han.'

Jess doesn't drink. Jess is a liar.

'What? Got something to say, Han?'

'Yep. Two words. Lucy and Williams.'

Okay then. If I'm going to play dirty, we'll play dirty.

I never told my best friend not to speak to me ever again when I didn't mean it, just because I'm stubborn. Because I'm full of fucking shit.

'Okay, Jessica.'

I never kissed Evan Jones.

'Bitch,' she says. 'We were only eight. And I only did it because you dared me. There weren't even any tongues. Alright then, fucker.'

I never cried listening to Cass Elliot.

'Fuck you.'

I never cut pictures of serial killers out of a magazine and stuck them on my wall just to piss my mother off.

'Suck my cock, Hannah. Okay...'

I never missed my mother.

'Yeah, yeah.'

I never missed my father.

'Aye, alright, Han. Whatever.'

I never fancied my English teacher.

'Piss off, Jess.'

I never wanted to go home.

Well neither of us drink, do we? Our cans are super-glued down to the table. As if we want to go home. Christmas or no Christmas. Christmas dinner or no Christmas dinner. We stare at them until Jess decides she's drinking hers but it's got nothing to do with the game because she definitely does not want to go home, alright? She takes her feet off the chair so that she can kick me, right in the shin and before she quickly pulls her leg away I kick her back, twice as hard. And it's not over yet. The questions keep on coming. We hit them back and forth across over the table like ping pong balls, aggressively, each one of us hoping one of the blows will knock the other out. We're trying to hurt each other and I don't know why. I never this, I never that. Okay and whatever and fuck you. Billy sits there awkwardly smoking his joint, the cloud of smoke like a halo above his hair which is gradually drying back to normal colour. It's then the flash appears outside the kitchen window. A shock of white lightning, like the sky just took a picture of us. And then the deep grumble of thunder. The rain gets louder. Jess gets drunker.

'I hope there's a storm,' she says. 'Fuck the snow. I love a good storm.'

'Well, I hope there's not a flood,' Billy says. 'I can't…'

'Yeah. We know. You can't swim.'

And then the jingling sound. From the mobile that's somehow survived the weight of her arse sitting on it all day. Bev must be up late, I think to myself. Drunk, no doubt, probably really badly, the most depressed she's ever been because it's nearly Christmas and she'll be missing Jess. Yesterday she left an answer-machine message. She'd bought Jess a present and it was under their Christmas tree waiting for her. Bev also said she'd seen my mother in Pandy and she looked very sad, like she hadn't slept in weeks.

FUCK and OFF. But Jess is thumbing the buttons on the keypad far too many times to be writing those two words.

'What you saying? Is it Bev?'

'Yeah. Course it's Bev.'

'What are you saying then?'

'Nothing, mun.'

She may as well tell me. I'll only go through her messages later when she's asleep, like I always do. I lean across the table and try to snatch it off her but she keeps hold of it.

'Fuck you doing, Han, you *psycho*?'

'What are *you* doing?'

Jess can't cope. Who do I think I am? Her mother? I'm not her mother! It's like living with the fucking Mafia, mun. She goes through the graveyard of cans on the table one by one, shaking them to see if there's any dregs left, but they're all empty.

'Fuck this,' she says, getting up with a dramatic scrape of the chair leg. 'I'm off to sleep.'

And I'd better not follow after her. Either of us. Because she wants to be on her own, alright?

Alright.

'Do you think I should go after her?'

Is Billy thick or what? Jess wants to be on her own and when Jess wants to be on her own, it's best to leave her.

'There's a Christmas tree up the attic,' he says. 'In a box. Maybe that will cheer her up. Will you help me get it down, Han?'

I tell him no. I will not help him get it down. A Christmas tree won't cheer Jess up. Now, kitchen taps running with vodka instead of water, *that* would. Can he get her that for Christmas? No. Didn't think so. I don't want to think about Christmas and I don't want to even talk at all. I just want to know what Jess said to Bev and it bugs me so bad that I can't stay down here just going over it in my head.

'Goodnight,' I say to him, although I don't mean it at all.

I walk up the stairs with my bag on my back. The landing light doesn't work so I light the way with my mobile and open the door to our bedroom which is also in darkness. Maybe she'll try to kiss me tonight. Maybe she'll apologise for the nasty things she said downstairs or maybe we'll just go to sleep. I call her name but she doesn't answer. Stumbled into Billy's room drunk again – she does that sometimes. I shine the light on my phone around again, a green beacon. I illuminate his single bed with no sheets, a balled-up, cover-less duvet thrown on a mattress. A wooden tower of wonky, broken drawers and on top a wad of bloodied tissue, two orange Bic razors and a lighter. Fag papers. Socks and one of Jess' bandanas strewn across the floor. But I don't find her.

I'm standing on the landing just staring at Marley's bedroom door and it all becomes glaringly, disgustingly obvious. It wasn't Bev who text her at all. Cass is singing. I can hear her. It's like she's actually here. Alive. Coming from a speaker booming through my head and this whole house. 'Baby I'm Yours'... yeah right! I push Marley's bedroom door open and this crazy, fucked-up planet freezes over. It just completely stops turning.

1

They say that when a baby is born it's the happiest moment of its mother's life. Ask mine and she'll tell you they're talking bloody rubbish.

She sits down on the settee next to me when she's found the albums in the drawer and then they're carefully placed on her grey skirt lap. The sticky labels on the front of the packs tell you what photographs you'll find in each. And this is the one she's been looking for. Its label reads … *Hannah King. Six Pounds Eight Ounces.* She's shuffling through the stack inside and I'm thinking, I must be honoured. I've never seen the flames like it, burning and blazing full blast behind the glass. The gas fire was turned up especially for me. And here it is. She gives it to me, a photograph of her. My mother. She's got long hair and she's lying on a bed wearing a hospital gown and long, white socks. She's cradling a baby wrapped in a blanket. That baby is me and I was born on a rainy Saturday night in August, and this is how it all went.

My mother is down the pub with Jill and the rest of her friends. Tonight's a one off. She doesn't normally go out on a Saturday night but they've had these tickets booked for months. They're there to see an artist who sings songs from the 60s. Lovely voice. It's the middle of summer, what feels like the hottest summer my mother has ever known despite the rain tonight, and she's as big as a whale. Imagine it. A whale in a bloody yellow-flowered frock and sweating cobs! What a sight she must've been.

Inside the pub it's like a sauna what with the lights and the people and the smoke. She's fanning her face with a beermat while Ray is calling the bingo numbers out onstage before the artist comes on and she doesn't win a penny. I was bad luck from the bloody start. Jill turns to her and she goes, that baby you got in there is a cowing Omen. Like that boy on that film, she said, and she wouldn't be surprised if I came out with 666 on my forehead. Jill might've been steaming, but she wasn't far wrong, you know.

Because on that clammy night in August, by their table adorned with ashtrays and various coloured bingo markers, under the hot lights and with Jill knocking the whiskys back like they were water, I was inside my mother's big belly just about to ruin not only her night, but her life. I kick like mental and her waters break. Cowing Hell, Jill screams, as she downs her drink before sprinting up the street in her heels to fetch Dad. Ray even announces it over the microphone. Baby King is on the way.

Dad fumbles around the coat pockets in the passage for his car keys. He doesn't understand ... I'm not due for another two weeks yet. Well Jill had never seen him in such a state but he managed to compose himself enough to drive down to the pub with Jill running on the pavement alongside him. Mum is out on the pub doorstep by the fag bucket, cursing me. Nine bloody quid she paid for that ticket and now she's going to miss it all. Trust me to come tonight. Her friends are also out on the doorstep with her and they're placing bets on how much I'm going to weigh. Jill's out of breath after running down the street but the cowing size on my mother, she won't be surprised if I'm a porker, at least a ten pounder. Then again Jill is always bloody dramatic. My mother is quite calm but Dad can't get her in that car quick enough. They soon speed off to Church Village hospital. Dad promised to ring as soon as there was any news because back then no one had mobile phones like they do now. And that's exactly what he did only Jill had her head halfway down the toilet when Ray interrupted the artist onstage to let everyone know that mother and baby were doing well.

I'm wheeled in my plastic cot box to the room on the ward where the other just-born babies are so that my mother can get some rest. I didn't come out without a fight, see. We're dressed in all-in-one suits with popper buttons, this row of blue and pink and white, of squirming toes and wrinkly fists. The lights on the ceiling are blinding and unlike the other babies, I'm not sleeping or quietly taking in this brand new, too-bright world. I'm cold. I didn't want to come out. I was happy inside my mother's big belly. So I scream and I don't stop. I want the world to know how I feel. I want my mother to know how angry I am at her for pushing me out. The other babies wake up and then they start screaming, too. I've

279

caused a bloody riot. My mother was sleeping fast until she heard me coming back down the corridor.

She's awful worried. Nothing, not swaying or swaddling or feeding, will stop me crying. Put a dummy in my gob and I spit it straight back out. She asks the midwife if she's sure everything's alright, if they examined me tidy after I came out, like ... even checks my forehead for numbers. And when Nanny comes to visit the next day my mother's a bath of sweat and a bag of nerves as she's rocking me, this baby with a blood-red face, the result of twenty-four hours' worth of screaming blue murder. Been like this since I came out, she tells her, I'm a bloody nightmare. Nanny in her pinny takes me off her, wraps my shawl up tighter. She strokes my cheek with one finger and kisses my head, a flat, thin layer of ginger locks because I've yet to develop my life-ruining curls. And then, looking down at me, Nanny speaks ... not a bloody nightmare, are you love? You're absolutely fucking lovely. It's the first time I hear her voice and from this exact moment on, I know that Nanny is on my side.

'The first night we brought you home I lay you in your cot and you fell asleep, only because I had my arm through the wooden bars. I pulled it out gently and crept out of the room, quiet as a mouse. Well if I did you started bloody screaming again.'

My mother stops her story to put all the 'Hannah King' albums into a Somerfield carrier bag.

'And when I put my arm back in the cot you stopped screaming, just like that. Like turning a bloody tap off. Your little blue eyes were swimming with tears and you gave me this look. I think that's when I knew,' she says.

'When you knew what?'

2

I'm walking through Ponty Park again. I'm surrounded by trees that are glistening with frost, that line the icy path either side of me. White lights wrapped around the branches that claw at the black sky. They look like glittery tree snakes. It's pretty, very Christmassy which is apt, since it is Christmas Eve after all. I've slipped six times and tonight couldn't be more different from the last time I was here, on that boiling hot day in the summer holidays. Even in my coat and gloves I'm freezing.

I'm only here because she asked me to come. I thought she'd deleted my number. I thought she might've even actually burned her mobile because I did call her. I called and called and I text and text but nothing, not even a FUCK OFF. It was only this morning that I heard off her.

meet me at 7. ponty park. benches by the bridge. oh, and im still yours. x

And that's where I find her.

Jess looks clean, the cleanest I've seen her in months, and she smells like a normal human being. It's been nine days since her father turned up on The Estate in his black jeep. I didn't recognise him at first. Well I did, it's not like I thought he was someone else, it's just that I didn't expect the person banging on the back door to be him. I went to open it because people had been knocking it a lot. I was to send whoever it was away, tell them to fuck off and leave us alone. I didn't have time to ask him any questions, and I had loads, because he pushed past me and headed straight for Marley who was by the sink filling money bags with the spoon. Marley didn't stand much of a chance. Even if he had fought back.

Jess' father picked him up, actually hung him by the hood of his black hoodie, and then he rammed his head face first into the sink until his blood ran through the watery grooves on the silver draining board. Think you're a big man, do you? Think you can drive around in your little fucking car with another man's daughter,

281

yeah? Let's see how hard you are, little boy. Those fists had already practised on Bev but this wasn't one blow that knocked Marley down. He was pounded repeatedly. In the chest and in the face, like a human punch bag. And when he finally sank to the floor Jess' father swung his leg back as if he was taking a penalty kick on the rugby field and smashed his steel-capped work boot into Marley's ribs. I didn't help him. I was enjoying it far too much for that.

Marley was lifted up by his neck and pinned to the kitchen wall. His faced looked so pathetic. Did he get the message yet? He nodded his head fast, this bloody, beat-up mess that fell back down to the floor again but that wasn't the end of his punishment. Jess' father went outside and I followed him, watched him open the boot of his jeep and take this pipe-shaped piece of metal with a sharp end out, watch him scrape it from one end of Marley's space car right to the other. The noise hurt my teeth but the rest of me felt amazing. All this was happening in front of people on The Estate who had come out of their fairy light-clad houses especially to watch. These were the same people who'd been knocking on our back door for the latest gossip. We were already the talk of The Estate and now *this*, some massive, angry bald guy fucking the great and powerful Marley's car up. This would be talked about for years to come. And since Marley was too much of a coward to come out, Jess' father shouted it loud enough for him to hear it all the way in the kitchen.

That's right, he yelled, waving his metal pipe thing like some massive bald caveman with a club, his furious breath lost in the freezing cold air … if Marley went near Jess, his *daughter*, ever again, then it would be his fucking throat he'd slash.

Jess was home and she'd told them everything. Yes, *everything*. It took him and Bev best part of a day to drag it out of her, mind. She was in a state up in her bedroom, sitting there on her bed with her music on. He said he'd take me back with him. All I had to do was get in his jeep. He even held the door open for me! My mother was worried sick but no one was angry with me. All they wanted to do was help. *Help*. Ha. Mr Matthews, this man who I hadn't seen for months and months and months, this man who abandoned Jess and fucked her up, this man who punched his wife, who was standing there in his Wales rugby shirt and bleeding knuckles, he was going to help *me*, was he? Come to rescue me like some kind of super hero? Fly me away in his jeep? No thanks. I was sixteen. I was fine and I wasn't, not today or ever, coming home.

'Alright?'

'Yeah, Han. I'm fine. Did you get the bus down then?'

'Yeah.'

'Tidy.'

Jess has lost her voice. It's all gravelly. She puts a fag in her mouth and in the light of her flame I can see her cheeks are glowing a reddy-pink with the cold, shining like plump cherries. And when she unzips her coat to put her fags back in the inside pocket, cheap and Spanish, I'm shocked to see that she's wearing a plain black polo shirt. No faces, no words.

'Where's Marc? What about Freddie?'

Burned them all, didn't she? Every single t-shirt because they stunk of the house, like weed and damp … like everything.

'You should've just got Bev to wash them.'

She did. Bev put them through the machine twice but they still came out smelling the same. Burned all her posters as well.

'Why?'

'Because I hate them all.'

I tell her that she doesn't mean it. How could she possibly hate Marc Bolan who is the most beautiful man in the world? And Freddie Mercury, her favourite. And Cass Elliot. Cass is just…

'Yeah I know,' she says. 'I know.'

We talk like this, through chattering teeth and in short snaps, because it's absolutely freezing and I'm not exaggerating. Under my coat I'm only wearing her white California Dreamin' t-shirt. I don't know what to say now really but at least there's something else to look at instead of each other. In front of us there's an ice rink where the gravel tennis courts usually are. At Christmas Ponty Park sort of turns into a baby Rockefeller Center with the lights and the ice and the people and the tree, and a hut that sells mulled wine in plastic cups. Of course New York's Christmas tree touches the sky, is picture perfect in beautiful, warm colour, whereas the one in Ponty Park is much more of a low budget job. Me and Jess are bookends on the frozen bench as we watch the skidding blades and the sliding legs and the arms that grab hopelessly at the air. The happy people in big coats and fluffy hats who scream and laugh like nothing's wrong.

'Tossers,' she says.

'Yeah.'

'So how's the happy couple doing, Han?'

'What?'

'You and him. How are you, like? Come on, tell me the Goss. You enjoying life together or what?'

'As if, Jess. We're not...'

'Whatever,' she croaks, cutting me off. 'I really don't want to know.'

Because he's nothing but a prick. There's just pricks everywhere! Or maybe they just follow her around. Like the Pied Piper of Pricks, Jess is. And another prick, her father ... she bets I had a shock seeing him turning up like that. Apparently he's picking her back up in an hour.

'Yeah. Just a bit.'

'Who does he think he is? Fat Pat don't want him anymore so I get back to my house right and he's there sleeping on our settee and our fridge is full of fucking food. All Christmas food. Dates, mince pies, his stupid stinking cheese and there was even a Terry's fucking chocolate fucking orange, mun.'

'What did she say when you got home then?'

'Old Bev?'

'Yeah.'

'Cried, didn't she? And you won't believe what else she did to me.'

No. She didn't slap her. As if. She did something a million times worse than that. She hugged her. Bev fucking *hugged* her.

'Can you believe it, Han?'

You'd swear Bev poured acid over her or something. I don't tell her that I've been home as well, just come from there actually, and my mother didn't hug me and unbelievably, she didn't even cry.

'Did Bev ring my mother when you told her ... you know?'

'Yeah. They were both crying on the phone.'

Jess lights herself a fag. She's been home less than two weeks and already things have gone back to normal. Fridge is full. The arguing's returned with a vengeance. And tomorrow will be the worst. Christmas Day is going to be absolutely fucking horrendous. Bev fussing with the roast potatoes. She'll be putting the plates out on the table and her father will be slicing the fucking turkey and they'll all be pulling crackers and fake smiling like everything isn't absolutely, chronically shit, you know?

'My mother hasn't even put our tree up.'

'Well you're lucky, Han. Bonkers Bev has gone completely bonkers. Like this is our last-ever Christmas. She even tried to get me in my jumper with the snowman on, know the one?'

'Yeah.'

'Well I told her straight, didn't I? Do I *look* like I want to be walking around with a flipping fucking snowman on me?'

Jess stamps her fag out in the twinkly, crispy grass by her feet. Oh yeah. She almost forgot. She unzips her coat again and fiddles around the pocket. Got me a present.

'Open your hand then.'

They're dropped gently into my palm – three silver hearts. Happy fucking Christmas.

'There used to be four though, didn't there?' she says.

'Yeah.'

'Well I lost one. Found them in my bedroom when I was having a clear out.'

Silence. Again.

'What are you thinking?' I ask her.

'I'm thinking that it's Christmas Eve.'

'Yeah..?'

'It's Christmas Eve and I'd tell you that I love you if I didn't hate you so much.'

'Oh.'

I put the silver hearts in my bag because now we really have run out of things to say. Come on, she decides, because her father will be back soon. But we don't go the way to the bus station, the place where she told him to pick her up from. I ask her where we're off. I'm freezing. *Jess*.

'I think you know exactly where we're going, Han.'

I stop walking. No way. Is she sick or what?

'Yeah, I'm sick, Han. But not as sick as you.'

Soon the blue glow from the ice rink is gone and the only light we're left with comes from the stars that are like silver candles that flick on and off above us. We're walking down the Taff trail again. Jess' fags are smoked and thrown over the bushes. I can't see them, they're just black shadows, but I know there aren't any blackberries sitting on the leaves today and I'm not thirsty, either. I light the way with my mobile screen, shine it down on the icy ground that cracks like glass under my trainers, trainers that are as shamefully dirty as the mud itself.

We move quickly because we're cold. Cold or scared. To think that last time we were sweating so bad … now my nose and toes are actual ice cubes. We walk and walk. I tell her that she's missed it, that we've gone too far, in the hope that it'll make her turn back but we keep on walking and slipping until she finds the D-shaped gap in the scruffy bushes. The branches have frozen to icicles, sharp and glistening and white, like shark's teeth. Then we're stumbling down the slippery bank in near darkness.

'Just come by here, Han. Don't be a baby.'

Of all the places she could've asked me to meet her. We could've met on the chapel roof or up on the Comp banking. It would've been cool to jump over the main gates and sit on the grass on Christmas Eve under the silver stars. Poetic, even. We could've burned it down if we wanted. But no. It had to be here because this is so Jess. So spooky. So dramatic. I stand next to her right by the river. She says I want to see someone about that bag, you know, get it surgically removed.

'Why didn't you just leave it in your house?'

'Because I'm not going back.'

Oh. Right. Going back *there*, am I?

'No I'm not, Jess.'

Whatever.

She unzips her coat again, digs around that inside pocket which must be massive, and says that it's absolutely mental, isn't it? *Life.* Absolutely mental and absolutely bonkers and most of all, it's got a wonderful way of kicking you in the tits when you really need it to be kind for once.

'My mother hugged me and it proper freaked me out so I went upstairs and emptied all my shit out of my bag on my bed and it was just there amongst it all.'

Jess cried for hours on her bedroom floor with Marc Bolan. Bev thought she was going to *top herself*, can you believe she said it? Of all the things to say. Those words actually came out of her mouth. Insensitive bitch. But Bev is thick as shit, isn't she? Hasn't got a clue about The Club, hasn't got a clue about anything. Jess turned 'Cosmic Dancer' up so loud she wouldn't be surprised if I heard it up on The Estate. And you know what she wished?

'What?'

'I wished I hadn't gone. I wished I hadn't told you to stay there with him. Why did you listen to me, Han?'

'You left, Jess. You left *me*.'

'Well I text you, didn't I? And don't forget you left me too, Han. Once. Don't you forget that.'

Silence. But she fills it. She's good at that. The Best.

'If we both left that night we could've listened to it together, couldn't we?'

Jess says we could've nicked Bev's vodka out of the cupboard, *all* of it, and listened to Cass Elliot in the purple lava lamp dark until it got light and then dark again. Or at least until our wires felt a bit looser and all the bad shit went away, like we used to. But it doesn't matter. We're both here now, aren't we? Down by the river Taff on Christmas flipping Eve. She blows it up, the blue balloon she found amongst her clothes and stuff. It must've come from the attic, Han, and then she ties it. It's a struggle with frozen, massive shovel-hand fingers. I look up and the stars are so clear it's like someone has drawn them on with a glitter pen and coloured them in.

'For Billy,' she says as she lets it go.

And I watch it, track its flight. It bobs above the frost dusty trees until I can't see it anymore. I'm not sure if Jess realises the irony, if she knows how mental life *really* is because the balloon disappears just like it did the last time we were here except tonight instead of lost in blue, it's lost in the black of a starry, Christmas Eve sky.

0

The kitchen window was somehow still intact despite the black rocks of rain that seemed louder since Billy had pushed past me by the back door and run out into The Estate. He was crying.

Marley put his clothes back on and said he was probably somewhere stupid, probably sitting up on the mountain with the fucking turbines, giving himself a shiny new cut. Because that's what self-harmers are like. It's all about the attention, all so someone can look at your arms and go, awh, there's fucking terrible. So we needed to calm the fuck down. We needed to Chill Out. And I agreed. I had to believe it because if something bad did happen, it would be all my fault. I was the one who walked down those stairs in the dark thinking, I will not let her leave me ... I will not let Jess leave me. I was the one who walked into the kitchen, radiating the colour green. Nuclear. I was the one who sent Billy upstairs.

One hour went by and then two and then seven and eight and twelve and in all that time the rain never stopped, never gave in. But he'd be back, you watch, like when he ran away from Barry Island and then turned up a day later. Yeah. This was exactly the same. Jess was smoking at a blistering pace but I knew she wasn't actually bothered about Billy. She didn't care that he might be bleeding to death up on the mountain with the turbines. If she did then she would've gone out looking for him. She was only worried that he'd throw us out when he got back. It was Billy's house after all, even if Marley did pay the rent.

We'd have to go home – to that place we'd forgotten about but not really. We'd have to somehow try to be those girls again, those girls we'd killed off and buried but not really. And what upset her the most was when Marley pushed her away. She screamed at him but he just laughed. Stupid bitch. He didn't even *fancy* her and her tiny fucking tits. He only fucked her because she was *there*. Because he *could*. And soon as Billy came back he'd explain how it was all her idea. He'd tell him – you know what girls are like. They're all slags. Dirty fucking slags. And you know what this one is like – do anything for a gram, Jess will. Cause we all knew what she did in Barry, didn't we? We were just two stupid girls they'd met on a chapel roof one night. Marley said it, something I could've told him weeks ago … we were nothing special.

I'm sitting on a bench in Ponty bus station. And when Jess let the balloon off just now I tried to imagine how the river was that night. Not calm like it was then under the stars and definitely nothing like the day we sat in the sun talking about dead dogs and shopping trolleys. That night Billy ran away from The Estate the river would've been high and swollen, the water wild and freezing cold. Maybe he sat on the bank and talked himself into it. The police couldn't say for sure whether he did it on purpose or whether he just fell in. Apparently lots of people have killed themselves down by the river Taff over the years, something of a hot spot, they said, something no one ever taught us in Geography. But we knew The Truth.

It's quite busy in the bus station. People are waiting to go home with bags bursting with last-minute Christmas presents and long rolls of wrapping paper that don't fit in them tidy. Jess' father picked her up about half an hour ago. She wouldn't get in the front, said she couldn't stand being that close to him, breathing him in, and when she climbed in the back she begged me to get in, too. Come on, Han. It was cold, mun, and Christmas fucking Eve. We'd sort it out because this was me and her, and we could *always* sort things out no matter how bad they were. Nah. I told her I'd be fine. Don't worry about me, just go. And then I watched her shut the door and leave and I swear to God, I don't know why I didn't just get in the stupid jeep. By now she'll be back in her bedroom. Warm. Marc Bolan will be singing 'Cosmic Dancer' to her and Cass Elliot will sort everything out the way only she can because her voice is medicine for all the problems nothing and no one else can fix.

I made Marley stop at the bottom of my street earlier. Scratched and dented, his car wasn't a space car anymore but it didn't take us long to get to Pandy because he drove fast even for his standards. We didn't say a thing. No see you around one day or plain goodbye. I got out and he screeched away like he was leaving an unwanted black bag of kittens behind. I walked up the street with my bag on my back like I'd made that walk a million times before. But this time I wasn't just coming home from school or Jess' or Nanny's. I was expecting to see fairy lights in our window because it's Christmas Eve, but the window was bare. I walked through the front door without knocking and without hesitating, like I'd only gone to the shop and come back.

My bedroom was a museum. Untouched. Like it had been frozen in time. My things were ancient artefacts, priceless paintings too precious and too delicate to move. My bed was made and my curtains were open and the books Laser Ludlow had given me were still on my side table, the exact same place I'd left them. Jeffrey Dahmer was there on the wall to welcome me back as was the black-and-white pencil sketch of Cass Elliot Jess drew me as a present a few weeks before the end of school. I pulled my coat off a hanger in my wardrobe because I never took it with me to Jess' house, because I didn't really plan on not coming home.

Downstairs my mother was ransacking the drawer for photographs. The fire was turned up full for the first time, I think, since it had been installed. The living room hadn't changed, either, except the Christmas tree wasn't where it should've been. I didn't ask her why she hadn't put it up or where her cards from all her friends were, or why I couldn't smell mince pies cooking in the oven. I was going to tell her The Truth, like Jess had told Bev. Maybe my mother would hug me, too. And this was it.

We'd done some really bad things and something *really* bad had happened but I was home now, look, and once Christmas was over with she could ring school and ask if I could come back. I missed Laser Ludlow like mental and I wanted to do my A Levels. I wanted to be back in Room 58 and I wanted someone to tell me that I wasn't a massive mess, that I wasn't crazy at all, but good at something. I wanted nice words. I *needed* to feel like I was worth something again. Mostly, I just wanted everything back the way it was.

But I didn't do that. I didn't tell The Truth. That would've been too easy, too simple for me. Instead I asked her for photographs. I don't know why. I told her that was the reason I was there. I was going to write a book about freckles and balloons and words and dolls and sherbet lemons and all the things I'd ever done. I was going to be a writer like I always said I would be and one day she'd be able to tell her friends good things about me. One day she wouldn't be ashamed to be my mother.

She could've stopped me, told me that she knew I was lying. Her and Bev had already cried together on the house phone so she must've known everything. But she went and told me the story of that rainy Saturday in August.

'I think that's when I knew you were trouble.'

'I thought you knew I was trouble when I said my first word?'

'No. Knew straight after you were born.'

It was weird. She was talking really calm. She wasn't angry with me like I'd planned, like I'd prepared for. So I decided I would be angry for her. I decided this wasn't my fault, it was hers. Because if she knew when I was born that I was trouble, *bad*, then she should've got rid of me somehow. Go on, shout at me ... I wanted her to. Tell me that you don't love me and that I've always got on your nerves with my questions and my lies and my general just being *alive*. I needed her to get it all out because I deserved it. But instead of shouting or hugging me, and even worse than crying, she said – You're mine, Hannah, whatever you are. And of course I bloody love you.

She didn't ask me to come home and I didn't tell her that I had nowhere else to go. She put the photographs in the carrier bag and then I put them in my own bag. I'm going through them by here on the bench and I'm in every single one. I've got freckles all over my face and my dimples are massive. I'm wearing a bonnet with a green trim, an orange curl flicking out of a woolly hole. I'm wearing my denim dungarees and I'm standing in Nanny's garden pulling a face because I didn't want my photo taken. I'm blowing candles out on a birthday cake. I'm sitting on the settee with Jess and we both have our thumbs up. I'm on the beach with my arm around Kyle's shoulder. I'm on my dad's knee. I'm riding his back. I'm holding a baby pigeon in front of our garden shed and I'm sitting on the bonnet of his car. And in those photographs with him, my smile is the biggest.

They make me think about The Story. How he once told me that I wouldn't find freedom in the Rhondda and how I decided that the reason it wasn't there was because it was in Danville – that place in the song we liked to sing. He promised to take us and when we showed up Joan Baez would be waiting, already tuning her guitar up ready to make my skin fizzy. I zip the photographs back up in my bag because I can't stand to think about it. I take my notebook out. Just the one. The pages inside are full but I can't bring myself to read any of the words. It's quite sad really. Its red cover doesn't sparkle so much anymore, the glitter badly faded, and it's kind of battered, stained. I didn't look after it the way I should have.

I look up and see the three familiar yellow numbers on the bus. It pulls into the stand in front of me and stops with a loud gush of its brakes. The revised festive timetable on the wall says it's the last one Home. The 120 bus goes everywhere and slowly, but it doesn't go to Danville. I really wish it did.

I won't tell you if me and Jess will ever be the same again. I won't tell you how *I* feel because the thing about words is that you can use thousands of them and put them all together and still they won't change a thing. And at the same time you can use just a few of them and change *everything*. I really did think they were safe things, things that no one could take away because they were yours. But the more I know, the more I read and hear, the more I think words may be the worst things God ever let us use. Worse than giving us guns and sticks and stones. Because words get you in trouble. They make rips you can't stitch up or Sellotape together. Words are bombs. Once you drop them that's it, you can't stop them from falling. Once you let words go you can't take them back, can't stop what happens next.

It took me a while but I know now that words are nasty little things and I'm done with them. And it's funny, isn't it? I did warn you. I told you right from the start that I'm the girl who lies so, really, you probably shouldn't believe a single word I've said.

Acknowledgements

Thank you…
Jacqui Jones, Penny Thomas, Maria Donovan and Rachel Trezise.

About the Author

Rhian Elizabeth was born in 1988. *Six Pounds Eight Ounces* is her first novel.

SEREN

Well chosen words

Seren is an independent publisher with a wide-ranging list which includes poetry, fiction, biography, art, translation, criticism and history. Many of our books and authors have been on longlists and shortlists for – or won – major literary prizes, among them the Costa Award, the Man Booker, the Desmond Elliott Prize, The Writers' Guild Award, Forward Prize, and TS Eliot Prize.

At the heart of our list is a good story told well or an idea or history presented interestingly or provocatively. We're international in authorship and readership though our roots are here in Wales (Seren means Star in Welsh), where we prove that writers from a small country with an intricate culture have a worldwide relevance.

Our aim is to publish work of the highest literary and artistic merit that also succeeds commercially in a competitive, fast changing environment. You can help us achieve this goal by reading more of our books – available from all good bookshops and increasingly as e-books. You can also buy them at 20% discount from our website, and get monthly updates about forthcoming titles, readings, launches and other news about Seren and the authors we publish.

www.serenbooks.com